KING ARTHUR
AND
THE RIDERS OF RHEGED

THE STORY OF
GWYR Y GOGLEDD
THE MEN OF THE NORTH?

Rheged Books

ISBN 0-951 9535-0-8

Printed in Great Britain by Antony Rowe Ltd, Chippenham, Wiltshire

Typeset from wordprocessor disk by Indent Typesetters, Kendal.

Published by Rheged books
P.O. Box 39 Kendal.
Cumbria LA8 8LS

CONTENTS

INTRODUCTION:
tradition, fact and fiction

Like wind rippling the pennants of many towered Camelot so tales of King Arthur and his knights have stirred the imaginations of generations. Yet we know now that Arthur – if ever he existed – belonged to a different world from that of the medieval knight. Sometimes that world is called the Dark Ages, sometimes it is described as post-Roman but whatever we choose to call the period it was a time when the old Roman province of Britain was lost to the Anglo Saxons.

Lowland Britain was, however, not conquered by the Anglo Saxons overnight. The image of coarsely dressed, hairy barbarians wading ashore to rape, pillage and settle in Britain as soon as Roman galleys laden with clean shaven, wine swilling legionaires disappeared over the horizon is a false one. True the first half of the fifth century was a time when ship loads of Germanic, Scandinavian and Irish raiders roamed the coast like Hell's Angels on a Bank Holiday but such raids were merely a recurrence of those which had begun whilst there was still a Roman army to guard the province. When the final elements of that army were withdrawn is unknown but it was certainly before AD410 – the year in which the Emperor, apparently in response to a whingeing letter, told those who claimed to be the government of Britain that in case they hadn't noticed there had been no troops in Britain for some time and there was no hope of any being sent. AD410 was, therefore, the date when Rome washed her hands of Britain, telling its citizens to look after their own defence; in much the sameway as post-war British governments treated Australia and New Zealand, and not for dissimilar reasons.

So the newly independent British organised their own defence employing foreign ("English") mercenaries or *foederati* as the Romans themselves had done. According to the sixth century British monk Gildas such professional troops were paid a "monthly allowance" in the form of "supplies" and such payments were accepted "for a long time" until, complaining they were "insufficient", and "purposely giving a false colour to individual incidents", "the barbarians" threatened industrial action, the breaking of their agreement and the plundering of "the whole island unless more lavish payment were heaped on them". The English, it would seem, had invented what was to become known as "the British Disease" and when the government of the day refused to negotiate fighting broke out. The Anglo Saxon attempt to take what they wanted of Britain had begun.

It is, however, unlikely that there were at first sufficient numbers of Anglo Saxons to mount a sustained offensive and the fighting was sporadic, a nibbling away at the edges of the old province, so it was not until cAD480 that the old fort at Pevensey in Sussex was lost to the foreigners. The loss of this fort seems to mark the beginning of more sustained warfare which culminated, Gildas tells us, in the battle of Mount Badon when the British led by one Ambrosious Aurelianus crushed the English. When and where the battle was fought is unknown but a date between AD500 and 520 is generally accepted.

The effect of the battle was to weaken the foreigners for more than a generation and the peace seems to have lasted until about 570 after which we again hear of significant Anglo Saxon gains. Between 570 and 580, for example, the English effectively broke through into the Bath-Gloucester area and by 590 seem to have controlled the Vale of York. Again, in 603 the Northumbrians defeated the embryonic kingdom of the Scots north west of the Clyde and in about 616 they were victorious at Chester.

Most of the old Roman province of Britain was, therefore, lost to the Anglo Saxons, not immediately after 410, nor in the fifth century, but between the years 570 and 616. The years around and after 570 then seem to be those which saw the end of that period of relative peace during which Gildas wrote. These years of British independence – commencing sometime before 410 and ending in the North West in 616 – were years during which the old Roman systems and traditions declined, were ammended, replaced, or simply taken over by other forms of organisation. By the end of the fifth century Britain had fragmented into a number of kingdoms whose territories coincided in general terms with pre-Roman tribal areas.

Rheged was one such kingdom and appears to have included most of what the Romans described as Brigantia and we call Northern England. The exploits of its king, Urien, and his son, Owen, are celebrated in the earliest surviving Welsh poetry and there too we learn they were descended from Coel Hen, Coel the Old, a figure better known for his bowl and fiddlers three. Medieval gossip also knew of Owen as the father of Saint Kentigern and made him a sometimes troublesome contemporary of Arthur. Strange then it is that Arthur should not feature in the early poems about Urien and Owen. The more so since the earliest known reference to Arthur is in connection with Catraeth,

Catterick, a place where Urien is said to have been "lord". And when later Welsh dynasties forged – quite literally – links with The Kings of Old it was with Urien and not Arthur. Could they be one and the same? Certainly some Welsh medieval writers did not use the latin form Artorius when writing of Arthur but the word Arctures which is thought to mean, Northern Bear.

This novel – for academic argument will never prove or disprove the theory that Urien was Arthur – seeks to explore further what we know of Urien and Owen, and of the similarities between their story and that of Arthur. In particuler it seeks to show that all of the battles attributed to Arthur can, with one exception, be explained if they were fought by Urien and Owen. That one exception is Mount Badon which, as we we have already learned from Gildas, also belonged to Ambrosius Aurelianus and may well have been borrowed from him by Arthur's supporters. On occasion, however, it has been necessary for me to introduce wholly fictitious characters and events. Some of these are drawn from Celtic mythology and tradition, for a secondary intention is to try to recapture something of the richness of tradition and belief (alien to the Roman world and church) which must have existed amongst the sixth century British. Indeed, Urien, Owen and Kentigern may themselves have been born of such traditions and myths; what we might call "fantasy" characters.

So it is that my sources – Gildas, Bede, the earliest surviving Welsh poems, folklore and tradition – are essentially the same as those available to Geoffrey of Monmouth who, in the twelfth century, wrote the first popular account of Arthur. Indeed those same sources were probably the "ancient book" he claimed to have copied as his story. To them, however, I have added material relating to St. Kentigern which Jocelyn of Furness recorded eight hundred years ago. Scholars usually dismiss this and much of the other material as dubious and whilst the bulk of the material undoubtedly can be so designated it is strange that a number of the details fit together to make a coherent and rational account for the sixth century. Such is the basis of my story and the way in which the "historical" and topographical details fitted together led me to conclude that if the story I am about to relate did not actually happen it – or something like it – was nevertheless known to or invented by Jocelyn.

As history, or psuedo-history, the events and battles relate to real topography and include by chance some of the best scenery in our island. I hope, therefore, that you will take the opportunity to follow the story on the ground; to follow the victorious armies of Urien Rheged and his grandson Kentigern; to relive sixth century Britain and those decisive years of glory and tragedy which spawned the legend of Arthur ... and the Riders of Rheged.

LINEAGE USED HERE

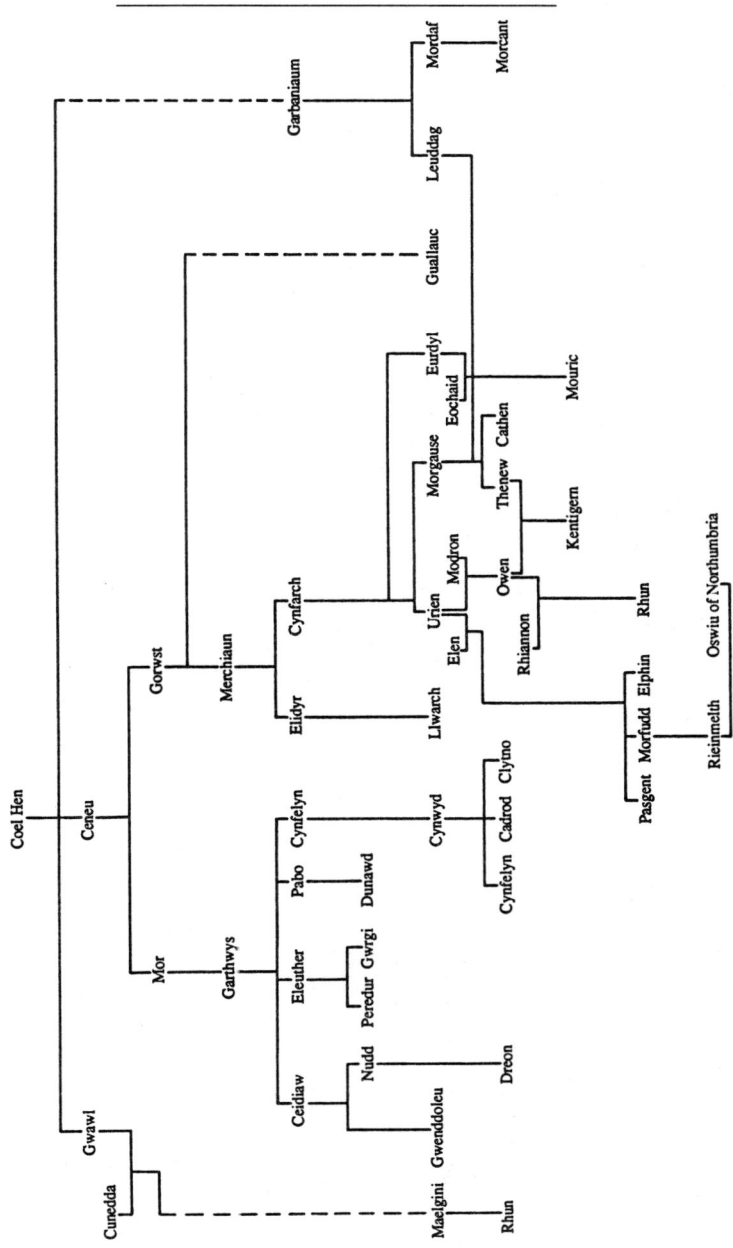

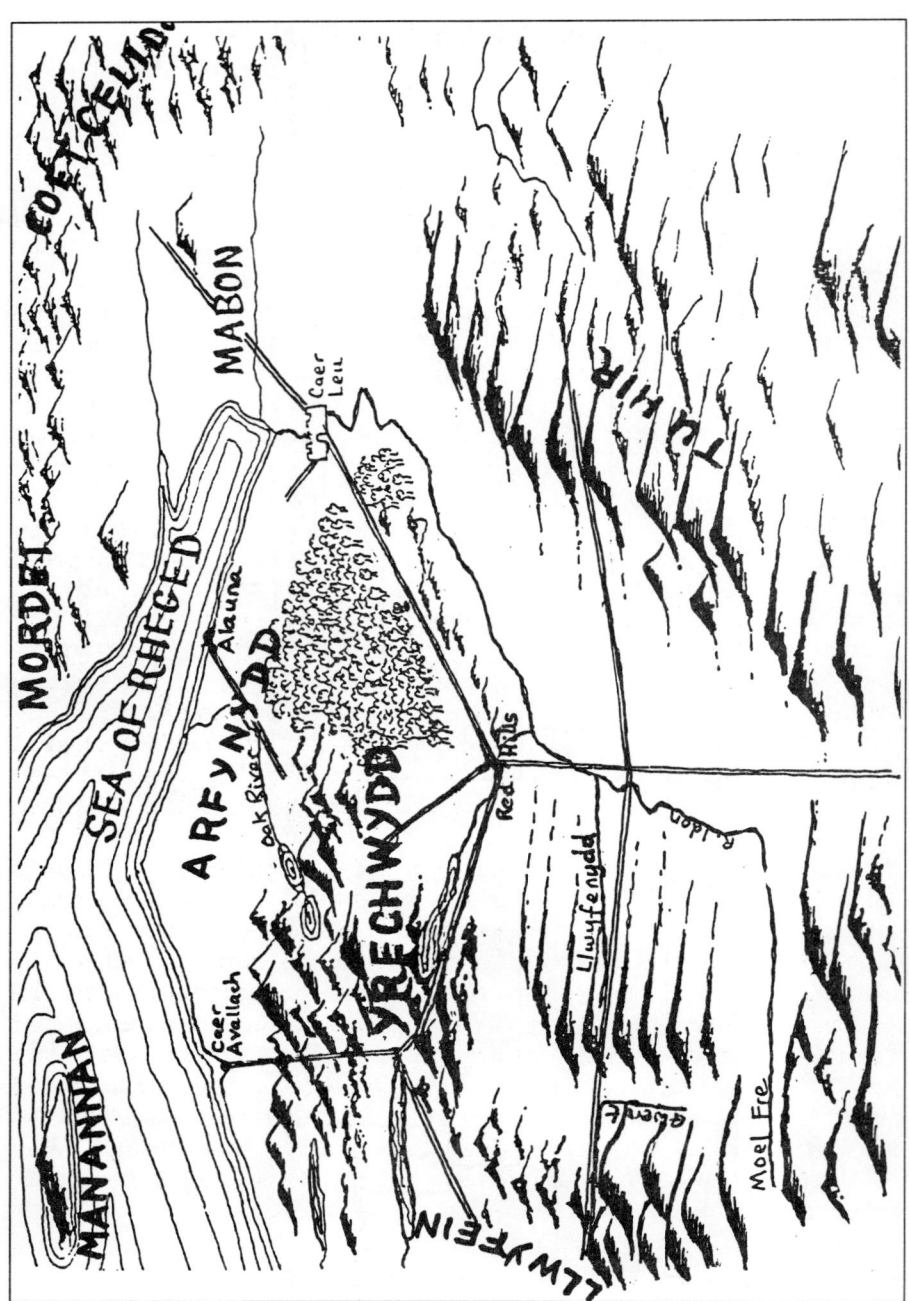

URIEN AND MODRON

Westward beyond the Lake Mountains the sun was setting. The brilliance of the day was passing from the land and the long grasping fingers of night were creeping across the rich fields and gentle slopes of green Llwyfenydd where Tuan stood guard. The young man wrapped his cloak about his slender shoulders trying to imprison the last of the sun's warmth whilst a flight of geese passed overhead, their wings rythmically beating the pale blue air. Tuan watched their effortless progress. It seemed to him that they were like some heavenly warband, free companions riding in unison to distant lands. He leant back against the gatepost and let his eyes roam half attentively across the still pastures whilst in his mind he rode with heroes past and dreamt of exploits yet to come.

Suddenly he tensed. Was it his imagination or was that a real horseman on the horizon? His eyes scanned anxiously across the green sward and fields of young barley searching for the apparition. An apparition! Tuan shuddered and sought the small leather pouch that dangled on a cord about his neck. "Holy Mother Brigit, let it not be elven". Reassuringly his fingers closed about the small flint arrowhead within its bag as he spied again the horseman, far to the south. "Only one," he muttered, half to himself half to the hounds that stretched at his feet and about the gateposts. Attentively one dog lifted its head briefly then, stretching its legs, it nuzzled comfortably into the dust, oblivious of the distant stranger.

Tuan watched as the silhouette galloped westward seeking to outpace the darkness which pursued. In his hand he twirled the ashen shaft of his spear, feeling its fine balance. Apprehensively he saw the rider turn onto the old Roman road but now the dogs, alerted by the drumbeat of hooves on the worn surface, were running out to greet the stranger. They ran to and fro across his path barking incessantly, but the rider came on, his pace not slackening, until at last he was before the gates and there, breathless, he drew rein. In front of him Tuan stood with his broad spear ready for the upward thrust should that be necessary. Around his feet the dogs were regrouping, growling. "Who rides thus to the Lord of Llwyfenydd?" called Tuan pulling his round, whitewashed shield closer to his chest.

"Cadwallon of the household of Cynfarch would speak with the Lord Urien".

Tuan moved sheepishly to one side, allowing the elder to pass, ashamed that he had not recognised the hoary hero. Often had he heard his father and uncles speak the name of Cadwallon and tell how this now grizzled warrior had been one of the Raven Riders who had fought with Cynfarch under Outigern. Then the Brython led by Outigern in the North and Ambrosius in the South had saved the West, driving the Loegrians from Caer Efrawg and establishing Rheged as the greatest of all the kingdoms of the Brython. But Cadwallon chose to ignore for the moment the revering eyes of the young guard. Digging his heels into the steaming flanks of his horse he urged it forward once more, clattering into the cobbled yard where an ostler ran forward to take the reins. Cadwallon swung himself from the saddle and massaging his muscles stared about the yard. Behind him was the gate and the doting eyes of Tuan; in front was the great hall, its circular stone wall barely visible below the roof of new reed thatch.

The inside of the hall was dark and its warmth and smell swept over Cadwallon making him feel drowsy and hungry. The smell of roasted meat and the rowdy banter assailed his nose and ears. Tired, he sank onto the bench at the entrance waiting for the doorkeeper to deliver his message. All about him the feast continued uninterrupted but Cadwallon was too tired to notice the glances cast in his direction. In the central hearth the fire leapt and crackled, sending sparks high into the rafters, casting its strong ruddy light on the firedogs which fenced it and upon the men, women and children seated around. Later its power would fade, its illumination become more fitful as the flames flickered to oblivion, but for the moment it roared and danced like the company about. Its yellow and orange tongues sparkled in their eyes, on their enamelled brooches and on the shield bedecked pillars. High above the blue wood smoke hung, drifting like clouds in the firmament. The air was heavy and the atmosphere soporific and Cadwallon had difficulty in shaking off the blue tendrils which were starting to ensnare his mind. With an effort he stood and peered after the doorkeeper.

His eyes found the porter whispering into the ear of Urien. Cynfarch's son was dressed in a linen shirt and short sleeved woollen tunic, his silver hair matched by the torc about his neck. To his right was the tall, full figure of Modron whose beauty the passing years had not sullied. Her long golden hair was coiled and bejewelled and the folds of her white linen dress were gathered on each ivory shoulder by gilded brooches fashioned like swans, the chain between them a necklace for her elegant throat.

Urien listened to the doorkeeper with impatience, his eyes fixed on the face of Cadwallon. Not yet dulled by the evening mead they sparkled in friendly recognition. Without waiting for the porter to withdraw, Urien stood and banging his broad hand upon the trestled table called for silence. "Hail, Cadwallon, and welcome. Yours shall be the choicest pieces and the purest mead, for there is none here who would gainsay your right to the champion's portion." Urien paused and looked at his sprawling companions with a fierce eye that warned them not to challenge the elderly rider. "But come, tell us first your news for I daresay it is that and not our company which brings you hither in such haste."

Cadwallon bowed and for a moment his face was lost in shadow. Urien acknowledged the gesture. "Your silence, old friend, proclaims the gravity of your unspoken news and no doubt if I had not cut my doorkeeper short he would have told me you wished us to talk alone. But, having betrayed your message, there is little point in us now withdrawing. Besides, there is none here whom I would judge unfit to listen to a Raven Rider and truth quickly learned stops false rumour and speculation, even amongst friends."

Cadwallon nodded and stepped forward to the edge of the throng. "The Lord Urien is as generous as ever, as generous as his famed forebear, Coel the Old. The Lord Urien ap Cynfarch is as perceptive as ever. His eyes like those of the falcon see his enemies when they are but specks in his domain. His mind like the seer and raven probes behind the eyes of mortal men. Nought is hidden from him and nought now shall be hidden from his company."

The old man paused as if summoning up his courage. "My lord, the King ... the King ... your father, is dying but it is not merely his body that is ailing, for in his mind he fights a foe whom he will not name to any of us. Yesterday morning, being so agitated, he set out from Catraeth to come to you in person. So we crossed Tu Hir by the high valleys and by nightfall reached his estate on the flanks of Moel Fre. This morning as the sun rose he seemed less troubled and we let him sleep on. Alas that we did not recognise that fateful sleep earlier; for as the sun moved south, sometimes clear in the sky sometimes hidden behind a peak, so our lord Cynfarch slipped in and out of consciousness. So he was when I left him to ride hither ... without his leave."

Cadwallon bowed his head, staring at the earthen floor. Far to his right Urien sat, his eyes glazed, his face ashen, Modron's arm resting comfortingly on his. "Did I not know in my heart what news you brought? Aye, and we are in your debt for that news. Tomorrow at first light I ride for Moel Fre. In the meantime let all gathered here offer

13

prayers, to whom or what I care not."

Urien rose and with the hand of Modron still clinging to his, left the hall. All around men stood and, gathering a last handful of food or draining their horns, began to disperse. Here and there small groups remained behind talking in hushed voices.

* * *

Urien could not sleep. He lay staring upwards at the blackness beneath the roof. Beyond those timbers was a whole universe: myriads of stars, their courses fixed, their life endless, their beginning unknown. A warrior, a knight, might count his life in only days or months, but his father and the peace he had wrought with his sword had lived so long that it was impossible to imagine the world without him. How odd that, until now, Urien had never thought his father might be called from them. A tear trickled down his cheek and landed on the soft flesh of Modron beside him. She put her arm around his chest and looked up to where she knew his head must be. "Do not weep, my love, for why should the Christian believing in heaven, or those who believe in the old gods and the Isle of the Blessed, weep for those who die? Should they not be pleased that those they loved have gone to their paradise? Should we then not be pleased for his sake? He will not regret his passing and nor must we. From now on he is, and was, no more than your grandfather and Coel himself, each ageless and as near to you as the other."

Urien smiled to himself. She was, as always, right; he should be glad for his father's sake, aye, and some would say for his own sake, too, for now he would be King, heir to Coel the Old. His would be the chance to be Guledig, High King of Prydein, and heir to Maxen Mascen, of whom it was said Rome itself did beg to be spared. Yet there was a paradox in what Modron had said that troubled Urien, for if the goal of the Christian was to worship God in heaven should not a believer, out of love for his brother, speed him to that paradise? Urien sought to give shape to the meaning of life but it eluded him. How dulled his mind had become by the years of peace and plenty. But even in his youth, finely honed by war, he could probably never have answered such questions. Urien shook his head. Questions about life were for young Kentigern to ask and answer. As for himself, Modron was right: God had given him a life and he would live it. He bent his head and kissed her tenderly.

* * *

14

He loved her then as he had always done and as on the day when he had first seen her. That day more than thirty years ago when, as a youth of sixteen, he had hunted with Pabo in his kingdom west of Yrechwydd. Together they had chased the quarry all morning. Their horses had sped over gentle ground, climbed rocky slopes and plunged into deep gullies until on the edge of another valley he had become separated from Pabo. There his own hounds had turned from the stag and darted into a wooded defile from which no amount of calling would bring them back. So he had followed them, the sound of the hunt shut out by the steep slope and canopy of trees as if he had entered some shee mound or cave: a magic cave of soft green light and sparkling, splashing, tumbling water.

He found his hounds at the bottom, baying, their noise drowned by the roar of the stream as it cascaded into a deep, rocky pool of brown water. From high overhead where the forest canopy was broken a single shaft of sunlight lit the pool and illuminated the face of the girl who bathed there, a rainbow behind her head. Not in all Rheged had Urien seen such beauty and like his hounds he was both afraid and entranced. Often in winter when seated at the fireside he had heard stories of enchanted woods but he had only half believed them until that moment. Then he had thought her a phantom of the place, one whom the men of old, and some still, worshipped, piling up gifts and erecting altars to such beings.

She had laughed at his muteness and, shaking the water from her long golden hair, had risen from the water and walked towards him.

"Is not Urien the son of Cynfarch pleased by what he sees?"

He had backed away at the mention of his name for no stranger could know that except by magic. Surely he thought she was the Morrigan who in the form he now beheld sought to entice him into the pool and there drown him. Yet her smile was one of reassurance. "Should lesser beings not know those who are to be set over them? Until this morning I had never seen anyone in my mirror except myself but today I saw a man who seemed to be Leu. Though his hair was dark his face shone like the sun. In his hand he held a great spear and all of Prydein knelt before him. This morning I saw the first born of Coel, Duke of the North."

She paused, her eyes searching his but Urien was already backing away again for how could an ordinary girl have seen the future? Seeing the fear in his eyes she too turned, walking towards her clothes which lay, Urien now saw, on a rock at the far end of the pool. "I am sorry if I frightened you. I really meant to tease. My mirror is this pool and I

thought you would be pleased to know your name had spread this far ...
Wouldn't you really like to be compared with Leu and Old Coel?"

As she asked the question she turned to face him and Urien saw the
sparkle of life had gone from her eyes. In that moment he knew she was
of this world and her ripe body was, like his own, mere flesh and blood.
Decisively he strode forward and lifting her off her feet carried her to
the verdant bank which lay beyond the bare rock fringe of the pool.
"It's I who should be sorry ... " he said, putting his hands about her
slender waist and kissing her on the shoulder. "And so you should be,"
she teased. Together they laughed; the spell was broken, and she was no
more a being from the Otherworld than he a god.

So they had laughed and talked, kissed and loved. Entwined together
on that warm grass they had gazed at the golden sun through the green
lattice high above their bed. "I shall call you Modron, my nymph," he
had whispered as his tongue played with the lobe of her ear.

"Then Modron shall be my name and you shall come for your son,
Owen, in a year's time, for that will be his name," she replied kissing his
chest again.

Urien lay back and ran his hand through her thick hair combing it
over her shoulders with his fingers. "I shall come before then."

"That will not be possible, it is not written, the Lord Pabo will not
allow it."

"Pabo is nothing and no family is greater than that of Coel as you
yourself said. No one will prevent you and me from moments such as
this."

"We will see." Modron cast her head back, stretching her long neck,
letting her toes dig aimlessly into the sand at the water's edge. Giggling
she rolled over onto her stomach and looked up at him. "You had better
return to the hunt. It is enough that Pabo and your friends hunt one
stag this day."

Urien had found his horse further downstream grazing a patch of
grass which had not been flattened by lovers. Gathering the reins he
began to lead the horse up the steep slope, the hounds running on
ahead, their tails high in the air.

Modron watched from her bed, her head propped on her elbows, her
breasts trailing in the grass. "Don't forget to ask where to come for me
and our son," she called, teasing him one more time. "At the end of this
valley, below the sea of Rheged and Manannan, in the glass of the
raven, there you must seek the swan that guards your treasure."

With that riddle they parted, and that night Pabo scolded Urien.
"Such a person is not fit to marry a son of Coel, either yourself or my

16

young Dunawd. Wise you were when you thought her the Morrigan, for she and her people are indeed not of this world. A hundred years ago or more they came, borne upon the back of Manannan in ships the like of which our people had not seen before. They claimed they were descended from the Tuatha De Danaan, the magicians of old, and who were we to gainsay such a story?" The elder paused, swirling the wine in his goblet. Its rippling surface reminded him of the sea that had brought Modron and her kind to the shores of his kingdom. The wine was bitter and Pabo tipped it onto the floor, studiously rubbing it into the dust with the sole of his boot before turning to look at Urien once more. "Surely it was magic when she saw you in her mirror and by magic that she ensnared you? My people say that sometimes they have seen her swimming in the form of a swan."

"Perhaps," replied Urien guardedly, for he did not wish to offend his embittered host – not yet at least. Besides, Modron had woven magic; the magic of a girl's ripe body held for the first time. Aye, and of that Pabo would know little. Urien glanced momentarily at the sour face of his host's wife and their young son Dunawd. "Perhaps," he repeated, his voice dreamy as he gazed into the fire. "Perhaps. Yet what warrior would not have taken such a prize, magic or otherwise? And if she is indeed of the Tuatha De Danaan I will chain her to this world by marriage."

Pabo drew back in horror. "You are a Christian prince, Urien, and even if you were not no man takes the treasures heaped at the side of holy pools. You must forget her ... "

Urien nodded faintly as if finally and reluctantly agreeing. There was no point in arguing. He was far from home, a guest and he could appreciate how Pabo felt about a possible alliance between a vassal of his and a prince of Llwyfenydd. So he did not discuss Modron again but neither did he forget her. Elfshot was lodged in Urien's heart and Modron had kindled a fire there which burned brighter with each passing day, until Samhain came and he returned at last to his father's hall.

There he had found his father waiting impatiently; for emissaries had come from the North, from Manau Gododdin. "From our cousin Garbaniaum ... " Cynfarch reminded him.

"A distant cousin," corrected Urien sensing but not clearly seeing some danger in their presence.

"Distant cousin or no, they ask for our help in expelling Dyfynwal of Clud from their lands. Garbaniaum has proposed a formal alliance and suggested it be sealed by the marriage of you and his daughter and I have agreed. What do you say?"

Cynfarch's words were like a stone cast into the still waters of a pond or at a glass mirror: plans which had been crystal clear were instantly disturbed; thoughts which had sparkled in his mind were shattered and suddenly no more. "What do I say? Why ask me when you have already sealed my destiny? Could you not have waited?" Urien retorted angrily. "What I say is this: that I refuse."

Now Cynfach's temper too began to flare. "Yes, I did wait for you. Three weeks have we waited. Three weeks while you enjoyed yourself hunting ... It is our way to be generous to our guests but how long could I keep them without an answer? Would you have it said that I was less generous than Old Coel himself? By my life, Urien, I dote on you but you test that love now ... "

Urien drew his father aside out of earshot of the emissaries. "Aye, you were right and I have no right to speak to you so. My temper rises with the steam of my horse for together we rode as quickly as we could; not to boast of stag or boar taken but of a greater prize. Father, I came indeed with all speed to ask your blessing upon my marriage; but not to Garbaniaum's daughter."

"To whom then?" whispered Cynfarch between clenched teeth.

"Modron, daughter of Avallach ... "

"Avallach is bound to Pabo. Knowing Pabo I doubt he would allow such a marriage. An alliance between you and his servant would be to take half his kingdom."

Urien had been calm, his mind working fast to think of how he might escape the destiny which had been put upon him and how instead he might weave his own future with that of Modron. He began by accepting there was much value in what his father had said. "I am not against an alliance with Manau Gododdin, and Goddeu come to that, for Nudd, too, is under Dyfynwal. Indeed they are our natural allies, lying as they do between us and the Picts, and if there can be a marriage alliance between those painted savages and Gwynedd it behoves us to seek friends where we can."

"Exactly," exclaimed Cynfarch. But his guard had been lowered, instead of anger he felt pride in his son's ready appreciation of the situation and quick grasp of politics. Urien saw his chance. "But Pabo, too, is inclined to listen with favour to the sirens of Gwynedd. Nor would a marriage alliance sealed by me and Garbaniaum's daughter necessarily bring us advantage in the North for he already has three sons, Leuddag, Dumngual and Bran, and it is they who will rule after him not I." Suddenly Urien was inspired. "What I am proposing will give us control both in the West and North. I will take Modron and, if necessary, drive out Pabo, whilst we will secure our alliance with Garbaniaum by offering Morgause's hand to Leuddag."

"Morgause? Your sister?" Cynfarch stroked his chin, thinking through the plan. "Would you have me force your sister and not yourself?"

"Ask her. I think she will not refuse. Leuddag is said to be not without admirers and many would wish to marry the heir to Gododdin. What greater kingdom could there be for a daughter of Cynfarch? As for me, I ask not for myself but for Modron and your grandson. Aye, father, Owen he will be called and I will have him acknowledged as legitimate heir. Father, as you love me and I you, so I love Modron and so will you. I ask for your blessing upon our marriage consummated in the greenwood and thus by ancient law already reality".

Cynfarch looked at his son, his eyes full of sadness and love. "So, it is Morgause."

Urien's father made as if he needed to relieve himself and quickly crossed the yard to the house of the women. He found his daughter braiding her long copper hair before a heavy bronze mirror held by her maid. Cynfarch dismissed the servant and peered down at the slim face, a face that reminded him of his dead wife; a face lightened by what Cynfarch had to say. Morgause threw her arms about her father's thick neck and kissed him on the cheek. "Garbaniaum has not agreed yet," her father cautioned. Then he laughed, "Not yet, my love. Not yet."

So Cynfarch had returned to the emissaries offering his daughter and his arms in the war against Dyfynwal of Clud. But those emmissaries had perceived more of the truth than either Cynfarch or Urien wished. "It is a sad day, Prince Cynfarch, when as great a warrior as you is trapped by his own son, your better judgement surrendered to his passions. Yes we accept your daughter and we will fight together but as Urien has refused the love of Manau Gododdin so She will refuse to love him and his heirs. This destiny we place upon him, that as he has set his bastard heir ... "

"Bastard? Bastard?" cried Urien drawing his sword. "See father, how right I was to insist that Owen should be acknowledged as legitimate by my formal marriage to Modron ... "

Urien stopped short, realising too late how he had been goaded into giving that information his father had concealed. Cynfarch put his hand on Urien's, urging patience. A sword cut away the emissary was intoning, inaudibly now, the geis: a destiny that now would remain unknown until it came to pass.

Angry with himself Urien bid them make haste, for he would not have it said that he was frightened.

It was midsummer when he had set off to find Modron and his son. Of her riddle he had been able to make little sense. Some of those he asked merely shrugged their shoulders unable to help. Others thought Modron had spoken of the Otherworld where, beyond the Sea of Glass, beyond the western ocean of which the Sea of Rheged and Manannan are mere fringes, a man might find the Isle of the Blessed and all he holds dear; but these advisers took it as proof that the girl was indeed the Morrigan. The Morrigan! The very name might freeze a man's heart. Upon such counsel Urien turned his back, wrapping his cloak about himself to keep away the chill of despair which was creeping over him. So winter passed and Beltane came and as the grass sprouted anew and leaves unfurled themselves from buds so new hope sprang in the heart of Urien. Besides the warm fire of Beltane he had sought out the wise woman and, guided by her, had set out at midsummer to find the Keeper of the Silent Stones. He travelled westwards but always north of the Oak River, careful to avoid Pabo's men. Whenever he could he rode under the cover of woods and thickets, making detours whenever he glimpsed smoke or sensed that he might be near a farm. Like a bear, stronger than any man yet shy of them, he kept to himself until on the evening of the third day he reached the fort of Setlocenia which some call Alauna.

There, where once merchants, soldiers, priest and whores had jostled together Urien found only silence. The ivy clad walls of the fort rose sheer from the cliff top, trees growing where sentries had once paced gazing, like Urien, across the Sea of Rheged to the lowlands of Mabon and the mountains of the Mordei. Westwards they stretched as far as the eye could see and where they touched the horizon they seemed to float, suspended between earth and heaven. But of Manannan there was no sign. The island lay invisible, wrapped in the cloak of the sea god. Urien turned his back on that adversary and descending the rubble-strewn stairs entered the town that had once gathered about the soldiers of Rome like children about the skirts of their mother.

From there a short ride brought him to the harbour where screeching seagulls dived about a curragh moored on the river side. Urien sat astride his horse examining the boat. What had Pabo said? " ... they came in ships the like of which our people had not seen before." Jumping down Urien ran his hand over the taut leather, feeling the ribs within: wondering. Was it in vessels like this that Modron's people had come and if so did this one too belong to them?

Suddenly Urien realised he was not alone. Beside him stood a gaunt figure dressed in the salt-stained leather jerkin and breeches of a sailor, his features lost in the shadow of a hood.

"Where did you come from?" stammered Urien.

The shadow smiled. "Now that is a question. My father would give you one answer, my mother another."

"And who are you?". Urien backed away, reaching for the reins of his horse but not taking his eyes off the figure.

The shadow followed. "Me? I am nothing. I am my mother's son. I am a sailor. I am a fishermen. I am Brian and I am Niall. I am the Guardian. I am the Ferryman. I am who I am and who you would have me be."

"I seek the Keeper of the Silent Stones."

"Foolish would be a Keeper if he did not ask who sought his charge."

"Urien, son of Cynfarch, seeks help. I am seeking Modron, daughter of Avallach. I was told the Keeper of the Stones might help me, and hither I came directed by one of the old faith … "

Urien had thought the figure shrank somewhat at the name of Avallach, and when it spoke it seemed its voice was wistful. "What they say is true. When Rome still watched, our people came: the Eoganacht. Pirates set against pirates some said but were the Romans not pirates too? Did not Bran himself steal Prydein from the giants he found here? Did Moses steal his holyland or was it God given? Of the Eoganacht I am, but I am not one. Keeper of the Stones I am. But see, night draws on. Come now and tomorrow I shall take you in my boat to seek your destiny."

The shadow led the way northwards, and as they walked, stepping over fallen columns and ducking under elder, hazel and birch, Urien's guide told of his journeys into the western sea, but of Avallach and Modron he said nought. Suddenly he stopped, his hand gripping Urien's arm. "Listen, he comes."

"I can hear nothing … "

"Sshh"

Then Urien heard the crashing in the undergrowth and a magnificent stag appeared in front of them less than ten paces away. Stag and men examined each other. "Behold the Horned One, Guardian of this place," whispered the figure at Urien's side.

"I thought you were the Guardian."

"Does not the trusted servant act as steward when his lord is absent? As the bishop is both servant and shepherd of his flock so am I to his kind. Blessed are you to be honoured by his presence and to have him gaze upon your countenance. It is the sign of victories to come. Do you plan war my friend?"

Urien turned to look at the figure by his side: how could he know what was planned for Pabo? But in that moment the stag turned and trotted from their view. Urien watched the beast go before turning once more to question his guide, but he too had vanished. Urien cursed himself for being a fool and began to search for his horse.

But before he had gone far he heard again his former guide: "Leave your horse if you desire that which you came to find". Urien spun round but whence the voice came he could not see. "He sees and yet he does not see. Darkness may hide many things from the unbeliever. Should not a man kneel before the Stones and ask for guidance?"

It seemed to Urien then that the voice came from the black shadow beneath a tangle of bushes, and dropping onto one knee he peered into the gloom.

"Aye, desire may overcome many fears and belief be sacrificed for gain", mocked the voice. "You thought this place the Otherworld but your need to find her made you stay. You do not worship the Horned One yet you seek his guidance. Do not be afraid for it is my destiny to serve you, and this is not the Otherworld though I live below the ground, like a fox driven to earth. Come, lord, and behold the place you seek."

A light flared and Urien found himself looking into what had once been a stable. High overhead pink fleshed roots festooned the rafters like enormous cobwebs and prised apart the slates like the gnarled fingers of some ancient giant. They were, Urien surmised, from bushes which, growing on the roof rubble, hid the building from view. But the dry air did not smell of earth and Urien glanced at the floor, surprised to see how little dust had settled between the cobbles.

It was not the building, however, which held Urien's attention but the contents. A number of small slabs were propped against the back wall, each carved with an image of a horned warrior whilst in the centre of the floor a stone phallus thrust more than four feet high; its top carved in the likeness of a human head, a torc about its neck. Urien stepped forward and sat crosslegged next to the figure he had followed from the harbour, watching as his companion placed a pine cone on the small fire alight on the floor. Finally, when the cone was glowing and the air filled with heavy scent, the Guardian turned and Urien saw for the first time his eyes. Dark eyes that bored into a man and then became deep, languid pools in which one might seek the bottom and see only oneself or a blackness like the abyss of time in which heroes and people unknown are momentarily glimpsed, like fish darting from one shadow to the next. With a blink the vision past and Urien beheld a smile. "Now we too can eat and talk some more."

They had talked late into the night. Of Brian himself Urien could learn little but the mysterious stranger talked easily of his many journeys and of ancient heroes until Urien was not quite sure which was which. And when at last he fell asleep it was to dream of Owen, Cu Chulainn and a horned warrior. Sometimes they were but one person, sometimes they struggled with each other and sometimes the face beneath the horns was that of Brian.

In the morning they had made ready the boat, loading skins of fresh water and stowing bundles of food wrapped in oiled leather. Brian had placed hurdles along the bottom and onto these they coaxed Urien's horse, waiting for the drugged feed to take effect before they could tie the beast and stow it aft. At midday they eased the boat out into the river, letting the ebb tide carry them down the narrow estuary towards the open sea. There they headed north of west and Urien was surprised to find that, even when loaded, the curragh seemed to skim the surface like a water beetle on a freshwater pond. With both of them rowing they made steady progress.

"Aren't we heading in the wrong direction?" called Urien over his shoulder.

"Not unless you want to see Pabo again," came the answer, borne by salt spray. "We could not have sailed out of sight of land and reached Avallach's by nightfall. Today we will beach below the mountains of the Mordei and tomorrow, if the weather holds, sail south."

It had been late in the afternoon of the second day when Brian pointed to a small rock on the eastern horizon. "There is our guide at whose feet you will find her whom you seek." Excitedly Urien moved forward, a hand shading his eyes as he tried to get a better view but, for what seemed an eternity, their new guide appeared not to grow in size. Impatiently Urien checked the foaming wake of their craft, reassuring himself that they were still moving. Three herring gulls soared and dived about the bows and Urien watched them jealously, wishing he were one. So the minutes passed and the rock became a mountain and the mountain Yrechwydd.

They made landfall on a golden beach a little to the north of a shallow bay. As soon as the prow nuzzled the soft sand Urien waded ashore straining to haul the boat far enough up to unload his horse. Behind him Brian too worked fast, anxious to be off as quickly as he could. So it was that when Urien had looked up from rubbing the stiff legs of his mount it was to find Brian pushing his boat back out to sea. "You will find her at the head of the bay," he called, a hint of bitterness or enmity in his voice. Then the tone changed. "Farewell, until we meet again, Urien son of Cynfarch. Farewell until you need me again."

Urien mounted and rode inland, climbing the first crest of sand dunes which bordered the beach. There he halted, surveying the shallow estuary which lay infront of him. Its edge was fringed with tall green reeds, its black water teeming with geese, ducks and waders. And on the far side, above a shallow cliff, there rose a smudge of smoke, a beacon to guide the sailor of Llwyfenydd. Behind him a strong wind was rising, sending grey clouds scudding across the pale blue evening sky. The marram grass and reeds began to bow and weave and in the open bay grey waves flecked with white spray drove against the pink cliffs. The light was fading and a storm was brewing.

Urien reached the far bank of the river just as the first drops of heavy rain began to fall. In front of him a meadow stretched to the ruins on the cliff top and to the building which nestled in their lee. Urien slowed, hoping he could catch the occupants by surprise. The rain was falling heavily now, whipping across his face, and his cloak flapped and snapped noisily in the wind. Yet above the tumult of the growing storm was the unmistakable cry of a baby.

A rain-soaked figure ran around one corner of the building, her bare feet splashing through the puddles that were rapidly forming beneath the eaves. Suddenly she stopped and looked towards Urien. "Urien!" Turning from her errand she ran out to greet him. "I knew you would come, you haven't changed at all."

Urien wiped the water from his eyes and looked down laughing. "But you have, for I heard little Owen cry just now."

"Come and see him."

Modron led Urien into the house and stood by his side looking first at the baby and then at the father. "Do you want to hold him?"

Urien hesitated.

"He who can put kings to flight so easily must be a great warrior," she observed.

"Of course. He takes after his father," retorted Urien recovering his composure and, putting his arm about her slender waist, lifting her up so their lips might touch once more.

Later, as the rain rattled against the shutters and oil lamps flickered in plaster niches, Modron's father had recounted for Urien something of the history of his people. They were, as Urien had already learned, descendants of the Eoganacht; Gaels who had come from Hibernia as foederati and been given land in return for military service. "So we are both part of and separate from Pabo's kingdom," exclaimed Avallach at last. Then he took Urien apart much as any father in law might. "You have heard tales of Modron." It was a statement as much as a question. "My family is indeed descended from the Tuatha De Danaan, the people of the goddess whom you call Brigit. Their skills, weapons and knowledge were without parallel but their enemies called it magic. Skilled beyond the understanding of all others they were but they were also mortal and so they married amongst the Gael and their blood was weakened until few now remain. Something of them remains in Modron and its seed, planted in Owen, is the dowry she gives you. It is a treasure to be prized above all others and to be guarded jealously."

"Aye, for few are descended from Brigit now," continued Avallach wistfully. His eyes were fastened upon those of Urien but they did not see him: they were looking far beyond into a world without limit, without time. "Perhaps one day the Tuatha De Danaan will regain their strength."

Suddenly Avallach returned, his eyes twinkling. Slapping Urien on the back he called for more wine and for another song. And when that was finished Avallach bade Urien tell of his journey. So Urien recounted his story; Modron's head against his lap. Once or twice when Urien expressed an interest in a particular place Avallach would add his knowledge to the story but it was noticeable that he did not speak of the Keeper of the Silent Stones.

The following day and with Owen carefully wrapped Modron led the way eastwards towards the mountains and, beyond them, Llwyfenydd. They rode quickly and soon were climbing upwards towards summer pastures and the fort which Rome had built to watch those grazing grounds. But the wolf had gone and instead of bellowing officers there were only lowing cows, bleating sheep and a single, lone stag which watched their progress from afar. So they travelled, in easy stages for the sake of Owen and his appetite, and within four days reached the lush limestone slopes of Llwyfenydd. And there, as Urien had predicted, his father had loved both Owen and Modron.

* * *

Urien looked down at her now. She was asleep, her head on his chest, her arms about his neck. She lay as she had all those years ago and, in truth, the passing years had hardly touched her. It was difficult to believe it had been so long ago. Since then Pabo had been driven out and forced to flee to Gwynedd with his son Dunawd. There his wife had died and he had entered a monastery. In the north Urien and Cynfarch had helped Nudd of Goddeu win back his kingdom and Owen had been brought up there as a foster brother to Dreon. Manau Gododdin had also prospered and there was peace with Clud and its new ruler Tudwal. Urien ran his hand down Modron's back and along her thigh. She was the gift of his father and his destiny.

In the morning she watched him depart for Moel Fre. She stood beside his horse, not looking up. Urien who had been shouting orders to the others turned and put a broad hand on her trembling shoulder. "Is there something ailing you, my love?"

Modron shook her head silently before looking up with watery eyes at his silver hair blowing in the early morning breeze. "Nothing." She shrugged her shoulders pretending to adjust one of the harness straps. "We both loved your father and yet in a way we both looked forward to this day when you would take the cloak of Coel the Old. I am very proud of you. You look so magnificent." Urien bent forward and pulled her to him, kissing her on the cheek, whispering in her ear, "And so are you". Then he was gone and Modron was left in the empty courtyard knowing in her heart that despite her words the life they had shared had changed for ever.

For a while Urien and his teulu followed the old road, its green surface rutted by wheels, its ditches yellow with marsh marigolds. Southwards they rode, passing a ruined farmstead where before the great plague children had played and grown and where now only nettles competed for height. Within an hour they had gained the top of the escarpment. Below them the sun glinted on the Gweryt as it wound its leisurely way between rich meadows and thick woods before turning south to plunge through its rocky gorge. Beyond that gorge, beyond the flat topped mountains silhouetted against the morning sun was the land of Urien's cousin, Llywarch. Like its ruler it was a gentle land of rolling hills and few mountains. The plain of Llwyfein stretched to the walls of Caer Legion and beyond, it extended to the mountains of Gwynedd, to the borders of Powys.

Urien and his retinue turned eastwards along the crest of limestone, leaving the old road to follow the Gweryt by itself. The undulating slopes of Llwyfenydd lay to their left now, the greensward dotted with white boulders and rock outcrops, hazel, birch and oak thickets, yellow gorse and carpets of cowslips. Here and there, watched over by small boys or old men, sheep and cattle grazed whilst pigs rooted amongst bare soil. Lower down were the farms and wooded slopes of the gentle sided valleys that led to the plain of Idon and Gwen Ystrad: a patchwork of dark green woodland, bright pasture, ripening corn and numerous farms. Overhead a sparrowhawk circled, gliding, watching for the slightest movement below. Suddenly, wings folded back, it plunged downwards and was lost to sight in a fold of the ground.

The teulu rode on, quickening its pace as it passed the first of the great shee mounds built when Leu, the fair haired one, was young and through which it was said one could enter the Otherworld. Now the good pastures were behind the riders. Before them was an area of bare, fissured rock, white stone and black crevices, the home of ferns and stunted trees, fox and wolf. Here it was not possible for the horses to move easily so the party swung away, descending the steep southern face of the escarpment, picking their way carefully between broken cliffs and loose stone, crossing narrow, grassed terraces until they reached the head of the Gweryt. The ground was flatter now and they were able to make good time. By mid afternoon they were able to look down into Moel Fre and upon the resting place of Cynfarch: his farm nestling in the verdant pastures at the entrance to the narrowest part of the valley between precipitous crags and cliffs, the domain of kite and eagle.

Cynfarch lay as Cadwallon had left him, drifting in and out of consciousness. "When he is awake he calls for you, my lord," informed the priest rising from his stool. "He fights for his life, warding off death with some invisible shield until you should arrive."

With a silent motion of his hand Urien dismissed the priest. Kneeling by the side of the pallet he began to call gently his father's name.

His name! From somewhere far off Cynfarch heard it being called. It echoed round the mountain tops and down rocky passages. Far off, his son was calling his name, calling to him. Gathering all that was left of his strength Cynfarch struggled back along the tunnel that joins this world and the next. "Urien, is that you?" He opened his eyes and peered through the mist of death, the door of the shee mound.

"Aye, father, Cadwallon sent for me."

"Cadwallon. 'Twas ever so. Always where he was needed. Alas, he too grows old, for in the future you will have need of many such as him ... " Cynfarch struggled to gather his thoughts and energy. "The peace is ending, Urien. The peace is ending. It is dying with me. In the east beyond Catraeth and Caer Efrawg the Loegrians grow stronger and seek to make war upon us again; to take our land and enslave the people of Prydein. No, not enslave. This time they fight not just to wrest lordship from our brothers, this time they are driving our people from the land. Aye, they come only as a trickle now but soon it will be a torrent unless you act. Urien. Urien, my son, my spies tell me the Loegrians add to their strength daily from across the sea and the

Morrigan too sides with them, driving some of our own into dark treaties. I have seen with my own eyes the refugees; our people driven from the land, women with young children crying for husbands and fathers, crying for food and water, huddled together, crying for vengeance. Not even the child's toy is spared the greed of the Loegrians now. Already their strength is such that a single battle will not suffice. The coming struggle will be a war. A war greater than that of Ambrosius and Outigern; for if we lose, all Prydein will be lost."

Cynfarch continued, racing against time. And his mind read that of his son. "No, not even the Raven Riders will be sufficient this time. Gather them about you for you will need them but seek also the Talismans with which the People of Brigit first guarded Prydein. It is because they have been lost that the Loegrian strength grows. Find them and you will free Prydein ... "

The old man's breath grew intermittent. He was falling back into the Otherworld. " ... the Talismans. Only one descended from the people of Brigit can use them ... Owen ... a lucky marriage for Prydein ... give Modron my love ... "

MYRDDIN and THE BEAUTIFUL HAG

They buried Cynfarch in a shee mound on the highest hill overlooking Moel Fre so that he might guard fertile Idon against its enemies for all eternity. And that night they held a feast and sang of his deeds and of a time before Flamebearer, King of the Northern Loegrians, came: of a time before the plague, of Coel; of a time older still, a time which seemed even nearer the Land of Promise to which Cynfarch had gone than that now slipping from them. They sang that night of the People of Brigit and, as they sang, Urien tried to recall all he had ever heard of the magic Talismans of Prydein.

But it was not a great deal and the following evening he began his journey to the head of the valley, there to stand vigil for the soul of his father and the land. There too, at the source of the river, he might ask its genius to help him find the Talismans and to reveal to him his destiny and the geis placed upon him in Moel Fre all those years ago.

What Urien saw that night and what he heard he would not tell, until two days later he returned to the warmth of Modron. Lying beside her he played absent-mindedly with a tress of her hair, twisting it around his forefinger, gazing upwards. "In that clearing I sat and waited wondering what the future would bring and what the geis was that had been placed upon me. I wanted to see the future but I could not. So I prayed and beads of sweat stood out on my brow and my shirt was wet. Then I dozed and my sleep was like that of a fever; many places came before my eyes and many things did I see, but none was I permitted to remember and I awoke to the certain knowledge I would never be able to see the future. Yet that no longer mattered for I was contented. Contented in the knowledge that if the future is fixed then all we do, all choices we think we make, are already decided. I saw then that life is like a cloud driven before the wind or a leaf borne upon a stream. Destiny carries us all forward regardless of our preference; that is the geis placed upon us. What was it Christ taught? Be not anxious for the morrow. See how the lilies of the field neither sow nor reap ... Every hair of your head is counted ... "

Modron heard his story and knew it to be true. War was coming and their world would not be, could not be, the same one they had known until now. Even so she could not help fighting that destiny. She rolled over and lay on top of Urien cupping his face in her hands, caressing him, seeking to arouse in him the power that would bring them together

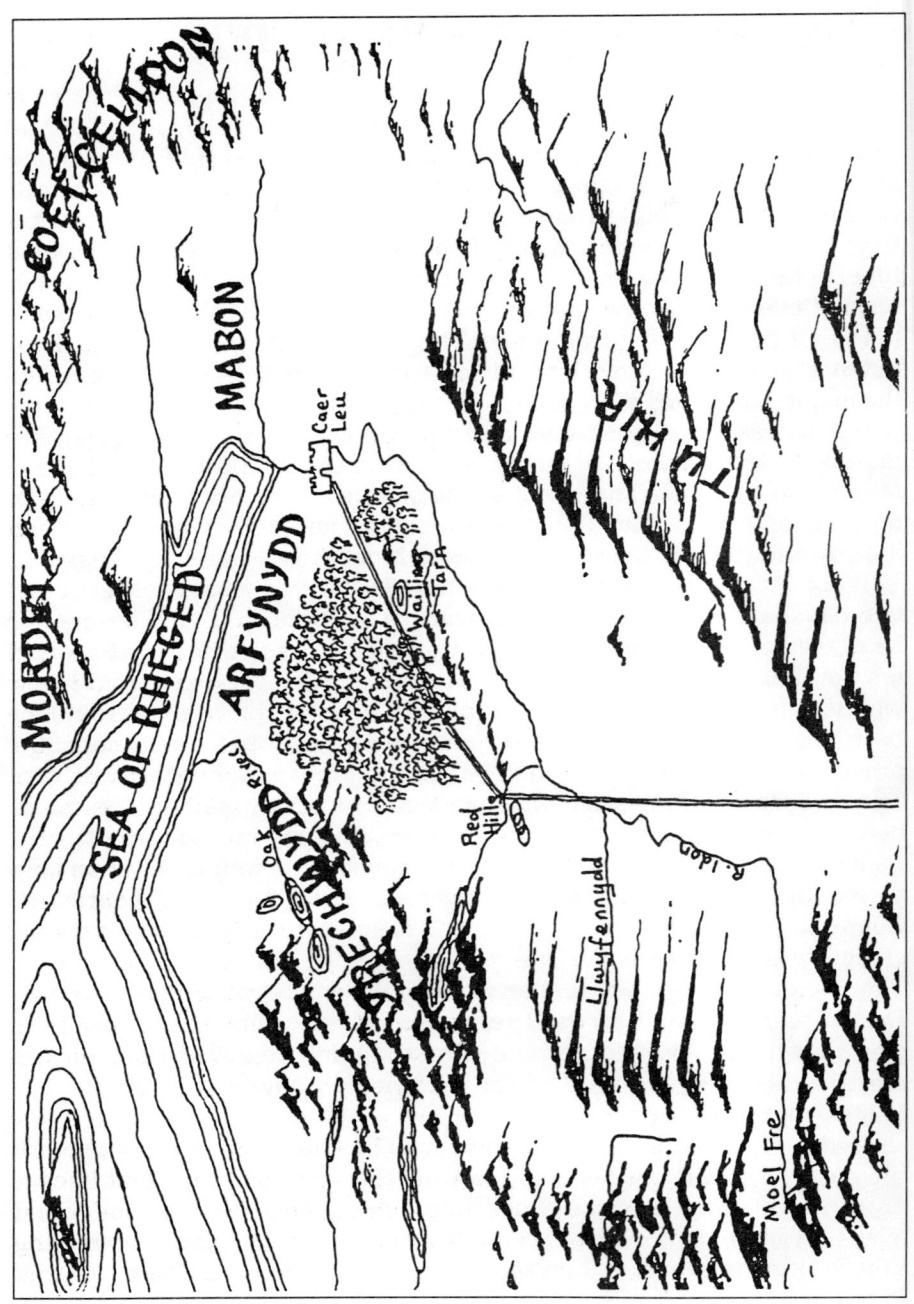

as they had always been. But they did not make love. Urien wanted to talk. He wanted to know all there was to know about the Talismans of Prydein. Surely she knew; for had not her father said she was one of the few descended from the Tuatha De Danann, the very people who had brought and wielded them.

Modron lay on top of him. When she had first met him she had wanted to put the lore of her ancestors away, wanting to be part of his world but now he wanted to speak of those things which she had wanted to forget. How could she refuse him she loved?

"There are many stories and many names," she began, her cheek against his chest. "To seek the Talismans will be like playing blind man's buff in a maze. The Gael, for example, call the Magic Ones the Tuatha De Danann whilst your ancestors called them the People of Brigit. So different people have different names for the same person or the same place. Even where the Tuatha came from is not known for certain but my father used to tell that they came in dark clouds from four great cities: Falias, Gorias, Finias and Murias. There they had learned science and craftmanship so that in every art they surpassed all other peoples of the world. In each city they learnt a different skill and from each city they brought a different Talisman. From Falias came the Stone of Destiny. Upon it in later times the High King of Hibernia would stand and if he were the rightful choice the stone would roar under him. From Gorias came the Invincible Sword from which none could escape when it was drawn from its sheath. From Finias came the Spear of Leu. No victory could be won against it and none against him who held it. And from Murias came the Cauldron of Ulph: a magic vessel in which a wounded warrior might be healed. Some say it gave eternal life, others that it could feast a host of men and never be empty. The Tuatha were wiser and more skilled than any but I have not inherited their arts. I am only partly of their stock and have not studied their ways as my father did ... "

Modron searched her mind for something her father had once told her, for some name. " ... once my father said another had studied with him but that they had quarelled; over what he never said. A druid was this other man. His name, I think, was Myrddin."

Kissing Urien, she slid her hand down his body seeking again that world of love and passion which they had long enjoyed together, but it was not the same, it would never be the same again. Thoughts of Myrddin occupied Urien now. Had he heard that name before? Urien could not recall. He mounted Modron and rode her indifferently, his thoughts far away seeking Myrddin, the Talismans of Prydein and his destiny. Perhaps Gwenddloeu who held to the old gods could help. Rolling off Modron, Urien resolved to ride to his foster brother as soon as the Royal Wedding was over.

Beside him Modron lay still, in a bed that no longer seemed like warm green grass by the side of a foaming stream. Her hand crept involuntarily to her neck. The chain that held the two gilded swans was broken.

* * *

The dykes were white with wild cherry and fragrant hawthorn when Urien, Modron and their retinue set out for the ceremony that would seal his right to the kingship, the marriage with the sovereignty of the land, the Royal Wedding to Rheged. They followed the old road northwards and were soon lost in the trees that crowded the lower slopes and valley floor. The bright sun filtered through the canopy and formed a patchwork of shadow and light across the highway. The ditches on either side were filled with cream, heavy scented meadowsweet. Overhead a hidden nightingale sang; a busy woodpecker could be heard in the foliage and somewhere an incessant cuckoo called. Below them was the broad gentle floor of the Idon, its countless farms hidden by trees and woodlands, and beyond, the massive ramparts of Tu Hir merged with the hazy sky which betokened a hot day. The genii of the plain, the spirits of the woods and fields seemed to be smiling upon the party and to promise a summer of abundance and a winter of plenty.

Across the floor of the great valley they travelled, past fields with well-maintained hedges, near neat homesteads, until late in the afternoon they reached the Redhills and the centre of Rheged. There, at the meeting place of Llwyfenydd, The Lake Mountains and the Forest, the People of Brigit had built three circular sanctuaries. There, at the meeting place of land, water and air, a man might meet his gods or seek to invoke the Powers. For more than two thousand years men had met there to restore the fertility of the land and kingship to the tribe. There the Romans had built a fort to watch the gatherings and guard the crossing of the river and there Ninian had come to build a little church and claim the area for Christ.

Urien looked at Ninian's colony huddled within a circular boundary bank that aped those of the People of Brigit. Within its wall he would spend the night and the following day ride forth to a ceremony older than Christ Himself. "How frail and transitory the monastery looks compared with the great stones of Brigit," he mused, "I sometimes wonder whether our new religion will endure as well as the old, whether there will still be a church here in two thousand, nay, even a thousand years time."

"Don't let them hear you say that," chaffed Modron pointing, to the chanting line of monks coming out to greet them. "They are for ever preaching the end of the world is near. Why should they need permanent houses when they expect to be taken at any time? In truth though I believe there will be a church here for centuries to come. Perhaps not that church, but a church. But so too will the places of the old religion and even the name of Urien and his great son Owen Caesarius will still be remembered here ... "

"Enough," laughed Urien. He placed his hand upon the thigh of the woman next to him and leaning across kissed her. His eyes promised a night of love but their signal was not returned; her brief gaiety had disappeared as fast as it had come for tomorrow he would bed another.

* * *

Owen had come during the night and now, in the light of dawn, he stood with his companions watching the monks go about their business. He dwarfed their frames: a giant amongst men. His golden hair hung like a mane about broad shoulders and his intense blue eyes flashed above a luxuriant moustache. Bronze wristguards shaped like snakes held the rippling muscles of his forearms and on his chest was an elaborately worked corslet of silver. His short kilt was of white linen bordered with gold embroidery, his sporran-guard crimson leather of exaggerated length. To women he was Maponus, the Divine Youth.

Standing amongst his companions he regaled them with stories of conquest, carving the air with large hands, drawing womanly curves and torrid scenes; gesticulating. Thus was the rising orb greeted by their bawdy laughter and the rhythmical chant of swaying monks. Owen watched the monks from the corners of his eyes: men who neither raided nor whored. Yet was not his own son, Kentigern, amongst such men? Kentigern! The thought, the name, the memory pierced Owen's heart. Suddenly silent, he brushed aside his comrades and strode towards the gate of the monastery where Eurdyl, her husband and son were tethering their mounts.

At that moment his mother emerged from her lodgings. "Owen", she cried, running across the courtyard and grasping both his hands. Holding him at arms length she cast a women's eye over him and his apparel. "You do your father proud."

"And you I hope."

"Of course." Modron reached up and kissed him on the cheek. "I shall ride with you and Urien and all the girls and women in Rheged will envy me."

Owen gave a mock bow and as he raised his head his eyes met those of Eurdyl. Eurdyl who was half sister to Urien and a few years Owen's junior. Strange then that he should have seen so little of her. Her mother, Cadwallon's sister, had married Cynfarch long after Urien's own mother had died. "She is grandfather's little indulgence," Urien would say, laughing. From the start he had doted on his baby sister and she, learning fast, had returned those feelings by wrapping him round her little finger.

"Like mistletoe about the great oak is she," Modron would mutter. "And one day she will be as poisonous."

So, increasingly, Owen had seen little of his aunt. The last time was at the age of fourteen, when she had been married to Eochaid, the stolid lord of Arfynydd. Since then she had borne a son, Mouric, and had, Owen judged now, become a woman a man might admire. Owen returned her solicitous glance with a smile. "We must see more of each other, aunt."

She laughed and looked at his sporran. "We will."

Pleased with himself Owen turned and mounted his horse, trotting through the gateway to join his mother and father. Behind them rode the great warband: three hundred picked warriors; three hundred gaily painted shields: three hundred burnished spears and pennons.

In the sunshine of the morning they rode to the three sanctuaries which were the centre of Rheged. The first circle was the smallest and with but a single entrance The second had two entrances and was guarded by large stones, whilst the third and largest was perched above the river, an enormous bank of stones, a white hall in a green meadow. Through its single entrance the cavalcade passed, the grey standing stones silent sentinels as they had been for countless centuries. When they were old Rome had not been born. Of all that the Romans had brought with them nothing had survived without decay. Even their government had not endured and Rome herself had handed back power to those from whom she had stolen it. So the old kingdoms had been restored and Rheged gathered in the great amphitheatre: the Ravens of the Brython returning to their nest after being startled by the passing Romans.

Inside the entrance the champions fanned out, taking their stations at the foot of the bank, their faces impassive. In the entrance Urien and Modron remained gazing towards the centre where a small hut had been specially built between the four stones which were the four corners of the kingdom. The hut's walls were of light wattle, woven from the sacred hazel tree, whilst its roof was thatched with grasses and heather so that it would smell like the summer meadow. Its doorway was closed by the skin of a white cow and in front of that a bronze cauldron hung from an iron tripod, its seething water heated by the holy fire of Brigit from which all others are lit. Now it was tended by the solitary figure of a hideous hag; one skilled in the old arts, bent double with old age and deformity, her face and body hidden by a large, hooded cloak of homespun wool. Modron glanced at Urien and then, with a great effort, she led him to the centre of the circle and the hag. "As the land gives sustenance to us so I freely give my husband that he might be King and the land continue to prosper."

She turned and walked to where Owen was standing with Eurdyl and Mouric. She walked with all the grace and majesty she possessed, betraying nothing of the revulsion and foreboding that she felt. Moreover she wished to remind all gathered there that she and not the hag was the real Sovereignty of the Land. Since she had come to Llwyfenydd had not the land prospered? Was it not now richer in cattle than even before the plague? The hag was her rival. Oh, she knew the crone only acted the part in an ageless ritual but together they had stolen something from her; they had stolen a part of her life with Urien.

No sooner had Modron reached her place in the outer ring than the drums began to beat. Now all heads turned twowards the entrance and the sound of the drums. Big drums beating out a slow, slow rhythm. Big drums beating time for three lines of swaying, straining men who, ropes over shoulders, hauled the Royal Cart towards the circle. Boom ... Boom ... Boom ... On they came, sweat glistening on brow, muscles tense, ropes taut, and always the sound of the drums keeping time. Boom ... Boom ... Boom. Through the entrance they came, the waggon creaking and lurching behind them. Through the entrance and towards Urien and the hag. Boom ... Boom ... Boom ... The drums echoed in Modron's head. She had wanted Urien to be the greatest king since Coel but she did not want this: her eyes began to fill with tears and she clutched Mouric's hand as if to comfort him.

The Royal Cart rumbled past in front of them, its wooden sides elaborately carved, its four large wheels made light by delicate spokes like those of the old war chariots in the poems of the bards. In its centre rode the horse of Cynfarch, Cadwallon holding it steady.

Like his mother, Owen shut his eyes tightly. The waggon reminded him of a time when he had been a little older than Mouric. It reminded him of another place but one where he had not been except in his dreams. His dreams! How many times had he seen that waggon and her riding there? ...

"It is like the story of Troy," whispered Mouric.

Owen opened his eyes and glanced at Eurdyl. With a toss of her head she flicked curls of long auburn hair from eyes fringed with long lashes. "His Christian tutor preferred the stories of pagan Rome and Greece to the traditions of the Brython ... but he has heard the warriors speak of his great cousin and now he is anxious to join him and hear the stories of our people."

Owen studied the freckled face of the boy trying to recall if he had looked like that all those years ago. Had Kentigern?

Modron's son shook himself free of his thoughts and ruffled Mouric's hair with his broad hand. "Heaven forbid that they should be like Helen and Paris. For the king from whom Helen was stolen killed Paris and laid waste his kingdom. That horse was a false one but the horse you see here signifies the divine kingship. Like all our horses it is descended from the speckled race of Mor Greidiawl. They come, it is said, from the land beyond the Sea of Rheged, from amongst the Mordei. It is said there are no people more skilled in horsemanship than the Mordei and that they are descended from the Great Queen herself and that the Romans were afraid of them, calling them cannibals."

The waggon had halted.

"Look, Mouric." Eurdyl put her arm around the boy's shoulder.

In front of them Cadwallon had descended from the cart and was now leading the horse towards the hag who was standing directly in front of the cauldron. Man and beast stopped in front of the woman who was holding a heavy axe. Slowly she raised her arms until they were above her head. Once, twice, thrice she passed the axe across the head of the animal, calling its name. Then, suddenly, the blade came down.

Owen could not explain the ceremony exactly to Mouric so Modron took up the story. "Long before the Romans came, the Great Queen ruled horse and men and no king could be crowned unless she allowed it. She whom you see here is but a token of she who was: the fairest of all. It is said the Mordei are the keepers of her horses now and that a few of her royal line still remain revealing themselves to those whom they choose."

As they talked the hag began to cut up the horse, placing the best portions in the steaming cauldron and pouring the blood into a hole in the ground. Now, as the meat cooked, there was time for the bards to declaim the ancestors of Urien; to tell, lest any should forget, of Coel the Old. It was his daughter, Gwawl, whom Cunedda of Gododdin had married, receiving as a dowry the land of Gwynedd; and it was his first son, Ceneu, from whom the Kings of the North now claimed descent: Guallauc of Elmet and Eleuther Gosgordmaur of Caer Efrawg; Leuddag and Bran of Manau Gododdin, beyond the land of Nudd; Pabo and his sons Dunawd and Samuel Penisel, now refugees from Urien; Gwenddoleu with whom Urien had been brought up as a foster brother: and Llywarch son of Elidyr Lydanwyn brother of Cynfarch. Then the bards told how the first son of Ceneu was Gurgust who inherited Valentia and the territory of Caer Efrawg, the city of the veterans east of Tu Hir. Like his father, Gurgust divided his inheritance between his sons: to the second born he gave Caer Efrawg whilst to the first, Merchiaun, he gave Valentia. That in turn was divided between Cynfarch, the first born, and Elidyr Lydonwyn. So Urien was proclaimed first son of the first son of the first son of the first son of the first son of Coel the Old. He more than any other could claim the right to be heir to Coel, High King of the North, Guledig.

"Will Rheged be divided as the inheritance of Coel and Ceneu was?" asked Mouric.

"No," replied Modron firmly, looking at Owen. "For Urien and I have only one son".

The swiftness and tone of the reply surprised even Modron. It was as if she were jealous for her son: but jealous of whom? Of Eurdyl and Mouric, of the hag? No, surely not. But who would come after Owen? To whom would he choose to hand the kingdom, the fertile land that was his and hers and not that of the hag?

Anger welled up inside Modron; anger that she was letting the crone embitter her and her feelings for those around. Or was there some devilish magic being worked to poison her and Urien? Strange emotions were sweeping over her. Unable to defeat them she shut them out of her consciousness by resolving to help Urien find the Talismans. The life they had known together in LLwyfenydd was ended. She accepted that now and determined to help him find his destiny; to become High King of all Prydein. Was that not what she had seen in her mirror all those years ago? Is that not what she had promised him then? Beyond her the bards were proclaiming messages of loyalty from Llywarch, Gwenddoleu and Nudd and as they did so Modron promised herself that one day all kings would pay homage to her Urien, and her son Owen.

Then the bards ceased. The cauldron's broth was ready and a great quiet descended upon the ring. The hag motioned Urien to come forward and drink.

"You drink from the wealth of the kingdom
You are bound by the truth
If you are false the land shall be waste."

Urien put down the wooden drinking bowl and wiped his hand across his greasy lips. Then with his hand in that of the hag he was led into the hut. Immediately the drums began to beat again: slowly at first then faster, faster, faster, louder, louder, louder. Suddenly they were silent, waiting for Urien.

In the stillness the words of the hag echoed in Modron's head: "If you are false the land shall become waste." How could they have any meaning for her Urien? For Owen, yes; but then he had not yet taken a wife. Modron shut her eyes and prayed. When she opened them it was to see Urien emerge from the hut, not with the hag but a beautiful girl, her lithe body and fertile breasts naked for all to see

"The old king Cynfarch slept with me and I was withered
Urien has restored me.
I am the bounteous lady
The Sovereignty of the Land".

* * *

The next day the party rode northwards through the forest to the Wailing Tarn and the Oenach. At first their road took them past neat homesteads and fields but soon these were left behind and the forest closed about them. Some of the trees, Owen told Mouric, were growing there before men first came to Prydein and amongst them Leu had hunted. "Did he hunt that stag do you think?" asked Mouric. Owen looked puzzled. "You know, the one that has been following us," persisted the boy.

Owen looked at his young aunt and winked. "Perhaps Leu did, and perhaps we might."

"For Owen is lord of this forest now," added Eurdyl.

They came to an abandoned clearing where deer were browsing amongst rank grass, bright dog daisies and rusty sorrel. "I don't think your stag will follow us further," laughed Owen casting his eye over Eurdyl's figure. "Not if he has any sense. You won't see finer hinds than they."

"Aye, and he's not the only horned one around here," murmured Eurdyl.

Owen nodded in the direction of Eochaid's back. "Better than being a boar."

Eurdyl laughed. "Mouric, why don't you go and tell your father about the stag and get Uncle to tell you how he and Modron first met."

After another hour the forest margins began to recede and they turned eastwards past the holy tarn to the gentle slopes of Caer Owen.

Urien walked along its decayed rampart leaving the sound of laughter behind. Northwards he could see smoke drifting upwards from Caer Leu; grey plumes that merged with the silver waters of the Sea of Rheged beyond which were the lowlands of Mabon and the hills of Coet Celidon. And beyond Coet Celidon? Beyond Coet Celidon was the future; the kingdoms of Aeron and Goddeu, Clud, Manau Gododdin and Bryneich. Bryneich, the home of Flamebearer!

Urien recalled the dying words of his father and wondered who else were their enemies and who would strike first.

* * *

During the next few days the weather held fair and Urien and Owen, accompanied by Mouric, were able to hunt in the forest and on the wastelands about the Tarn. Mouric proved to be a skilled horseman and Owen took to tutoring him in other arts, not all of which reached the ears of Eurdyl and Modron. For his part Urien, his thoughts elsewhere, was content to let Owen take his young cousin under his wing as if he were a substitute for Kentigern.

So the days before the Oenach passed and in the evenings, when all were gathered around the hearth and the smell of the day's success filled the hall, the bards sang of past heroes. Yet even now Urien only half listened, lying back in his chair, his legs stretched towards the fire, his mind wandering. But always his mind came back to the same question. Where and how were the Talismans to be found and had anyone heard of Myrddin of whom Avallach had spoken?

Standing behind him, Modron rested her hands on his shoulders and gently kissed the wispy hair of his crown "Gwenddoleu might know of Myrddin".

Urien reached up and put a hand on hers. "Aye, I'd thought of that and have sent a messenger to him. I had hoped for news by now. Do you think Kentigern might help too?"

Modron shook her head. "It is unlikely he has heard anymore of the Talismans than we. But he might have heard of a druid such as Myrddin, and whether such a person is still alive, and besides he could give us news from the North."

"Then tomorrow I will send him a letter."

"You will say nothing of Owen?"

"No, but not because I do not want to." Their hands tightened in unspoken sadness.

The following day the messenger came from Gwenddoleu, asking to speak to Urien alone. "The lord Gwenddoleu sends his greetings and asks if you will hunt with him after the Oenach. Of your query he says he knows of Myrddin and that the druid will come to you in his own time and in his own fashion, perhaps as himself, perhaps as a beast of the forest or a bird of the air."

* * *

That year it seemed half Rheged had gathered for the Oenach. Shrill children chased each other between groups of talking, laughing, drinking people. Pedlars cried their wares: ribbons of linen, silver bracelets, gilded brooches and knives of the best iron. Leather and basket workers busied themselves and smiths hammered at their anvils producing whatever was wanted. Tethered cattle and horses stamped their hooves. Penned sheep bleated and grunting pigs furrowed the ground between thickets as they awaited sale or slaughter.

For three days they celebrated as their forebears had, with eisteddfod and sport, whilst Urien sat in judgement between quarrelsome neighbours. He made murderers pay recompense to the relatives of the dead and those who had injured another were made to provide for their victims until they should recover. Thus he adminstered the law of the Brython which had prevailed for a thousand years before Rome brought her barbaric penalities and Christianity.

On the fourth night, after most of the multitude had drifted home, Urien awoke suddenly, conscious of someone in the room. At the foot of the bed the figure stood, tall and hooded, black against the shadows. Half asleep Urien saw the figure as any one might, imbuing it with all the demonic attributes that lay in the secret fears of his mind. For, at night time when elves and spirits walk abroad, the secret thoughts of all men wander through their senses glimpsed momentarily by a sudden awakening. So Urien, thus awoken, fought to recover his senses and drive back such fears. Drawing his sword from its place alongside his bed he hesitatingly challenged the spectre.

"It is not right for a great king and warrior to fear," soothed the apparition in a voice which was neither young nor old. "Now you do not know me, yet often of late have you dreamt and spoken of me.

My country is the region of the summer stars.
I was with my lord in the highest sphere,
On the fall of Lucifer into the depth of hell;

I have borne a banner before Alexander;
I know the names of the stars from north to south;
I have been on the Galaxy at the throne of the Distributor;
I was in Canaan when Absalom was slain;
I conveyed Awen to the level of the vale of Hebron;
I was in the court of Don before the birth of Gwydion.
I have been three periods in the prison of Arianrhod;
I have been the chief director of the work of the tower of Nimrod.
I am a wonder whose origin is not known.
I am what men want me to be.
I am Brian and I am Niall
I am Myrddin and a thousand years hence,
When this generation shall be but a dream
I will be Merlin."

"Myrddin! " exclaimed Urien in a voice which should have woken Modron. Anxiously he glanced towards the figure sleeping contentedly by his side but she did not move.

"Do not waken her," commanded the spectral figure, "for she and I ... her father and I once quarrelled and, besides, my words are for you alone."

"Is that why you have come at this hour?"

"I come when I may, for I serve many but not least the mystery of this place. When you became King did you not maintain a vigil until the mysteries came to you? So must one skilled in those mysteries order his life. For my part I would ask you to keep vigil with me now."

The figure moved towards the door, pausing there to give Urien time to dress. Soon they were slipping across the courtyard, shadows amongst shadows. No dog barked, no sentry challenged; the hilltop lay cloaked in a deep sleep. Through the gates they passed and along the hollow road that plunged downwards to the Tarn. Urien was held captive by the stranger and his words, as if Myrddin were Ogma first champion of Leu.

The countryside about was lit not by the golden globe of Leu, but by She of the Night. The grass was silver, the air cold and the water like a glass mirror. Patches of mist hung over its surface and amongst the reed beds, light grey in the yellow light. All around was silence.

Myrddin led the King through the drifting mist and thickets which Urien did not recall having ever seen before until at last they came to a small crannog amongst a reed bed. Its sides were made of wattles woven together and at its centre was a wooden statue, its surface black and polished by age. Myrddin genuflected before the image and then turned to Urien, the moon lighting high cheek bones and round, owl-like eyes. If Myrddin heard Urien gasp he gave no sign, but said, "Behold the goddess of this lake. Once she was feted by all men and it was in her honour that the oenachs were instigated here. And at each Gathering she would leave this secret place, riding amongst her people upon a waggon hauled by men. So she inspired the poets, athletes and judges who met in her name and into her keeping, to her glory, warriors gave the spoils of victory."

Myrddin moved to the water's edge and knelt down, feeling for something in the water. The cold seemed not to penetrate his bare body and it was some time before, grunting with satisfaction, he stopped searching and began to haul on something heavy. Slowly a large, dripping leather bag emerged from the water and, as Myrddin landed his catch, there was a clink of metal.

Urien watched the druid unwind the rope around the neck of the bag, gasping as the contents cascaded out: gold, silver, bronze; weapons and ornaments. Myrddin rummaged amongst the treasure. "These are the gifts given long ago to the Lady of the Lake. They were hidden here when Venutius, King of the cantrefs you now rule, was forced to retreat before the eagles of Rome. He failed to hold Catraeth against the foreigner and so lost his lands. That you must never forget."

With a cry of triumph Myrddin found what he had been searching for and stood up. In his hand he held a sword. A sword different from any Urien had seen before. "You have been invested with a hazel wand but now the gods through our Lady here invest you with this sword ... " Myrddin paused briefly, his eyes upon the King's. "No, it is not the sword which you seek. It is but a sword of the Caesars; for you shall be called Caesar, Imperator, and your kingdom shall stretch from sea to sea ... "

"But you know of the Talismans?" interjected Urien excitedly.

"Aye, I have heard of them and that there was a fifth, the head of Bran himself. But where they are I do not know. Perhaps some were carried into the Otherworld beyond the doors of the shee mounds for there the People of Brigit still live called by ignorant folk elves and fairies. They are a people who do not grow old and they are beautiful beyond imagination, but they are dangerous. No man may cross the people of the shee mounds without feeling their wrath sooner or later. Perhaps they keep the Talismans to spite us mortals; but I think not for how could those Talismans guard Prydein if they are not hidden in this world?"

Myrddin cackled. "Ordinary folk say the circles of the People of Brigit were built by giants. Giants! So much have we forgotten of their arts. So much have we to learn. Their magic was wrought before iron was tamed and so we can protect ourselves from their wrath by its magic but what does that profit us?" Suddenly his voice became bitter. "Why should we need to protect ourselves against them? Because we drove them into the Otherworld! There they took their arts and secrets. Sometimes they might bestow a gift on those who help them and so we now must hope. Until then their knowledge remains lost. Two thousand years ago those secrets were lost and two thousand years from now they will still be hidden unless they choose to tell us. Some call their arts sorcery but they never were. Is not all science and knowledge sorcery and fable to those who do not understand?"

"You do not need to speak, Urien ap Cynfarch! Do you not yet know what you must do? Have you not understood? Did you not stand on yonder ramparts and see Rheged as a flock from which the wolves must be driven back? So must you act for tomorrow a messenger will come telling you that Flamebearer attacks Goddeu. You must drive him back, and in time you must drive off other wolves until such time as we might find and secure the Talismans ... "

"I gave you the sword of the Caesars because you must act like your father Coel and not like Vortigern. When you defeat your enemy do not simply take hostages and return home but establish garrisons and set your men to rule over the defeated. So the Caesars maintained their rule and so must you."

"And what of your future, Myrddin?" asked Urien. "You spoke before of our searching for the Talismans. Will you join my teulu, for a king needs an adviser?"

The druid shook his head. "I cannot join your court; yet I will serve you in my own fashion and to the best of my ability. You are a Christian and the power within me cannot tolerate talk of the Cross; and mine eyes are burnt by the shrines and temples of your god. Your wife and son too ... they have the blood of the Tuatha De Danaan in them and I prefer not to be reminded ... "

Myrddin stooped and began to replace the bag in its hiding place whilst Urien watched in silence wondering what he had been going to say. Cynfarch's son remembered how Modron spoke of a quarrel between the druid and her father.

Myrddin finished and stood, blinking, in front of Urien. "Does the Christian Church not have schisms and the Christians of one sect persecute those of another? Why then should the Old Ones not also have differed? I did not call the Tuatha De Danaan sorcerers, for they came to a land already wise. A land which was already raising shee mounds and stones. The Children of Light they called themselves and they were the first to work metal, to pull a blade from the stone. They worshipped the sun and said he was a god, Leu, but otherwise they practised a Craft not unlike our own. But they set themselves apart from our Craft, and in their circles raised cones of power against us. So they turned their backs on Mother Earth and we drove them from the Great Mother into the Otherworld and banished them from seeing Leu, for the power of the Mother is greater than all others.

"But just as the Mother can be good and give bountiful harvests so can she be spiteful and send famine. For this reason there are two Crafts: the White and the Black. I am of the White Craft; the Morrigan of the Black. She has more power than any for she is both one and three. Like me she can shapechange but The Mother has also given her the power to bestow death where she chooses.

"This then is how I will help you. Whilst you search for the Talismans I will use the White Craft to keep the Morrigan from you, for should she alight on you, in whatever guise, you will fail. But see, the night is ending. You must return to your bed and tell no one of what you have seen and heard ... "

So Urien found Modron as he had left her and when he awoke in the morning he wondered if he had dreamt of Myrddin. But in his scabbard there was a strange sword and later messengers arrived with news from Goddeu. Flamebearer had struck, the long peace had ended and the war begun.

GWENDDOLEU AND FLAMEBEARER

Mouric ran his hone along the edge of the sword for the last time and held up the blade for inspection as he had seen the warriors around him do. Satisfied he stood up and slid it into the scabbard which hung newly from his belt. Now he was ready for battle.

It had been his mother's idea that he he should stay with Urien and his cousin and accompany them in the defence of Goddeu. Slipping her arm beneath that of Urien she had taken him aside, extolling the virtues of Owen and noting how he would complement what Eochaid had taught the boy. And as on numerous occasions past Urien looked down at the woman beside him and seeing only his little sister had agreed to her request. So when Eochaid returned westward Eurdyl had remained in Caer Owen, watching her nephew teach her son the finer tricks of sword play, running eagerly to bandage the nick which somehow Mouric had managed to make on the glistening, bronze skin of his teacher's thigh. And so now Mouric prepared for battle with the rest of his uncle's teulu.

Urien had given him a new pony and later that morning, two days after the messengers had arrived from Goddeu, he and the others rode north to Caer Leu: a place very different from the farmsteads of Arfynydd and Llwyfenydd. The city lay on a spur above the Idon, a huddle of buildings with the semblance of civic pride standing amongst the fields which kept its population alive. Roads, filthy yet passable, led between dilapidated buildings and open spaces of rubble and weed and along one they rode now, crossing the Idon by the stone bridge which lay beneath the hall Urien maintained at the northern end of the city.

From there they climbed the hill to the ruined fort where Cunedda had first been stationed by Coel. "Here Cunedda married Coel's daughter and from here he and his warband moved south to expel the Gael from Gwynedd," explained Owen.

"And now we ride north to begin the completion of the task begun by Coel and Vortigern," Urien added as Mouric rode by his side. "We ride to halt the Loegrian advance and one day when we are ready we will expel them like the Gael."

"But isn't Modron of the Gael?" asked Mouric innocently. "Mother said she is."

"Aye, but some were good and some bad, some useful, others not so. The bee stings us but we encourage it to breed so that we might have

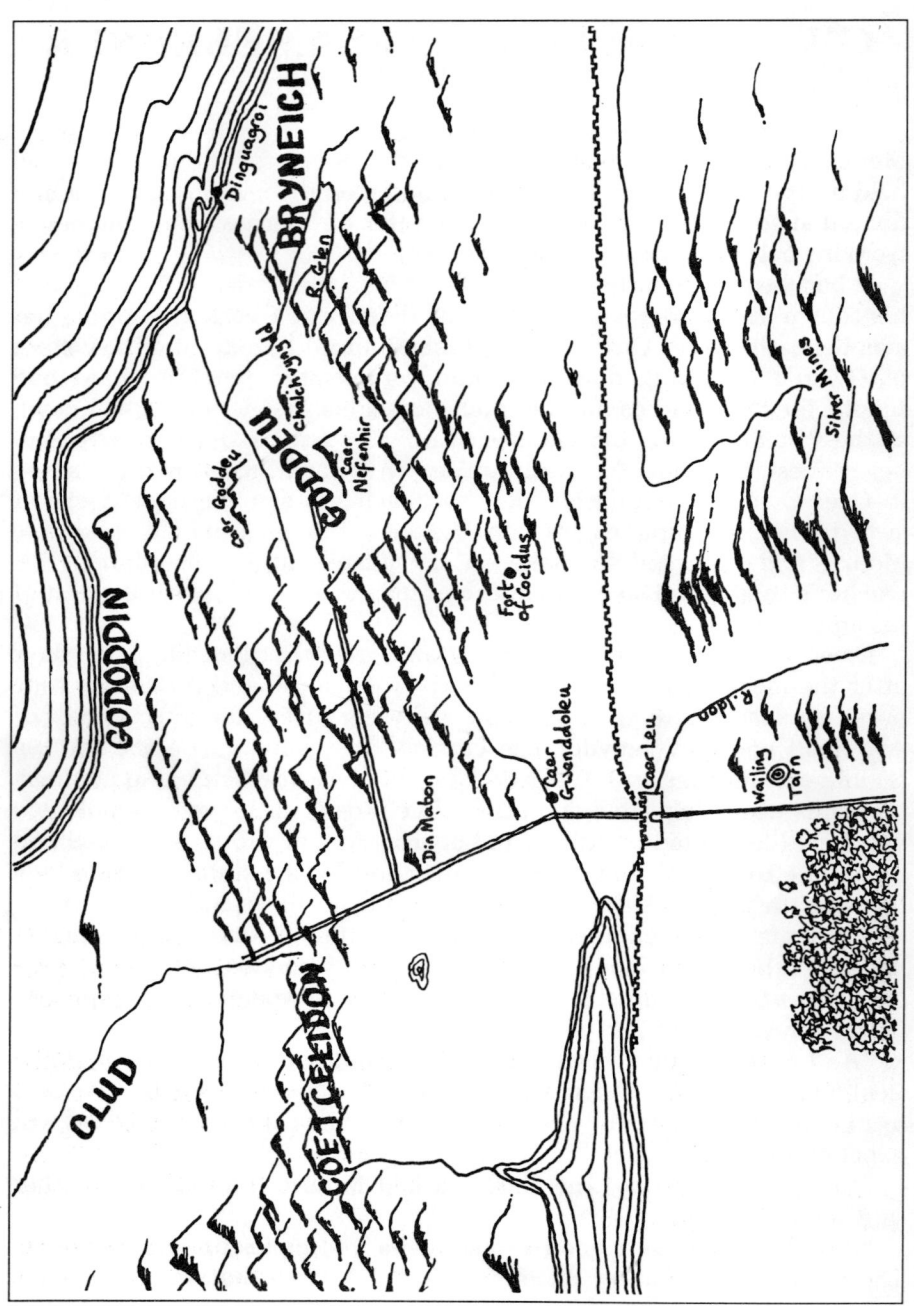

BRYNEICH

Dinguayroi

R. Glen

Plas Chalkynys

Caer Nefenhir

GODODIN

GODDEU

caer Goddeu

Fort of Cocidus

Silver Mines

CLUD

GODODDIN

Din Maibon

Caer Gwenddoleu

Caer Leu

R. Iddon

Wailing Tarn

COET CEIDDON

honey, but we encourage it to breed in its own house not in ours."

"Then will we let the Loegrians live in their own place?"

"For the moment, yes."

"That is what Vortigern said," interjected Owen. "Their own place is across the sea not here in Prydein."

"Tis true what Owen says," admitted Urien, "but had they stayed like the people of Modron there would have been no trouble. They were greedy though and sought to drive our people into the sea. So it was they and not us who started the war."

"Like Flamebearer now," added Mouric as they passed beneath the north gateway of the deserted fort. "When will we be ready to drive them into the sea?"

"When we are strong enough. When we have gathered all we need. For foolish is the warrior who goes out to battle without first having donned what armour he has and what weapons he needs ... " Urien paused, his thoughts far away " ... until then, until the moment is right we shall merely pen them in their land like swine, until the time has come to cull and slaughter as we need. And as we think so do they. They are not ready, yet, to make war, only forays to test our strength and resolve."

Ahead of them lay the wooded mosslands. Stagnant pools, beds of reed, thickets of willow and strands of alder lay to either side of their causeway but where the land was more open they could glimpse the hills of Celidon to the north and the flat topped hill of Din Mabon at the entrance to the pass of Clud. Owen pointed eastwards, showing Mouric the lie of the land and the valley which led to Goddeu. "And where our road forks, north west to Clud and north east to Goddeu, that is where Gwenddoleu lives. None may pass north or south without his permission."

"Did not Urien learn with Gwenddoleu as I with you?" asked Mouric.

Owen laughed. "In a way. Urien was fostered with Keidaw, father of Gwenddoleu after the fashion of our people that he might learn the arts of manhood ... "

"And from the very first day we became great friends," interrupted Urien. "You will find Gwenddoleu my elder, if only by a few years, but the power of his right arm will not have diminished if I am any judge of men. No man could wish for a better companion, and if he still adheres to the old religion, if he still keeps the fire of Brigit tended by virgins, then who are we to object?"

"Are they the same virgins you were telling me about?" Mouric asked Owen.

Owen looked embarrassed and cleared his throat but Urien had not heard the boy.

"Its typical of Gwenddoleu that he should not see the political advantages of adherence to the new religion," he continued, to himself. "And yet, and yet, may not the keepers of the fire of Brigit know of the Talismans?" Relieved by the thought he turned to Mouric: "Did you say something?"

Eurdyl's son shook his head.

"Hail, King Urien," mocked the large figure standing in the courtyard, a broad grin on his ruddy face.

Urien looked sternly down. "Should not a prince bend his knee to his sovereign Lord?" Then laughing at the pained expression of his friend he leapt from his horse and slapped Gwenddoleu on the back. Together they turned and strode towards the hall and the waiting feast.

"You should not jest so with an old man, lest he drops dead in front of you," complained Gwenddoleu smiling once more.

"If that happened," replied Urien, "I would send for my Kentigern, for rumour has it he brought his old priest's robin back to life when the other boys killed it."

"There is a difference between a tiny robin and an old bird like me. It will take more than Kentigern to save this flesh ... Myrddin, perhaps, but not your Kentigern."

"Ah, Myrddin! You know he came to me the other night and gave me this magnificent sword." Urien drew the blade from its scabbard casting his eye over it as he had so many times in the last few days. "Tell me, is he here now?"

Gwenddoleu detected the childish excitement in his friend's voice and laughed. "No. He has gone on one of his many journeys: across the western sea, into Coet Celidon, to the Gael, to Rome perhaps. Who knows where his spirit takes him, but when he returns it seems as if he is fuller of wisdom and power than before, younger rather than older. You and I, my friend, are in the wrong business. Give up your kingdom and become a priest."

"Nay, Gwenddoleu, I would not be a priest for then I would have to spend my time trying to be what I am not. As rulers we must defend our people by scheming, plotting and killing the subjects of others. Our virility ensures the fertility of the land, an abundance of flocks. Can there be another way and if there were would we choose it?"

Suddenly Urein realised they had been standing in the doorway of the hall talking for some time and that their followers were waiting to partake of Gwenddoleu's hospitality. "But come, warriors are not sustained by such thoughts but by the salmon from your doorstep, the venison from your back yard, by pale mead and foreign wine."

The wine and conviviality did not, however, lure Urien's mind from the matter at hand and as the evening became night and the night morning the talk turned to war and Flamebearer, Flamdwyn. "If my guess is right," Urien told his friend, "Flamdwyn intends to take Chalchvynyd and thus partition half of Nudd's land. Then ... " Urien cut a piece of meat in two and devoured one half. "We will need all the men we can get."

"So," added Owen, "I and Mouric will ride in the morning to Mabon and the muster. It will give you two schoolboys time to play together."

Urien and Gwenddoleu looked at each other and at Owen, laughing. Owen poured himself some more wine before sinking back into his couch to watch the two friends, and the maids who came to fill their glasses. He doubted such pretty girls could be maidens, especially the big one, but he would soon find out and the fire he would light would not be Brigit's.

* * *

It was midday before Owen departed for his estates in Mabon.

"How many days will it take from there to Goddeu?" asked Mouric.

"Two at the most. After we have gathered my men."

Mouric nodded, pretending to be unconcerned. "How many men do you think they will have? Are they like us? Have you fought them before?"

"Not so fast," laughed his cousin. "For you as for me this will be the first time I have fought the Loegrians. But I have seen them and they are mortal like us. Which is just as well for we can lop their heads off more easily than if they had two." Owen had drawn his sword and severed a branch they were passing, watching Mouric from the corner of his eye. "Don't worry. It's alright, all men feel like you before going on their first raid."

"But it's not a raid is it? It will be a battle. Mother says uncle Urien says it is the beginning of a war which could mean we all will be killed or driven from the land."

"And ears that flap are more easily severed than those pinned back."

Mouric ignored his cousin. "What are the Talismans of Prydein? Mother says we need to find them if we are to win, but I never heard my Christian tutor speak of them."

Owen considered the question for a moment. Why should Eurdyl concern herself with the Talismans? He shook his head. Surely he was being unnecessarily apprehensive; Eurdyl would simply have repeated a chance remark overheard and Mouric be asking an innocent question. Even so Owen found himself answering cautiously: "I will tell you only what you need to know. They were the first gifts The Fairie made in Prydein: since then there have been others, some good, some bad."

"Is that why we say good luck and bad luck?"

"Yes. An amulet, a gift from a lover might bring good luck, warding off evil just as the Lucks or Talismans will help the Brython deflect the blows of our enemies or protect us against the Morrigan. For remember, even the strongest of mortals can be brought low should she choose: I might perish and you be left. War is like a culling: men and the Morrigan select and choose those who are to survive. Long ago they chose the stock of Coel to triumph and you are one of us ... "

Owen passed Mouric a flask of sweet mead. "So, drink and be a warrior. Live for today for what will happen tomorrow or the day after is already decided and there is nought you can do, least of all worry. If the Morrigan pleases she will give you victory, if she chooses you will perish."

"Then is the destiny of Prydein already decided!"

"Aye, and though it be the work of the Fates and the Morrigan men will still say it was the work of Owen and his cousin Mouric."

* * *

With Owen and Mouric gone, the others rode eastward to the shrine of Cocidius. Gwenddoleu had nodded his understanding when Urien suggested they might hunt in that area for Myrddin had spoken to him of his friend's quest.

"Do you remember the legend of Cocidius, my friend?" asked Gwenddoleu as they looked down upon the old fort at the centre of its natural ampitheatre. "How he fought with Leu against the first inhabitants of Prydein defeating all but two warriors who long after the battle was ended fought on, living in the woods and feeding on the people of Brigit until Cocidius trapped them whilst they were in the form of ravens."

"Aye, and like Cocidius we must be, trapping the Loegrians and imprisoning them before they consume the Cymri. For as the legend says, if ever the ravens escape or be freed Prydein will be lost."

The shrine was different from how Urien remembered it, as if it were used more than before, and the air was heavy with the scent of burning pine cones. It reminded him of that place where, long ago, he had first met Myrddin though he had not known then who he was. Now, as then, it was a while before his eyes became accustomed to the dull red light and the details of the place. The far wall was dominated by the statue of Cocidius; warrior and hunter, half man, half owl, his hands holding spear and shield, a feathered cloak about his shoulders. And to his left there hung the caged ravens, their feathers purple in the reflected firelight. Yet it was neither they nor Cocidius who held Urien's attention but the figure seated in the rafters high above: a figure dressed in a cape of feathers watching the supplicant from its perch.

Urien studied the figure for some time before asking, hesitatingly, "Myrddin?" The shape moved slightly and there was a rustling of its cloak. "Welcome to one of my homes, Urien of Llwyfenydd. Do you come to worship the powers of this place or merely to ask for help in your need as men do now of the Christian God; believing in Him when it suits them and following their own ways when it does not? Nay, I do not condemn, for that is your own affair. Yet I tell you this that it pleased you and will please you to love one of the virgin attendants of this fire . Yes, Urien, though you scorn what you see, in your necessity you came to the Old Ones and they will repay you ... ." The final words were almost inaudible, drowned by the harsh calls of the ravens as they flung themselves against the walls of their cage making it rock violently. When Urien glanced upwards again it was to find Myrddin gone. Urien turned and stumbled over something lying on the floor.

"Cadwallon!" exclaimed Urien as he picked himself up and recognised the prostrate body jerking spasmodically. Running to the door he called for Gwenddoleu. "Quick, bring men with spears!"

Urien knelt beside the old warrior whilst Gwenddoleu's men interlaced their spears to form a makeshift stretcher. "What ails him?" asked Gwenddoleu anxiously. Urien rose, "I do not know but I remember a wise woman living close to here ... "

" ... and so she does still," exclaimed Gwenddoleu, signalling to his men to carry Cadwallon to the small hut tucked into the hillside above the stream.

Outside its door an old woman sat spinning, betraying no knowledge of their approach. Urien motioned for Gwenddoleu to call to her.

"Reverend Mother, fair keeper of wisdom, your son asks you to bestow your healing powers upon his servant Cadwallon."

"What you say is both true and untrue for Cadwallon is not yet his servant," cackled the old woman as she continued her craft. "Bring him whom you call Cadwallon here for as I spin the future so may I weave the threads of life to restore him."

At her command then they carried the unconscious Cadwallon into her hut and set him down in front of the slow burning peat fire. She followed them in and bent down to examine her charge. "Go, for you can do no more. Leave him beside the Fire of Brigit from which each year all men kindle their own hearth that his spirit might be renewed again. The pattern of life is woven and the thread cannot be undone. If my herbs are shown in its design he will recover, if they are not you will not see him in this life again."

Urien followed the others down the slope and then stopped. "You go on," he commanded, "There is something I must ask the crone."

The old woman looked up. "Did I not say you should go? What is it that is more important than the life of your servant?"

"The soul of Prydein, the lives of all the Brython!"

The old woman rose. "Many things I know but not that which you seek. Nay, do not puzzle how I know what you seek, for the Lord of Beasts told me".

"But surely your lore, the lore of those who keep the Fire must contain some clue?"

The old woman threw back her head and laughed, her bare gums black with age. "Aye, we keep the Fire but that is all Leu gave Cocidius. If it were otherwise do you think Myrddin would not have discovered what you seek? Like him you must seek elsewhere. Our ancestors called themselves the People of Brigit yet they were not. As our hearths are kindled from the Fire of Brigit but remain ordinary, so are we to the real People of Brigit."

Once more she bent to feel Cadwallon's brow, leaving Urien to return to his companions and his quest.

"What I cannot understand is how and why Cadwallon came to be present in the shrine," murmured Urien.

Gwenddoleu thought for a moment. "Perhaps he simply wanted to renew a vow. At any rate he has paid the penalty. And you? Did you find anything?"

Urien shook his head.

"So, now we face the Loegrians alone? Will it matter?"

Urien urged his horse forward. "No, not this time."

* * *

Owen had sent word from the hosting of Mabon that in order to save time he would march separately from Urien and Gwenddoleu: that he would take the old road through Celidon and meet them at the head of Goddeu. When he heard the news Urien was furious. "Save time be damned!" roared Urien, "It is the sickness which is upon him again. He whom women call Maponus is mortally wounded by love, love for a dead women. After twenty years you would think he could forget her, but no! God, who will reign after me? Why did you not give me other sons that Rheged might not fear the future?"

Gwenddoleu put his arm on his friend's. "Nay, don't talk so. Many would be proud to have but one son like Owen. Come, you know as well as I that it will save at least one day and that day could make all the difference. Even I know that."

Urien shrugged, apparently not persuaded. Striding from the hall he shouted for his horse, Saran and the others. "Sound the trumpet. We move now, now."

They had been following the river for about an hour when Urien reined in and turned to Gwenddoleu. "Why do I have such a son?"

"Because you are who you are and if you did not have him you would not be happy and you would not be Urien. As you felt for Modron so he felt for Thenew. You were prepared to risk your father's kingdom, he..." the thought flashed through Gwenddoleu's mind that perhaps Urien might never have loved Modron. It was a foolish thought but one which might be turned to advantage. " ... or did you calculate that by stealing Modron you would have a pretext to steal Pabo's kingdom? You should be proud of Owen. He is a man and more than a man. When the prospect of battle is there he will think of nought else but the severing of heads."

Urien laughed. "Aye, you're right; you're right." Then, kicking the flanks of his horse he trotted forward, towards the rim of distant hills, Goddeu and Flamdwyn.

It was late afternoon when they crossed the pass and descended into Goddeu. In front of them rose the conical hill that was both guardian of pass and plain: the hosting place of Dreon. There they found Owen, a broad smile on his face and a cup in his hand. "I hope you will not be as slow in battle," he called.

Urien looked at Gwenddoleu and shook his head. "If only Flamdwyn knew who opposes him he would join Pabo in a monastery, or whatever Woden has."

Dreon was waiting with news of the enemy. Flamdwyn had sent messengers, boastful messengers, claiming that the land was his, that Dreon should be his subject and send hostages to ensure his good faith. None had been sent and Dreon had replied saying that the dogs who had been fed from their master's table were greedy now in presuming to take the food themselves, and he had called Flamdwyn a pirate.

"That will please him," chuckled Gwenddoleu.

"And no doubt goad him. How many days do you think it will be before he reaches you?" asked Urien.

"Tomorrow."

Gwenddoleu winked at Owen. Urien pretended not to notice. "Then the sooner we spy out the land and make our plans the better. And after that we can feast and you, Dreon, can tell me of your father for it is a long time since I saw old Nudd."

Together the allies climbed to the top of the mountain, to the citadel of Caer Nefenhir. From its walls, protected by huge ditches carved long before man first came there, one could see almost all the land of Nudd. Westwards and as far as the eye could see were the mountains of Celidon, serried ridges pale grey in the afternoon light. Northwards were the twin peaks of Caer Goddeu and beyond them the southern hills of the Gododdin, one time home of Thenew. Eastwards the plain stretched to the sea and there at the south eastern corner of the plain, three days ride away, was Dinguagroi, the rock which Flamdwyn had made his own.

Bryneich itself, the land of Flamdwyn and the Northern Loegrians, lay behind the hills which formed the southern edge of the plain and could, Urien observed, only be reached by either passing beneath the walls of Dinguagroi or through one of the valleys near Chalchvynyd. Urien pointed the hill out to Mouric. "See how it lies in the centre of the plain and overlooks the valleys. Whoever controls Chalchyvynyd controls Goddeu. There Flamdwyn will come and there we shall meet him."

So it was that the next day the armies of Dreon and Rheged marched down river to Chalchyvynyd and there turned south east towards the southern hills. They halted on a wooded hilltop overlooking the broadest of the four valleys that led to and from Bryneich. "Why don't we ambush Flamdwyn?" asked Mouric. "It will be easy in a valley like that one."

Owen shook his head. "We don't know which valley they will use"

"And if we divide our forces to cover every possible route we will not have enough men at any place to ensure victory," added Urien. "On the otherhand Flamdwyn will probably divide his forces, some coming up the plain from Dinguagroi and some through the valleys in front of us. From here, then, we can watch all the fox's holes."

"What do you call this place?" Mouric asked Dreon.

"This is Llwyfein and yonder river is the Glen. Beyond that pass, where the valley opens onto the plain of Bryneich, our ancestors built a great fort and there now Flamdwyn has a palace."

"Then we will burn it after the battle!" cried Mouric.

"Aye. We will burn it," agreed Owen. "But before we do that we will play with the fox. The men of Rheged will hide in the wood and let Flamdwyn surround Dreon thinking he has him cornered like a chicken."

"When it is really he who will be surrounded."

"Exactly! But first we must get some sleep."

The evening's drink made Mouric sleep soundly and when he awoke it was to find several columns of smoke drifting up into the still, eastern sky. "See, Flamdwyn is already on the move," observed Dreon who had come down the slope and now stood beside the boy. "There is yet time for us to order ourselves."

"But how do we know they are not already near?"

Dreon thought he detected an urgency in the boy's voice that had not been there the day before. "Don't worry. Those are our signal fires you see. Stay close to Urien and not Owen and you will be all right."

By midday the warning fires had been replaced by runners. As Urien had predicted, Flamdwyn had divided his forces and now they were advancing in four groups. Not long after, Mouric saw the first of the enemy moving through the tall grass. They had obviously seen Dreon and were waiting for reinforcements. Mouric studied them closely, they looked no different from those about him. "No different except they don't belong here," Owen reminded him. "Appearance means nothing. Remember the Morrigan and how she can ensnare us by her beauty."

The Morrigan! Urien gripped afresh the sword Myrddin had given him, feeling its balance, praying the druid could keep the Morrigan from their backs that day.

In front of them the Loegrians were encircling Dreon's tiny force. At their head was a tall, bearded man; Flamdwyn. His black surcoat was embroidered with flames and flames wrought in burnished gold adorned his helm, tongues kindled into life by the sun, striking fear into the heart of those who beheld him. Striding forward now he called to Dreon: "The dog stands on the table and says give me the food, master, or I shall devour you. Where are my hostages, Dreon?"

ELEUTHER and TALIESIN

"Is it true the lord Owen killed one hundred men alone and that Flamdwyn is dead?" asked the maid as she plaited Modron's hair.

Modron turned quickly, pulling her tresses from the girl's fingers. "I know no more than what the messenger said and he did not mention Flamdwyn."

"But they say in the kitchen ... "

"All that they say in the kitchen is not true ... "

The girl turned pale with the sudden realisation that her man might not be returning as she had been told.

"Why don't we ride out to meet them," cried Eurdyl rising. "It will be good to see our Mouric and Eochaid, Urien and Owen once more."

"Owen!" Modron gave Eurdyl a glance of disapproval but before she could say anything the other had gone, calling for her mount.

"Wait for me," called Owen's mother.

They found the army enveloped in a cloud of dust, its progress slowed by the large numbers of captured cattle. Flies hung round both man and beast, briefly landing before flitting away: hooves drummed on the baked track and tails whisked in the summer heat.

"Is it true you killed a hundred men?" Eurdyl asked Owen as she rode between him and Mouric.

Modron's son blew a fly from his nose. "Not quite but I did loose count."

"You should not have come like this. It is not fitting," Urien told Modron.

"And why not? You were not angry with Eurdyl."

"She is but a girl."

"A girl!" snorted Modron.

Urien rode on in silence. He and Modron were growing apart with each new day, and with the passing of their youth the peace was passing from the land. What then did the future hold?

"Somehow Flamdwyn managed to escape," he complained that night as they lay awake. "We have gained only a respite, there will be no peace 'till one of us has driven the other into the sea."

"But when that time comes the Brython will be stronger than now whilst the Loegrian will have only regained that which they had."

"Perhaps. But this I know, that without luck we shall not prevail ... "

"The Talismans! Is there nothing else you think of now that they

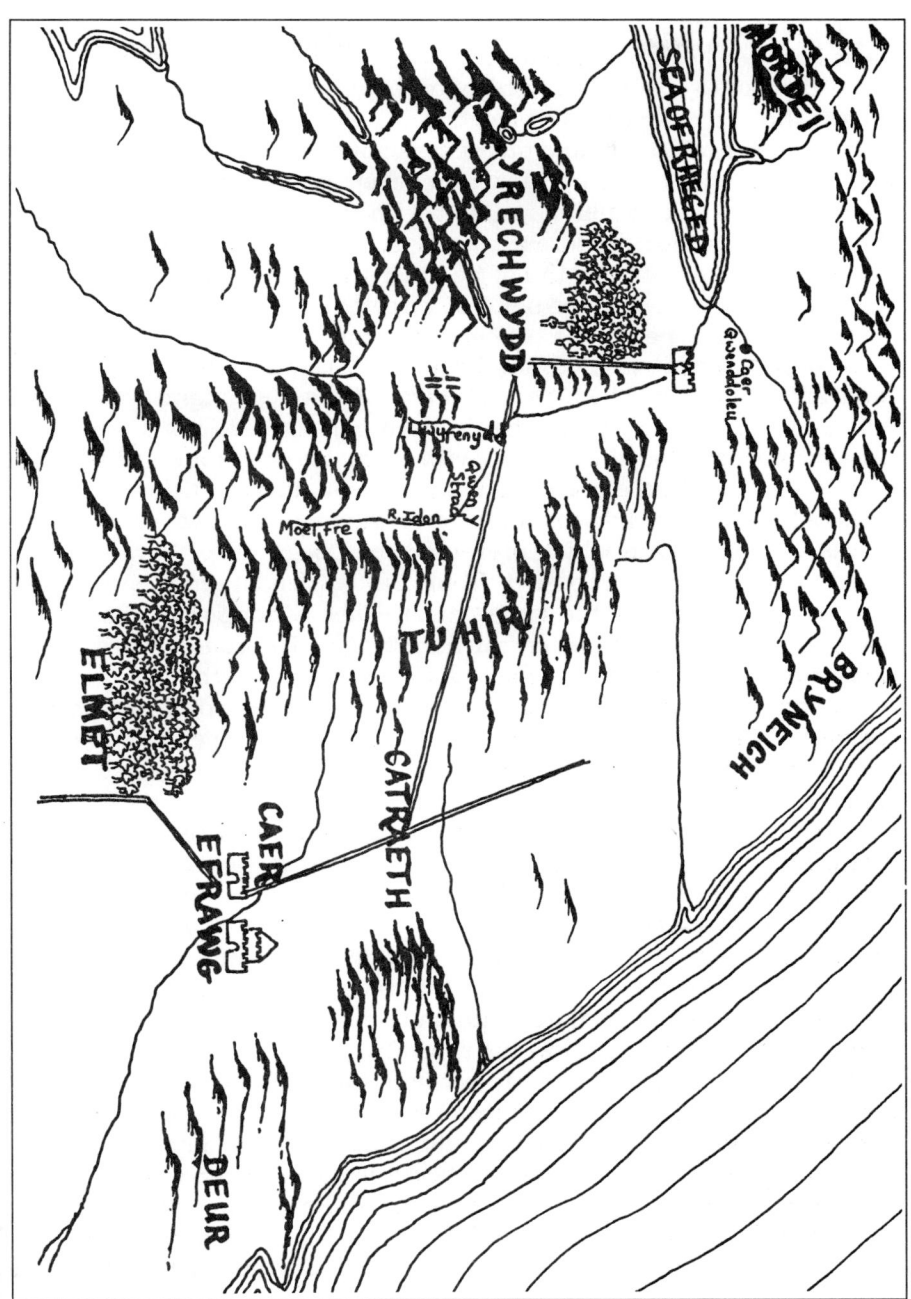

come between us so?" cried Modron turning over. Relenting she turned back and ran her finger lighty across his chest. "Once there was only one Talisman to ensure the fertility of the land. One Spear of Leu." Her fingers slid down beneath the sheet.

Urien slept fitfully. In and out of consciousness he slipped, dream and reality inseparable. Was it a dream when he saw an exhausted owl perch by his side and tell of its fight with the Morrigan, exhorting him to find the Talismans before all was lost? Perhaps, but in the morning Urien was certain of one thing: he must ride to the eastern lands and seek the Spear of Leu as the owl had directed.

As soon as the spoils of victory had been divided they left Gwenddoleu and travelled southwards. With them rode Eurdyl and Mouric for she had asked it they could. "For so we might broaden our education," she told her brother and he had agreed, but Modron had insisted Eochaid too should ride with them. So they journeyed, first to Caer Owen and thence to LLwfenydd and from there to Catraeth.

Like his father, Owen knew the strategic importance of that cantref. It was a great bastion which prevented the Loegrians of Bryneich from effectively uniting with those of Deur. But it was not only the foreigner who coveted Catreath; the kingdoms of Caer Efrawg and Elmet to its south also laid claim. Thus no ruler west of Tu Hir could afford to stay away from the city too long and, as Urien had given the frontier lands of Mabon to his son, so his own father had given him that rich cantref. It was the key to movement east of Tu Hir and whoever held that key controlled the destiny of the North.

They had been in the city a week when the messenger came. "Greetings from the Lord Eleuther to his nephew. The Lord of Caer Efrawg says it is not good that two great kings, uncle and nephew, should be so near and not yet see each other: it is not wise for the Brython to be divided. Let Caer Efrawg feast the Lord of Catreath, the victor of Argoed Llwyfain, as it does Guallauc, King of Elmet."

Urien weighed the words, trying to determine what lay behind the invitation. Eleuther Gosgordmaur had married Cynfarch's sister but now he was an old man and his sons Gwrgi and Peredur were by all accounts the effective rulers. From whom then did the invitation come? Surely not from those two whelps? Had Gosgordmaur exerted his frail frame in a final effort to counter his sons' and Guallauc's influence? "We are always pleased to receive news of your master who rode with my father and Outigern to drive back the Loegrians from Cear Efrawg. The enemy knows his power and trembles. Wise is Eleuther when he says let brother not fight brother, let the Brython be united. Tell

Eleuther then that it pleases us to visit Caer Efrawg and Elmet there to hold counsel."

* * *

Leaving Modron and the others with half the teulu in Catraeth, Urien and Owen followed the great highway southwards. They found the two sons of Eleuther waiting for them at the border of their own land. Of the two Peredur was the pleasanter and it was by his vigilance that the Loegrians had been kept from the walls of the city. He rode now with Urien whilst Owen and Gwrgi followed behind in silence; Gwrgi the cruel, whom men called, 'Garwlwyd,' rough grey.

So the unlikely allies approached Caer Efrawg, the matchless jewel of the plain; its cream walls rising either side of the great river. Through the streets they rode, amongst merchants, craftsmen and farmers; Brython, Loegrians and others from more distant lands. Through the noise and bustle they rode until they came to the towers of the fortress where the she-wolf of the Tiber had marshalled her eagles against the Brython, and Eleuther now held court. Amongst the decay of past glory he now sat, upon a high throne in a deep alcove in the Hall of Emperors. Like some old statue he sat, his hair long and white, his beard reaching to his knees, whilst all around was activity; the preparation for a great feast.

It was a feast fit for kings but Urien could not enjoy it. Like a lofted hawk watching for any sign that might betray its prey Urien studied the two young men seated below him. And whilst they ate, the bard of each king sang the praise of his lord, but neither Urien's poet nor Eleuther's could match Guallauc's man. He claimed his name was Taliesin and, as he excelled the other poets, so he claimed his lord surpassed the other kings and was Guledig. Urien was not pleased. Had he not shouldered the task of defending Prydein? Was not his the aspiration and right to be called Guledig? He remembered Myrddin's promise to send him a bard to sing his praises and wound his adversaries; yet here he was, himself the wounded party.

Eleuther sensed the need to cool the fevered temperature of such wounds. "It is a happy day for me that Urien should come to my house for he is a son of whom a father can be proud. Many times did Cynfarch and I feast and ride together and I look forward to that pleasure again, soon. Yet before I see him I would see his sons and mine agree to maintain the peace between themselves."

"As my father says, so I do," said Peredur rising, a glass in hand. "For who will be able to stand against the sons of Coel should they fight together? As I have driven back the Loegrian from the gates of Caer Efrawg and as Urien has driven him from Goddeu what is there we cannot do?"

Gwrgi stood a little unsteadily. In his hand he held a joint of meat and now he tore a large strip of flesh from it so that his cheeks bulged and he could barely speak. "As my father says, so I do, for together we shall rip the enemy apart and feast upon his lands."

Guallauc stood next, holding up his hand for silence. "Though I am not Eleuther's son I would speak. Though I am not Eleuther's son I would that men should call me so. Let then my arms join those of the Coeling that together the final victory might be ours."

Urien sat unmoved, trying to decide how to counter the words of bard and men. Slowly he rose, and no man stirred. "There can be no victory unless a bard record it but the time has come for deeds not words. And whilst we sing our praises and proclaim what might be, there is one here who has done what we promise and without whose doing we would not be here. Eleuther Gosgordmaur, Eleuther of the Great Army!"

Owen stood and raised his goblet, echoing his father, and all around men joined in unison. "Eleuther! Eleuther!"

Later, when the feast had finally ended, Eleuther called for Urien to join him in his own bedchamber. The old man motioned for Urien to sit beside him. "Caer Efrawg is pleased to see you but I sent for thee not. Why mine sons invited thee hither I know not, yet I may guess. For a day before they sent to thee there came a messenger from the west ... Nay, do not look so surprised for though I am old I have still my flies upon the wall."

"And I am in your debt, for there might yet be time ... "

"I did not send to warn thee for I judged it more prudent first to extract promises from my kin."

"No, you did right but with your blessing I would ride north at first light."

Urien paused and then put his hand on Eleuther's. "But before I go there is one thing I would ask. Before he died my father, your friend, charged me with a task and I have made that my destiny ... "

" ... and now thou seekest the Talismans of Prydein."

"You know of them?"

"I know of one, the Spear of Leu. How do I know? How did your father know to send for Myrddin? Is it surprising that one as old as I should know something of what once was? As for that which thou now seeks it is beyond thine present reach. In Deur it stands, guardian of the coast. Come closer and I will tell thee where to find it when thou art ready."

Behind them, unseen, a curtain moved and a shadow slipped from the room.

* * *

Eleuther's story was fleshed out by the messenger waiting in Catraeth. An army of Picts and their followers had crossed the Sea of Rheged from the area of the Mordei and had raided, were raiding still, Llwyfenydd. Urien nodded. "The Morrigan stretches her wings, our enemies flex their muscles."

"But why did they not attack whilst you were in Goddeu?" asked Modron anxiously.

Urien turned away from the window where he had been standing. "It is unlikely the Picts would ally themselves with the Loegrians, but with Brython like Guallauc ... ? Like a stag surrounded by baying hounds is Rheged. First I must lunge this way and then the other, warding off one enemy and then another. But sooner or later one dog will get through and we will be brought down. Then will all the dogs descend upon the Lord of the Forest, those who helped in the kill and those who stood by and watched."

"This would not have happened if Eochaid had stayed behind as I had wanted," said Eurdyl, looking at Modron.

"Aye, that's as may be, but first we have to deal with those who raid our land and steal our cattle. Tomorrow before dawn I will take the teulu, leaving Owen and the rest of you here, in case Gwrgi and his friends cannot wait to feast upon Catraeth."

"Then let me ride with you," cried Eochaid.

"And me," called another.

A stranger stepped from the shadows where Modron had concealed him. Taliesin bowed, "For there can be no victory unless a bard is there."

Then taking up his lyre, he began to play:
"Let me now sing of that great battle
Upon a Saturday morn,
When four warbands of Bryneich came
Without a day's delay.
Shouted boastful Flamdwyn
Have the hostages come? Are they ready?
Answered Owain
They have not come, they are not ready

61

For a cub of Coel must be sore pressed
Before he'd yield to thee.
Then shouted Urien of Yrechwydd
Arise! Death to Flamdwyn and his kind.
Before the wood of Llwyfain
I saw many a dead man
Upon that Saturday morn.

"Welcome indeed!" cried Urien "Now indeed is victory assured. Yet ... yet how came you here before us when only Eleuther and I knew of my return?"

Taliesin smiled. "Should not a good bard be a fly upon the wall?"

"Perhaps, but if he betrays what he hears then he will be swatted." Urien laughed at his own joke. "So, let us to bed, for tomorrow we have much work to do."

* * *

By the time the eastern sky had begun to lighten, the small army had ridden north west from the city, following the great road which would take them across Tu Hir and north of the Idon. By taking that road and not the one to Moel Fre they might hope to outflank the enemy, to reach the ford of Lech Wen before the Picts. Now, in the first light of day the horses sped over the cobbled track climbing towards the broad pass. They reached its western end by midday and there within an old posting station, above a farm, they halted. Below them a green and gold mosaic of fields and woods stretched to distant, hazy, blue mountains: a land Taliesin had not seen before; the land of Urien and Modron. But it was a land marred: marred by the palls of smoke which billowed into the cloudless sky as if from a hundred pyres.

But the smoke did not merely show the corruption of the peace, it showed the enemy were still active, oblivious to their impending fate. "See how far they still are to the south," Urien told Taliesin, pointing out another orange speck which had appeared amongst the green landscape. "Such fires are beacons betraying their position."

"Beacons to inflame our passion and valour," added Taliesin

"Catraeth's men are up at dawn
For their conquering prince.
Urien is he, far famed chieftain
Strong in war, true Christian lord.
Pictland's men shall know him
Neither field nor forest spared."

Taliesin paused, looking up, "how does the rest go my Lord?"

"Like the wind," laughed Urien. "See, here come fresh mounts." He pointed to the column of men and horses winding its way up from the narrow valley below. "Yesterday, when you were but a fly upon the wall, an annoyance in Caer Efrawg, I sent messengers into Moel Fre to gather as many mounts as possible and to meet us here. For a good general knows what to ask of his men and horses."

"Who can defeat a lord who sees the future?" asked Taliesin admiringly.

Urien smiled but did not reply.

Soon the men of Catraeth were galloping down into the valley of the Idon, pennants and cloaks streaming behind, the air rushing upon their faces. Like the helm wind which descends the walls of Tu Hir they rode; past the ruined fort at the mouth of Moel Fre they galloped, along the floor of Idon towards the ford of Lech Wen and the fort of Guinnion. And there as dusk was settling they learnt they were in time, that the enemy had not yet passed back across the river.

"The enemy must ford the river here," explained Urien in the morning. "And whilst fording the river they will be at a disadavantage."

Taliesin nodded his understanding as they cantered across the meadow towards the river's edge and the small army which Urien had deployed along the cliff top and amongst the trees and bushes either side of the road. Moving forward under the cover of the bushes they looked across at the meadows in the bend of the river opposite. In the distance a wall of flame was beginning to engulf a field of ripe barley, the crackling of its flames drowned by the shouts of the raiders marshalling cattle and other booty for the crosssing.

On they came, silver, glistening spray thrown into the air, but at the top of the steep river bank they found the way between the dykes too narrow to take the full width of their column. As the leading cattle and horses halted momentarily, jostling to squeeze into the funnel of the lane, those climbing behind began to slip back, unable to maintain their hold. Men and beasts slithered into each other or rolled into the river below. Cattle bellowed, men cursed and shouted; a cacophony of panic above which there rose the strident notes of a horn, Urien sounding the attack. On horse and on foot, on dry land and in the river men fought; in green field and in red waters until at last the Picts, seeing they were hopelessly outnumbered and unable to advance or retreat, surrendered. Wet and weary they stood upon the sand banks, arms crossed, isolated; the loneliness of defeat.

Urien stepped over the bloated body of Tuan and pushed the charred gate to one side. Here and there wisps of blue smoke curled upwards from the heaps of torn thatch and half burnt timbers which had been his hall. Like a doused hearth ringed by stones the farmstead lay smouldering upon the hillside within its wall. Wearily Urien clambered onto his horse and trotted across the green slopes, riding he knew not where. Where now the prophecies of glory? But was not all war so? Would not all of Prydein smoulder thus, aye and be lifeless too, unless he won through? Angrily Urien drove his heels into the flanks of his horse, resolving to make good the losses of his people; to restore the land which had been his and Modron's world.

Throughout the next week, with Taliesin and most of the warband returned to Catraeth, he busied himself. But at nightime he would sit brooding, staring into the hearth. And so it was that the stranger found him, head bowed, a mead cup in his hand. Urien did not look up, he did not need to. "Isn't it strange that flames such as these, flames by which a man cooks and warms himself should also bring him ruin and pain, destruction of house, goods and crops?"

"It is so, my lord," comforted Myrddin, "but it is not the flames themselves which bring good and pleasure, terror and destruction, but the way they are used. The fates, blowing this way and that, may fan the conflagration until it has consumed all, but it is man who first kindles the fire. No, not only the fates, for man himself may fan the flames for his own purposes. Many great fires can be started from smouldering coals but where they are kept, how and when they are used is up to us. A foolish man will store them badly or fan them until they consume him and his possessions but the wise man knows where to keep the fire, when to use it and when to extinguish it. It is a king's duty to control and force the flames and in them forge his country's destiny. Never forget that the sword with which you were invested and which you wield over your fellow men was drawn from stone, in a fire kindled and controlled by men." Myrddin paused briefly. "Is not the sword worked to perfection by being plunged time and time again into the fire? So are you tested now that you might have greater strength than before. From the smouldering fires of defeat you will, you have been, pulled that you might better lead the Brython and thus give them the final victory."

The King examined the face of the druid for a long time, weighing his words. Surely here was no Taliesin with flattering words, no poet with barbed sarcasm but one who sought to give order and meaning to life.

"Tis true," he cried striding to the door and calling for wine and the finest goblets, choice meats and ripe fruit. "Come let us celebrate, for soon the Mordei and the whole of the North shall know my strength."

Myrddin ate ravenously, as if no morsel had passed his lips in days until, finally satisfied, he wiped his hand across his drawn yet ageless face. "It was, my lord, not the assuaging of my hunger which brought me here ... "

Urien stretched his legs towards the fire. "Go on, good counsellor."

" ... there is a matter which you already know but which you will not recognise: that which wearies you and saps your strength. To speak of it is why I came, though you know it in your heart. No king, Urien, no renowned battle leader like you frets over a raid like this. But a king is himself the sovereignty of the land. Its prosperity is his, when he is prosperous it is, when he is marred it is also ... "

"Aye, I know it," cried Urien, agitated. Rising suddenly, he began to pace the room. "It was but a few months ago when I cast my eye over these fields and farms congratulating myself and Modron for the prosperity we had brought. I took the credit then and now must take the blame."

"Not you, my lord."

Urien spun round, his face beginning to colour. "Who then? Modron?"

Myrddin nodded. "Already men point to her having only the one son, saying that as she is barren so the land is."

Urien shook his head. "If that were so why was the land not barren before now?"

"Because she was not Queen and you not King," answered Myrddin firmly. Then, dropping his voice, he continued. "Did she not persuade you against your better judgement to take Eochaid to Catraeth? Urien, the darkness which your father saw and feared grows stronger and it cannot be wished away. Only one summer since his passing, one summer since you saw this once fertile valley as your creation, and already there has been war in the west and east. What more proof do you want that the Morrigan stretches her wings casting a shadow over you and this land? Do you not remember the chained birds of Cocidius and how they sought to escape? For a generation they had not appeared so, not since the victory of Outigern and your father. Little wonder that they should try to strike at you, his son. And if not you, your son. I left you then to seek the Morrigan and distract her familiars but she takes her toll. Did you not see me by your bed? Urien, the time has come when I must use all my power, all the cunning and skills I have ever learnt, to help you and the Brython and thus drained I will die. Like a drone I live to perform one task and when that is done to the best of my ability I shall die. But in dying I will, I hope, have given sustenance to the royal bee that it and its kind may survive and with it the future of the hive. Urien, you are the royal bee. Without you the hive, the kingdom, Prydein, will not survive. You must give the hive more sons."

"It is the Queen's duty to do that and she has given the world Owen."

"As you say, but Modron is not full queen. She whom you mated with at the coronation, she is the real sovereign of this land and now she bears you another son."

"That was but a ritual, Myrddin."

"To you it may only have been a ritual but to others it was real. You accepted the kingship willingly and now you must accept, nay acknowledge, your new son."

Urien contemplated the words of Myrddin in silence. And when at last he spoke it was with a heavy heart. "And what of Modron, what will become of her?"

"The ancient laws allow a man to take a secondary wife to get sons. Modron will be your principal wife ... Should you wish it."

"I will not have Modron hurt, Myrddin," avowed Urien.

"But will you see the girl or her baby suffer?"

* * *

The next day Urien and Myrddin rode alone towards Yrechwydd. At first they rode in silence, each lost in his own thoughts. "Gwenddoleu says you have learned from many people and places," ventured Urien.

"Then Gwenddoleu is right. He who would be wise should listen and watch. Did I not tell you I have been with Caesar and stood with Coel? We cannot understand ourselves without knowing what has been. As the Christian examines his former thoughts and actions to learn how to better himself, so we must know past faults and mistakes. You will not allow raiders to reach Gwen Ystrad again because you have learnt your lesson. Thus is the future built upon the past."

"And what does the past tell me to do?"

"Outigern defeated his enemies but could not prevent them from rebelling, nor could he influence those beyond his own borders. Have you never thought why Gwynedd could not reinstate Pabo after you had expelled him? It is not enough to win a battle like that of Argoed Llwyfain. You must hold down those you have defeated by building forts or placing your own man as ruler over them. Would Llwyfenydd have been raided if you had been here or Eochaid in Arfynydd as Eurdyl had suggested ?"

Myrddin watched Urien from the corner of his eye. Satisfied his words had struck home, he allowed himself a smile.

They had come to the lip of the valley which separates Llwyfenydd from Yrechwydd and where, countless centuries before, a great avenue of stones had been built. From there a broad shelf of rock led northwards, high above the valley floor. Myrddin followed it until he came to a wood and there he halted, whistling softly, summoning two shadows from amongst the tress. To Urien's great surprise and delight one was Cadwallon. "Is that really you, old friend?" he called, leaping from his horse, "or is it from the shee mound that you come."

"Nay, but peace and contentment I have found. True, part of me will not obey my command, but that is only to be expected in an old man like me." Cadwallon laughed. "But see, I have brought my lord a present."

Urien studied the girl whom he had seen only briefly at his coronation. She was dressed in a loose linen tunic embroidered with gold and a cloak trimmed with fur. Long dark hair fell about her shoulders and cascaded down her back and such was her beauty that for a time Urien could only stare. Then he walked towards her through the bracken.

" You know I don't even know your name, your proper name I mean."

"Elen, my lord."

"Elen! It is a pretty name, as beautiful as its owner." He stroked her hair, slowly but there was a pain in his voice.

"My lord is troubled? Perhaps he is angry." Worried, Elen looked briefly at Myrddin.

"Troubled, yes, but angry, no. How could I be angry? . If I were my son I would not hesitate to bed you, but I am not he, and already I have a wife. You understand?"

Her eyes examined the ground. "Yes, my lord."

Urien put his hand under her chin and lifted up her face so that his eyes could speak to hers. "Then do not be afraid, I bear you no ill. Neither you nor my son will ever want. Before he is twelve months old I will have given him the lands of the Mordei from which the Pictish raiders came. Until then, return with Cadwallon to the breast of Cocidius where I might find you again." Then, drawing her chin towards his, he kissed her.

OWEN AND THENEW

There was something wrong. Urien had changed, like the land that lay before Modron now. She had first sensed it when she dismounted in the courtyard upon her return from Catraeth, for his embrace had been more intense than usual, as if he were deliberately trying to prove he loved her and no other. She had tried to discuss it with him that night as they lay alone together but he had only shrugged his shoulders and said there was nothing wrong. So for much of the night she had lain awake by the side of the snoring figure, her body and mind unsatisfied, trying to imagine what troubled him. Surely the very fact he could not tell her was proof enough that all was not well. It was, she mused, as if the Morrigan had sunk her talons into his shoulder, and poison from the diabolical wound was slowly consuming him. No, not just him; them.

So Modron had cried herself to sleep and now she sat upon a shee mound at the head of Llwyfenydd. What had brought her to that place she did not know except that it was somehow part of her, her future and her past. In front of her, northwards, the devastation seemed to stretch as far as the eye could see, even to the Redhills. The Redhills! In her mind Modron saw a beautiful hag and heard again the words: "If you are false the land shall become waste". Then she saw herself and Urien at Caer Gwenddoleu and heard her own words: "Once there was only one talisman and that was enough to ensure the fertility of the land. Now the land must grow old with you and me."

"No, it cannot be," she cried. She covered her face with her hands and for the second time that day, wept. The tears streamed down her face and her chest heaved until, exhausted, she slept.

She awoke late in the afternoon with the certain knowledge that Urien had not been wounded by the Morrigan alone. Standing unsteadily she brushed the grass from the folds of linen and strode back across the limestone to the hall, determined to find out from the servants who had visited Urien in her absence.

"You did not tell me Myrddin came to see you here," she complained as they lay alone together. "What did he have to say? What did you talk about?"

Beside her Urien lay still. He had promised himself she would not be hurt, for the bonds between them were too strong to be broken overnight, even by Myrddin. He wanted to tell her all, of Elen and the child, but could not. So he answered her; "Of what must be done, how I

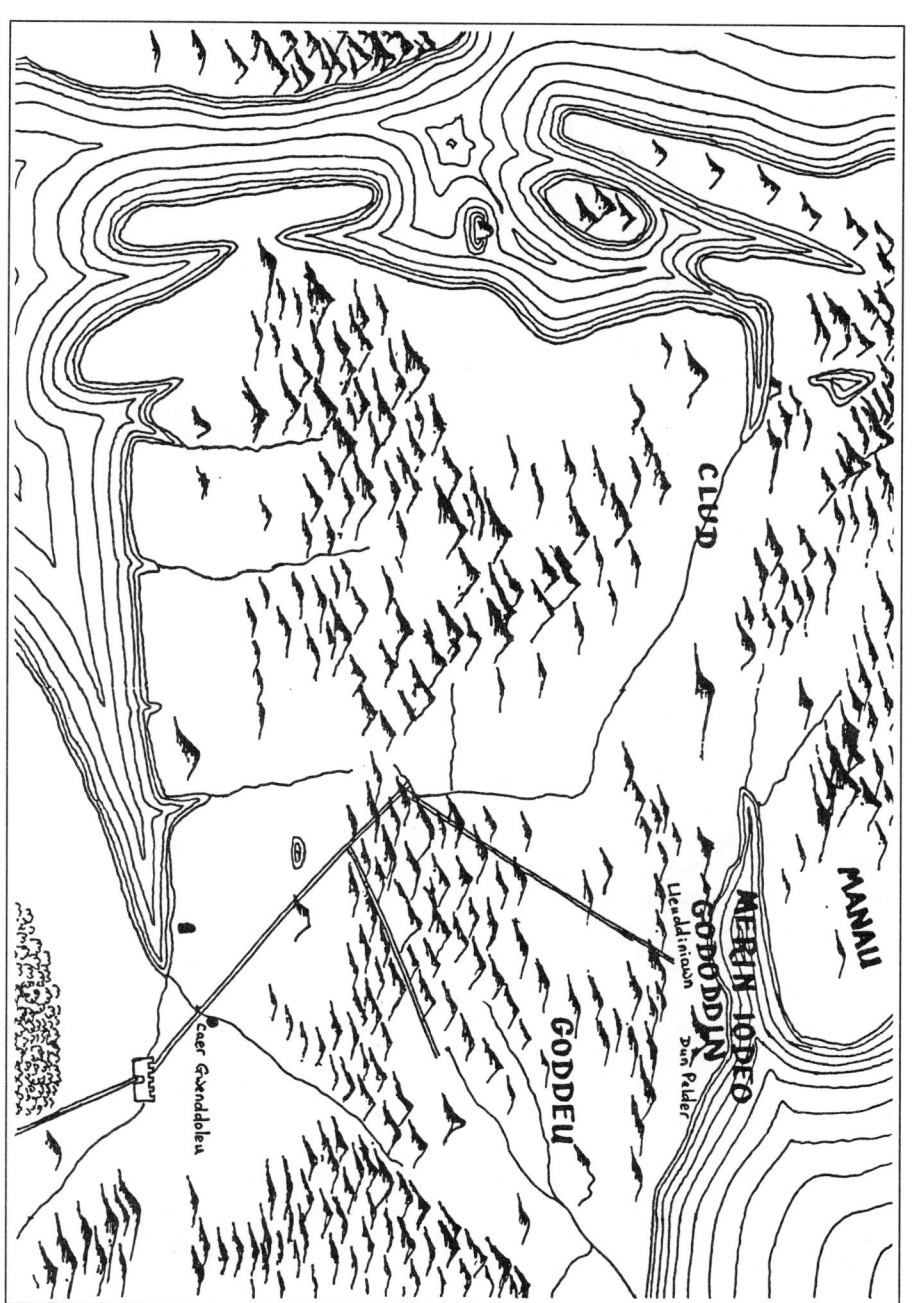

69

must garrison the land as Rome and Coel once did."

"And? Did he not speak of the marring of the land which we once thought so beautiful, the creation of our love, our Idon?"

"Aye, he spoke of that." Urien turned on his side to look at the woman beside him. "He said that men say the land is barren because we are, that we have only one son."

"And you believed him!" Modron threw the bed cover back and crossing to the hearth sat by its warmth, hugging her knees. "Don't you realise he is just using you, and me, to gain revenge for his quarrel with my father?"

Across the room, in what had been their bed, Urien shrugged his shoulders. This was not what he had wanted.

So Samhain came and winter followed summer. And throughout the winter the warband feasted and drank the music of Taliesin:

"Catraeth's men are up at dawn
For their conquering prince.
Urien is he, far famed chieftain
Strong in war, true Christian lord.
Pictland's men shall know him
Neither field nor forest spared.
Like waves roaring on the shore
I saw savage men of war
Morning fray, Gwen Ystrad your post
A thin rampart, reavers, battle gore.
At the ford I saw men stained with blood
Downing arms for a grey haired lord."

For Modron the songs of Taliesin were a balm, telling her men would rememeber the burnt homesteads as Urien's victory; that Llwyfenydd was becoming whole again. Yet she could never quite forget what had been said, what thought, and in her heart she knew Llwyfenydd was marred for ever. And, as it was marred, so was their marriage. The love of Urien had sustained her throughout the years but now, as it began to wane, so she began to feel older. Each day she examined herself in the mirror searching for some new grey hair.

Nor could Urien find peace of mind. Taliesin's praise only served to remind him of what was left unfinished; not a cattle raid, not a battle, but a war: a war that would seal the destiny of Prydein for all time. In his dreams he saw waifs standing amongst smoking ruins, their hands raised in supplication; three hundred generations as yet unborn: the children of the West. But with mead and wine came greater certainty. Why should he fail? Was it not his destiny to drive out the foreigner;

and had he not Myrddin to help him? Myrddin! How many times had he thought of the druid these last few months and seen the swelling womb of Elen; a child unborn.

By springtime Urien was active, determined to punish the Picts of the Mordei as soon as possible. Gone now was the languid lord of Llwyfenydd and in his place there rode the confident King of Rheged, Lord of Catraeth, Yrechwydd, Arfyndd and Llwyfenydd, Overlord of Mabon and Cear Leu, Victor of Lech Wen and Llwyfain. Even before Beltane messengers had gone out calling men to the hosting.

Urien planned to depart the day after the great festival. "All Prydein will learn to fear Urien and know the price of challenging him," he told Modron.

"And you will light a fire in the hearts of our people," she responded, her worries momentarily forgotten. As in the old days, she asked if she might go with him as far as the hosting but Urien shook his head. "From now on you must rule while I am away. You must stay here to reassure the people and watch for the covetous hands of Eleuther's sons and Guallauc."

"I am not strong enough."

"You are as strong as any man. You made me what I am and amongst our people a woman may rule as well as a man. Besides you are Llwyfenydd ... "

Modron nodded. She did not need him to say more. What could he say? What could she? She who loved him still. With moist, fearful eyes she kissed him gently on the forehead and with love and regret in her voice spoke to him of how she would return to Catraeth to watch over that place.

In that spring Urien and Modron turned their backs upon the past and Urien rode north, to Gwenddoleu; to Elen and his little son whom Myrddin had called Pasgent.

He found them in a small hut on the edge of a clearing deep in the forest, watched over by Cadwallon and his new wife. A slow peat fire was burning in the centre of the cottage and Elen lay beyond it, a small bundle tucked up against her face. For a moment or two Urien did not move. He simply stood in the doorway contemplating the scene. Within that house, within those circular walls, was a peace which he had not known since his father died: war and rumours of war had not penetrated, could not penetrate, that world. Silently he crossed the floor and looked down at Elen as she slept. Here too Urien saw the peace and tranquillity he had yearned for all winter: the tranquillity of innocence. In that moment he knew that he was right to come, that he did indeed want another son, that he needed Elen as well as Modron.

* * *

For Modron there was only pain. Pain as she fought to dismiss the knowledge of what would be from her mind. The pain of thinking that somehow she had failed them both; Urien and her son. For if Owen's glory reflected on her so did his shame. Now as she rode to Catraeth she recalled that which Owen drank and whored to forget, and she wondered how it could have been.

Then he had been sixteen and had ridden to Dun Pelder with his foster-father Nudd to visit his aunt Morgause and uncle Leuddag. "There is no finer fort in the North than Dun Pelder," Nudd had told him when first they set out. And so it was, for the hill dominated the plain, its steep sides rising from undulating fields; rocky walls from fertile soils. "Its top was girt with ramparts before the Romans came and here they and the Gododdin became friends. Within these walls purple-robed emissaries sought audience and then, it is said, its pillars were embellished with gold and its tables laid with silver. But the power of the Gododdin could not last; Cunedda went south and the Loegrians came to Bryneich and the wealth – most of it at least – was lost. Yet Lleudag and his kin have not forgotten, and so they count themselves the equal of your father and grandfather."

"But was it not my father who freed them from Dyfynwal of Clud?" asked Owen.

Nudd shrugged his shoulders. "We all have poor memories when it suits us Owen, just as we all have ears for praise."

"So beware of Leuddag's other nephew Morcant," warned Dreon. "He does not merely dream. Caten, your own cousin, does whatever he says. If Morcant asked for half his kingdom he would give it."

Dreon moved his horse nearer to Owen's, waiting for his father to ride out of earshot. "Now Caten's sister, Thenew, is something different altogether." Dreon made a gesture and both the boys laughed.

"Aye, your cousin Thenew is a beauty by all accounts," added Nudd eyeing the two youths over his shoulder.

Nor was Owen disappointed by what he saw. Although two years younger than himself Thenew was already a woman. Owen studied the curves beneath her white linen dress, the slender waist emphasised by a cord of gold, and the perfect feet shod in crimson sandles with gold filigree work. From that moment he had eyes only for her, watching her every move, watching her slip from the feast and not return.

Pretending he needed to make room for more wine he had followed

72

her, finding her standing on the highest point of Dun Pelder gazing northwards over the plain of Lleuddiniawn to the great estuary of Merin Iodeo and the land of Manau beyond. The wind had pressed the thin linen against her body so that it seemed to Owen she was wrapped in an ethereal mist, her hair shimmering in the sunlight.

"What do you see, cousin?" she had asked without turning to look at him, indicating with a sweep of her slender, manicured hand the view northwards. "Do you, too, see my destiny out there?"

"I see nought but Olwen standing before me. Her head yellower than the flowers of the broom; her flesh whiter than the foam of the wave; her palms and fingers whiter than the flowers of the meliot among the small pebbles of a gushing spring. No eyes are fairer than hers, not even the eye of the mewed hawk nor the eye of the thrice-mewed falcon. Whiter than the breast of a white swan are her two breasts ... " Owen had been standing a little behind her, looking over her shoulder, and now he put his hands gently on her breasts and pressed his lips against her neck.

"What are you doing?" she cried as she pushed his hands from her and fled down the slope, leaving him to gaze, unseeing, over the land beneath his feet.

His thoughts were shattered by a dagger at his throat.

"She is mine," whispered a voice full of venom. "Your father might have stolen from Pabo but you will not steal from me."

"She would not marry a snake like you, Morcant", retorted Owen without moving.

The mention of his own name had thrown Morcant momentarily off guard and Owen took the opportunity to jab his elbow into his assailant's stomach. Then, twisting free he brought his fist up and sent Morcant crashing to the ground. blood trickling from his mouth. Within minutes all of Dun Pelder had learned what had happened and the reason why: Caten had seen to that. Soon Owen found himself overpowered, his back bared to Leuddag's whip.

When Owen regained consciousness it was to hear Morgause berating her husband. "What kind of a fool are you to treat one of our guests so? Would you have men say Lleudag has no justice? Would you punish and then sit in judgement?"

"Justice! Why should I give justice to a man who tries to rape my daughter and defile my kingdom?"

"Because he is not the only one who would have his way with our daughter, not your daughter, our daughter, our kingdom."

Morgause had been pointing at Morcant but Leuddag was not listening to her, instead his ear was turned to that of a counsellor.

Turning on Morgause he spat on the ground. "Our kingdom is it? So, now we know where we stand. Well, in the morning your nephew and his friends can go back to their cess pits and you, too, if you wish."

Later that night Morgause sent for Owen. "I will not apologise for Leuddag. What he said was wrong but the intent was not." She held up her hand. "No, I know you cannot see, for you were not told, you did not ask. Thenew can no more be yours than Morcant's; not at least until Leuddag's heir begets a daughter. Until that time Thenew must serve as the sovereignty of this land. As long as she remains whole so will the kingdom."

"Is that what she wants?"

"It is not a question of what she wants ... Oh, I know you must be thinking of how your father took your mother, and I don't blame you, but Thenew can never give you happiness. Tomorrow you must ride away and tomorrow you must forget her, for if you do not you will never find peace. Find another love and forget her. And forget this place, for there are those here who bear a grudge against your father."

So it was that Owen, Nudd and Dreon left Dun Pelder, with Owen nursing his wounds and the injustice of Leuddag and the men of Gododdin. An injustice that no man could let go unavenged. As Owen nursed it so the image of Thenew grew until he could think of nought else but her: her and revenge. Throughout that summer the vision of Thenew haunted him: the tall grass swaying in the wind reminded him of her hair and he saw the curves of her body in the shadows, in the hillsides, wherever he looked. Unable or unwilling to heed the advice of Morgause, Owen let his passions consume him. So Samhain, the night of mischief, came: a time when Otherworld beings play tricks on mere mortals and boys dress as girls and girls as boys. With Samhain came an idea.

It was in disguise that Owen had returned to Dun Pelder to watch and wait for her who consumed his body and soul. There he found a living with Leuddag's swineherd and learned that the virgin daughter of the king descended each day to the holy spring in the wooded defile on the north side of the fort to serve as the lady of that fountain. But to that place no man could descend. So Owen waited and bided his time, waiting until the swineherd and his wife were away at market. Then, clad in an old dress and shawl he began to stalk his prey. Of the valley he saw nought but in his mind he saw Thenew standing upon the hilltop, her hair streaming in the wind, each strand a silken flail encouraging his bitterness and unrequited lust. Goaded by such images he stumbled blindly along the twisting path between the rocks and bushes. They tore at his skin and cut his feet and hands but he did not notice their lacerations.

It was as he rounded one corner in the narrow path that he saw her, sitting about one hundred paces from him by the side of a small spring. She was wearing a white dress as he remembered her; but now it was of wool, protection against the first incursions of winter. In her hands she was plaiting a garland of green reeds and was so engrossed by the task that she seemed not to have noticed the intruder. All the same Owen could take no chances. Turning towards the steep hillside he began to gather dry sticks as if for kindling but all the time working his way towards her, Lleudag's daughter. Instinctively he knew she was watching him as he shuffled along, bent as if with age, the shawl drawn over his head. Twenty paces from her he stopped; by now he had a sizeable bundle of sticks, one which an old woman would have found difficult to lift.

From her rocky perch Thenew watched as the old woman tried, unsuccessfully, to lift her load onto her back. "Let me help you," she called, sliding down the slab of rock onto the path. Owen had pretended not to hear, turning his back on Thenew and stooping lower as if again trying to raise the bundle. Thenew reached round and laid her hand on the old woman's. Suddenly she let out a stifled cry as Owen grasped her wrists and twisting round forced her to the ground. He lay on top of her now, his eyes tightly closed as he saw again the black face of Leuddag and the jeering smiles of Caten and Morcant. He felt her body in his arms and heard again Morcant whispering, "She is mine", and as her blood trickled between his legs he laughed, "Now, Leuddag the Just, is your kingdom defiled in accordance with your law."

At last Owen was satiated and in that moment, drained of all his pent up love and anger, he looked down for the first time at the sobbing girl. The girl he had loved and worshipped on the summit of Dun Pelder was no more; he had destroyed her, and with her part of himself as his aunt had foretold. With an anguished cry he stumbled to his feet and ran blindly up the path and from the valley.

* * *

Thenew told none of the affair, hoping above hope that she need not mention it. But as the months went by so her anguish grew and with it the need to seek help from the Christian virgin. Placing a small cross of twigs in the shrine by the side of her spring she prayed night and day for help. "Great Mother, I was sent here to serve a goddess whom I now acknowledge to be false. As you gave birth to a holy son yet remained pure, so grant that I, being sullied, may have no child."

Betrayed at last, however, by her swollen body she was dragged before her father and his advisers. Like wolves they circled her, their eyes full of hatred and malice. It was Leuddag who gave the first blow. "Cursed I was the day you came into this world for now men say I am not fit to be King. Not in all its years has Dun Pelder felt such shame and now men say its days are numbered, that its walls will soon be abandoned, its glories forgotten. Will you not even now lessen that shame by telling us who the father is?"

Thenew shook her head, her once golden hair matted with mud. Angrily Lleudag grabbed a tangled tress and twisting it around his hand pulled her face close to his. "You might not tell us yet, but before you depart from here you will." In an instance she was thrown to the ground, her head banging against the boot of Morcant. Slowly, he withdrew his foot from beneath her head and then malevolantly kicked her in the ribs, sending her rolling back to Leuddag. The King looked down at the girl curled up at his feet, her hands protectively around her swelling waist, for Morcant's kick had awakened the child within. Few would recognise her now as the proud beauty who had beguiled a host, none there would now own to having ever dreamed of sleeping with her.

But for a moment she had a respite, for Leuddag's brother Bran had returned from his search of the defiled valley. He had brought with him the small cross Thenew had placed by her spring, and the story of the swineherd and his wife. Leuddag listened to Bran in silence and then, crushing the cross in his hand he looked down at her who had once been his daughter, his pride and joy. "The spear of Mabon has pierced our goddess, the knot of her powers has been broken. He whom some call Maponus, the divine youth, the hunter, has hunted in and fouled our land. He gave no maiden price except the fear of destruction of our country. He is a thief who takes without paying and upon him I swear this destiny: let him not know love except it shall destroy him; may he never have another child except that in the moment of its birth he shall die. Cursed be Rheged and his offspring."

Thenew looked up, studying the face of him who had once doted on her. But the smile was gone, the narrow lips set firm, the eyes cold; eyes filled with hate and fear. "You condemn me as you did him without listening to my tale. He forced me, goaded by passion, you condemn me in malice and ignorance. Did I not know as well as any of you what our laws and traditions say? But what good was such knowledge to me when I was overpowered by the spring? How will your punishment redress that wrong? Will I be made whole again? Oh yes, it is easy for you to say I should have resisted, you who dare not bring him to justice. As a murderer may be made to look after the family of those he has wronged so should Owen be made to acknowledge his son."

Leuddag laughed derisively, hauling her to her feet by her hair. "I would not give him or you such pleasure. And that is not our law. Stay with us you shall not, nor to him will you and your child go. As the land is destroyed so shall you be and all that belonged to you. Your bed, your clothes, even the waggon upon which you were pleased to ride and be feted at festivals must perish that the land might be clean once more. Your memory shall be expunged for ever and none will speak your name. It will be as if you never were for you are not my child."

Thenew looked at him and at those about. "I did not ask to be your goddess. Had I been but a servant you would have laughed to see me raped, bringing the child up as one of your own. Instead you created an idol and seek to punish me for straying from the taboos you placed around that image. Who then is guilty? You have cursed me and him; you have crushed the cross and the hope I had, and in so doing you have destroyed those who might have saved you. Cursed indeed are you for now the land will certainly be lost and the Gododdin shall not endure. Not because of me but because of you."

"Enough!" cried Leuddag raising his hands not in anger, not to strike her but as protection against her words. "Our laws are our laws. If we do not abide by them the people will not know their place, the kingdom will be lost. The law requires your death. If you do not die Gododdin will perish in anarchy with no man respecting the law." With a wave of his hand he summoned the guards. "You know what to do."

Outside Leuddag's hall they had prepared her waggon. In its centre where at festivals a holy statue would be placed they had erected a post roughly carved to look like a phallus and to this they tied her. Then, lifting the shafts, they propelled her waggon to the steepest slope and there they let go. At first the cart moved slowly down the slope, then it began to gather momentum. Above her sobs Thenew could just make out the words of her father: "Many times has our goddess ridden in that holy car before the people but now she has been betrayed. As her sanctuary is broken so shall her cart be ... " But Thenew could not make out his final words for they were lost in her own cries, the rumbling of the heavy wooden wheels and the creaking of the cart as it plunged, bumping and jolting between bushes and rocky outcrops. Once, twice it nearly overturned and then lifting in the air for the third time it landed backwards with the pole pointing downhill. The waggon rumbled forward for a few more paces before the shafts stuck in the ground. For a moment it looked as if the slender timbers would snap under the weight of the moving cart but they held firm and the waggon finally shuddered to a halt; Thenew unconscious in its middle.

She awoke aware of the pains in her womb and of voices near by. The King and those around him were scrambling down the steep slope as fast as they could. "Tis the goddess looking after her own," she heard one wail. She thought it might have been Caten but she could not be sure. "Shut up, you snivelling bastard," came the reply in her father's voice.

They had reached her now and she was conscious of their eyes but she could not see them for the pain of labour had closed her own. "Lever the wheels up and get that shaft free," she heard her father command.

"No. Fate has intervened here." It was the voice of a priest. "Take her from here and cast her adrift upon the sea for even the land has refused to accept her blood. Let the powers of the ocean do with her as they please."

When she awoke again it was to find herself trussed on the sandy shore of Merin Iodeo, with the tang of salt in the air, the screech of seagulls and the gentle sound of waves lapping a flat beach. Rough hands dumped her in a coracle and dragged the basket towards the sea. There a guard held her boat steady whilst another cut her bonds, then together they gave a final shove. Thenew watched them wading back towards the shore and then looked around for a paddle but there was none. She was at the mercy of the sea and sky now, drifting eastwards and northwards away from those who had once called her theirs, away from her home.

RHIANNON

"My lord, wake up," persisted the servant shaking Owen by the shoulder. "The King, your father is here."

Owen opened an eye. "Huh?" Slowly the words of the servant sank in.

"It is morning, my lord."

Owen pushed himself from the rush covered floor, bumping his head on the table under which he had fallen asleep. The bump did nothing to ease his sore head. Somewhat unsteadily he made his way to the door and peered out. The bright light hurt his eyes and he rapidly withdrew.

"A good night?" enquired Urien following him into the dark interior of the hall. "You should get a good woman and have children."

"I had a good woman and I have a son of sorts," retorted Owen brushing past his father to the courtyard where he could plunge his head into a bucket of water. Urien quickly changed the subject. "Have you had any reports of the Picts?"

His son shook the water from his blond, curly hair. "Not since Gwen Ystrad. They have it seems gone to ground."

"Aye, but perhaps only for the winter."

"Perhaps." Owen adjusted his breeches. "Perhaps we will catch them as they stick their little snouts out of their hole smelling the first air of summer. Perhaps we will catch them in their hole."

"If we move fast. Is the hosting arranged?"

Owen nodded, crumbs of fresh bread falling from his bulging mouth.

The hosting place of Mabon lay at the head of the Sea of Rheged where the lands of Owen met those of Gwenddoleu. There, on the shore, neither in one cantref nor the other, neither on land nor in water, were those holy stones where men could meet for war yet be at peace. There Urien gathered his ravens. They came in groups each with his own chief; some on horseback, some on foot; some with spears, some with swords.

It was evening before Eochaid's troop came splashing through the waters of the estuary, silver ripples across the red surface of the westering sun. Soon they were trotting over the soft sand and short grass, splashing through the saline pools and shallow channels, scattering the sheep which grazed there.

"Welcome!" called Urien. "I was beginning to think my sister had chained you to her bed."

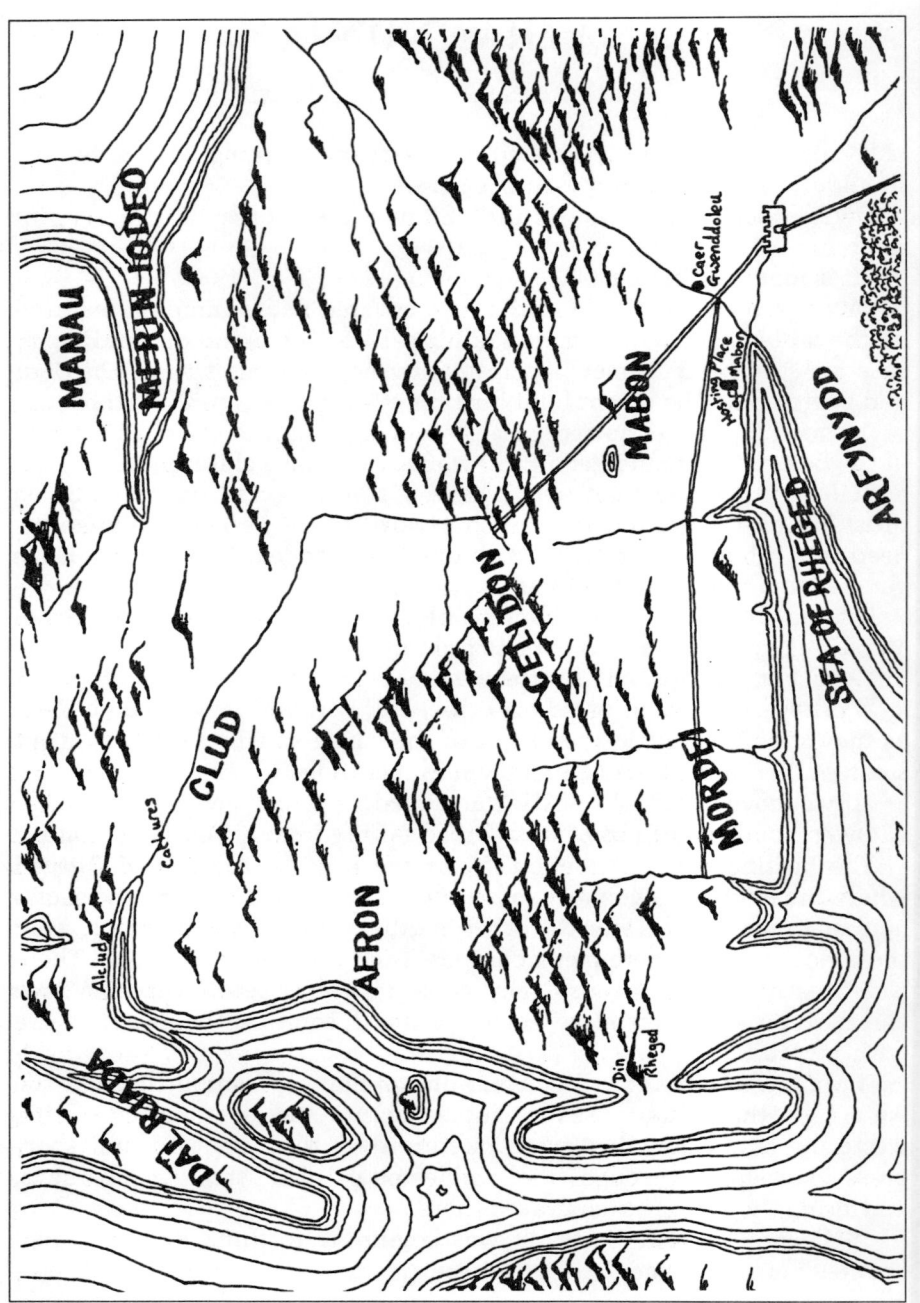

MANAU

MERIN IODEO

CAL RYDDA

CLUD

Cathures

Alclud

AFRON

CELIDON

MABON

Hunting Place
of Mabon

Caer
Gwenddoleu

MORDEI

Din
Rheged

SEA OF RHEGED

ARFYNYDD

"Nay, but she has chained him to herself" snorted Owen. "Look. Is it not she that rides between him and Mouric."

Eurdyl dismounted and tossing back her head ran her fingers through her hair to comb it. "Greetings, brother." Turning to look at Owen she smiled. "And to Maponus."

Conscious of Eochaid's glance Owen addressed Eurdyl's husband. "Welcome is the warband of Arfynydd to this place; a place set aside for men and women to meet, on the appointed day. Yet is this a hosting and not an oenach. To what then do we owe the pleasure of the lady Eurdyl's company?"

"I came to ride with you, my brother, husband and son." Eurdyl put an arm around Mouric's shoulder. "For so he wishes ... But I told him I would only come if my brother also wished it," she added coyly, her eyes upon Urien.

"I can see no real harm in it," he replied. "After all, I doubt that we will be hard pressed by the Mordei."

"So who will guard Arfynydd?" retorted Owen, Modron's son. Recognising now he had been mistaken about Eurdyl's intentions he turned to his father. "You would not let Modron come even as far as Caer Gwenddoleu. This is no place for a woman."

"Enough!" cried Urien. "Do I not have enough problems with our real enemies without having family squabbles. I have made my mind up and there is no more to be said. Come."

Eurdyl followed, giving Owen a withering look as she passed him by.

Inside his tent Urien took a piece of leather from his pack and unfolded it on the ground. "Do you know what this is?" he asked Mouric, who was standing behind his father. The boy shook his head. It did not look like a book to him. "Nor is it a book, though it sets down all that is known about Prydein," Urien told him. "It is a map. See, this line is yonder coast, here Yrechwydd."

"And here Arfynydd," added Mouric, excitedly.

"Exactly. We will make a general of you yet." Urien ruffled the boy's hair. Would Pasgent grow to be as quick as this boy he wondered.

Sighing, he turned his attention back to the map. "This area is Mabon, here the Mordei and in this place their lair. Destroy that and we destroy them. So, we will move fast lest they bolt from their holes when first news of our coming reaches them."

Eochaid nodded. "Catch them before they flee into the forest or some bog to hide their cattle, eh?"

"Before they can hide themselves, for it is they and not their cattle we must hunt." Urien saw the look of puzzlement on the faces of those around. "Have you forgotten that it was through them that Maelgini of Gwynedd sent Bridei to be king amongst the northern Picts?" he asked. "They are a link in a chain which might one day fetter Rheged, better to remove that chain once and for all than to leave it broken. So must we sweep the Picts from the land of the Mordei and, thus freeing that land, bind it to ourselves. The ravens of Rheged will spread their wings and all shall see their power. Many will clamour for their protection and shelter and to ride with us. The land then must not be burnt as they burnt Llwyfenydd, only their lair must we destroy."

Gwenddoleu looked from the map to the face of his friend, understanding now his promise to Elen and Pasgent.

The next day they moved westwards, following the old road to the head of the estuary which formed the boundary between Rheged and the Mordei and there they camped. At first light they forded the river, their feet sure on the cobbles which engineers had laid centuries before. Owen led the way for he had allotted himself that task, prefering to be alone than send the wrong signals to Eurdyl and Eochaid. Besides, he had a feeling that somewhere ahead his destiny lay. What that was he did not know but for the moment he was content to be alone.

After a while they found themselves riding south of a line of hills shaped like shee mounds. "Do you think they are an omen?" asked Mouric who had galloped forward to be with his cousin.

Owen shook his head. "You imagine them as shee mounds if you wish, or they can be ... "

"Breasts?"

Owen laughed. They had come a long way from Mouric's first school room. Even so, he could not shake off the feeling he had had since they crossed the estuary, and he thought he glimpsed horsemen amongst those shapes: flitting shadows in the corner of his eye. But when he turned or stopped none could he see. So they rode on, passing hurriedly abandoned farmsteads whose gates stood open, their yards quiet except for the occasional hen or lame cow left because it could not keep pace with those who had fled. Everywhere there were the signs of hurried departures; fires still burning, meat or broth simmering in cauldrons.

"There is almost enough to feed an army," observed Gwenddoleu with a broad grin on his face.

"Aye, but none is the Cauldron of Ulph for which I seek," reflected Urien. "Still, let the men take what they can carry, but no more, for we have not time to drive the spoils of war nor have we yet deserved them."

"What is the Cauldron of Ulph?" Mouric asked Owen.

Owen looked at his cousin. Was this what Christian learning brought, ignorance of the lore of the Brython? How long would it be before children forgot, nay were not taught, of the magic cauldron? "It is said it was brought by the People of Brigit long ago and that it could feed an army and not be emptied, nor need filling. So was one of its uses and even now some people compare the generosity of Old Coel with it, though 'tis certain he never possessed it. The more is the pity for now the Brython have need of its greatest property: the making whole of those wounded in battle."

* * *

That night they feasted upon the spoils of war, cattle and sheep, mead and beer; their fires guardians against the night. Within the grassy ramparts of a fort long since abandoned they camped, protected by its double banks, overlooking the crossing of a river. South and west were distant peaks, the walls of the enemy, grey against the evening sun. And far to the north, beyond slopes of yellow green pasture, were the massed trees of Western Celidon: a land where the plough was a stranger. What manner of people inhabited that place Owen could only surmise for he had heard strange tales about the Mordei; that some were cannibals, some shape shifters. He shivered. Were they the shadows he had seen earlier?

Unable to settle he had joined the guards and now stood on the outer rampart, watching the column of horsemen approaching from the north. "See how they carry their shields on their arms and their spears at the ready, lord", whispered the man on Owen's left.

Owen nodded. "Aye. You had best bid our men arm themselves."

"But what kind of men would attack at this time of day?" asked the other.

"What kind of men indeed," reflected Owen, his sense of unease greater than ever.

The riders had halted at the bottom of the steep slope, along the river's edge. All except three who had begun to climb upwards and Owen noted with admiration the ease with which their mounts seemed to negotiate the steep ground. The three riders halted some fifty paces from Owen where he could see that two were youths of about fourteen years. The third, who was old enough to be their father, manouvered his horse nearer to Owen. "I would speak with the King of Rheged."

"The King would be foolish to let those he does not know approach him thus," replied Owen, rubbing his thumb uneasily along the shaft of his spear.

The stranger nodded. "It is proper that a man should be so wary; yet should he not fear more those who come to him in peace with offerings and malice in their hearts? Did not Judas betray Christ with the kiss of peace and friendship? If I had intended harm would I not have come along the high ground and not to the bottom of a cliff? If I had wished to ride with your head and that of your father dangling from my mount would I have let you gird yourselves with ramparts this night? No, I would have struck you down whilst you were strung out along the road that brought you hither."

"Then who in this wild place speaks the name of the Christian god?"

"Cynfelyn and his brothers Clytno and Cadrod. Our grandfather who bore my name was the brother of Eleuther and came here in the days of Outigern to stop the Gael expanding eastwards."

"And so you seek an alliance with us against the Gael?" asked Owen.

Cynfelyn shook his head. "Not against the Gael but the Picts. They it was who stole our land and drove us like beasts to find what grazing we could amongst the wilds of Western Celidon so that no man spoke my name except to call me Cynfelyn the Rough."

Owen relaxed. He had not noticed it before but his feeling of unease had vanished. "Your horses are weary, Cynfelyn, and unless you deceive me you have come far. Let your men graze their mounts where they stand and take from mine what drink they will."

"Your eyesight is like the sharp eyed hawk, my lord, for we have indeed ridden hard this day for we were up before daybreak to find your trail. My men will be pleased to share with the men of Mabon but there is yet another amongst them whom I would bring with me to meet your father."

Owen nodded his assent and watched in silence as Cynfelyn sent Clytno cantering back towards the others. Presently he returned, riding beside another youth who sat astride a pure white stallion.

"My teacher once told me of a race known to Rome and Greece as Amazons. Is your warband made of such creatures, Cynfelyn?" exclaimed Owen as he surveyed appreciatively the ample breasts that stretched tight the girl's leather jerkin and her bare, bronzed thighs. What would he not give to ride between them?

"Has Owen Rheged not seen a woman before that he stares thus," taunted the girl, reining her horse. "You said these were men, Cynfelyn, but I see only boys."

Cynfelyn's face coloured. "She means no harm, my lord. She is the apple of my eye and I have perhaps spoiled her over much. Yet does that not place a greater value upon her, for I brought her as a sign of my good intentions, that should your father wish she should be hostage.

Rhiannon is her name."

The thought of her being hostage appealed to Owen, but before he could reply his father arrived. "It is good that a man freely offers hostages but if he has broken his oath to one lord will he not break those given to the second?"

Cynfelyn dismounted. "What you say is true, great King, but I have given no hostages to the Northmen and in truth they demanded none, for who but a fool would demand pledges from an outlaw? Yet once I was not so and I rode with your father to drive back the enemies of my people. So now, let me ride with you."

Urien nodded, uncommitted. Could Cynfelyn be trusted? Perhaps, perhaps not. Yet surely he might be useful? Moving to one side he gestured for Cynfelyn and his band to join him and his men, for they had much to talk about. Of immediate concern was the strength and whereabouts of the Picts, and then there was the question of the Talismans. Surely a people who had kept to themselves for so long must have information which others had lost?

"Aye, I have heard of the Talismans," said Cynfelyn when Urien finally broached the subject. "But who has not? Yet ... " and the man of Mordei paused "I did once hear something; a snippet of idle conversation, the chance remark of a trader. Certain it is that he was not one of the Brython but I think his story was true and that he was of the Scotti, for men say only they would be stupid enough to think Cynfelyn had riches." Cynfelyn laughed quietly to himself, glancing at Rhiannon. "Aye, he was of the Scotti for he knew also more than he would tell. But of this he did speak, that in the time of his grandfather his people had brought out of Erin a stone upon which, in the days of old, those who would be King must stand. Perhaps it is the Talisman of Falias, the Stone of Destiny."

Urien stroked his chin thoughtfully. "A Scotti you say, a man of Dal Riada beyond Clud?" Cynfelyn nodded almost absent mindedly, for he had turned his attention to the lady Eurdyl as she watched a strangely silent Owen, her eyes burning with resentment. But it was not at her Owen looked now. Cynfelyn wondered if Urien too had noticed, or had he discovered a weakness in the great man, an over indulgence of his sister? The man of the Mordei cast his eye upon Owen: aye, and of his offspring too.

Urien's son still smarted from the greeting of Rhiannon, vowing silently he would show her what kind of man he was and make her smart below his whip. He chewed slowly on his food, savouring the thought, watching her over the rim of his brimming cup. He surveyed her round face with its full, moist lips and large, sparkling eyes fringed with long lashes. He measured her full curves and contrasted her golden skin with the black leather. Here was one worthy of Maponus. He smiled at her, "Let's hope they soon retire to bed, that we may."

But he had misjudged her. Her laughter dashed his hopes, wounding him more deeply than before. "It is indeed true what they say of you, that you pick what fruit takes your fancy. But you are like a small child who sees a red berry and immediately plucks it for eating without first asking whether it is poisonous. Like a child you reach for the warmth and brightness of the fire without heed to the dangers. Who or what am I, Owen, that you think I should share your bed this night?"

Urien had risen and with him Cynfelyn and his daughter, leaving Owen alone with her words and his own thoughts. He slept fitfully then for before his eyes there drifted many women: some dressed as Rhiannon, some as Amazons; some whores, some nuns. The Amazons stood over him, whips in hand, demanding that he serve them, but he had no more to give. Why would they not let him alone? The whores, some with the face of Eurdyl, called him to bed but they were hideous creatures, haggard with their work. From them he drew back in horror unable to find satisfaction. Nor did the nuns allow him respite for he knew, without seeing their faces, that they were Thenew. He covered his eyes but what use was that when they were in his mind, images conjured up by Rhiannon, by her words of truth? Aye, Owen recognised that now and with that recognition came respect. So at last he fell into a deep and untroubled sleep and when eventually he awoke it was to find the others breakfasting; Eurdyl's composure returned. But of Rhiannon there was no sign.

Anxiously Owen looked about whilst pretending to be unconcerned. Cynfelyn smiled. "With the blessing of your father and his sister she has gone."

"What?" Owen turned on his aunt and then his father. "Was she not to be our hostage? Why then have you let her go?"

Urien rose and crossed to where his son, Modron's son, stood. "Am I not King that I cannot make my own decisions? Is it not the place of a king to be generous as well as severe? What greater generosity than the sons of Coel should let the hostage freely offered return."

Cynfelyn continued to smile at Owen. "Even so, as your father set her free, Rhiannon knew you would be angry. So she left you a token." He pointed to the ground behind Owen where a magnificent mare was grazing. "She is called Clovenhoof."

Owen's anger evaporated. He crossed to the horse and patted its flanks, feeling its long legs, letting her nuzzle him. "Everytime I ride you, I will think of Rhiannon," he whispered.

* * *

At the end of that day they reached the estuary separating them from their goal and there they camped, watching the lightning breaking about the distant mountains and listening to the thunder. Some of the men, the less experienced, were mumbling amongst themselves. It was, they said, a bad omen. Urien's response was swift. "Their gods are afraid," he told them. "They dare not come near. Like their people they dare not challenge us. All day they have watched and done nothing. They strut and parade themselves and make threatening noises, but only beyond our reach. They see how the ravens have come announcing their doom; their gods moan, knowing that tomorrow their servants will be carrion flesh." He seized a shield and banged it with the hilt of his sword. Behind him Gwenddoleu did the same, then Cynfelyn and Owen, until all the men were copying their lord. The noise rolled down the slope and across the valley towards the Picts: the thunder of Rheged, the vengeance of Llwyfenydd.

In the morning they swooped in three columns: Urien and Cynfelyn; Owen and Eochaid; Gwenddoleu and the kin of Cynfelyn. The sun filled the valley, and on the fresh green slopes glistening with dew were myriad points of glinting steel. Owen and Eochaid led the attack, trying to force the crossing but it was well guarded. At Urien's command they fell back, feigning retreat, drawing the blood of the Northmen. And in that moment, though few knew it, Eochaid perished, an arrow in his back. So the battle raged and it was mid afternoon before Urien and Cynfelyn were able to cross the river and drive back those who guarded the ford. From there, with half the battle still raging east of the river, they advanced towards the fortress.

Urien surveyed its walls with dismay: here was no earthen rampart carelessly thrown up as defence against prowling wolves in the moment of Rome's departure, but massive walls of stone laced with timber. The fort was like a limpet fastened upon a rock: protection against the tide. Waves of warriors would not break into that place. What then was to be done?

"Smoke them out," advised Cynfelyn. "It has worked before and the wind which gathers will be our ally."

Urien smiled grimly. "Quick. Fetch fire and those most skilled with bows."

Some arrows fell short, others were extinguished in flight but enough reached their target. As darkness began to fall the first flames began to lick walls and roofs. Now the wind was blowing like a gale, roaring through the valleys, shrieking like a banshee. Fanned as if by bellows, its nozzle the rock gullies, the flames leaped ever higher. So intense was the heat that the timbers of the walls burst into flame and the stone began to melt. To those who looked on, it seemed as if that hill had become a shee mound, the melted stone the face and eyes of those entombed within. "They sowed the wind and have reaped the whirlwind," observed Urien. "Let us hope the smoke is seen in Caer Efrawg and amongst all our enemies that they might know the vengeance of LLwyfenydd and the power of Rheged."

The following morning, whilst the rocky hilltop still glowed like the setting sun, they buried Eochaid. Eurdyl gazed down at the lips drained of blood and upon the eyes that would see no more. She turned to Owen by her side. "Let me lean on you." Reluctantly he put his arm around her shoulder and drew her to him, listening to her sobs. And high above, seated on a rocky ledge, Myrddin watched them all; biding his time, waiting for Eurdyl to come to him, for Urien to be alone.

* * *

"A great victory, my friend," said Gwenddoleu. "Where now will the Guledig lead us?"

"To the ends of the earth," Urien laughed. "Aye, to the ends of the earth for there, as Myrddin has said, I should plant our seed, build a fort and garrison it with men of Rheged."

"And there at the edge of the western ocean will your footprint remain in the sands of time," exclaimed Taliesin.

"Perhaps. But not if we linger here much longer. Besides there are the other Talismans yet to find, we have a trail yet to follow."

For one and a half days they travelled westwards until no more than a league of water separated them from Hibernia, Prydein from the next world. Here, where Prydein ended, the land was shaped like a hammer, an island of high ground joined to the mainland by a marshy isthmus; the home of curlew and lapwing, oyster catcher and gannet, tern and cormorant, gull and wigeon. Here the rule of Rome had ended and, in the days of Ninian, the Gael had settled.

"When will we attack?" asked Gwenddoleu.

Urien shook his head. "A man may use weapons other than a blade to gain his ends: the satyrist a sharp tongue, the priest silvered words, a king diplomacy. Beyond that peninsula is Erin and all the islands from here northwards belong to them. They are a great power. What would it benefit us to stir up such a hornet's nest? Besides, have not their cousins in Dal Riada got the Stone of Destiny?"

"Will you send envoys then?"

Urien shook his head. "The wind blows upon our faces from their land but the whispers of our coming echo around their halls. In a day, two at most, we shall hear from them and exchange gifts. Then we shall turn north, for the men of Aeron have need of us."

Urien clapped his friend on the back. "Do not look so puzzled. You ask how I know these things and I will tell you. A little bird told me."

The envoys from Aeron were waiting for Urien when he returned from hunting with Allmuir, lord of the Gael, and they spoke of their land beyond the mountains. It was, they said, a place where Coel the Old had once held sway and now lay buried, and they spoke of raiding by the King of Clud and bid Urien become their Protector, even as Coel had been.

So it was that Urien and Owen turned north with Clytno and Cadrod as hostages leaving Cynfelyn and Gwenddoleu to consolidate their hold on the Mordei by the building of a fort. And within four days of leaving Dun Rheged they stood before the tomb of their ancestor with Corocticus, lord of that place, by their side.

"The power of Clud is naught compared with that which grows in the east," Urien told his host. "And should we lose? ... Where would the Brython go then, across the western ocean? Aye, for there lies the Land of Promise, the abode of the dead. Our choice then is simple, destroy or be destroyed. So we must unite the Brython and make allies of those we call our foes ... "

"So you will not help us fight Clud?"

"Nay, I did not say that, but one day they must join us if we are to stand a chance."

"Unnatural allies I say."

"Perhaps. Yet in defeat might they not join us more readily than as our equals?"

"I'll drink to that," laughed Corocticus. "And me, too," added Owen. "Tomorrow you can take us hunting and if by chance it is close to Clud so much the better ... "

* * *

Urien pointed to a small, conical hill "Can we see Clud from there?"

Corocticus nodded, "And if the weather is fair, Dal Riada too."

Urien smiled to himself. "Then have I a desire to rest upon its summit whilst you and the other youngsters continue your sport."

Corocticus nodded and turning, galloped after Owen.

Urien ascended the hill alone to find the view as Corocticus had described. Westwards, where a pale bank of cloud hung in the clear firmament, was the land of the Scotti, Dal Riada, and the Stone of Destiny. Urien recalled what he had heard of these people and of how Conall had ruled there since Bridei King of the Picts had killed Gabron and weakened their power: they were a people anxious to find allies against the Picts, and Clud too. Urien smiled to himself. Yes, they would make good allies.

With that thought he turned his eyes towards Clud. Before Coel ruled, Rome had given that kingdom to Paternus. Now Tudwal was King, dwelling upon the great rock which rose sheer above the northern edge of the estuary. His brother Elidyr it was who had married the daughter of Maelgini allying Clud with Gwynedd, Bridei and the Picts. Urien let his eyes follow the estuary, from where he surmised the rock of Alclud to be, to its head and Cathures where his own grandson, Kentigern, had been bishop less than three years.

His grandson! Urien had never seen him, but both he and Modron had always questioned closely those who knew of the boy's progress. The lad it seemed had been lucky for the waves had protected him and his mother when man would succour neither. The wind and waves had carried him and his mother far out to sea until they were hidden from Gododdin and then delivered them to the northern shore. How horrific that journey had been only Thenew could tell: she in the final stages of labour and the boat bobbing up and down. Bracing herself against the wickerwork she had called to God or anyone who might hear for help. And, suddenly, as if those prayers were heeded, the motion of the vessel had changed and the side which she rested against ground to a halt on the sandy shore. Exhausted by her ordeal, and that not yet finished, she had made to climb out of the boat but it had simply tipped over, spilling her into the shallows. Slowly she had crawled forward, inching away from the water and up the beach. Each movement of her legs had brought a sharper pain, yet still she crawled forward fighting for breath, her clothes torn and her hair matted, until she was beyond the line of seaweed where, finally, she collapsed.

Regaining consciousness she had found herself by a heap of glowing ashes, the remains of a fire lit by some shepherds the previous day. In great pain she had gathered the unburnt sticks within her reach and, with the wind to help her turn the eddying sparks into tiny flames, she had rekindled the fire. It was by the light and warmth of those flames fanned by fate that Kentigern had been born; and it was their flickering

90

which brought the shepherds to the spot once more.

Having taken the strangers to the shelter of their huts the shepherds had soon begun to argue amongst themselves. Who was she that had been driven there by Manannan, lord of the waves? In fear they had hurried to the Christian holyman, Servanus, who lived nearby. At first he had not believed them, but when at last he returned with them it was to find mother and child sleeping peacefully, shepherds watching over them, as had happened once before, in a distant land before Rome had conquered Prydein. Servanus stooped and looked closely at the strangers. They were no supernaturals, just a little soul with a wretched girl to protect him and speak his name.

As soon as they were able to travel Servanus had the pair brought to him, for the shepherds still regarded them with dread and he feared for their safety. Again he wondered who she was, the waif of Merin Iodeo. Her hands had done no work and only those who were high born or who had served the gods had such hands. Each time he asked she would only shake her head and say it did not matter, that she was of no importance. But her child she insisted should be called Kentigern, Foremost Prince, after his father and because of what he would be.

Nor was Servanus alone in wondering who the girl might be. Not long after Kentigern was weaned Morcant had arrived with his soldiers, for it was in his land they had been cast ashore. "I have come to return the girl to her father, the guilty to her judge," he boasted to Servanus, his eyes cruel and gloating.

Servanus barred his way. "She was judged and given to fate for punishment; but fate found them innocent and gave them to me for safe keeping, that their destiny might be fulfilled."

"She is guilty of fornication with Rheged."

"She is guilty only of carrying his child; and it was the intention of the father to lure the mind of her, a virgin, towards marriage with himself. Do not presume to think the conception of this blessed child hath contracted the taint of fornication when God and the waves he directs have declared they both shall live. As Leuddag dedicated them to his gods so has God dedicated them to Himself. Think carefully, therefore, my lord, before you lay a hand on them."

Morcant turned purple, the veins stood out on his forehead and he began to shake with rage. He would not be cheated of the bastard of Rheged nor of his revenge upon her, but who dare defy his god or gods? "Have a care, holyman, have a care," was all he could splutter as he stormed from the hut, summoning his men to follow.

When he was gone Thenew raised her head from her pallet and

extended an arm to Servanus. "Thank you. I should not have brought this trouble upon you, I should have told you who I was and then there would have been no trouble."

"Do you really think I had not guessed who you were?"

Thenew lay back on her pillow and smiled up at him. "Do you really think Owen wanted to force me to marry him?"

Servanus nodded and brushed away the tear from her cheek.

"Then I forgive him."

"I know."

"Father, you spoke also of us being dedicated to God. I think that is what I want. You know I prayed to Mary and not the old gods when I was in need of help."

"Did I not say even I occasionally get news?" Servanus reached into his robe and produced some broken twigs which had once been bound with plaited reed. "Morgause sends her love."

For five years Kentigern and his mother lived with Servanus, until the time had come for the boy to be taken into the school which adjoined their little church. "And now, my dear," Servanus told Thenew, "it is time that you too fulfilled your pledge to God and took the veil." Thenew nodded trying to hold back the tears. Kentigern had become all to her. Would he remember her as his mother and know how she had loved him? Many nights did she cry herself to sleep, his face pictured in her mind like an icon upon the wall of her cell. Sometimes she could hear him crying and calling her name but she could not go to him, to comfort him, to love him as she wanted. Instead she had to bite her lip and bury her head in the folds of the pillow, praying furiously that he and she might one day find peace and be together again.

As the years passed it seemed her prayers were being answered for the boy was quick and anxious to learn. At the board none could beat him at Wooden Wisdom; one king after another would fall to him. Servanus watched the boy in silence, nodding with satisfaction. To him Kentigern was Munghu, My Dear One. But his peers, especially those tutored by Morcant, seeing how their teacher favoured the bastard, had shunned him, taking every opportunity to get him into trouble and a beating; for the ways of the world are not simply abolished by the erection of monastic walls. So Kentigern found himself alone, climbing the rampart which had for so long been the edge of his world and venturing into that other world of mortal men. There amongst its woods and warm fields he could run free and his imagination could soar like the birds.

On one such day, having wandered farther than usual, he found himself by the side of a small stream. In front of him was a man kneeling, his arms outstretched, his eyes turned heavenwards. As still as stone was the figure yet from his mouth came music like the tinkling of the stream.

"The Lord is my rock
my fortress and my deliverer;
My God is my rock
in whom I take refuge.
He is my shield and the horn of my salvation,
my stronghold ... "

Quietly Kentigern fell to his knees by the side of the hermit and took up the psalm:

"You give me your shield of victory,
and your right hand sustains me;
You stoop down to make me great ...
You have made me the head of nations ...
He gives his king great victories ... "

"What is your name?" asked the hermit when they had finished.

"Kentigern."

"Ah, yes, I might have guessed ... " The old man waved his hands, gesturing at the sky and trees. "Have I not seen you when you have come into my world seeking the solitude which I seek? I have made it my business to know."

"Will you not tell me about yourself then?" asked Kentigern.

For a while the hermit sat in silence his head bowed as if in prayer. Then, suddenly, he looked up "Very well, just this once. Fergus is my name. My parents lived by the rock of Alclud but that was long ago ... " He paused, as if it pained him to remember such things. "Have you heard of that place, Kentigern? Alas, it should be where the kings of Clud have built their fortress, for upon its top a man like me might be wholly sufficient, without need to see others. 'Twas certainly in search of such a place that I came hither. Before then I was amongst the armies of Gabran of Dal Riada as they marched against Kernach. Driven back by Bridei I chose this life, living by myself as I had made children orphans."

Kentigern was fascinated by the idea of Alclud. Was it like Dun Pelder he wondered. Not that he had seen his mother's home but he had his own ideas. "Is it the rock of which the psalm speaks?"

Fergus laughed. "Perhaps, perhaps not. But this I know that each man must find his own rock upon which to build his life. There he might feel secure and there, except for unforseen disaster, he might hope to die. My parents, certainly, are buried nearby the rock of Alclud and sometimes I think I too would like to be buried with them. But for one such as I that is impossible." He paused again and when he looked up Kentigern saw his eyes were moist, but whether in sadness or mirth Owen's son could not tell.

With that they departed though they promised to meet again. Each week they joined in prayer but then there came a day when Fergus did not appear. Anxiously Kentigern had raced through the forest, following the faint path that the hermit had made. But all to no avail. Fergus lay on his bed, his hearth cold. Gently Kentigern kissed his forehead, promising he would be buried with his parents as he had wished. Then, he folded his friend's arms and bound them with rope.

Later that day, having said farewell to Servanus, he returned with a waggon drawn by two white oxen, beasts of the forest which served the spirits of the trees. But first Servanus had made him promise he would return. "Kentigern, Munghu, my dearest son! Light of mine eyes, staff of my old age. Call to mind the days that are past, and remember the years that are gone by; how I took you up when you came forth from your mother's womb, nourished you, taught you, trained you even to this hour. Do not despise me, nor neglect my grey hairs but return, that in no long time you may close my eyes."

Kentigern carried his friend's body towards Alclud and the place of which Fergus had spoken, Cathures. But no grave could Kentigern find; for the place was deserted, a wilderness. Near to the head of a small valley, however, he found a spring of crystal water the sound of which reminded him of the stream where Fergus and he had first met, and nearby a grove of yew trees. Kentigern smiled to himself, here amongst the once sacred mugna tree he, Munghu, would inter his friend and make his own home: his promise to Servanus momentarily forgotten.

Soon word of the young hermit of Cathures reached Alclud and the ears of Ethni of Dal Riada, Tudwal's wife. By him she had a son, Ridderch, who had been baptised by the Gael and now she wanted him to have a Christian education.

"Christian learning is one thing, to be taught by a son of Rheged is another," complained Tudwal.

"I doubt he considers himself a son of Rheged. Never has his natural father set eyes upon him or sent him word."

Tudwal considered what Ethni had said and as he did so another thought came to him: might it not profit Clud to place a weevil in the apple of Rheged? He smiled. "You are right, my dear, I will ride to Cathures tomorrow and speak with this young man of yours."

At first Kentigern had declined the offer. "I am too young. I am but a poor man. True I was born of one who had been a princess but she was also one whom God chose to disinherit. Should I now go against the will of God? I have not known the pleasures of a court nor do I wish to."

"Just so," answered Tudwal, noting how Kentigern had spoken of himself. "But as God chose to raise you in poverty that you might become wise, so should Ridderch be taught by you. Shall not the poor and meek be exalted and the exalted cast down? Shall not the one who knows poverty, hardship and the wickedness of men counsel those who are set above men? Has your mother's suffering been in vain that you will not take your place amongst your peers?"

The eyes of Kentigern searched those of Tudwal, his mind struggling to remember that which he had come to forget. He dimly recalled his mother's face; a face of tears. To him she was a woman with outstretched arms, calling for her son. For what purpose had Tudwal invoked her? To taunt him? Or did he really speak from love? Had he known her?

"For my mother's sake then. But not in Alclud. This is my home, here might I be found. And you shall know me as a man of poverty, calling me Munghu not Kentigern."

* * *

Urien sighed and then, turning his back on Clud and Cathures, rode slowly down the hill, his mind still occupied with thoughts of what had been and what might be. How different, it seemed, were Kentigern and his father. Yet was there not something of Owen in his son: a single-mindedness of purpose which had manifested itself when Kentigern had turned his back on Servanus and not returned as he had promised? And then there was the way the youth had, apparently, ingratiated himself with Tudwal, moving easily amongst the court of Clud when it suited him. In the mind of Urien there was no doubt Kentigern was his father's son, one born to rule. But not as a king.

Suddenly Urien's thoughts turned to little Pasgent and in his mind he saw him nestling in his mother's arms, feeding at her breasts.

* * *

Corocticus' bailiff, Mordaf, pointed to the large herd of horses running down the opposite hillside. They had left Urien far to the north and now, upon the northern slopes of Celidon, they paused, gazing across the narrow valley. The bailiff was right: never before had Owen seen such magnificent beasts and it seemed to him their gallop was slow, like

Kulhwch running before the house of Olwen. Like ripening barley rippling in the breeze; like the shadows of scudding clouds upon a hillside, they moved across the land.

"See how they are led by that white stallion?" called Mordaf over his shoulder, for he had already set off in their direction, galloping down the gentle slope.

Owen nudged Clovenhoof forward and soon they had caught up with Mordaf. "They are no ordinary horses, lord, but those descended from the speckled race of Mor Greidiawl which the Men of Old first found ruling the land, by whose goodness kingship is still passed to those chosen to govern and upon whom only the royal may ride. See how they are led by Swanmane who answers to none but Rhiannon."

Rhiannon! Owen turned to look enquiringly at the man who had brought him here.

"Her people range far and wide for they have no land of their own," observed his guide, his eyes to the front as if he had not seen Owen's.

"They have land of their own now."

The man of Aeron shook his head. "Cynfelyn has land now. Not Rhiannon, and the people are hers; they do what she tells them, not Cynfelyn."

Intrigued, Owen urged Clovenhoof forward, racing after Swanmane. Soon he had left the others far behind and he alone ran with the herd. Like a flock of birds changing direction they swung to the right, passing over the ridge top and down into the valley beyond. Suddenly the pace of Swanmane slowed until she was merely trotting, but all around the herd plunged on, flowing round its leader like a river round a boulder. Owen too had slowed and now he and Swanmane were alone, the valley silent. Swanmane turned and trotted towards Owen, gently nuzzling Clovenhoof. Then as swiftly as he had stopped, Swanmane galloped after the others.

"Didn't you manage to catch them?" queried Mordaf as at last he climbed up onto the ridge where Owen was waiting. Owen nodded. Mordaf was silent for a moment. "Think you not your own mount is one of them? I have never seen anyone ride as fast as you, none save her."

"Her?"

"Rhiannon."

* * *

Myrddin pricked up his ears. Like a stag allerted by distant noise or a foreign smell wafted upon the breeze he sensed something was not as it should be. Urien had need of Cynfelyn and so Myrddin had let them be, but he sensed danger in Owen and Rhiannon. He rose from his bed of bracken and trotted down the slope towards Aeron.

In her bed Eurdyl dreamed of Owen. He had come to her silently and now he stood above her, his legs astride her body. Grinning he loosened his broad, studded belt and let it fall onto the rushes. Slowly she drew up her knees arching her back, and then ... and then he was gone. Eurdyl awoke to an unsatiated aching between her thighs and an empty bed; a bed which had been empty longer than she cared to remember. Flinging her pillow against the wall she cursed her Eochaid, but most of all she cursed Owen.

In the morning, naked except for her torn dress, she flung herself upon Urien crying for help. "What has happened, child?" he cried, pulling her to his shoulder and gently stroking her hair. "What ails thee?"

For a long time she sobbed and each time she shook her head saying he would not believe her, until at last, holding her at length he spoke to her sternly. "It was Owen wasn't it?"

She nodded. "I tried to resist him but he was so insistent. For months now he has pursued me and my protestations have counted for nought. No, not even mention of Eochaid's name could stop him; rather he laughed saying that one day ... " She burst into tears. " ... and ... and.."

"And Owen was next to Eochaid when he fell," murmured Urien.

"Nay, lord, it cannot be so. You do the boy an injustice," protested Corocticus, his arm on Urien's. "Send for him that he may answer his accuser."

Owen's father shrugged him off. "Eurdyl would not lie. Do I not know my own son? It is as Myrddin said it was but I did not believe him. Would that I had, for Eochaid might still have been alive."

"How can you believe this of your own son?"

"My only son? Is he really mine? Would that I should not see his face again. My only son? Then let him be alone and, as you seek to protect him, I will leave him as your protector – for the moment. So let me not tarry longer here. Today Eurdyl and I will return south, to Caer Gwenddoleu."

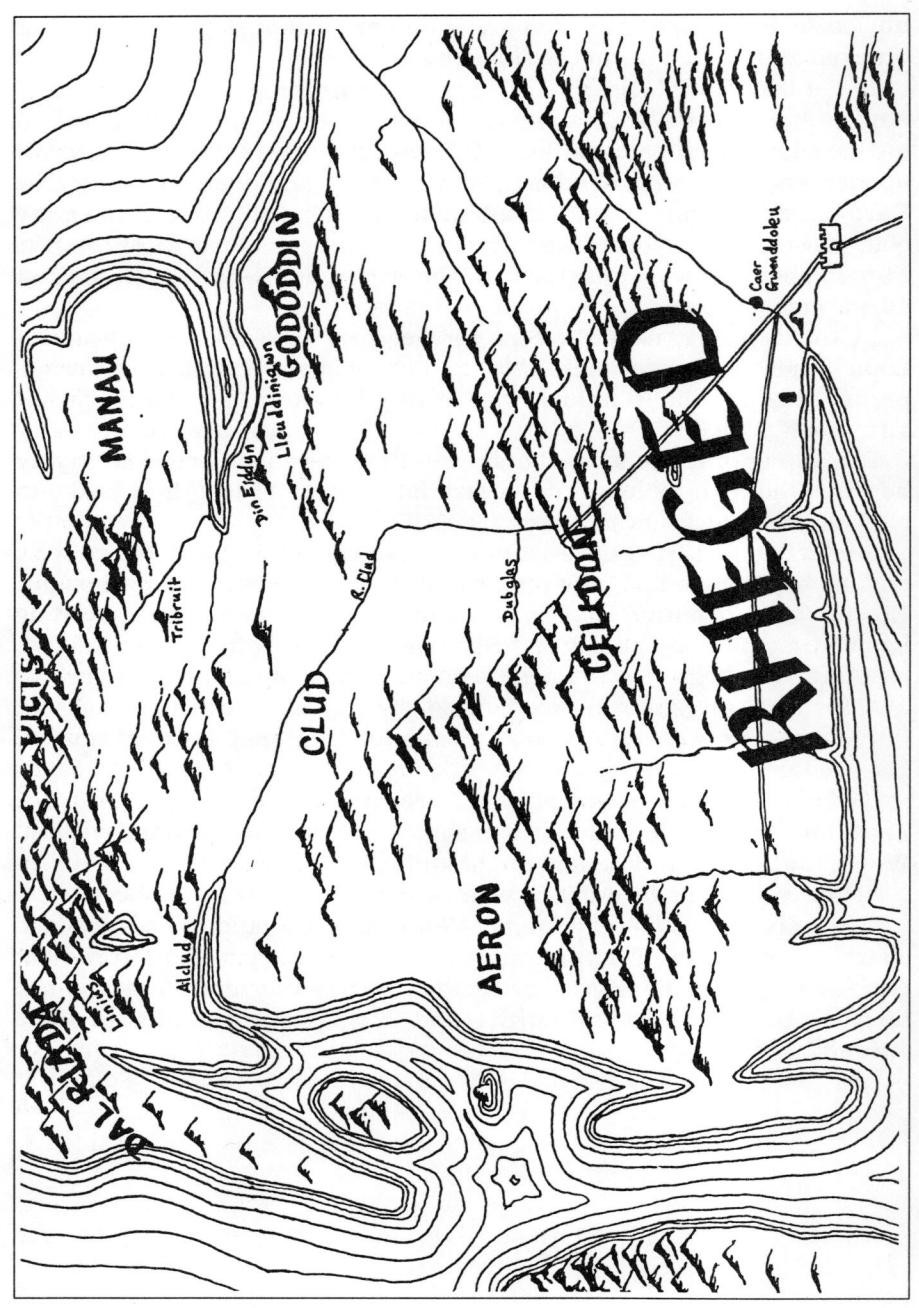

KENTIGERN and RIDDERCH.

The slopes of Llwyfenydd were white. The deep snow lay in drifts against the dykes, its surface sculptured by the wind. It filled the hollows, smoothing out the irregularities of the ground. Here and there tufts of dun coloured grass poked through the surface, tangles of stalks beaded with white crystals. Hedges and trees were similarly clothed, only the yew and holly retained their summer hue.

It was the same throughout Gwen Ystrad. It was a landscape of white, stony grey and woody black. A landscape in which little moved. Occasionally a lone fox would make a sortie across the frozen mantle, and a few birds flitted from tree to tree, their song momentarily forgotten. Even the wolf gathered into his pack despaired; his nightly howls louder and closer to the farms than for many a year. But louder still was the whistling, bitter wind as it whipped the loose snow into the face of man and beast. Nor yet was there any sign of an end to the cold. Above, the heaviness of the solid, grey sky presaged more snow. Whenever man moved he did so out of necessity, checking and feeding the livestock, the collection of firewood, water and food. Then, thankfully, he would scuttle back to the warmth of his hearth and family.

Modron and the others sat close to the great fire, but she could not get warm. Now she listened not to the boasts of warriors and the songs of Taliesin but to the howling wind, and the bitterness she felt was for Myrddin. Like the cold wind blowing from Celidon he blighted all that was in his way. Lifting raw eyes she watched dispassionately as Taliesin sang the praises of his lord. How gullible, how fragile was her Urien. Even now, as he claimed to disown their son, she knew she could not abandon him: he was part of her. She shook her head in disbelief that it could be happening to them. How? Why? What had possessed Urien to believe such a thing of Owen? She closed her eyes and felt the tears trickling down her cheeks; streams of emotion welling up from her heart. Had she not always known Eurdyl to be poisonous and sought to protect Owen from her? And had not her father sought to warn them against Myrddin? She wiped the tears from her face determinedly. Myrddin and Eurdyl had to be destroyed.

Outside, Leenauc pulled his woollen cloak close about himself, his booted feet crunching the freshly fallen snow as he made his way across the yard to the wood pile to get more logs. Engrossed in transferring the snow-topped timber into the cradle of his arms he did not see the two figures stumbling across the fields. They were upon him before he had time to call the guard.

"Do not be afraid, my son, we seek the court of Urien Rheged," called the older of the two.

"Then you need look no further," replied the servant, casting his eye quickly over the strangers. The man who had spoken was well built, even though his face was slightly drawn. He was wrapped in a thick but plain cloak, the surface of which was speckled with frost. The second figure was smaller and Leenauc, unable to see the face beneath the fur trimmed hood, thought it might be a woman or a boy of ten or twelve. "You had better come this way. You must be in need of a good warm and mulled ale," he added at last.

"It would be wise to recover a little before we speak to the King."

Leenauc stopped in his tracks and looked again at the elder of the two. "And who should I say you are if I am asked?"

"If you are asked, say, 'He who was lost is found'."

"He who was lost is found," repeated Leenauc, trying to remember the message and think what it could mean. Now he began to be afraid. The riddle made no sense to him and he knew how those of the Otherworld might visit kings at just such a time to ensure fertility in the coming year. Aye, and here was one, a female perhaps, whose face he could not see. Watching them from the corner of his eye Leenauc stooped to pick up the logs he had dropped. To his great surprise the elder of the two strangers bent down to help. Leenauc said nothing but as quickly as he could he led them to the great hall.

The doorkeeper pointed to a bench against the outer wall. "It's far from the fire yet hot enough to begin thawing out." He nodded to a guard and, slipping past them, returned with two tankards of hot ale. "There are two places nearer the fire, over there," he informed them, pointing to a space amongst the shadowy figures.

The elder thanked him kindly but declined the offer.

"I would prefer to sit beside a good hearth again, father," pleaded the other.

"For your sake, then," answered the taller, rising and unfastening his cloak.

From behind their pillar Leenauc and his friends watched. The taller of the two was clad in plain, undyed wools, the other, they could see now, was a boy.

From her place next to her brother, Eurdyl too watched as they picked their way between the warriors. She was glad she had not to ride in the present weather and wondered what had made them battle against the forces of winter. Who were they, for she could not remember seeing them before? And yet ... there was something about the elder that was familiar to her, but she struggled to find a name or place. Finally she summoned the porter.

"Who are they?"

"I do not know, lady. They came seeking your brother but first asked if they could warm themselves. Walked here they did, so I thought it best to get some warmth back into them."

"Did they give no clue as to who they are?"

"Well, the father of the boy told Leenauc, 'He who was lost is found'."

Like the servant before her, Eurdyl repeated the riddle, her eyes still upon the strangers. Mouric, seated on the other side to Urien, leant across. "What is it mother, you look puzzled?" Then seeing the direction of her gaze he asked what the servant had said. Eurdyl turned her head slowly. "He who was lost is found."

For a moment Mouric stared in disbelief and then he laughed. "The prodigal son. My Christian learning was not a waste after all ... "

"Prodigal son!" roared Urien, pushing back his bench and striding round the hall towards the door. "I'll not have him here." Suddenly he halted. "Who? Who are you that look like my Owen but are not?"

Leenauc dropped his logs. "Oh God, it is elven!"

"Not elven but a saint," reassured Modron who had raced after her husband to stop him making an even greater fool of himself. "Its Kentigern. I know its Kentigern." Her eyes filled with tears of joy and there was a lump in her throat. Gently taking Kentigern's face in her hands she kissed him on the forehead.

Urien stared in disbelief and then laughed with relief and joy. "You don't kiss priests like that."

"Well, to me he is not a priest, he is my grandson, he is ... "

"Munghu."

Modron looked at the boy beside Kentigern. Grinning at her he repeated, "He is called Munghu."

"And what then is your name?"

The boy straightened and, looking from her to Urien and back, proclaimed himself, "Ridderch, rightful King of Clud."

Urien raised an eyebrow. Here was something he had not expected, not yet at least. "Rightful?" he repeated. "Has another taken your place? Is that why you journeyed here in the worst winter for a generation? But what of Tudwal, your father?"

Kentigern motioned for the boy to be silent. "At harvest time King Tudwal was taken ill. No one knew what ailed him though some suspected poison. I was sent for, though why any should think I could help I knew not, not then at least. It was in my arms that he died, three days later, of a high fever. The people had not time to finish grieving before Morcant arrived with his men and, supported by Caten, was made regent. For a month or two there was little trouble and then the rumours began."

"That you had murdered Tudwal?"

"Aye, then I knew why I had been called to his bedside ... But who would believe me innocent when Corocticus their enemy had feasted you? It was easy to say you had got me to poison Tudwal that you might rule in Alclud. Then I wished I had done as Servanus wanted and returned to him: arrogant, selfish man that I am. Had they attacked me then, it would not have mattered; but they struck at the Church and I began to fear for Ridderch. So we plotted our escape. It was to be one day after lessons, when the darkness of night might protect us, but Caten suspected and came to collect the boy ... "

" ... and so Munghu hit him and killed him," added Ridderch, his eyes alight with with youthful admiration. Urien noticed their glint and thought he detected glee rather than innocent admiration: the boy was not perhaps what Kentigern thought. Yet Kentigern's feeling of guilt would be a useful ally.

"And so you came here," exclaimed Modron, clapping her hands in joy and admiring her clever grandson. "From evil comes good."

"Indeed," added Urien and then, turning to Ridderch, "Well, young man, there is a place set aside for kings in the halls of warriors. Come, and we will plan your return."

"Munghu said I could count on you," answered the boy as he walked proudly alongside his host, around the blazing hearth to the seats of honour.

Ridderch ate ravenously whilst Urien talked of how they would drive Morcant back and help the boy rule until he was of age. Perhaps, added the Lord of Rheged, he would like to have Morcant's head upon a stake over the high gate of Alclud. The idea was an appealing one and Ridderch held aloft a piece of meat at the end of his knife, savouring the idea. The warm fat and blood ran down the blade and over his hand. "Then indeed shall Morcant get what he has always wanted, to be the highest in the land. Yet I think it would be unwise for you to rule as regent in his stead, for might not men say he was right after all, that Urien Rheged had my father poisoned?"

Urien was silent. He had misjudged the boy, aye, and perhaps the opportunity. For the moment he must bide his time and watch. "You have learned much and well, my boy," he replied as if in praise but stressing the word boy. "But if neither Kentigern nor I can return with you, you must remain here."

"Then men would say you held me hostage."

Urien shrugged his shoulders, biting deeply into an apple. "It would seem then there is little we can do. It is a problem and no mistake."

Ridderch began to get agitated. "Perhaps the mistake was to come here."

Urien spat out two pips and took another large bite. "No, no, Kentigern's advice was sound ... Unless of course you wanted to stay with Morcant, and then what would men have said? No, you did right to flee hither and, by so doing, point the finger at Morcant. And he now can blame Cathen, thanks to Kentigern. But by coming here you have also shown how you believe me to be innocent. There is then no reason why I cannot help. Still, in deference to you we will find another regent." "Yet one whom I can trust," he added silently. "But come we have talked enough as kings, tell me about yourself and what you like."

Modron had been watching Kentigern as a mother a long lost son, forgetful of his age and station. "You have not eaten any meat."

"I do not eat such things, grandmother, only bread and cheese with milk and water, for many have no more. Today in a moment of weakness I allowed myself mulled ale ... "

"Surely you cannot really prefer that life?" asked Eurdyl who had been listening to both conversations. "Besides, the world expects its rulers to feast."

Kentigern smiled benevolently: so this was his father's accuser? "Yes, the world expects but that is not to say they need to, nor am I a ruler. I eat enough for my needs and so I hope do not take from the mouths of others. I enjoy life; life that God has given, the beauty of this world. Of that I am thankful. I see the world around and am satisfied, I contemplate its beauty and am intoxicated."

Modron sat silently, weighing Kentigern's words. She had hoped he might be her and Owen's ally but he was clearly his own man with his own ambitions, his own purpose. What that was and how she might use it she must find out, but not immediately. "We must talk some more, you and I," she said, smiling.

"Tell me Kentigern," sneered Eurdyl, "does the world need druids?"

"No more than it need harlots."

Modron smiled to herself. Yes, she and Kentigern could do business.

* * *

It was many weeks before the snows melted. During those days Urien talked often with his grandson; for in the time that had passed since Caer Gwenddoleu the power Myrddin held over him had begun to wane. "You spoke of the world needing many kinds of men: smiths, shepherds and priests. Does it not also need warriors? Is it not necessary for the shepherd to hunt the wolf that his flock and that of his neighbours might go in safety? Must not a kingdom, a nation, fight to save itself, as the Church destroys heretics lest itself be destroyed?"

Kentigern did not speak for some time, as if he were not sure how to answer. "One day all men will live in peace. Swords will indeed be turned into ploughshares and there will be an abundance of goodness for everyman. But that time has not yet come and until it does the good king and the Church must defend themselves. Perhaps that way is to use evil to destroy evil but it is a choice we must make. Which, indeed is wrong? To watch one's sheep torn apart or to slay those who would attack them?"

"Then why do you trouble yourself with Cathen's death?"

"Because I could have driven the wolf from my sheep, I need not have killed him."

"It was chance. There are casualties in all war."

"Why do you speak of war?"

"Why do I speak ... ?" Urien looked at his grandson with amazement. He thought he understood him, that he might be able to use him. Was he a mere cleric after all, or did he possess ambition, the desire to stamp his authority upon the land? And if the latter, whose authority? Could Urien, could Rheged, count on Kentigern; or did Kentigern make his own plans, perhaps even with Ridderch?

Urien decided deeds were stronger than words and that he would give Kentigern enough rope to do what he wanted, but tethered he would be.

Modron and Kentigern, too, talked often. They talked of his mother, of his home by the River Clud and of his hopes for the future. "Can you not forgive your father, your earthly father?" she asked.

Kentigern shrugged. "I do not know him."

"If you did, would it help?"

"Perhaps, perhaps not. For when a father and his son know each other they often seem to disagree."

"Sometimes, and sometimes husbands and wives quarrel and then make up, and in the making up love is borne anew and reaffirmed. But sometimes they quarrel because another has come between them ... So it is between us here. It was Myrddin who drove your father from me and Urien. Will you not help me drive him from the land?"

"Willingly, but you will forgive me if I have my own reasons."

"Yes, anything." For the first time in months, Modron began to feel hope.

"You know Myrddin will not come here whilst you have still some power," observed Kentigern.

Modron nodded. Relieved to have found an ally, she did not ask how Kentigern knew of the power she had rediscovered within herself; a power of which her father had once spoken to Urien and of which Myrddin was afraid.

Kentigern looked at her. "So, if I am to drive Myrddin from the land I must be free to seek him out."

* * *

With the melting of the snows Kentigern was anxious to be off, talking readily of his wish to fulfil the promise he had made to himself. For the last time he sat at the family hearth.

"In the days of Coel there was a bishop in these lands, a presbyter in Caer Leu. I have given you permission to preach where you will; will you not be my bishop?" asked Urien.

Kentigern smiled. "When I left Servanus it was to be alone and live like the monks of Dal Riada and Hibernia: a silent cormorant upon a rock. But that, it seems, is not as easy as I thought. First Tudwal and now you, invite me to be a robin amongst ravens. Do I not already have one flock to watch, a king to advise as Myrddin advises you ... " Owen's son paused, noting how Urien had scowled at Modron; the sign of a wound that festered. "One day I must return to the rock of Clud."

But Urien had regained his composure. "Your answer is as I thought. But the shepherd does not desert his new lambs, rather he nourishes them until they are strong and able to stand on their own. Will you not agree to a greater flock: one bishop in Clud and Rheged?"

"We will see."

"And in the meantime, Ridderch will remain with us, learning those skills important to a king which you could not teach."

"Aye, he needs your help and your teaching if he is to regain his kingdom. Future generations will thank us for that. We have, I think, much to give. Together we could mould the future of Prydein. You as High King and I as bishop. Kentigern in Rheged, Munghu in Clud."

Kentigern chuckled to himself and Urien too seemed pleased. "The idea has much to commend it... You as bishop, I as High King."

"But first, I have a promise to fulfil." Kentigern climbed onto his horse and waving farewell rode northwards towards the land of Gwenddoleu and Myrddin. But of Elen and Pasgent he knew not, not yet at least.

* * *

Gwenddoleu, seated before the perpetual fire he kept within his hall, welcomed the grandson of Urien and offspring of Owen. Had he brought a message from them? Did he come to ask for help in restoring Ridderch? Or had he grown tired of the poetry of Taliesin and wanted to hear from the bard's mentor, Myrddin?

Kentigern studied his grandfather's friend: he was indeed a fool. Oh yes, he had come to hear from Myrddin but not in admiration. "No, I did not grow tired of Taliesin's poetry, but it is because of Myrddin that I come hither. You said he was the mentor of Taliesin and that might be true in part but I never heard that from him. Taliesin indeed differs from Myrddin in his belief in the one true God ... "

"Ah, so now we know why you came," interrupted a voice from the shadows.

It was a voice neither young nor old, neither soft nor harsh, a voice Kentigern had not heard before, although he knew its owner. Now he saw his enemy for the first time: a golden torque about his neck, a feathered cloak upon his shoulders, a hazel wand in his hand: the proclaimer of kings, adviser to Urien. Here was he whom Kentigern had come to fight. But for the moment it suited him to ignore the druid for if he could win over Gwenddoleu then Myrddin's power would be seriously weakened. So he turned to Gwenddoleu once more. "In a few weeks you will join my father and grandfather, Ridderch and Dreon. Then you will set Clud free, but there will have to be death before there can be freedom and justice in that land. So also my Lord died, that your people might be freed from the dark powers which hold them in slavery and misery."

"They are not held in slavery and misery," retorted Myrddin. "It is you who would fetter their freedom. On May Eve do not our young ones, boys and girls, celebrate their freedom in the woods by reaffirming the forces which multiply the flocks and give crops in abundance? Would you let them do that if they wished? Would you let them dance naked about the fire of Brigit to celebrate the fertility which perpetuates life and brings the seasons to follow each other, day to follow night? Would those who choose not to worship the new God be allowed to dissent? Would you let me go free?... "

"Freedom to worship? The People of Brigit? Who are you to talk of them? You who boasts of how your people drove them into the Otherworld unable to stand their light," snarled Kentigern, but Myrddin would not be drawn.

Owen's son saw his chance. "Gwenddoleu! Your people might be free in body but their minds are snared by the invisible threads of Ogma, and if their minds are enslaved how can their bodies be free? Myrddin says he dwelt then as now. Did he then burn our fellow countrymen in wicker cages? Is that his freedom? Is a man free when his gods demand: 'sacrifice to me a lamb or I will send pestilence upon your flock; give me bread or I shall flatten your crops with thunder'? My God does not need to be bribed with sacrifices for he sacrificed himself. Myrddin says no harm comes from a girl or boy lying down amongst the trees on May Eve, but who asks the ugly to the woods? For some there is indeed pleasure but for others unhappiness. No man can pursue his own wants unchecked without bringing misery to another. If one man is rich then another must be poor. Thus Christ taught us to think before we act, to do naught that might hurt our neighbour."

"So we see the Christian God of love: not the love of the forest but the love of a man for his neighbour. If then I am filled with passion for the wife of another, like Trystan and Esyllt, should he out of love for his neighbour not give her to me?" mocked Myrddin.

"The Christian would not covet his neighbour's wife."

"But until all freely choose to become Christian you would prohibit covetousness. Thus you make slaves of men," crowed Myrddin triumphantly, his face beaming with the delight of one who has his enemy at his mercy.

Kentigern eyed the grinning creature by the side of Gwenddoleu calmly, for none is vanquished until dead and many, believing they are victors, are slain by those they wounded first. "I would prohibit covetousness, not to spite you or any man, but to prevent hurt to him whose wife you sought."

Gwenddoleu watched Kentigern with the fascination of one who sees but does not immediately recognise danger. Here was a match for Myrddin, one who could return blow for blow, a champion like his father. Indeed his very face reminded Gwenddoleu of Owen. A power which could transform the offspring of so great a warrior into a person living the life chosen by Kentigern was a force indeed. Had Urien not said the Christian priests were powerful allies? But how much did Kentigern know? All this talk of coveting, did he know about Elen? Whatever else he must not be allowed to wander freely in the land.

Myrddin too had seen the danger. "My lord King, let this priest who preaches humility yet who accepts a title ... "

"I did not want to be bishop."

"No, but your fellow travellers have such titles and make places of honour for themselves ... "

"Only because the Church needs rulers to guide it. A good bishop chooses to eat and live no differently from the farmhand except he is able to study and pray more. Those bishops who live as kings I renounce, as Christ would."

"No matter, good priest. I say good for that is what you tell the world you are ... "

"No. As God is my witness I have never claimed that, but I have taught we should all strive to attain goodness even though it is impossible. Christ alone was perfect goodness," replied Kentigern defensively, for now he was having to fight both the druid and the temper he had inherited from his father. His anger was beginning to blind him; better to stand his ground than to stumble going forward.

Myrddin saw his chance and advanced. "So, your religion strives for what it knows it cannot attain. That is something to offer the people indeed."

The druid sensed victory. His gloating face looked right and left, calling upon the warband, friends of Urien and Owen, to laugh with him. Then he was holding up his rod to demand silence. Now he turned to address Gwenddoleu: like a gladiator before his emperor he sought permission to make the final thrust. "I say to you who have kept faith with the powers men found in this land when first they came, that Kentigern should be allowed to preach if he can answer one question."

Gwenddoleu leant forward in his chair, his eyes slowly searching those of Kentigern; for he sensed whatever the outcome he, Rheged and all Prydein would be the loser. Like the ravens of Cocidius he felt shackled by powers beyond his own control and comprehension. Powers which if unleashed, like those birds, would destroy him and the world he loved. And when at last he spoke his voice was heavy with sadness. "Are you agreeable, Kentigern?" The son of Owen nodded, like Gwydion baring his neck for the stroke of Ulph. "Then before all you present I swear upon myself that whatever is decided by these two I will abide by and shall not change until I die. Let Myrddin strike the first blow. If Kentigern can return it he shall preach here, if not, let him leave this place in peace."

Myrddin paused, savouring the moment. In front of him was one born of Modron's stock, the blood of Avallach in his veins. His eyes glinted in the firelight; they burned with loathing, hatred and fear. "You teach Christ's death was necessary for the salvation of mankind: that his death was the willing and loving sacrifice made for us by the good God. Why then do you say Judas' betrayal was evil, for without Judas there could have been no sacrifice?"

* * *

Owen stood on the shore watching the sunset. He had hoped that by remaining in Aeron he might see Rhiannon again, but in that hope he had been frustrated. Was there some geis upon himself ... Aye, he had heard Lleudag had sworn one. Owen kicked the sand cursing himself for that day long ago. Yet he felt as if the injustice now done to him, Eurdyl's false accusation, made him one with Thenew. He could understand now how she must have felt and with that came new shame and guilt. Who could forgive him? "Oh God, help me," he called. But there was no answer. He stumbled alone along the shore blinded by the salty waters of his own eyes.

Westward was the swell of the ocean, rolling forward like the inexorable forces which control a man; sometimes benign, sometimes murderous. Could man ever hope to tame such primeval forces? Forces which move to their own pattern and purpose, so that man can only hope to propitiate or deflect them, or, learning their direction, ride with them. Like Thenew and Kentigern...

Owen stopped and wiped the back of his hand across his eyes, gazing across the darkening waters towards the silhouette of islands whose names he did not know. Was he, Owen, condemned for all time to drift amongst such islands, seeking the happiness of others but not tasting it himself? Raising his hands to his lips he again called for help; and again there was no answer except the murmur of the waves breaking gently over black rocks, their white foam breaking and surging like the mane of a horse.

A horse! Even here he could not escape Rhiannon. Owen ran from the beach and leapt onto Clovenhoof. Galloping away, he tried to shut out the thought, tried to forget. But how could he when it was her horse, her gift? Owen brought his whip cracking down; again and again. Where they galloped he knew not, whither they went he cared not; if only he could escape and find peace. He was tormented by thoughts of what he had lost, thoughts which burned inside his skull. But there was no escaping them. Like the hounds of hell they pursued him baying at his heels.

Morning found him upon the slopes of western Celidon where the grey mist, not yet dispersed by the benevolent sun, hung about the slopes and garlanded the hilltops. Yet still he galloped onwards, Clovenhoof's nostrils flaring as she fought for breath, her mouth foaming like the waves they had left far behind. Onwards they rode until at last Clovenhoof fell, exhausted, and with her Owen.

Where they were Owen did not know but he was alone in a boat: its sides were of copper, its keel of bronze and in it were oars for three hundred men. The sea upon which he drifted was perfectly flat and from its surface there rose many islands, but how far off they were he could not tell, for their colours and shapes were mirrored in the water and the horizon was one with the sky. Suddenly he found himself rowing, for though the boat was sufficient for a warband it was no bigger than he. As he pulled upon those blades his face was set against the place from which he had come: two great mountains, a shee mound upon each; the peaks of Magmell. He looked again and it seemed to him they were not mountains but the breasts of Mother Earth, the shee mounds nipples by which man is fed and given life. A third time he looked and this time the mountains seemed to him to be like the horns of a shee mound, thighs between which a man enters this life and the next.

So he rowed on and as he drew near to the first island he saw above him dark shapes wheeling in the sky. They swooped upon anything that moved and the smell of putrefaction was in the air. Like owls they vomited balls of whatever they had consumed, and these they hurled at Owen and as they fell about him he saw they were the heads of those he had slain. The claws of the birds were as long as spears, their beaks iron flesh hooks and when they called to each other it was like war trumpets upon ramparts. They were the familiars of the Morrigan, so he rowed on.

The second island was full of horses racing. How many there were he could not tell, but as they galloped around the mountain each revolved inside its skin, the ground shook, the sea was made to boil and the steam from their coats and nostrils hid them from his sight. So he rowed on.

On the third island there were horses also but they were like the beasts of hell and with their horns they tore the flesh from each other. Each day they were made whole and each day they fought, until their bones were white.

About the fourth island there was a white fog of milling, but the flour settled in the water and made further progress impossible. So Owen turned away and as he departed he heard the miller call: "Half the corn of your country is ground here. Here comes to be ground all that men begrudge to one another."

So Owen rowed on and two more islands he visited before he came to the last. There he found a rainbow of leaping salmon and twenty-seven women, but the face of each was that of Thenew and no sooner had he stepped ashore than they fell upon him and kissed him. But they were decaying corpses, their eyes bright with maggots, the waving tresses of their hair writhing worms. From that place for which he had searched so long, Owen now fled.

He awoke to find himself upon a shee mound. Rubbing his head, he looked around for Clovenhoof but of her he could find no trace. Somewhat unsteadily he began to walk upstream, towards a mountain from where he might be able spot a landmark he knew. It was, however, further than he had anticipated and the sun had long passed its zenith when he threaded his way past the last boulders and whin bushes onto the open ridge. Immediately a spear point touched his chest. "Morcant's men!" gasped Owen. "What a fool I've been."

A hand grabbed him from behind, and a voice whispered into his ear "A fool, perhaps, but not Morcant's men." Suddenly and to gails of laughter he was spun round.

"Rhiannon!"

She bowed, "Who else. None move – or sleep – here, except I allow them." There was laughter again. "All morning and much of the afternoon we have waited for the divine youth to struggle up here."

Owen felt his face redden. "You could at least have ridden down for me."

"Not the way you treat a horse, my present ... "

"I thought it was a hostage."

"Well, in that case you are now mine." As fast as lightening she grabbed his arm and threw him to the floor, pressing her knife to his throat and Owen noticed it was of copper not iron. Above him the other women stood, dressed and armed much as Rhiannon herself, their hair irridescent against the afternoon sun. Again there was laughter. Rhiannon took her knee from his chest and straightened herself. "Come, I will take you to my house and tomorrow we shall return you to Corocticus and your men." She held out her hand and pulled Owen swiftly to his feet.

Their horses were waiting behind a group of boulders; all except Clovenhoof. "Aye, you do well to wonder where she has gone, my lord," commented Rhiannon seeing his puzzled look. "Can you blame her. I hope you will not treat your future wife so." Rhiannon and her companions exchanged knowing glances and smiles. "So we have got you something a little more to your taste, something to teach you to respect horses," they laughed, pointing to an old mare which looked as though it would barely carry his weight. Yet carry him it did, albeit somewhat more slowly than Clovenhoof might. Owen rode alongside Rhiannon and behind the others. He had much to think about, not least the swaying curves of those who rode before him. "We are all that are left now. Cynfelyn has gone with your father," Rhiannon told him. "But I think you will agree we can defend our land as well as any man."

"Your land?" queried Owen. "I thought Corocticus said you had none, roaming where you will?" Rhiannon smiled and shrugged her shoulders. "If someone had settled half of Llwyfenydd without your permission would you stop calling it your land?"

"No, but ... we never knew Corocticus had taken this land from you."

"Ah, not Corocticus, not his father, nor his father's father but long ago when Leu strode these hills and warriors feasted from the Cauldron of Ulph. Until my people were driven underground." Her voice was sad and her eyes glazed. Suddenly she blinked. "Do I not cease to amaze you?"

"Aye, and frighten me." He laughed. "And there are not many times I have said that." He reached over to slap her thigh, not in anger and lust as he had once planned, more in play; but then withdrew his hand "Those bruises look like the weals of a horse whip, do they hurt?"

She winced a little to tease him. "What do you think? But I got his throat with my dagger."

They were descending another low ridge and Rhiannon pointed to the far side of the river, to the hut between two conical peaks. It was a building unlike any of the halls of Llwyfenydd. True, it was circular, but its roof of turf reached to the ground so that it was difficult to tell where one began and the other finished. A number of similar buildings were dotted nearby at the head of the valley and from them began to emerge older women and children, their attention attracted by the jingling harness. Rhiannon's companions had broken away, cantering across the long, brown grass towards their families, leaving Owen and Rhiannon to trot forward alone.

In front of Rhiannon's door an old woman was waiting, her grey hair gathered in a bun held in place by a white boar's tusk, her blue eyes moving from the girl to Owen and back again. "Luned was my nurse, my mother and father," explained Rhiannon as they dismounted.

Owen stopped. "But I thought Cynfelyn ... "

"No, but it suited us both, his people and mine. It was simpler, two groups of outlaws living together, in the same area."

Luned nodded knowingly, her creased face smiling, her eyes twinkling: "Welcome, my lord."

Owen examined the dark interior of the hut; the loom and glowing fire, the milk, cheese and oatcakes. Rhiannon and Luned watched him in amusement. "Is it possible we would have survived here if we had demanded wine, meats and white bread? But tonight will be different, tonight we shall roast a boar to welcome you to our house."

Luned watched Owen and Rhiannon. "My lord looks better already," she observed.

"And so he feels, but tomorrow he must return to Aeron if his old mount will allow."

"If I allow," teased Rhiannon, putting her arms around his neck, "for don't forget you are my hostage, to do with as I please."

* * *

Kentigern stood in the doorway of his wattle hut looking northwards to where the horsemen were fording the river. Triumphantly they rode towards him, he who had been forced to retreat by Myrddin. Now as he watched the column snake closer he promised himself that before he died he would see such riders trampling down the walls of Cocidius; that the fire of Brigit would be extinguished by the cross. But that day was yet some time away, a moment to be dreamed of, a moment to be worked for. Kentigern stepped forward, raising his hand in blessing. "Greetings to the defenders of justice, the hope of the Brython."

"You've heard then?" asked Urien looking down from the back of his mount. Kentigern nodded. Who had not heard how Urien, his flank protected by the unseen presence of Owen in Aeron, had driven Morcant from the Dubglas, chasing him to the rock of Clyde, cornering him against Conall of Dal Riada? Of how Morcant had sworn allegiance to Urien and his descendants? The men of Llwyfenydd had conquered at Tribruit and forced the gates of Manau. Ridderch had been restored, Nudd made regent and Cynfelyn installed in Dun Eiddyn; whilst Bridei had acknowledged Christ.

"Will you not ride with us to Modron?"

Kentigern shook his head. "I have work here, plans to bring to fruition."

Urien nodded. "So I am told."

It was with a heavy heart that Urien rode south, but it was not the parting from Kentigern which saddened him, rather it was the abandonment of Elen. Often had he thought of her and Pasgent as he rode the northern marches, met Conall and marshalled men. Where Modron was once supreme another now ruled.

Urien had ridden to her at the first opportunity after his return, cantering across the meadow in front of the farmhouse towards the tiny boy who played by its door. It had worried him that Elen had not emerged. Surely Cadwallon would have got a message to Gwenddoleu if anything were wrong?

The boy had run off calling for Cadwallon and Urien had entered the house alone. He halted just inside the doorway, his left hand upon the jamb. In front of him, seated by the hearth, was Elen, suckling another baby. "We were expecting you," she said lifting her eyes briefly from the little soul contentedly feeding at her breast. She worked two fingers around her nipple and the baby began to suck with renewed vigour. Elen looked up again and smiled. "Don't worry, it is no one's child except my lord the King's. Pasgent has a sister."

"A daughter!" he cried almost in disbelief. "A daughter," he repeated, his head turned to look back through the door as if the whole world was waiting in the meadow.

"Ssh ... " chided Elen as she moved to one side to allow Urien to sit next to her. Pasgent too had slipped in and stood behind her shoulder, an arm about her neck, the thumb of his free hand in his mouth. His head was laid against Elen's, his large eyes surveying the stranger. "And what of Pasgent. Do you like your little sister?" asked Urien crouching before the boy. Pasgent said nothing, but hid his face in his mother's hair.

"Pasgent, he is your father," she soothed. The boy peeped at Urien and then hid his face again.

"I have told him about you often, but you are away so long."

"I know and I wish it were not so ... and I too forget." Urien leant across and kissed Elen's cheek for her head was once more turned momentarily to the baby. "For her mother is almost as beautiful as she."

"Be off, before you disturb us any more." Elen gave Urien a playful push that sent him reeling backwards, laughing. Pasgent, watching, concluded the stranger presented no threat. "Go and show your father your treasures," Elen told him.

"Treasure!" exclaimed Urien. Pasgent nodded, his eyes not leaving those of his father. Silently he slipped his hand into that of Urien and led him from the hut.

Together they crossed to the middle of the field, to where a small ridge of grey rock broke through the turf. The sun had warmed the stone and a butterfly fluttered lazily into the air. Urien sat himself upon the mossy surface amidst lime coloured lichens whilst Pasgent, delving into a crevice, sought out his yellow and black banded snail shells, fossils and feathers. "My, what treasure," Urien observed, picking up one of the feathers and smoothing its ruffled edes. "Do you know what colour this is? It is black. It comes from the raven, a bird which helps men in battle. So you must learn to listen to the ravens for they will give you great wisdom and tell you what might be."

Pasgent had seated himself next to Urien, his treasures temporarily forgotten. "Listen to the raven. If it calls, 'grob, grob,' warriors are coming. If it calls long, it is women who come. If it calls from the north east end of the house, robbers are about to steal the horses. If it calls from the house door, strangers or soldiers are coming. If it calls from the edge of the storehouse there will be much to eat. If it speaks with a small voice, 'err, err,' there will be sickness in the house or amongst the cattle. If it calls, 'coin, coin,' from the sheepfold then wolves are coming. If it goes with you on a journey or flies in front of you, you will prosper and fresh meat will be given to you. If it calls from a high tree then it is the death tidings of a young lord ... "

Urien paused and looked down. Pasgent was asleep, his body snuggled between his father's arm and body. Urien smiled and lay back, listening to the cattle tearing mouthfuls of fresh grass and to the droning of the bees as they moved between the red poppies, white dog daisies and blue scabious. Here he could forget.

When he had woken it was to find Elen sitting by his side and Pasgent helping Cadwallon drive the two milch cows towards the byre. Urien reached out and put his hand on Elen's knee, "He should make a good cattle raider."

"Perhaps, but in such a place as this he will learn only the ways of a farmer and not those of a king."

Urien kept his eyes on the boy. "Don't you think I wish I could take you all away from here, to Llwyfenydd? But it cannot be. Do not ask me again lest our speaking of it puts that day beyond our reach. One day it will be possible, I promise you."

"Perhaps a raven will tell me when that will be," she called lightly as she scampered from him towards the house. Urien ran after her and caught her by the waist, carrying her struggling into the dark interior. "Now don't make a sound or you will wake the baby."

"What shall we call her?" he asked as he lay on the furs of the bed. Elen leant across and checked her sleeping bundle. "Morfudd."

"Morfudd," repeated Urien. "I wonder what Kentigern would think if he knew."

MAELGINI

The fire roared in the centre of the hall, the trestles were loaded and all about was the sound of merriment and of feasting. Taliesin circled the hearth, his eyes upon each warrior; three hundred men in a circle about their lord.

> "Throughout the year
> This man has poured out
> Wine, bragget and mead,
> The reward of valour.
> Each went on campaign,
> Eager for combat
> His steed beneath him,
> Set to raid Manau."

Modron looked on, her hand upon the arm of Urien. How different it had been but two days before. Then she had been seated upon the shee mound at the head of Llwyfenydd gazing northwards, straining her eyes for any sign that Urien might be returning. Upon that sward, where once before she had found comfort, she had waited, looking towards Caer Leu whilst her thoughts sought to give form to the darkness she felt. A darkness that had been in her mind for many a day; the ache of foreboding, its reality certain, its character unseen. She had ceased to dream of the future as if it would not be and only the past remained. A past that kept her loving Urien but in a manner different from before ... Before Myrddin had come and the Morrigan had called their names. Where now was Urien?

Modron had felt a cloak placed about her shoulders and looking up saw the kind face of Taliesin. He had smiled then and offered words of comfort.

> "I could have no joy
> Should Urien be slain,
> A bier his fate
> His wife made a widow.
> A strong steadfast man is he,
> My faithful King
> My bulwark; chief."

So, now by the great hearth, Taliesin sang the praises of Rheged's King: a lord whose deeds were beyond boasting; a prince whose achievements were numbered in cattle and not the words of storytellers

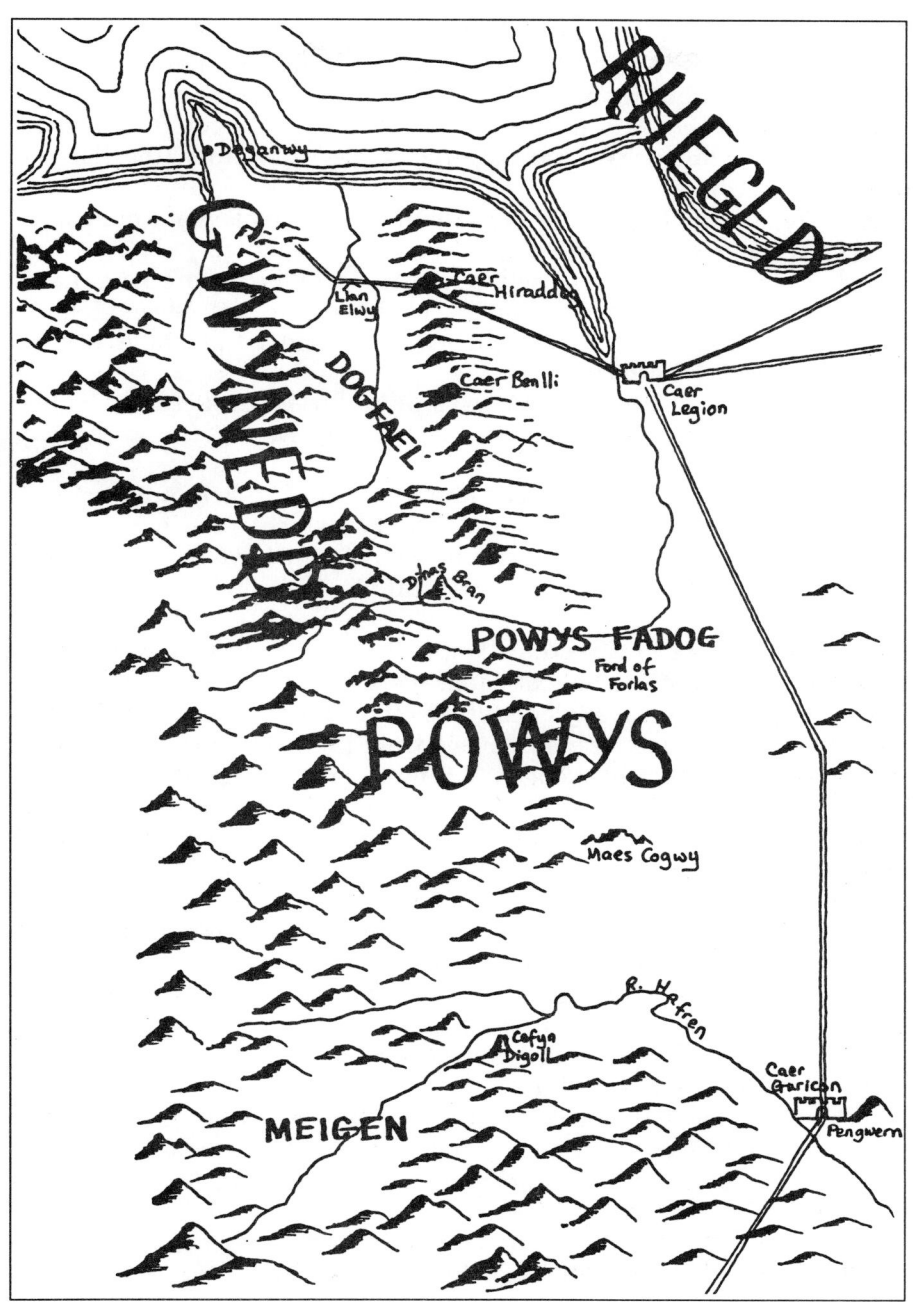

RHEGED

GWYNEDD

Deganwy

Llan Elwy

DOGFAEL

Caer Hiraddog

Caer Benlli

Caer Legion

Dinas Bran

POWYS FADOG

Ford of Forlas

POWYS

Maes Cogwy

R. Hafren

Cefyn Digoll

Caer Garicon

MEIGEN

Pengwern

embroidering by the hearth. For the moment, however, it was a time to gallop or stroll through the mead mists; to enjoy the world they shrouded, a world fashioned to the likeness of each man and containing none so great as he. And for the moment too, Modron could forget, the darkness of doubt driven back by the flames of victory, the light of laughter.

But alone with Urien it was different. "I thought you would have returned earlier, I was worried about you," she confided.

Urien lay still, an arm loosely about her shoulder; more from habit than any desire. "I had business to attend to at Gwenddoleu's. Kentigern it seems upset him and Myrddin, and I thought it best to soothe the ruffled feathers."

"Myrddin!" spat Modron. "Always Myrddin. He has cast a shadow over our lives, seeking to divide us. It is a pity Kentigern did not clip his wings."

"What are you saying, woman? Myrddin means to help not hurt us," retorted Urien. "There is no shadow save that which grows in the east: a darkness which threatens to snuff out the light we have kept alive since the days of Coel. I, we, need Myrddin's help, but even that is not enough.

"Well, I don't need Myrddin's help. Nor I think does he want mine, for have you not noticed how he shuns me? No moth is he to my flame."

Nor did spring bring any comfort to either for with the return of the geese, heralds of summer, came news from the north and south. From the north, Dreon sent messengers telling of how the first great frost of winter had brought the bitterness of his father's death. For Urien especially the news was unwelcome. Nudd had been a friend of Cynfarch. Of all who had ridden with Outigern only Eleuther and Cadwallon now remained. But there was still more bad news from the north: Cynfelyn reported some of Cathen's followers had invited Morcant to be King in Lleuddiniawn amongst the Gododdin.

"And what news from the south?" demanded Urien, turning on the messengers sent by his cousin Llywarch.

"None that is good, my Lord, for men of Gwynedd have attacked our southern lands, driving off many cattle."

Urien considered the news for a while. "So; the wind, herald of the storm to come, begins to rise. At first it was but a mere gust, a thing easily shrugged off, but now it begins to blow constant. Soon, soon will be the storm of which my father spoke."

"Then you think Gwynedd and Manau act together?"

Cynfarch's son looked at his wife. "If only coincidence why should

Gwynedd attack so early? Surely they intend to draw our strength that Morcant can have his way beside Merin Ideo." He turned back to Llywarch's man. "What think you? What other intelligence might there be from Llwyfein?"

"None from Llywfein, my Lord, but from Gwynedd perhaps; for a monk coming from there and on his way to see Kentigern ... "

Kentigern? Urien raised an eyebrow. He had given his grandson rope, was he about to hang himself? Urien motioned for the messenger to continue.

" ... why he was going to Kentigern we did not ask, judging him to be your grandson, but he did tell us how Maelgini, dreaming of his own death, had sent for a Christian priest and upon his advice entered a monastery, giving up the crown and his bed. Ludis, his brother's son rules now in his stead."

"Then Ludis may simply be anxious to prove himself and know nothing of Morcant's plans," mused Urien. "And yet ... and yet ... Will not a rotten apple lying next to the unspoilt make that corrupt too?"

"Like a stag surrounded by snapping dogs must you fend off first one foe and then another," quoted Eurdyl, recalling words spoken in Catreath.

Urien's eyes glinted appreciatively. "What my sister says is true and perhaps Gwynedd and Manau are not the only dogs abroad, for turning to fight Gwynedd will we not have Elmet and the sons of Eleuther on our backs?"

"Where then will you strike first?" asked Modron.

"First!" exclaimed Urien. "What they will not expect, if they act together, is an attack upon them both at once. This then is what we shall do. Llywarch will fortify his defences against Elmet by the building of a fort like that we raised against the Gael; and when that is done and our backs secure, we will turn upon Gwynedd whilst Owen moves to the aid of Cynfelyn."

"Oh, it suits you now to call upon Owen!" reproved Modron.

"It is his duty."

"And what of Kentigern?" asked Eurdyl innocently.

Urien looked at his sister. "Aye, what of master Kentigern? I think it is time he paid us another visit."

* * *

Kentigern bowed before his family, a smile on his face. "Sad I am to abandon God's family, yet glad I am to see my own once more."

"Are you?" asked Urien in a tone which suggested he thought

Kentigern a liar. "Has a messenger not come to you from out of Gwynedd, and did not Gwynedd then attack our cousin LLywarch's lands?"

Kentigern continued to smile. "Of the latter I know nothing, of the other no messenger has come to me but a monk and not from Gwynedd, though I dare say he came through those lands." He laughed now. "The man of whom you speak came from another called Dewi, bidding me journey to him to have theological discourse and ... "

" ... and you would of course not have gone without my permission?"

Kentigern shook his head. "Ask your messenger whether he found me at home or on the road here. "

"No, there is no need. You and I it seems are fellow travellers. You wish to journey through Gwynedd to see Dewi? I shall see that the door to Gwynedd is open, and if it is not then I shall break it down. Tomorrow we must talk some more, for there is much I would know of your friend and his land."

Modron seated herself next to the hearth and bid Kentigern join her that he might tell of all he had done since they last met; "and especially your battle with Myrddin".

Kentigern smiled. "Then with him we shall begin for it is my intention, now more than ever, that he shall be the last of his kind."

Modron put her hand on his. "Be careful. Eurdyl is an ally of Myrddin."

"Aye, but why?"

"To thwart me, perhaps, but why should she want to do that? Because of who she is. Her mother was introduced to Cynfarch by Myrddin; she is his child, his eyes and ears. And her uncle, Cadwallon, once he was a friend, now I am not so sure ... Whenever I ask Urien about him he changes the subject as if there is something wrong, something I should not know. Did you hear or see anything of him on your travels?"

Kentigern shook his head. "In the meantime we have to keep Urien and Myrddin apart. A campaign in the south might not be a bad idea. And if you accompanied him it may be possible to raise the seige and repair the damage caused by Myrddin. So too might we gain a respite until we are ready to attack again."

"But will Urien agree?"

"In time. For Myrddin is not the only one who can perch upon the shoulders of kings and whisper in their ears."

* * *

From the hosting place at the stone of Brandreth, and with Kentigern by his side, Urien led his men southwards along the great road through the gorge of the Gweryt, past the cataract of brown waters which pours forth like the brew of Llasar. To left and right the hill sides rose steeply above them: black and green, rock and grass, mossy ledge and clinging tree. Soon they were splashing through the grey waters of the ford, below the walls of a fort built to guard that place, its dismal mists and brilliant sunlight. Onwards they rode and within a few hours were in a land of broad fields and neat farmsteads; the northern edge of Llwyfein, the domain of Llywarch.

Within a week, their numbers swelled by Llywarch's men, they reached Caer Legion. The great fortress lay amongst verdant pastures above a slow, wide river. In the days of the Caesars there had been bustling life within its red walls, the crunch of nailed boots marching in unison upon its paved roads, the shouts of orders given and obeyed: but now it lay empty, a monument to the exigencies of conquest. Since the time of Mascen Guledig and the birth of the kingdoms it had lain empty, a shell belonging to none, the meeting place of Rheged, Gwynedd and Powys.

"We will camp inside the old walls," Urien told the others. "For though they are riven like the shield of a fallen champion we may make them serviceable."

"What need have the people of Rheged for such walls? What good did they do Rome?" called Llywarch. "Must not the Brython trust in their swords and spears? Have they not Urien ap Cynfarch for their shield?"

Urien clapped his hand on his cousin's shoulder. "The voice of Llywarch is like a war trumpet stirring the hearts of men. Yet as eagles building walls about their young must we be. Today it is the cunning work of man which we seek to wrap around ourselves, tomorrow we must seek the protection of our gods."

"And with your permission I will seek out men's allegiances to God and you," added Kentigern. "For there is a monastery not far from here: a place where weary travellers might disgorge rumour and what they have seen, and much knowledge is stored."

Urien contemplated the idea. Was Kentigern trying to trick him or did he simply want to talk with his brothers? What was the knowledge of which he had spoken? The Talismans? Was it possible knowledge about them lay amongst Christian cells? Certainly that would explain why Myrddin knew little of them. Myrddin! Kentigern's presence had made him almost forget the druid. "Aye, you may go, but go no further, for I need to know where I might find you."

"Your messengers will find me upon my knees, praying for your souls!"

The following day the men busied themselves as Urien directed, piling rubble into the breeches of the walls, securely blocking the eastern and northern gates and piling beams across the western one. Now only the southern portal remained open and Urien sent messengers westwards to taunt Ludis: "As Coel sent Cunedda to Gwynedd to expel the Gael, so have I come hither to expel Gwynedd from the lands of Coel. The Bear has come from the North, his claws are sharp, his temper roused by the firebrands thrust in his face. Let Gwynedd now acknowledge the heir of Coel and send hostages, before he takes them by force."

"Do you think he will?"

Urien eyed Llywarch. He had been going to say "Would you?" but thought he might not get the reply intended, for his cousin was not the greatest of warriors. Like many of the Brython he had grown up in an age which had known only peace; his weapon the lyre rather than the sword. Urien shook his head. "I would not. Nor do I anticipate him doing so. So we goad him and bait our trap."

"But why do we not assault Gwynedd directly?" asked Mouric. "Is not Rheged the greatest of all the kingdoms of the Brython?"

His uncle smiled. "Does my sister's son not yet understand? Some of our men we have had to send eastwards to protect our backs." He pointed to the distant rim of hills. "Beyond them is Elmet and other potential enemies. See where the hills dip and there is a high pass. There we have built a new fort and posted some of our men ... "

"Whilst even more men are with Owen in the North," added Llywarch.

Urien ignored his cousin. " ... so we have little advantage over Gwynedd save that which this place gives. Here we will wait."

The next morning Urien was woken by his armourbearer, Saran. "They are here, my lord: Ludis and the men of Gwynedd."

"And what of our men?" Urien was standing now and throwing his breastplate over his shoulders.

"Ready," stammered Saran as he ran alongside the striding figure, trying to fasten his buckles.

Soon Urien was on the ramparts next to Mouric and Llywarch. To either side the walls were lined with their men, watching, pointing and talking excitedly. Before them was the river and beyond that the host of Gwynedd, the sun upon their faces, their numbers lost in the trees behind. Saran finally finished fastening his master's armour and, picking up the helmet, placed it in the outstretched hands of Urien.

"Ludis it seems has not split his forces," observed Llywarch.

"Perhaps not. But look ... Listen ... " A murmur rippled through the men of Gwynedd and their ranks began to part.

"What is it?" asked Llywarch.

Urien ignored the question. The murmur became a roar, the roar of laughter, of jeering. "Look, there it is," cried Mouric pointing to the cart which began to roll between the columns of Ludis.

"Do you see what I see?" Llywarch was laughing now and with him Urien.

"Aye, it is a bear, a caged bear!"

A runner whispered in the ear of Urien and his laughter turned to a grin of determination. "The enemy have surrounded us as I hoped. We have goaded him into believing we are caged. Now we have no need to attack across the river. The advantage is already ours, he has taken the bait and the trap is sprung."

All around was the cacophony of battle: the strident calls of horns, the roar of voices charging forward, the cries of those wounded, the prayers of the dying; a thousand, two thousand voices wafted on the breeze, carried heavenwards to those who might hear. The men of Gwynedd had charged forward, confident in numbers but had found the task more difficult than they thought. Like waves around a rock they surged and broke: the stones red with gore, the gaps filled with corpses. By midday the tide began to ebb and Urien signalled to Mouric. Silently the beams of the western gate were removed and the men of Arfynydd sallied forth trapping their enemies between the ramparts and a wall of steel.

Many fell that day before the Morrigan was satiated, but of Ludis there was no sign: he had scrambled to safety, leaving his boasts lying on the muddy slopes, amongst the broken spears and mangled bodies. Throughout the night the fires burned, a hundred pyres releasing the souls of those whose prayers had not been heard: the stench of war.

* * *

Urien assembled his men and those of Llywarch outside the walls of the fortress. Behind him rode Saran, his spear transformed into a standard by the small image of a boar found amongst the ruins. Its red ribbons fluttered in the breeze as Urien spoke. "Men of Llwyfenydd, Arfynydd and Llwyfein, warriors and heroes. In the days of old when the land had been wasted, its inhabitants captured and only Pryderi, Manannan, Cigfa and Rhiannon remained free, a white boar led them to a magic, deserted fort. There they laid hands upon a bowl and claimed the kingship of the Isle and Pryderi restored prosperity to the land. Hither we came to these deserted walls, to defend our land, to fulfil our destiny and here too we found this boar. Is it not an assurance of victory? Like Pryderi shall we not now lay claim to our land and restore freedom to its people? As Gwydion protector of Leu was the first to take pigs into Gwynedd shall we not do the same?"

Six hundred voices answered him, six hundred blades were raised, six hundred flashing suns. With Urien at its head the host of Rheged turned and swept down the gentle slope towards the river, towards Gwynedd and the den of Deganwy.

As they crossed the river Urien noticed a curragh moored amongst the reeds. He could have sworn it had not been there the day before and it triggered in his mind a distant memory, of a similar boat below similar walls; of a time when he had wanted nothing more than to see his son. His son! Now he had two yet the world knew of only one. And now, as then, Myrddin was waiting for him; a hooded shadow amongst the trees.

"How long have you been here?" asked Urien as they rode side by side.

"Long enough to hear your speech. We will make a bard of you yet."

Urien smiled. "What need have I to be a bard when I have Taliesin, aye, and Llywarch?"

"Just so, and wise is he who knows his strengths and limitations. For the true bard is skilled in knowledge as well as poetry so that he might be counted as wise as any druid ... "

Urien had ceased to smile. What did Myrddin mean? Why had he come now? What did he know? Myrddin put a finger to his lips. "Of some things I will speak now, of others when we are alone. We have spoken of bards and, as Llywarch's lyre sometimes graces him with a tune, so might any man stumble upon the truth. You spoke before of how Pryderi and the other champions laid hands upon that magic bowl which could restore the land."

Urien halted briefly. "I had not thought of that. You mean the Cauldron of Ulph is here?"

Myrddin shrugged his shoulders. "I don't mean anything, I just wondered. I just wondered if that is what you thought." He wanted to ask if Kentigern had spoken of the Talismans but could not. To do so would show his own weakness and strengthen the Christian's hand.

By the evening they had reached Caer Hiraddog and camped within its walls, secure against man and the wind which buffeted that bare top.

At their feet, below precipitous slopes, lay the fertile valley of Dogfael on the far side of which were the foothills and mountains of Gwynedd proper and, to the north, the headland of Deganwy.

"Do you not feel how the wind blows from the West?" murmured Urien.

Myrddin shook his head. "No, that wind is spent. It blows now along these slopes and ledges from the South. That way destiny lies."

Urien nodded. "This place reminds me of another where you and I once stood, gazing across at the mountains of Yrechwydd. Then you took me to see Elen, before Pasgent was born. Then Elen was nought to me, Modron my all … "

"We have come a long way since then, lord … "

"And have a long way still to go I fear."

Myrddin shrugged his shoulders. "Perhaps, perhaps not. How often climbing a hill do you look up and see the skyline thinking it to be the top, only to find it is but a crest and that the summit lies beyond? Then you learn to think each skyline false until, suddenly, one such proves to be your goal. So men live their lives, climbing each slope, surmounting each crest in the hope that they might finally find that which they seek."

"But some never reach the top, some fall and are killed." Urien pointed to the cliff beneath their feet. "Come, tell me what other news you bring."

"From Elen; that she, Pasgent and Morfudd are well. And that you have another son, Elphin."

"Elphin! Aye, I like the name."

In the morning Urien said farewell to Myrddin and moved south towards the great road which led to Deganwy and, beyond the mountains, to Caer Segeint, Mon and the western sea. Mon, where the druids had been hunted by the men of Rome and forced to hide in wild places, wandering in secret, their lore of the Old Ones disguised in the stories of new gods and heroes. Urien looked back towards Caer Hirradog searching for Myrddin, but the ramparts were deserted except for a single stag silhouetted against the red, eastern sky. Urien turned westwards, following the road Mascen had used when carrying retribution from Mon to Rome so that the eagle was seen no more above the towers of Caer Segeint.

It was with such thoughts, thoughts of all that had been and of what might yet be, that Urien occupied his mind as they descended to the valley floor. In front of them their path stretched into the distance, heading for the low ridge which lay in the centre of the plain between two rivers. There the emissaries were waiting, their horses grazing below a farm. Signalling for Llywarch and his men to halt and guard the rear, Urien rode forward noting how the men of Gwynedd carried their shields on their backs.

"The Lord Ludis sends greetings and hostages to the sons of Coel," they called to Urien, who had halted on the eastern side of the river, his shield on his arm.

"They are welcome, for no man should wish to shed blood unnecessarily. Let then the land of Dogfael, the land between Gwynedd and Rheged, belong neither to one nor the other. Here at the meeting of three cantrefs let men give perpetual thanks to God and Kentigern build a monastery. Let it be a place of peace and let the hostages offered by Gwynedd be returned to their king and those he holds returned whence he took them."

Urien watched whilst the men opposite discussed his terms amongst themselves. After a while they turned back to him. "We will take your message to our lord but until our return you should wait there."

"Why should I camp upon damp ground when yonder dry ridge is there for the taking," called Urien angrily. "Aye, and then I will take my message in person to Deganwy if needs must."

Again Ludis' men discussed the terms. "It is agreed. Here you might camp until our return."

Urien bowed in mock thanks and calling for Llywarch and Mouric to follow, began to ford the river. On the opposite side the men of Gwynedd scrambled for their horses and disappeared down the other side of the ridge as quickly as they could.

That night, as they were seated by the fire, Llywarch asked his cousin what his plans were, why he had asked for that place to be given to Kentigern and how he could be sure his grandson would obey.

Urien warmed his hands before the fire. "As we rode south from Gweryt did you not tell us the story of Setanata whom the Gael call Cu Chulainn? Of how, single handed that champion defended his country against the onslaught of its enemies? Here on the banks of the Elwy a man might do the same, for whoever commands this point commands Dogfael and those who would come and go between Gwynedd and Rheged."

"Aye, a champion of old might, but a man and Kentigern at that?"

Urien smiled: perhaps Ludis too would underestimate Kentigern. "That is precisely why he is suited to hold this ground. Ludis can claim he gave nothing away save to the Church and by that claim he might hope to stave off his downfall. Is it not in our interests to have a weak ruler in Gwynedd? As Rome created client kingdoms beyond her

frontiers so we might buy peace with land such as this ... " He laughed.
" ... Kentigern did us a favour by going off to his monastery, for Ludis'
men can see he is not amongst us and can therefore think he is not
my tool."

Llywarch nodded in appreciation of the plan. "But how can you be
certain Kentigern will come?"

Again Urien smiled. "Do you remember how news of Maelgini
reached you?"

"By a monk who sought Kentigern."

"Exactly, and that monk came from Dewi, a holyman who lives some
days from here. It seems he and Kentigern are of a like mind and
anxious to counter the growth of the teachings of Pelagius, which they
regard as heresy. Gwynedd adheres to that heresy and Dewi asked for
Kentigern's help in combatting it. A church on the Elwy would be a
perfect base from which to operate."

"A base from which to strike at Gwynedd?" laughed Llywarch.

"A buffer at least," continued Urien, unwilling to add he hoped
Kentigern's energies would now be turned from stirring up trouble in
Rheged. "Moreover, the king to the south of here, Brocmael of Powys, is
an enemy of the heretics too. He is descended from Cadell, a servant
whom Germanus set up in the north of Powys when he fought against
Pelagius and his Gaelic allies in the days of Vortigern. From that day to
this there has been enmity between the house of Cadell and the
descendants of Vortigern who still rule in southern Powys. Until the
battle of Caer Legion Brocmael was crushed between the Pelagians,
now with our Kentigern to help he can turn the tables and recover his
lands. He shall be an arm of steel beneath the robes of Kentigern.
Together they shall watch and contain our enemies. Descended from a
servant, Brocmael shall be our servant, though we might reward him
with great lands."

"Why then did Brocmael not join us at Caer Legion? Because he had
given hostages to Gwynedd?"

"The same hostages I demanded Ludis return: Brocmael's brother
Maye, lord of Dogfael, and his son Asaph. Their imprisonment is our
good fortune, for if Brocmael had helped us we would have been in his
debt, now he is in ours."

"And the great lands you will reward him with? Are they Southern
Powys?"

"Aye, for that way destiny and our quest lie."

It was the following morning when the emissaries from Gwynedd
returned, this time standing on the western side of the western river.

"The Lord Ludis is agreed to your proposals providing that you give a sign of peace. Thus says Ludis, the son of Cunedda the Great: when Kentigern comes hither then shall Maye of Dogfael and his son Asaph be returned, but into the keeping of Kentigern. Let Asaph be a hostage of God."

Urien listened in stoney-faced silence, his hand upon the arm of Llywarch urging caution. "Let no man say the King of Rheged breaks the vows he has given. Yet for the sake of peace he will grant the request of your lord."

Two days later a group of riders came from the south, their leader a tall man with a somewhat triangular face and thick black beard. Beside him, to the surprise of Llywarch, rode Kentigern. They halted at the ford and the stranger sought out Urien. "Hail Arctures, Northern Bear. Like Pryderi you have freed this land and the land of Powys Fadog from the plague which afflicted it. Brocmael ap Cyngen salutes the prince of Rheged and swears allegiance to him, his son and kin. From this day forth the men of Powys shall remember Gwyr y Gogledd, The Men of the North."

Urien stood at the entrance to the farmhouse. "Welcome is the son of Cyngen. Welcome to my hall, such as it is."

The man of Powys laughed. "Then is my task so much the easier for I came to invite you to Powys Fadog and the hall of my fathers."

* * *

With Llywarch and half the men of Llwyfenydd left to guard Llanelwy, as Urien had come to call their farm, Urien and Brocmael journeyed south following the river to its head. Its valley reminded Urien of the Idon; its floor dotted with numerous trees and white walled farms; its left hand side a steep rampart, its conical peaks capped by ancient forts. Brocamel pointed to one. "There Germanus pursued Benlli. There he killed him and gave this land to my ancestors. Dogfael and the land of my brother lies behind us now, in front is Powys Fadog and my inheritance."

Onwards they travelled, passing over a low shoulder into a shallow basin, the eastern rim of which Urien had seen from Caer Legion. Soon they were cautiously edging their way down the narrow track of a deep valley where streams tumbled in long white columns from cliff tops and dark brown buzzards glided along rocky ledges. The stream they followed led them southwards and where the narrow valley widened to become a green basin in the mountains was a knoll surmounted by a cross. "It was here Germanus defeated Benlli and his allies, the Gael

128

and the Mordei as they marched towards Caer Guricon," explained Urien's host as they rode across the clearing towards the concourse gathered there. "It was a victory of the Church and so to the Church belongs this land, but Dinas Bran was given to Cadell." Brocmael pointed to the conical hill visible to their left, its top ringed by a high rampart.

At the foot of the hill was a tall woman with auburn hair and a dress of gold and crimson. Beside her were two men, one auburn like her the other dark like Brocmael, and next to them a small boy on a pony. Brocmael introduced them to Urien: first the lady Cigfa, then Dingad and then Cynan and his little son Selyf.

"The house of Cadell welcomes the new Germanus and would be honoured if he would foster my son," said Cynan the auburn haired.

Urien looked at Selyf astride his pony, his freckled face beaming mischievously. He reminded Urien of Pasgent and would make him a good companion. Yet how could that be whilst Elen and the children remainded hidden? Urien forced himself to smile. "It would be good for Owen to have a little brother."

With Selyf leading the way, Urien and his hosts climbed the winding path towards the summit of Dinas Bran, the place of which Kentigern had spoken in Llwyfenydd. "Tell me about this place," said Urien nonchalantly. "Was this Bran he of whom legend speaks, the Bran who was brother of Manannan?"

Brocmael shrugged. "Some say so, that it was here, after he had been mortally wounded, his friends brought his apotropaic head at the start of their seven year journey."

Urien nodded, noting the shape of the hill itself. Could Bran's companions have returned and buried the Talisman here?

From Dinas Bran Urien could look down into the closed world that had been given to Cadell, and about the foot of which the oenach would soon be held and bards compete in song. From there too, he was able to explore the land of Brocmael; riding over the southern rim of hills to the ford of Forlas at the edge of the great plain.

The plain stretched to the horizon and beyond: northwards to Caer Legion and Llwyfein, eastwards to the Loegrians, and southwards to Hafren and the place where some said a magic sword lay buried: the Sword of Gorias?

"How far south does your land extend?" Urien asked Brocmael.

"To Maes Cogwy, but beyond that lies Southern Powys."

Urien smiled. "Then I think it is time you showed me Maes Cogwy."

It was not far from the ford of Forlas to Maes Cogwy, to that old fort which lay to the east of the high ground; a low, flat topped hill protected by more ramparts than Urien had ever seen before. Once they had defied the arts and wiles of warriors, protecting the crowded interior of houses, barns and workshops; but now they fell before Urien and Brocmael, the interior deserted except for brambles, gorse and thickets of advancing hazel and ash. At the south-east corner they halted and Brocmael, at the request of Urien, pointed out that part of Powys ruled by the descendants of Vortigern, allies of Gwynedd.

"See that conical mountain at the entrance to the valley? That is Cefyn Digoll, the watch tower of Eliud whose lands lie beyond that pass and about Meigen in the upper Hafren."

Urien nodded. Of that place too Kentigern had spoken. For beyond it was Dewi, his ally.

"Now follow the eastern edge of the hills again," continued Brocmael. "See how they sweep gently round towards the east to meet the Hafren as it flows south. The isolated peak to the east is Pengwern behind Caer Guricon."

"And how far is that?"

"A day's ride. There Constantine rules, as far east as the Grey Wood, Luitcoyt. Before Mascen Guledig, before Vortigern, all our people were ruled from there ... "

The voice of Brocmael trailed off in a note of sadness, as if the loss of that greatness was difficult to bear.

"And so it shall be again," promised Urien. "Powys shall be united once more under Brocmael and his son Cynan and they shall rule from Pengwern all the lands of which you have spoken."

* * *

The grassy slope outside the monastery buildings was yellow with the sun of the late summer evening and the air was oppressive. Pabo sat on the stone bench beneath the eaves of the library reading again, this time aloud, the pamphlet which had caused so much controversy in Rome. Maelgini was only half listening. True he believed, like Pelagius, that men controlled their own destinies but he did not go along with all the extreme talk of the holyman's disciples. Priests should stick to things about God: whichever of their fellow countrymen had written that pamphlet had deserved to be condemned. Rome had found it difficult enough to maintain itself against the barbarians without having to face rebellion within. People needed strong leaders and surely no one could grumble if those who risked their lives to defend others were rewarded with more. The greater the risk, the greater the reward: anyone could plough and sow. People who believed the words written in that book were either mad or senile like Pabo, a man who had forgotten he had once been a king.

Maelgini was bored. He shut out the words of the old fool and sauntered down to the stream to watch the trout swimming in the brown waters. Even they had leaders, for did not the biggest fish bully the others for the best lies in the pool? He bent his tall frame and picking up a smooth stone from the bank tossed it idly into the water, watching the fish dart to safety and the ripples of light spread ever wider to obscure his view. Once his armies had radiated from the mountains of Gwynedd and men had run from them, hiding in this hole or that. Then there had been few south of Rheged who did not know his name and his anger had been like the roaring of the dragon in the days of Lludd. Now he had given up that power and chosen a purgatory of peace and inaction in the hope of salvation. It was a hope which with every passing day and hour seemed more remote; a promise as empty as the words of the Emperor in the days of Vortigern. Maelgini regretted giving up the kingship. He should have been like the Coeling gang, ruling until they died, believing their actions were preordained, their deeds decided by higher authority.

He turned and began to climb, slowly, the steps towards the main buildings and his cell. There was no particular hurry, there was nothing to do when he got there except sleep or read: time passed slowly in that place if at all. Suddenly he halted, watching the figure running towards him, bounding down the steps two at a time. The figure was unmistakably that of Dunawd, son of Pabo, for years of inaction had lent extra weight to an already broad frame and the gait was necessarily less than athletic. Maelgini watched the bouncing folds of skin and wondered what drove Dunawd to such exertions. In the year that he had been in the monastery he had become something of a father to Dunawd. He had been able to tell a different story to the old man who was now leant against the wall of the library, his eyes closed, his book fallen from his lap; he had stirred the imagination with tales of battle and aroused passions and hatred for the Coeling.

Dunawd halted in front of the former king, his thick lips opening and closing without uttering a sound except the gulping of air, his small dark eyes trying unsuccessfully to convey the news. Maelgini despised the bag of excess flesh yet he had recognised in it a cynical spirit not unlike his own and he could wait.

"You should not exert yourself, dear friend, for nothing is urgent here."

"My news does not concern this place," gasped Dunawd beginning to recover. "There is talk in the village of dishonour in Gwynedd, of lands given to Rheged, of Urien encamped on our doorstep. All that you achieved has been lost."

Maelgini turned pale, his cheeks like autumn leaves; and like autumn leaves blowing in the chill winds that are harbingers of winter he began to shake with anger. "When I saw that crane on the march against Cadoc I knew there would be disaster but I did not think the bird of ill omen meant this. It was to escape the prophecy that I came hither and thus have I brought it to pass. I should have known better, what a fool to be guided by superstitions." His eyes which had been turned heavenwards alighted on the buildings huddled on the mountainside. "Pelagius was right: there are no hidden fates, no predetermined courses, men determine their own destinies. Ludis was defeated, not because God was on the side of Rheged, but because he was weak."

"You say Ludis was weak, my lord?" There was the sound of expectation and cruelty in Dunawd's voice.

"Aye, for no kin of mine is he that has betrayed me. Let no man speak his name again. From this moment he is as dead as the vellum upon which sermons are written."

Maelgini thrust Dunawd aside and strode angrily and decisively up the steps.

Dunawd found him in the entrance of his hut gazing at the bare wall opposite, searching for inspiration amongst the blocks of unhewn stone held together by their own weight. Maelgini continued to examine the wall of the room for some time and when at last he spoke it was without turning, as if the words were for himself alone. "It would not be seemly for me to depose him, he must meet with an accident." He paused. "Better still, be murdered by someone from Rheged. First Tudwal and now Ludis, who would not believe the hand of the Coeling lay behind both?" He chuckled; a coarse, rasping laugh which sounded hollow in that cell. Suddenly he turned to face Pabo's son. "I shall take back my kingdom and I see us taking back yours."

* * *

Gwyn sat next to Ludis in the Hall of Kings beneath the citadel of Deganwy. Her long flaxen hair shone in the lamp light, the white linen of her dress almost transparent whilst on either side were heaped tables of food and drink. Gwyn sat in the midst of laughing men and women. It was a time to celebrate, not the loss of lands but the triumphs of the hunt and the end of mourning for Maelgini's wife, mother of Rhun, who had died suddenly.

Here and there young men who had succumbed to the bragget lay sprawled amongst the rushes. Ludis too was beginning to totter. Gwyn picked a cherry from the bowl in front of her, holding its stalk lightly between the painted nails of two slender fingers, twisting it to and fro before slowly putting it between her milk-white teeth. There she held the fruit, teasing Kodicum the handsome champion of Ludis. Her large, dark eyes had been upon him all evening: when she flicked her long golden plaits over her ivory shoulders had not their eyes met? When she loosened the white laces between her full breasts as if the air was hot, had their eyes not met? So Gwyn teased and enticed him who sat at the top of the next table: a man of broad shoulders and thick curly hair, a warrior with a moustache turned up in the manner of the old heroes; a man of many conquests. She wanted him to be a god to her, to feel his strong hands around her heavy breasts and on her thighs; to celebrate with cornucopia and not the delicate glasses of distant lands. Nor was Kodicum unresponsive, for Ludis had given him no reward. He watched the long tongue of Gwyn playing about the cherry and when he was sure she was watching took an apple and thrust his dagger upwards into its core.

But Ludis was not too drunk to ignore their signals. He had been watching them for some time and now he leaped across the table, hauling Kodicum from his place. "My lord is quick to defend that which is his," sneered the Champion pulling the hands of the king from his tunic. "It is a pity he were not so bold in defending our lands."

Ludis reached for his dagger but the drink had made him slow. His blade had not left its sheath before Kodicum's sank into his stomach, the apple crushed upon its hilt. Ludis fell to the floor, the red pulp of blood and apple between his fingers. Instantly there were people by his side, friends and servants, but so great was their concern and stupor that they forgot about Kodicum who slipped quietly out into the night.

That night Ludis slept upon a bier and in the morning his friends bore him from the hall of his fathers. A morning when the sound of the wind blowing through the bent trees was like the roar of the sea beneath the fort; as if winter had come early to the land. The rain drifted in vertical squalls across the hillside like spray from crashing waves and the greyness of the ocean was inseparable from the sky. Through the driving, stinging rain, between the drenched flowers of gorse upon the lower slopes of Deganwy they carried Ludis; their feet slipping in the mud, the wind pushing and tearing at their backs.

Eastwards they carried Ludis, through the wooded valley and its shelter from the wind and rain, until they came to the monastery and there they laid him, with his father whom Maelgini had defeated in battle. His uncle watched them now, his cloak wrapped about himself, his grey hair streaming in the wind. But the rain had stopped and behind him the sky had begun to brighten. An arc of rainbow rose from the glistening, silver bracken of the valley floor and the birds in the coppice, shaking dry their plumage, began to sing once more. It was as if the primeval forces themselves were celebrating the return of the Dragon.

THE HIGH KING

Maelgini sat once more in the hall of Deganwy, a brimming cup in one hand, the other upon the thigh of Gwyn. The hall was filled with laughter and dancing, the celebration of victories past and of homesteads burning. A strong king had returned to Gwynedd and in the spring there would be war. Gwyn of the white breasts would be given Kentigern's head as Salome received John's; and Rheged would be driven beyond Caer Legion. It was a time to look forward to victories to come, a time to drink and feast, a time to live.

For a month they celebrated the return of the Dragon: until the leaves had begun to fall and the cattle to return from the high pastures; until news came that Kodicum had been seen in Llanelwy. There he had fled fearing Maelgini whose orders he had obeyed, for it was not in the new King's interest that the assassin should live. But in seeking sanctuary with Kentigern he aided his master's plot still further for now Ludis' death could be laid squarely at the door of Rheged. Maelgini had expressed dismay but not surprise at the news, vowing that he would bring back the champion in chains.

"Like a bear," added Dunawd.

"Like the Bear," repeated his mentor.

Their warband halted before Llanelwy and Maelgini rode forward alone, a monk's habit over his mail, a staff instead of a sword.

"Holy Kentigern, let us talk in peace."

"If it is of peace that you want to talk why do you come against me with an army, breaking the pledges which Ludis gave?"

"Was I the first to break pledges? Is not Kodicum within your gate? Was I the first to bring an army hither? Did you not come here with three hundred warriors, borne upon the wings of the raven? Why was it necessary for me to leave my monastery and an incorruptible crown and assume again that which I so willingly gave up? For the love of our fellow men let us avoid bloodshed. Surrender Kodicum and let Rheged show itself contrite by withdrawing to Caer Legion. Let that place and not this be sanctified as a place of peace between our lands; a place where men may go to trade and meet without fear."

Kentigern looked down impassively from the wall newly built about his monastery. His eyes surveyed the seated figure and the loose cloth about shoulders bent with age if not sin. Should he condemn or pity Maelgini? Until a man learns what is good or bad is he not like a child

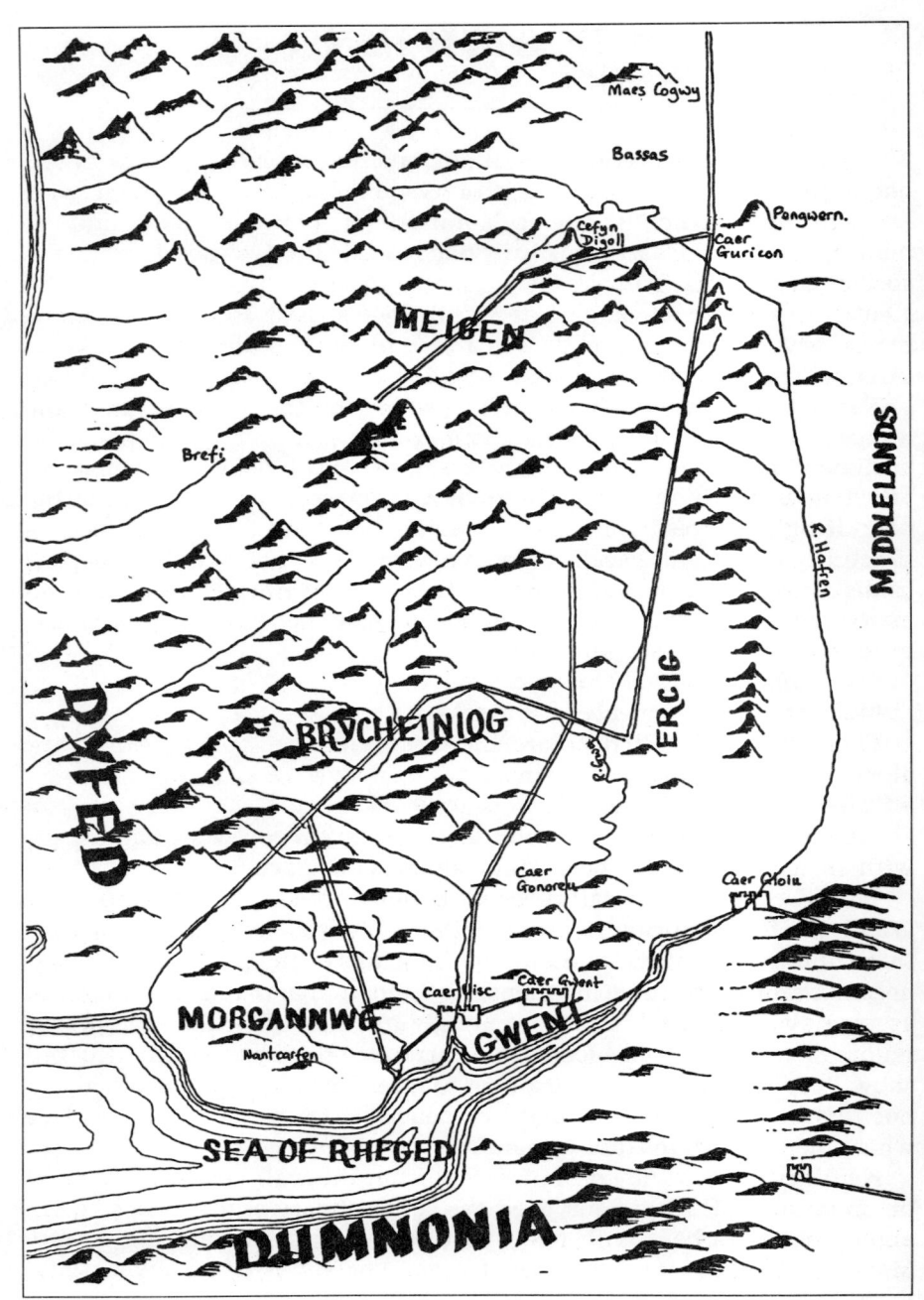

Maes Cogwy

Bassas

Pengwern.

Cefyn Digoll

Caer Guricon

MEIGEN

Brefi

MIDDLELANDS

R. Hafren

DYFED

BRYCHEINIOG

ERCIG

R. Cam

Caer Ffolu

Caer Gonoreu

MORGANNWG

Caer Uisc

Caer Gwent

Nantcarfen

GWENT

SEA OF RHEGED

DUMNONIA

136

unable to be condemned: to transgress but not to sin? Were not Adam and Eve naked yet innocent until they acquired the knowledge of right and wrong? Was it not for them Christ descended into hell?

Thus it was that Kentigern looked down and saw a man, mortal like himself and it was from sorrow and not anger that he now spoke. "Brother, are you blind to your lies? Why if you wish no blood to be spent do you ask for Kodicum? Why do you speak of forgiveness but demand retribution? Do not add to the sins already heaped over you like a cairn over the dead, for Ludis was not murdered by Kodicum but by you. It was in your deserted cell that he first hid. The wake you made a marriage feast and now you come here with an army, not to see justice but to make mischief. As God loves the repentance of the sinner, return now to your own monastery; turn back lest God strikes you down. Assume the wings of an angel not those of a dragon lest the flames of hell burst forth and consume you."

Maelgini steadied his horse, his eyes blazing, his staff held high. "Whelp of Rheged, do not condemn and you shall not be condemned. You came here because the talons of Rheged had torn more flesh than those of Gwynedd; you were borne upon the back of the raven and not the wings of the dove. You say I come to work mischief but do you not wish to convert my people with force, to loose the bear upon those you call heretic. Should I stand by whilst your holy soldiers plan violence against my people? Who is the greater sinner: he who openly admits, aye even flaunts, his sins or he who plans violence and claims it is for God he does such things? If it is the will of God that I am what I am, then how can I be condemned? By what shall we test his will? With soldiers you guard your altar, let us test His will by their art. Come forth, Kentigern, and face me man to man."

Gwynedd's protector said no more and waited for no reply. They had talked enough, it was time for the singing of blades and arrows not psalms. Maelgini turned from the gates of Llanelwy and galloped back to the western ford. In front of him his men stood in battle array, waiting for his signal: in them he would trust. But as he galloped towards them, his horse striding across the soft meadow land that lay beside the river, a hoof sank into the ground bringing low man and beast.

* * *

Urien smiled. He laughed at the thought of Maelgini being nursed by Kentigern and of his ceding more land to the monastery "in gratitude". In gratitude! Had he, Urien, not been vindicated? And from the North too the news had been good. Morcant had been defeated and Cynfelyn restored to Lleuddiniawn: whilst Cadrod had been betrothed to Dreon's young sister, Gwrygon. Aye, there was much to celebrate that winter and much to look forward to.

Urien had returned to Llwyfenydd once he had seen Kentigern securely installed in Llanelwy; but in the spring he would return with Modron, for so he had promised their grandson. Besides, he had become anxious that sooner rather than later Modron might learn of Elen and the children.

"It will be like old times," he had hastened to assure her.

Yet how could it be like old times? The peace which a generation had known was ended and where once he loved only one, now there were others: Elen, Pasgent, Elphin and Morfudd. Yet it was a love different from that which he and Modron had once shared: it was the love of an old man seeking to cheat time.

Modron was part of his past, part still of him, and for that reason he wanted her to accompany him. But that was not the only reason: he wanted, he needed her now because he could not afford to alienate Owen and Kentigern, her offspring, her blood ... Her blood! Why did he think of them as hers not his? Was it simply because he had others now by Elen? Perhaps, but in his gut he had a feeling that it was more than that. Whatever the reason, he had agreed to Owen being given command over the North.

"For who else is there to rule in our stead?" Modron asked, looking from Urien to Eurdyl, to Mouric. Then, clapping her hands in delight, she cried "And Eurdyl, and Mouric can come with us, for did you not say how Owen's pupil proved himself at Caer Legion, and tell me once of how Myrddin advised you to set your own men as governors along our borders? You would like to be a king, wouldn't you Mouric?"

"If that is what my uncle wants," replied Eurdyl's son.

Urien smiled. "Of course. Rheged, no, Prydein, needs you and us in Gwent."

* * *

"Tell me about Gwent," said Mouric as they rode south, "and why I am needed there."

Urien thought for a moment, for of the Sword of Gorias he would not speak. "It is a land far beyond the borders of Rheged, beyond Powys even. It is a land they say where houses are still built in the Roman style and the rich might yet be seen in chariots. A land which is Christian and yet does not hold the beliefs of Kentigern."

138

"A land ripe for taking?"

Urien laughed, the phrase was one he had heard Owen teach the boy.

"And when I am King?"

"I shall be High King, Guledig. Not since Ambrosius and Outigern has there been a High King ... " Urien's voice trailed off. "Then, as now, the Brython and Loegrians were locked in a struggle to decide the future of Prydein."

"Then the Brython were triumphant and so shall they be again," added Modron, sensing Urien's unspoken fear.

Modron was happier than she had been for many months. She felt she had won a battle with Eurdyl and regained the initiative in the war between them. The darkness and cloud which had gathered about her for so long seemed to be dissipating the further they rode from Llwyfenydd. Llwyfenydd! Once she and Urien had seen it as their creation but now it was a place of memories, some good, some bad; a place to leave and seek a future in the South. Besides was not her ally, Kentigern, there too?

He was waiting for them at Caer Legion and considered carefully what she had to tell him.

"And has there been any sign of Myrddin?"

Modron shook her head. "Nor did I feel his presence. No, rather did I feel relief the further we came from Llwyfenydd."

"And yet you say Eurdyl was pleased to come with you?"

"Not at first, but later, yes."

Kentigern fingered his crucifix, weighing the words.

"Is there anything wrong?" asked Modron anxiously.

"Perhaps. Perhaps not. What I cannot understand is why you feel Myrddin has not, is not, following you and why Eurdyl was pleased to."

"I thought she came because Urien had promised to make Mouric a king in a land where the luxuries of old Rome have not been entirely forgotten, for such things would appeal to her and she would be the real ruler in all but name."

"You think that is all there is?"

Modron shrugged. Kentigern's questions were beginning to make her doubt that all was really well. The sun which had shone briefly on their journey south was disappearing behind cloud once more and in her heart she knew that cloud was the coming storm. Not the storm of which Urien spoke but one far greater in which the forces imprisoned for generations would be unleashed, like the ravens of Cocidius.

"Oh, Kentigern," she cried. "I don't know. I can't think anymore. I am getting old. I don't even know why we have come here and where we are going."

Kentigern patted her hand. "It is alright. We all grow old. It is our nature ... "

" ... but not mine. You don't understand ... "

"Sssh," comforted Kentigern. "You have had much to put up with. As for why you have come here and where you are going, that is easily put to rights. Urien plans to strike at Gwent, as he told you and Mouric. But first he will attack Southern Powys and restore that to Brocmael and his line. Cynan is to meet us here and we will move south whilst Mouric will join Brocmael in Dinas Bran and move south from there."

"And you?"

"For the moment I must do as my master bids and watch Gwynedd. Then I shall travel to Dyfed to meet Dewi and conclude a treaty with Dyfed which lies to the west of Gwent ... "

"You speak of your grandfather as your master, as if you do not wish to do these things?"

Kentigern smiled. "I am my own master and I have only one master and He is Christ. What then I do is for Him."

"God and gods! Priests and druids. Between you, you and Myrddin will destroy Prydein. Poor Urien."

"No!" cried Kentigern. "I seek not to destroy and bring death, but life. Urien seeks to defend our people from their earthly enemies, I to defend them from their spiritual foes. Heretics and pagans, Gwynedd, Gwent and Bryneich, they are our enemies and Urien's victories will be those of the Church!"

* * *

It was as Kentigern had explained. Soon they were joined by Cynan and a small warband, whilst Mouric, accompanied by Kentigern, rode to Dinas Bran. With them went Modron and Eurdyl, for Urien was anxious they should be safe and comfortable.

A day later Urien struck southwards along the great highway which divided Brocmael from Constantine; Powys Fadog from the lands to the east. The road to Caer Guricon led them across the great plain, the high sun upon their faces. By the middle of the second day they reached the small sandstone hill of which Brocmael had spoken in secret the year before. Now Urien, Llywarch, Cynan and Selyf climbed to the top, their path taking them through strands of ash and rowan, bramble and honeysuckle, tall bracken and foxglove. They found its summit deserted, the home of wild strawberry, trefoil and speedwell.

"Where is Maes Cogwy?" asked Urien as Cynan pointed westwards to where the hills of Powys swept in a great arc beneath brooding clouds towards the Hafren. Upon that river was Caer Guricon and beyond that the peak of Pengwern.

Urien nodded in remembrance and pointed to the gap in the centre of the western hills and to the higher of the two sentinel peaks at its entrance. "Cefyn Digoll?"

"Aye, and the gates of Meigen."

"So if we advance across country from here we will cross your father's path at Bassas as arranged?"

"Aye"

Urien nodded appreciatively, casting his eyes from the peak of Digoll to that of Pengwern and back. "Aye, your father and I spoke of Bassas when we stood upon the ramparts of Maes Cogwy. It is the bar which closes the door to the lands of Vortigern, for none can advance from there to Caer Guricon without exposing his flank to attack from Meigen or Ercig, nor can one attack Cefyn Digoll without being exposed to Caer Guricon."

Llywarch looked puzzled. "But why not leave Bassas to Brocmael, and ourselves continue on to Pengwern or Caer Guricon?"

"Because we need to draw Constantine, Eliud and Eldat to crush them with one blow."

The sun had disappeared behind advancing clouds as Urien finished speaking and the wind began to catch their cloaks and hair. Soon they were riding towards the storm, along the low ridge of ground that ran westwards from their lookout, and by the end of the afternoon the wall of grey rain they had seen from afar had enveloped them; heavy rain that came in torrents so they were soaked in no time at all and the track became mud. The horses hooves and their feet sank into the glutinous soil and progress was slowed. It was late evening when, splattered and caked in mud, they finally reached the cheerful fires of Brocmael and Mouric and the news that Constantine and his allies were camped nearby.

Urien had hardly breakfasted when the envoys arrived. "The sons of Vortigern ask why Urien the Coeling comes against them. Has he lost his way that he comes so far south? Have they attacked his flocks, his herds or burned his homesteads that he comes against them with arms?"

"I have not come to wage war, but to unite the Brython and restore the inheritance of Vortigern as I have that of Coel. Vortigern sought to defend the land against the foreigner but because lesser kings than he would not accept his rule he had to employ foreigners. But they turned on him and now threaten us. I have then come to seek help as Vortigern

141

did. Are we not Cumbroges, fellow countrymen? Then join with me for those who do not I will trample in the mud. Thus says Arctures: accept me and mine as overlords in Powys or let us try our might in combat."

"You cannot surely expect them to accept your terms," exclaimed Llywarch when the messengers had departed. Urien shook his head. "No, but one can always pray."

Soon the envoys returned. "Thus says the Lord Constantine. Rome divided Prydein into three: the land of the Picts, the land which Coel took and the land which Vortigern ruled. Is Urien ap Cynfarch greater than the Caesars that he thinks he can rule the South as well as the North? If so then let him prove he is such a man, let him prove he has the right to be called Guledig, let him meet Constantine, son of Vortimer, upon the causeway between us and there decide who should rule Prydein."

"And if I win?"

"Then shall all Powys acknowledge thee Guledig; and Eliud and Eldat shall serve you and yours as they do now Constantine."

The smile had gone from the face of Cynan. "You will not go, my lord? Constantine is but my age."

Urien pretended not to hear. He was examining his sword. The sword given to him by Myrddin, the sword of the Caesars given to him by She of the Lake. Would it not then triumph upon a causeway between marshes? Would it not make him Guledig? Trusting in it, Myrddin and a silent prayer to Mary that if she helped him now he would help her triumph over the Pelagians, Urien gave his answer.

The causeway stretched into the mist leaving Urien and Constantine alone. Like Urien, Constantine was equipped with spear, shield and sword; for since the days of Leu had champions fought thus. But the son of Vortimer was, as Cynan had said, younger than Urien, perhaps the age of Owen. He wore a coat of mail the colour of the clouds, and upon his feet boots the colour of the mud. He halted, saluting Cynfarch's son. "Is there time for you to be Guledig in this world, old man?"

"Time to release the wind from your stomach and your head from your shoulders," retorted Urien throwing his spear at the stationary figure. The tall figure laughed, deflecting the missile with his shield as if he were flicking away a troublesome fly. "You will have to do better than that, old man," he taunted, hurling his own spear at Urien, shattering his shield and knocking him backwards so that he began to slither and loose his grip on the muddy path. Seizing his chance Constantine rushed forward slashing his sword downwards. With an effort Urien dug his feet into firm ground and parried the blow with his own blade but the momentum of Constantine's charge sent him sprawling in the mud. Above him the sword of Constantine poised and then came crashing down, and with it its owner, skewered on the blade of Myrddin.

Urien lay for a moment beneath the heavy body trying to regain his composure. then slowly, he began to worm his way free. When at last he was able to stagger to his feet it was to find a sharp pain in his own right arm. With difficulty he rolled Constantine over and with his left arm pulled his sword free. Then with his feet he nudged Constantine to the edge of the causeway watching him roll down its side into the water.

* * *

The anxious eyes of Modron examined those of Urien, her hands upon the splints and linen with which the bone setter had mended his arm. "Does it still hurt?"

"Not much, and it's just as well if everyone is going to touch it," grumbled Urien before laughing.

He had sent for her, his sister and Kentigern to join him in Pengwern. Now they sat in Brocmael's new hall drinking Constantine's beer, eating from the forest of the Middlelands, listening to the praise of Taliesin:

"His the triumph
And fair lands,
The Bear of the North.
He slays, he commands,
He cherishes, he honours,
None dare challenge him now.

Arctures lay back and listened to the music of Taliesin but he could not rest. Victories he had wrought and extensive were his lands; more extensive even than those of Coel, for with the apple of Constantine had come the whole orchard. His now was the choice of which kingdom to prune and which to leave, which to keep and which to burn. He now was the master of the Brython and of their destiny as Myrddin had foretold. Urien thought of Myrddin and of Elen and of the children: his heirs.

"How can they be your heirs and serve the Brython when they have no one to learn from, none to acknowledge them?" he heard Myrddin ask.

Urien started. Had he been dreaming or had Myrddin really been there? Surely Myrddin was in the north? But if not why had he come south and why was he remaining hidden like a shadow?

"Are you alright, brother?" asked Eurdyl.

143

"Huh?" Urien looked at his sister seated by his side. She must have come whilst he dozed.

"Are you alright?"

"Yes, yes, I'm fine. It's old age: I must have dozed off," he laughed.

"Not old age, just the pain of your arm. Rest, for you have much yet to do."

"Aye." He put his hand on her knee. "It's strange you know but I never noticed your eyes before... How black and like those of Myrddin."

"Then you must rest indeed." Eurdyl lifted Urien's hand and placed it in his own lap and then rose. For a moment she looked down at the sleeping figure. "Sleep well Urien of Llwyfenydd, for Myrddin has need of thee."

* * *

Urien sent for Kentigern. "Many months ago you spoke to me of Dewi and of your desire to talk to him as one churchman to another. If that is still your wish Eliud here will help you."

Kentigern studied the figure next to Urien. A proud man perhaps: a defeated man certainly and one who could not yet be trusted; that is why Urien had spoken of Kentigern's mission as he had. Owen's son bowed. "Then I would be grateful to you both." He turned to face Eliud, listening.

"It is easy to find Dewi," said Eliud. "From here follow the Hafron to its head and the mountain of the Five Peaks, the centre of the land of the Western Cumbroges. From there, should you be a crow flying high and straight, it is the same distance to Mon as Caer Gwent. Again, fly from Caer Legion to Arberth, palace of old Vortepor of Dyfed, and you will find the mountain halfway. From that mountain you will be able to gaze upon all the children of Don: Aeron, between you and the western sea, where Cinglas holds sway; Dyfed, greatest of all the kingdoms of Deheubarth, to the south; Gwynedd to the north, and Powys to the east. From there it is but a short journey to Brefi, the home of him you seek."

"Then I will start tomorrow, with your permission, grandfather," said Kentigern.

"When will he be back?" asked Modron looking westward to the peak of Cefyn Digoll and the gates of Meigen.

Urien shrugged. "Before winter perhaps, perhaps before spring. He is a free spirit, we think we have tamed him but we have not. But whenever he comes, we will be waiting."

Modron turned, "Aye, we will be waiting. But do we wait for the same thing?"

If Urien understood her remark he chose to ignore it. "Brocmael and I are agreed we should spend winter here and next summer march south to enforce that which Kentigern and Dewi will promulgate: the suppression of Pelagius and all who follow him. Amongst such is Cadog, lord of Morgannwg, a land to the east of Dyfed. As Vortepor fails with age Cadog has grown in strength, attacking Brychan and seizing Gwent; a land without a king."

Modron looked at Mouric. He had grown in stature since they had met at the Redhills. Now he was a man and looked every inch a king, but he was his mother's tool. And if his mother's, Myrddin's too. "So we shall put our cuckoo in their nest," she said.

"As Kentigern was in Gwynedd and is now in Dyfed!" added Urien laughing.

* * *

The cloak of winter had been lifted from Pengwern. Where icicles had hung from eaves, the white-bibbed sparrow and martin now flew, darting in and out of the thatch and wall tops, whilst around them Urien and his allies prepared to move south. For Urien it was a time of hope. Soon he would lay claim to all the Talismans, and then turn upon the Loegrians. Then, too, he could find time to be with Elen and the children. He remembered the last time he had seen them and had fallen asleep in the warm meadow. Then he had found peace, and now he longed for that peace again. That once he had found peace only with Modron, that he gave no thought to Owen seemed not to trouble him: he had discarded them, as a child a toy; they were forgotten until he needed them. The High Kingship, the Talismans and Elen were the only thoughts that occupied him now. Seeds sown and nurtured by Myrddin; seeds which had become plants and which soon would bear fruit.

So the warbands of Powys and Rheged assembled about the walls of Caer Guricon. Brocmael alone was to remain behind and with him Modron and Eurdyl. "Until we send for you to join us in Caer Gwent," Urien told them, kissing Modron briefly.

Soon the long columns were across the river and in the sound of jingling harness and cantering horses, in the anticipation of battles to come, he could forget. Onwards they rode, the claws of Arctures stretching into the lands of Eldat and Cadog, Ercig and Gwent.

Their path took them across clay lands dotted with farms, cornfields and woods, towards the gap in the distant hills; but it was midday before they reached the entrance to that valley, the gateway to the South. Steep slopes rose to ruined forts, the watch towers of the Men of

Old. Through that valley they passed, until they came to a broad basin filled with the fragrance of sweet vernal, bright light and the fierce heat of the afternoon sun. In the still air butterflies busied themselves, lingering with folded, upright wings upon the dog daises, meadow saxifrage and golden dandelions, before suddenly fluttering away. Beneath them grasshoppers basked in the sun, their noise momentarily stilled by the presence of danger. And in the trees a perched corn bunting sang, watching the men and horses speed beneath.

"The road threads the valleys together like beads," observed Mouric.

Urien nodded, "That way Rome could control them, skewering the heart of every kingdom that lay between the Middlelands and the mountains of the west."

"So many kingdoms did they bind together with their roads from Caer Guricon that they called this land Powys," volunteered Eliud, "and to them Vortigern added Ercig, denying the Gael any more land beyond Dyfed ... "

" ... and Germanus planted Cadell in Dinas Bran to stop the the Gael of Gwynedd reaching the city of Vortigern," noted Cynan scornfully.

Eliud ignored the son of Cadell. "So Vortigern made his son Pascent king in Built and Ercig and his descendants still maintain that trust."

Urien noted with satisfaction the enmity between his allies and urged them forward. So it was by evening on the second day when they reached Ercig and the valley of the Gwy, the second of the great rivers to rise upon the mountain of the Five Peaks where Kentigern had journeyed the winter before. It was a broad fertile valley and its fields of corn and hay stretched westwards to flat-topped mountains silhouetted against the setting sun. Eliud pointed to them: "Beyond them, along this valley is Brycheiniog."

Mouric examined the land of Ercig carefully, wondering if Gwent would be the same. Here were numerous farms and the ruins of stone buildings whose inhabitants Vortigern had sought to protect. But it had been an unequal struggle and the patterns which Don had woven into her land were emerging again; the people living in the forts where their ancestors had before Caesar came. So Eldat had established himself above the old city, providing himself with a fort from which he could watch the valley and the northern road.

The warbands turned towards Eldat's hall upon that high hill, following the track through a coppice of slender hazel and ash. Upwards they climbed, emerging from the green tunnel of trees into the golden light of the setting sun. There Eldat was waiting, his silvered mail said to have been worn by Vortigern himself, glinting in the dying light. Kentigern too was waiting there with news from the west: Brycheiniog had been attacked by Cadog and sought the protection of Arctures. Urien nodded with satisfaction. Kentigern had done well. "And who is your friend?" he asked casting an eye over Kentigern's tall, dark-skinned companion.

"Theodoric, son of Budic, King of Llydaw."

"Llydaw?" Urien raised an eyebrow. Was not that part of Gaul, the area where the remnants of Mascen's continental army had been settled and later joined by others from Prydein? Theodoric nodded, adding that after his father's death Macliavus had been elected King with the help of Conomorus of Dumnonia and he himself had been forced to flee, seeking patronage where he could.

"My father had spoken of the strength of Vortepor and how he was an enemy of Conomorus and so I set my sail towards him. But how could such an old man help? For ten years I drifted without hope. For ten years; until a man of God came out of the North and spoke to me of Arctures, the splendid prince of Prydein."

"And it is from Llydaw that Cadog has recently returned," added Kentigern.

Urien smiled, there could be no better news. Llydaw would be the jewel in the diadem of the High Kingship. "Welcome indeed is Theodoric but what gift can I give him when I have brought no wealth hither but my arms, save that I give him honour and the promise we shall make him King again."

"Those are priceless gifts indeed, lord," said Theodoric. "So do I give myself to your service."

"A valuable gift, too," acknowledged Urien. "Come let us and Kentigern talk."

The next day Urien sent Cynan, Llywarch, Eldat and Mouric towards Gwent, whilst he, Kentigern and the others moved westwards, following the river towards Brycheiniog. There they feasted upon the hill of Crug that is in the centre of that kingdom. And there the bards sang of Gwydion, the son of Don, and of his sister Aranrhod who gave birth to Dylan and Leu Llawgyffes. There too they sang of how Gwydion and Math fashioned for Leu a woman of flowers and called her Blodeuedd; and of how Blodeuedd, falling in love with Gronw, lord of Penllyn, tricked Leu into revealing his geis that he might be killed.

And as he listened, Urien dozed and dreamt that he himself was upon a grassy bank by the side of a pool, a girl astride his body, a face like that of Modron. "In a year's time you will come for your son for it is not right that he should remain hidden here," she told him. He looked again and it was the face of Elen.

He awoke to find Owen's son by his side. "Are you all right?" asked Kentigern.

"You're sweating as if you have a fever."

"No, I'm all right," Urien assured him hastily, wondering if in his sleep he had called her name; betrayed his secret. "I was just snatching some rest, for tomorrow I shall doze in Morgannwg."

It was Rhain, King of Brycheiniog, who led them upwards that next day onto the southern rim of the mountains and the high escarpment which slopes gently towards the sea and Nantcarfen. There they galloped freely over the springy turf of the mountain tops, beneath the azure dome of a perfect summer's day. Between gorse and furze they cantered; around the head of a small valley they swept, a small river sparkling below them. Along the edge of a limestone scar they raced, high above cliffs where a solitary yew clung like a hermit and the peregrine falcon had his home. Like them whose hooves drummed upon the turf the falcon wheeled, stretching his wings in effortless flight, searching for his prey far below.

It was the afternoon of the second day when they stood above the plain of Morgannwg beyond which were the cream sands and silver sea of Hafren, and in the middle of that sea two islands like stepping stones. Theodoric pointed to the hills and valleys on the far side of the estuary. "There lies Dumnonia ruled now by Constantine. That plain you see marks the boundary between his lands and those of Aurelius Caninus. There Ambrosius drew his strength when he and Vortigern contended for Caer Gloiu and Gwent."

"And beyond them, far to the east lies Caer Lundein where, it is said, the Head of Bran lies buried," added Kentigern.

Urien blanched. Did then the Head not lie in Dinas Bran? "Surely it cannot be in Caer Lundein," he reasoned. "For that city has been held by the Loegrians for more than three generations. How can that be if the Head is buried to protect the Brython? Surely it must be in land still held by us?"

"It need not be so," said Kentigern. "Have you not considered the Talismans may only work in the hands of the right people, like the Blessed Sacrament in the hands of the true priest?"

Urien studied the face of his grandson. How much did he know? He must question Kentigern again, but for the moment there was a more immediate task. Urien called to Rhain and bid him lead them to Penychen, Nantcarfen and the fort of the heretic Cadog.

They found Penychen a land of steep-sided valleys and flat-topped ridges; a place of large farms, sweet meadows and woods. The fort of Cadog was built upon the end of one such ridge overlooking more open ground. There his ancestors had come, leaving their nearby villa and gathering about them the remnants of their former life, the clinging rags of imperial Rome. At the foot of that hill their estate workers lived and there too Cadog had built his church.

Kentigern looked about him. "It seems our friend has fled."

"Nay, master, he left yesterday morning with his men to drive back Eldat from Caer Gwent," volunteered an elderly servant who was busy sweeping the floor of the hall.

"Then it is as we planned," cried Urien, wishing to assert his authority once more over his own prince-bishop.

Remounting, they rode east. There they found the warband of Cadog streaming back towards Caer Daff. A ragged column of grim faced men; some with helms, some with hair matted with blood; some with shields, others slumped over their mounts, spears broken. They halted in the heat, a hundred flies about their heads. Cadog was resting in an orchard, a broken sword across his lap. Urien told the others to stay back and rode forward alone, looking down with pity, an emotion he felt Kentigern would not share. "Does not the husbandman fear the wind from the north which can kill the blossom of the trees and blacken young crops?" he asked. "Wise he will be if he plants a tree or seed which is from the North, one that knows the way of the wind. Coarser than the produce of the south may such fruit be but it alone can stand against the winter which is spreading from the east."

Cadog looked up, his face rimmed with dust, blood upon his cheeks. "The words of The Bear are wise, let his men and mine ride together, feast and heal their wounds, and in the summer of next year let there be a synod, a gathering of the church to judge between me and my accusers."

"Like that which Constantine the Great held?"

"There is none more fitting than you to call one, you who are now High King in all but name."

Urien held out his hand and, wincing with pain, pulled Cadog to his feet.

"Your arm? Is it hurt?" asked Cadog, concerned.

"A badly mended break. It's just as well you didn't come at me with that broken sword or you might have killed me."

"Aye, but it's no use like that. A king who is marred is no king. Do you not remember Nudd, who led the people of Don in their first battle with those they found in this land and who there lost his hand and thus his right to the kingship?"

"And he was given a silver hand until his old one could grow again?" added Urien, refraining from mentioning the Sword of Gorias which Nudd had wielded.

Cadog nodded. "Between Gwent and Caer Gloiu there is a shrine belonging to him and there people still go for healing, casting into the waters a model of their foot or arm or whatever they want healed. People think I don't know they still go ... "

"But it is a king's duty to know these things?" laughed Urien. "Will you not take me there?"

* * *

The place agreed for the great oenach and synod was Caer Uisc at the head of the estuary which divided Gwent from Morgannwg, a place neither in one kingdom nor the next. There the men of Rome had first landed when they pursued Caractacus towards the mountains of Brycheiniog and there they built a fortress. Later other ships had come laden with grain, wine and spices. But all that was long past and now the river was empty, the walls and streets deserted except for the church and school built amongst the ruins long ago by Tathan, a monk of the Gael. His successor now was Dubricus, a wizened man bent double with age; for he was born when Tathan was yet alive and he had been educated by those who had spoken with the holyman.

From there Urien sent Kentigern to Dyfed and, Theodoric and Eldat to bring Modron and Eurdyl and news from the north.

"Did you send Theodoric on purpose?" asked Modron when she and Urien were alone again. "He fair turned her head with tales of Gaul, blue seas and vineyards."

"Aye, he would."

"Then why do you encourage him and Eurdyl? That one day men might say Arctures ruled in Llydaw?"

Urien laughed. "Is it that transparent? Certainly I promised Theodoric a throne, and that promise I will keep."

"By making him regent here?"

Urien nodded. "For it will be a long time, if ever, before Theodoric regains Llydaw. So I give him wood painted in imitation of gold, and he gives me a jewel."

Modron looked at Urien. She would have said he was indeed changed beyond all recognition but now she wondered if that were really so. When Urien had driven Pabo from his land she had clapped her hands and laughed as Eurdyl might. Was Urien really any different now? Was it Modron then who had changed?

"Do you not think they should marry then?" asked Urien.

Modron shook her head. "Oh no, it's a splendid idea." "Splendid," she repeated to herself. "Especially if Theodoric takes her across the seas."

"And you," she continued aloud, "you have changed for I see your arm no longer gives you pain."

"Oh, that." Urien looked down and patted his elbow. "It's fine now. Cadog got me to bathe it in the pool of Nudd."

Modron stood back from her husband, her eyes searching his face quizzically. "I suppose you didn't tell Cadog why you really went to that shrine." She laughed. "But did you know Nudd has a shrine in Caer Lundein too, and that the Loegrians there call him Lludd?"

"Caer Lundein?" Urien's smile died and the blood drained from his face. "How can they know of the Talismans?"

"Why should they not know, are there not Brython still in that city?"

"But what if the foreigners control the Sword, aye, and the Head of Bran?"

Modron shook her head. "Have you not considered that it is not the Talismans themselves that are important but the control of the land where they are said to be. If you controlled Caer Lundein as well as Deur, Dal Riada, Caer Legion and Gwent would you not control the whole of Prydein and thus have already won? Is not that why your father told you to seek the Talismans?".

"But Myrddin says I must control the Talismans themselves.."

"Aye, but why? For his own ends not yours."

* * *

Eurdyl and Theodoric were married by Kentigern upon May Eve and not long after Eliud and Rhain returned, the first of many to come to the great oenach. They came in straggling lines, bright shapes in the light green fields of that spring: tall men upon horses, mail glinting in the sunlight; women and children clad in red and yellow silks, the whitest of linen. Like the flowers of the meadow they gathered about the walls of Caer Uisc: Theodoric and Cynan, Eliud and Eldat, Rhain, Conmail, Farinmail and Condidon, kings of the lands about Caer Gloiu and the Hafren. But Vortepor was too old to travel. Instead he sent messengers proclaiming he had named his grandson Artorius, "The Latin name of Arctures, for Urien has restored the power of Old Rome and his son shall be called Caesarius." Messengers too came from Dreon, Corocticus, Ridderch, Cynfelyn, Conall, Peredur, Guallauc and Catraut, from all the kings of the North and all the cities of the south and east which had not yet been lost to the Loegrians. And in Caer Gwent the bishops and holymen gathered about Kentigern and Dubricus: Dewi, Seiriol, Cadfan, Cynidr, Dunawd, Tebaus, Maedog and Gildas. Gildas who had brought Ridderch's greetings, a man whose brother had been killed in raiding between Rheged and Clud; a man whom Ridderch could trust.

Upon the appointed morning Urien rode towards the assembly, the clasps of his armour gilded and enamelled with blue, a crimson cloak upon his back. Beside him rode Modron, her high cheeks flushed once more with hope, her hair coiled and pinned by clasps matching those of Urien. Her dress was gathered with a silver belt and upon her feet were shoes of gold and azure like those fashioned by Gwydion and Manawydan when they alone stood against the evil in the land. Through the meadows they passed, between yellow coltsfoot and cowslips, sweet violets and bluebells. Beneath oak, elm and hazel they rode. Golden sunlight streamed into the valley from a blue sky and cream coloured clouds banked up over the hills, as if heaven itself were drawing up seats to watch the multitude gathered below. In the warmth, white butterflies stretched their wings and bees droned about the yellow flowers of gorse whilst overhead the chaffinch, wood warbler and thrush sang their chorus.

On that morning they proclaimed Urien, Guledig, High King, Dux Bellorum; and amongst the trees a hidden stag watched, alert.

WOODEN WISDOM

"Your move," said Modron.

The tables were empty. Where once there had been a feast there were now only crumbs and pools of spilled drink. The guests had gone and Urien sat alone with Modron by the fire playing Wooden Wisdom.

"It is your move," Modron reminded him.

"I know."

"How could such a great king become so easily trapped?" she teased, forgetful of the gulf which had but months before existed between them. Here in Caer Uisc she had begun to forget the shadows of the Morrigan; and the sun glinting upon the meadow had rekindled in her something of the love they had once enjoyed. But the fire which Modron sought to stir into new life was no more than embers, a fitful glowing, a memory in the heart of Urien.

"There must be something..." he murmured, his attention concentrated upon the board.

"There is something, my lord."

Urien looked briefly up, nodded a greeting to Kentigern and resumed his survey of the board.

"My lord, what I have to say is very important," persisted Kentigern.

"Oh, very well. We will have to call it a draw." Urien rose, but his relief was shortlived. Instinctively he knew what news Kentigern brought and his eyes strayed to the small scroll which his grandson was turning in his hands.

Urien sat down and motioned for Kentigern to do the same. Owen's son shook his head. "Does my grandfather not remember the story of Saul and David? How Saul consulted the Witch of Endor and fell from grace so God annointed David in his stead?"

"The Witch of Endor? Do you mean Myrddin?" asked Modron, a hand on Urien's shoulder.

Kentigern looked briefly at his grandmother. "Yes, the matter concerns that druid, for I do not doubt it was by his arts the woman of whom I speak beguiled the King."

Modron let her hand fall to her side. "What do you mean? What are you saying?"

"That Urien has taken another for his wife and by her has three children."

"Is it true?" Modron asked Urien. She wanted to say, "Tell me it isn't

153

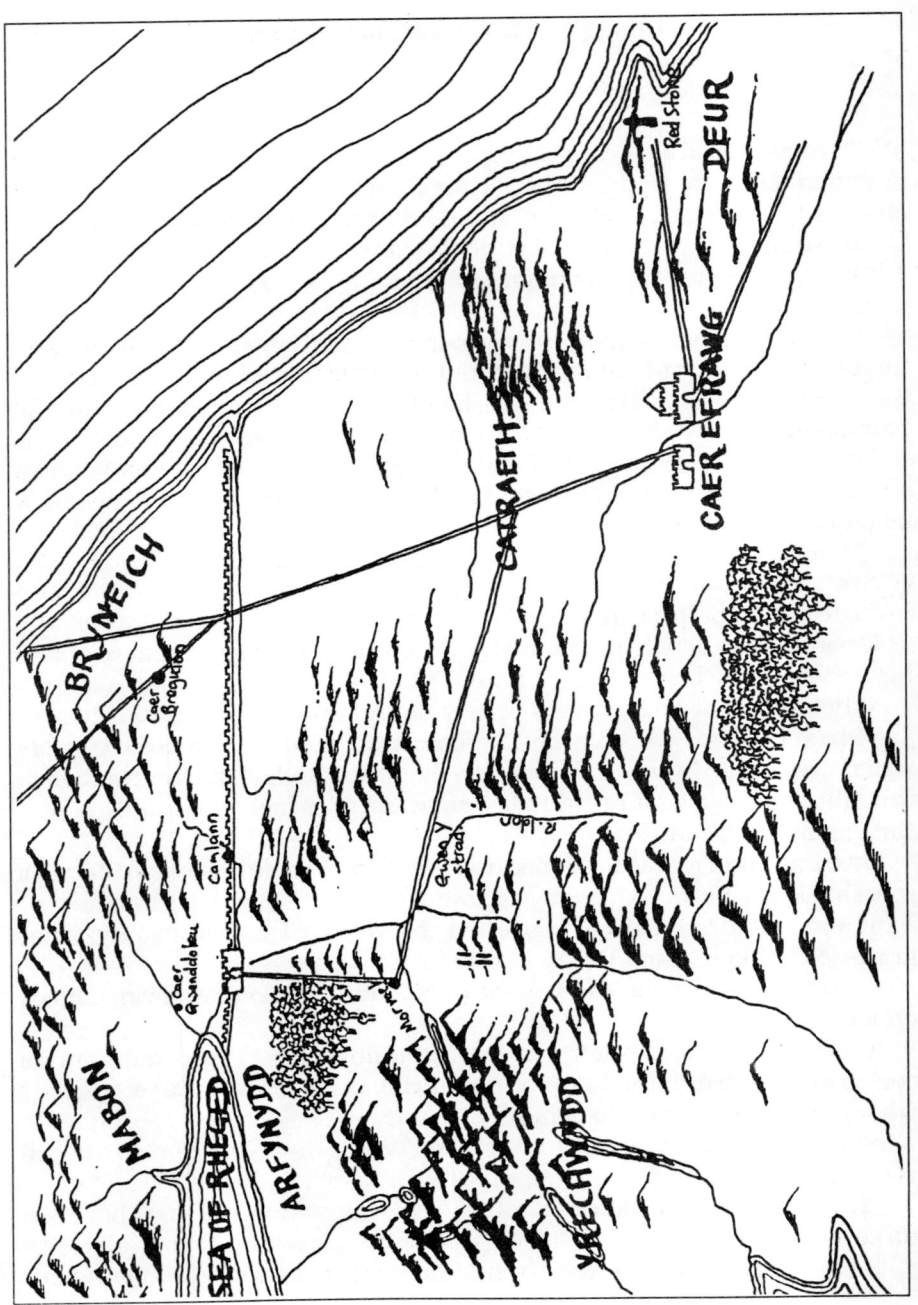

154

so," but in her heart and mind she knew Kentigern spoke the truth. The shadow which she had first felt when Urien was made King now had shape. But she had lived with that shadow for so long, she could only feel empty.

Urien put his head in his hands. "It was for Prydein's sake. I only wanted more sons. I didn't want to love her. I didn't love her ... not at first. Even now my love for her is different from my love for you ... "

"A king must be without blemish," continued Kentigern.

"When Solomon took Bathsheba, the Lord forgave him," retorted Urien.

"Only the Lord can forgive."

"Nay, men and women can too – if they wish!" cried Urien rising to his feet, knocking over his stool. He reached out for Modron but she backed away.

"How can you speak so, you who would not forgive Owen even when the accusations against him were false? If you want us to forgive you then say he is truly innocent, that he will be your one and only heir!"

"How can I, they are all my children."

"No, they are the work of Myrddin. I shall return to my people and my father's land. Where you go, to whom you go I care not now. You are free Urien ap Cynfarch. The High King is free to be his own master."

"I must go in search of the Talismans," muttered Urien, seizing upon a matter he thought she might agree with. But he was mistaken.

"Duty! Destiny! They have come to rule your life. Wise you were when once you said no man can know his destiny. One of the foolish kings of Prydein you have become, a tool of Myrddin."

"No, he has always spoken true ... "

" ... foretelling you would be High King, no doubt. And no doubt he told you I was elven ... "

"Is it not the Otherworld of which you now speak, the land of your father? Is Owen then, elven? My son!" Urien laughed sarcastically. "Your son! There too Myrddin was right. Aye, and you, for I was indeed a fool."

Modron shook her head; even now she loved him. "No fool, only a frail mortal. The battle of which you have dreamed and for which you have prepared, seeking out the Talismans, will be of no consequence compared with that which Myrddin plans. The Morrigan is indeed abroad and seeks to destroy the Children of Light ... "

"You are mad!" cried Urien.

"Mad! Perhaps, for is it not amongst such that seers might be counted? Does your beloved Myrddin go into a trance and foam at the

155

mouth? Was it by such means he blinded you so that you would not see the Morrigan ... "

"No, he keeps her from us. Was it not he who brought us together?"

Modron paused. Why had Myrddin, disguised as keeper of the silent stones, helped carry Urien to her all those years ago? Why?

* * *

Myrddin found Urien slumped in his chair staring at the flies which crawled across his lap.

"She has gone, Myrddin. I have lost her and with her part of me."

"Aye lord, but you have gained another and the world will rejoice to hear Arctures has other heirs, that the sovereignty of the land is ensured. She would not wish to see you thus ... "

"She? Who is she? Modron, Elen, the Morrigan? Why did you let Kentigern find out?"

"Lord, I know how bitter must be your feelings yet you must not grieve. How many times did Elen ask you to declare her openly and how many times did you say wait? But we cannot wait longer, so did Kentigern tell Modron that which you would not. What did you do wrong? Love two women? Want more heirs, not for your own sake but for your people? Will they then condemn you? No, rather they look towards you all the more, awaiting your word, your command. You are a warrior, a king, and there is work to be done, a destiny still unfulfilled. Your army waits, the Brython wait, your children wait. Go to them and rejoice in their love."

Urien rose and straightened himself. "Aye, it is time to return. We have stayed too long ... Where are Mouric and Eurdyl?"

A servant ran from the hall and returned shortly with Urien's nephew and sister.

Behind them strode Theodoric. Urien bid them sit. "I have stayed too long here and must return north. You must guard this place now ... "

"Never fear, you can trust us," said Eurdyl, looking from her brother to Myrddin.

"But what of the Talismans?"

Urien sighed. "Four are at my command: the Stone of Destiny in Dal Riada, the Cauldron of Ulph in Caer Legion, the Head of Bran in Powys and the Sword of Gorias here. It only remains to take the Spear of Leu." He shook his head. "They tried to trick me, saying some lay in Caer Lundein and that only the right people could use them ... "

"Modron! Kentigern!" spat Eurdyl. "What do they know. Trust Myrddin."

Urien patted Eurdyl's hand. " I am tired ... tired. Time alone will tell. If it is my destiny to drive out the Loegrians then they were wrong, but if it is not my destiny, well then, such questions do not matter. Come, let us drink to your future here and across the seas."

"That the name of Arctures, Artorius, may be renowned and feared there too," added Theodoric.

Urien smiled wanly and raised his goblet.

* * *

Urien returned to the North but he did not tarry in Llwyfenydd, for around its hearths there danced ghosts of all that had been, memories of past happiness. Once, he had wished he and Elen could enjoy together the sweet pastures of Llwyfenydd, but now that opportunity had come he could not grasp it: such are the tricks fate plays upon men. So Urien turned his back upon the valley which had been his home for forty years and rode northwards; beyond the Redhills, beyond Caer Leu, to Elen. She was waiting for him and helped him dismount.

"I am sorry," she began, putting her hands about his neck and resting her head against his shoulder.

Urien pulled her face to his and saw she had been crying. "Nay, lass, you have nothing to be sorry for. Besides, now the world acknowledges you and the children. Now our enemies will fear us all the more, for if I shall die Owen will spring into my place, and after him Pasgent and after him Elphin ... "

Elen had begun to cry again. "Sorry," apologised Urien. "I didn't mean ... You know what I meant."

Their embrace was cut short by the children tugging at his cloak. Urien looked down at them; their faces red with eating blackberries. "Princes and princesses should not be seen with dirty faces," he teased, stooping to hoist them in his arms. "My, someone is heavy ... or perhaps your father is getting too old."

"Our father is not old, he is the greatest king in the whole world," answered Pasgent as he was lowered to the ground.

"Perhaps so, but what does that make you?"

Pasgent thought for a while. "The greatest prince in all the world".

Elen giggled.

"Don't let your big brother hear you say that," said Urien laughing.

"I have no big brother," pronounced Pasgent solemnly, looking at his mother.

Urien straightened and put his hand on Elen's. "I cannot forget him now. Strange isn't it?"

Elen smiled and kissed him on the forehead. "I don't mind. If Modron had accepted me and the children it would have been so anyway. But don't tell Myrddin."

"Myrddin will be happy for me. He is a good servant ... "

"He is the servant of none but himself ... " Elen broke off. "I should not have said that. Never, never repeat it."

Urien paused. First Modron and now her? In his stomach he began to feel fear. Stooping, he picked up Morfudd. "The first thing we must do is to take you away from here ... Mother will be with you," he added hastily, seeing their faces begin to pucker. "From now on we will all be together."

The following day they set out for Gwenddoleu's. Pasgent rode on his pony alongside his father whilst Elen and the others folowed in a waggon. Every so often they would pass a farmstead and the people would rush out to watch the strange cavalcade. "Are they looking at me?" Pasgent would ask, trying not to stare back.

"I expect so. All the world will want to look at so important a prince." Urien turned and grinned at Elen.

Caer Gwenddoleu was a place very different from the world the children had known, a place only imagined from the tales of Cadwallon; a place of a dozen large buildings and cobbled yards; of industry, baking, hammering. The children gazed around, excited yet apprehensive, whilst their cart rumbled across the outer yard, splashing through muddy puddles, scattering hens and hissing geese. They halted outside the largest building and Urien lifted each of the children down and then with Pasgent and Elphin clutching his hands tightly he led them towards the porch. Elen followed with Morfudd.

Gwenddoleu had prepared a great feast with acrobats and clowns to entertain the children. The tumbling men reminded Pasgent of the frogs he used to watch leaping from stone to stone by the side of the stream, the clowns the quick magpie and slow limping Cadwallon. And so entranced were the children they did not see the man stooping to whisper into their father's ear: "Hello daddy."

Urien turned as best he could without disturbing Pasgent and Elphin who were seated on his knees. Elen too had turned. Owen was older than she had imagined, though no less handsome. He kissed her gently on the cheek and she blushed. It was not what she had expected from one with his reputation, nor from the son of Modron. Urien too noted the change in his eldest son and wondered, but his thoughts were interrupted by the shifting of Pasgent, resentful of the interuption of the entertainment. Owen put a finger to his own grinning lips and stole away, leaving his brothers and sister in peace.

In the morning, when they were rested, he came to them again. "You don't know me, do you?" he said, kneeling on one knee and looking from one to the other as they backed away. "But I have watched you." Owen looked up at his father and Elen. "The hunter too must learn what creatures come and go in the forest. Does not each animal and bird tell in its own way that there are strangers in the land? So I watched; sometimes from the trees, sometimes by the stream, sometimes on the rooftop ... "

"Like the raven!" cried Pasgent, his eyes wide with wonder as he propped himself against Urien's leg.

"Like the raven," repeated Owen.

Elen moved to one side to allow Owen room to sit beside his father.

"It is good to see you," Urien began, a tremor in his voice. "But if you knew my secret why did you not tell your mother?"

Owen paused for a moment. "Perhaps I should, and many will say I am a fool to forgive, but what is past is past. Besides, I came to tell you that what my mother said in Caer Uisc is true: Myrddin is simply using you. For your sake, for the sake of Prydein do not listen to him ... "

"Is this the real reason why you came here? Not to forgive but to drive Myrddin from me?" cried Urien, rising.

"Father!" Owen stopped. "Very well. When you went south I swore to protect these lands and that I will still do. For the sake of Prydein and my children. Should you need me I will be with Rhiannon for with her I have found happiness."

* * *

Owen and Rhiannon were married according to the customs of her people. Customs whose origins were unknown. Perhaps they were made when men first tamed the speckled race of Mor Gweidiawl and iron was unknown, for it was with gold that they were wed, their mounts unshod. It was upon horses they came and upon horses they sat: symbols of the kingdom a man and woman would build together. Like a king, Owen and his friends demanded the bride, whilst she and her friends defended her pride. To refuse him entry she had galloped away and in pursuit they had followed, certain this time that Swanmane would not outpace them. Yet she taxed them hard before, fatigued, they caught her and Owen carried off his bride.

It was May Eve, Beltane, the time when the People of Brigit had first invaded the land, the time to celebrate the coming of summer and plenty. The seed was sown and in the days to come friendships would

159

blossom sustaining both body and soul. Around the tall staves the maidens danced, weaving their ribbons and charms, and from such webs few escaped. It was a time to renew the future and celebrate the birth of summer, the golden days of warmth and abundance.

For nine days they feasted and sang, drank and slept not knowing the hour; for so Owen and Rhiannon would live, not counting the passing of the years but feasting upon each other, intoxicated with love. Then they journeyed to their new home, along dry tracks and across pastures yellow with cowslips; beneath shady trees and copses carpeted with bluebells and ivory woodruff with which to scent the linen of their bed. The birds sang to them and the river at their side murmured their praises. Golden sunlight poured through the white flowers of the rowan trees, rainbows in the spray of foaming pools, and from the limpid brown waters rose the salmon, its food the unsuspecting fly. Rhiannon pointed, laughing, "Was it not the salmon that led Gwrhyr to release Maponus from his prison?"

So it was that they came to the border of his land and hers, where Owen had built a house upon a peak, a green helm rising from high precipitous slopes. To the north and west lay hilltop pastures and the sport of summer; east and south was the luxuriant vegetation of the valley floors. Between her land and his they lived: a paradise between this world and the next. Between earth and heaven they loved, watching the sun and rain fertilise the earth in the womb of the sky.

There the months passed like scudding clouds upon a summer's day. And with their passing the body of Rhiannon swelled like the heads of golden corn which filled the fields that year. It was a summer to remember: a summer of abundance and peace; the peace of Rheged. Aye, and of Urien, Gold King of the North, for who could doubt such was the reward of the High King and his new wife Elen? As Myrddin had said, so it had come to pass.

Through those long, hot days of autumn Owen waited; waited for the moment of which he had dreamed so long: the birth of his child. Boy or girl, what did it matter? Soon he would be a father. But it was from the east the messengers first came, riders who brought no gifts of gold, perfume or spices but news of rebellion. Flamdwyn had broken the oaths given after the battle of the Glen and had gathered new forces, some said from across the seas.

"I should have known it was too good to last," sighed Owen. The warrior clamoured for action, the father urged him to stay. In his mind he saw for the first time the tumult and pain of war; the rending of shields and spilling of guts and, as if for the first time, he heard the cries of the wounded and dying, voices calling to those they loved. In his mind he heard the banshee, the calling of the Morrigan, the summons of the Otherworld. "Autumn has come to Myrddin's summer. Here is one thing he did not prophesy!"

"And so he should be shown to be responsible. It is he who lulled Rheged and your father that the Brython forgot their enemies," derided his wife.

Owen shook his head. "No, I swore I would defend these lands and I will not have men say Owen broke his promise. Then certainly men will say I have no right to rule, neither me nor my heir." He patted Rhiannon's womb gently and laughed. "You forget I have responsibilities now, and like the honest husbandman of whom my other son speaks must earn my keep ... Besides, should Modron's son and not Myrddin be seen to defend the Brython?"

Rhiannon smiled resignedly. "I know. Go with our blessing and our love. Go, and amongst the men of Bryneich carve the future of our child."

"So, you want to be rid of me, huh?" laughed Owen, reaching down to pick her up.

"Careful," answered Rhiannon. "I don't want you to tire yourself."

"In your condition, I won't ... " Owen paused. "Nor could that big serving girl interest me now."

Three days later Owen and his warband rode eastward. Rhiannon had risen from her bed and, wrapped in a warm cloak to keep out the chill morning air, waited in the courtyard whilst the horses were made ready. Owen stood beside Swanmane, whom now he would ride, his arms about Rhiannon, his eyes and lips fixed on hers. Behind them the horse clattered impatiently upon the cobbles. "You had best be off," laughed Rhiannon peeping over the shoulder of Owen.

"Aye, take care of yourself and the little one." Then, with one more kiss, he climbed onto Swanmane and was gone. At the bend beyond the gates he turned to look once more, a shadow in the mist which hung about the hilltop. Rhiannon stayed for a moment longer, listening to the joyous chorus of birds heralding the new day.

At the foot of the mountain Owen turned eastwards; the mist was high above them and the sky was red.

* * *

Urien stood upon the ramparts of Camlann gazing anxiously eastwards, watching for the fires that would tell of victory. It had been three days since Owen, spurning the help of Gwenddoleu, had ridden along the old wall to Caer Breguion, the fort which guarded the eastern door of Rheged. Across its valley, past its walls the Loegrians would have to come to reach the western plains. But it would not be in his lifetime, nor in that of his son. Urien put his arm about the shoulder of Pasgent, praying to God that the Loegrians would never see Llwyfenydd except as slaves.

So the lord of Rheged waited, his eyes upon the wall which ran before him: a dark cord stretching through the evening mist, a girdle across the green mantle of Prydein. Not a girdle that brought fertility to the land like the belt of Brigit but a symbol of the sterility which comes from the minds of men – treasure poured out for war.

It was another two days before Owen came home, Swanmane tethered to the side of the waggon. Inside and hidden from view by the leather canopy Myrddin plied his skill. Urien had sent for him as soon as the news came that Owen had been wounded, for who was more skilled in the lore of healing than Myrddin? So together, he and Urien had ridden east and now Myrddin sought to clean and bind the wound: "Mother of the earth receive not your son before he sees his own. She of the waters of life, quench the fires of his fever. Keeper of the sacred fire, consume the bad and heal the wound. Blessed trinity of the unseen ones without whom there can be no life, claim not his. Give power to the hands of your servant Myrddin and wisdom to his mind that men may see the glory of Rheged rise and may glorify yourselves."

Rhiannon was waiting below the walls of Caer Owen, at the edge of the Wailing Tarn where Myrddin had first promised Urien he would fight the Morrigan. She nodded to Urien. "Greetings to Owen's father."

"It is good to see you again but I wish ... what can I do, what can I say?"

"There is nought you can say for this was always his destiny, his geis, but there is one thing you can do, and that is why I am here. In yonder fort waits Modron and it would be better if you were to come no further. I will take him home."

Urien nodded. "Aye, I wronged the lad, and Modron too. I have no claim on him now. He gave his life for me who would give him nought."

Urien climbed onto his horse and watched as the wagon, empty now except for his first son, moved slowly away.

When again it stopped, Modron drew back the curtain and, with the help of Luned, climbed in. Owen lay between linen sheets on a bed of hay, his shirt torn back, his body wrapped in clean white bandages. A single brown stain above his chest indicated where the wound had last bled. "There is nothing more we can do now but wait." She motioned to the men to lift Owen and carry him to his bed. Rhiannon stooped to kiss the ashen face of Modron's son. Had he not always been Modron's; conceived by her and carried by her, until Urien had come to her father's house? Rhiannon sat next to Owen's pallet, tracing her fingers lightly across his forehead, feeling the yet warm flesh, the contours of his face. "We are taking you home, Owen, we are taking you home."

Once Owen woke and, as if to comfort Rhiannon, drew her hand to his lips telling her, "I shall not die before I see our child".

"I know," she comforted. "It is your geis and it must be mine too. Do you forgive me, that, by loving you, I brought about your death?"

Owen nodded. "Did you really love me?"

"Of course."

"Then I forgive you."

Rhiannon laughed lightly and shook his hand gently. "Now my prince you have at last growm wise. Sleep and when you next awake it will be to see that of which you have dreamed so long."

They called the boy Rhun, and Rhiannon had him placed between her and his father. "Where Owen can see him," she told Luned and Modron.

Perhaps it was the calling of his own name, perhaps it was awareness of a new life next to his that awoke Owen for the last time. Slowly and gently, he stroked the back of his hand along the tiny face. "In death is my victory. The Morrigan has taken yet has she given ... "

Rhiannon wiped a tear from his face. "Aye, and you have come home as I promised." She paused briefly "Do you not yet understand? You never did ask why my knife was of bronze ... " She pulled it from its sheath, letting the light dance along its length. "Do you not remember how you awoke upon a shee mound to find Clovenhoof gone and in her stead me, whip marks upon my flanks? Did you not dream of the peaks of Magmell and find my house between two hills?"

Owen began to laugh. "I never guessed you were elven, of the Otherworld, your house a shee mound."

"Such is the power we shapechangers have that such things can be hidden from mortal men. For since the time when our people were driven underground by the likes of Myrddin our daughters have sometimes been given to ordinary men. But you were not ordinary, Owen, for your mother too is elven, though her father kept that from her. It was above Llwyfenydd that she first felt it, the call of the shee mound, her true home. And when in your dream you journeyed across the glass sea, when you came to me you too returned to that home, a land which is part of you and me, a part of us all."

* * *

At Kentigern's request they buried Owen in newly consecrated ground
at the southern edge of his land. About his grave they placed four
stones, one for each corner of the kingdom, for that place was the centre
of the land and he the centre of their hearts. There, within sight of
Llwyfenydd, Yrechwydd, Arfynydd and the hills of Mabon they buried
him. Two more stones they placed upon his grave, one at his head, the
other at his foot for if a man has no beginning and no end how can he
have lived, how can he have died?

Urien, Gwenddoleu, Elen and the boys watched from a distance,
hidden by trees. Some said Elen should be pleased, for now her children
were Urien's heirs; but she felt only sadness, remembering the time
Owen had come to them in Caer Gwenddoleu. But she knew her sadness
was nothing compared with the torment of Urien. He had turned his
eldest son from his gates and cursed him, and that son had repaid him
by doing his bidding, riding to his death. Once, when a little girl, she
had heard a Christian priest preaching and now his words came back to
her: "He gave his life for thee." Elen put her arm round Urien's waist
and laid her head against his shoulder.

Urien had sent Taliesin to give the oration and now his voice wafted
to them across the meadow:

"Soul of Owen ap Urien
May the Lord care for its needs.
Let us not cease to praise him
For who was there to equal
Llwyfenyddd's splendid lord,
A green mound now his dwelling.
Reaper of foes, despoiler,
When he cut down Flamdwyn
It were no more than sleeping,
The green sward now his pillow.
Splendid in pied armour
And generous gifts of steeds,
Wealth beyond measure he poured out
Before the earth received him.
Soul of Owen ap Urien
May the Lord care for its needs."

Beside her Elen felt Urien's body begin to shake. Reaching up, she
pulled him to her, comforting, stroking his thin silver hair. Behind her
she could hear Kentigern. "How should it avail us to ask why he died?
Was he not a man searching for his soul, that vessel, that holy grail

which contains and controls his destiny? Let no man say he did not find that for which he searched, for he tasted the cup of life and found its wine sweet."

When the others had gone Urien stood, head bowed, by the side of Owen. And when at last he looked up it was to see the highest summit of Tu Hir. Somewhere beyond that purple top, a hundred miles or more, were the Loegrians. A hundred miles, a thousand miles, it did not matter now: nought could save them from his fury, for the Bear had been wounded, goaded by fate and his own folly. He turned to Gwenddoleu, his eyes red and angry. "He died for us! Did he die for nothing? Shall we leave him unavenged? No, we owe him that. It was his destiny I hear some say and so it was. And so now I lay this destiny upon all men that they should avenge him and drive the Loegrians from this land. Let no man say he died in vain."

* * *

Throughout the winter Arctures made his plans and prepared for war. The war of which his father had spoken all those years before. So from Manau to Morgannwg, from Llanelwy to Caer Efrawg messengers, winged their way. Prydein was filled with the sound of hammering. In innumerable fires ore yielded up its contents, a thousand blades, five thousand spears.

By early summer the Brython were ready to swarm; Morcant, Ridderch and Cynfelyn; Dreon, Gwenddoleu and Urien; Llywarch, Guallauc and Peredur; Kentigern, Mouric and Brocmael. Three times three were the armies gathered, with three more to guard Gwynedd and the South. It was a time when no man could refuse to fight and, indeed, Urien had summoned all who were eligible to the hosting. At the western end of Gwen Ystrad they gathered, below the stony pass to Catraeth, upon the green banks of Idon. There, where Rome had built a fort to guard convoys of corn and silver, the men of Llwyfenydd met now. Many had brought with them their women and children and it seemed to Pasgent, as he looked down from the old grey walls, that all the world was encamped there. With gathering excitement he and Elphin watched as daily the ranks swelled. Blue smoke rose into the air from countless fires, each with its own group of men and women; some rowdy, some whispering, some laughing, some kissing. Here and there carcasses roasted and a skin or two of drink was passed round. Wives, smiths and cobblers made last minute adjustments to belts, jerkins, helmets and boots. Between the waggons and carts, tethered horses tugged at their ropes or grazed the area within reach, their swishing tails driving off flies like their riders would the Loegrians. And between them all ran the children, playing tag, squealing with delight.

At last, however, the day came when all was ready. Pasgent and Elphin sat astride their ponies, apprehensive yet anxious to be moving. Urien had insisted they go with him and Myrddin so that they might learn about the world and the world see them and know Arctures had heirs. It was a plan Elen had been only too pleased to accept and yet now, as the moment for their departure came, she could not help but cry. Standing on tip-toe she reached up for the lips of Urien. "Take care of the boys. Pasgent! Elphin! take care of your father."

The two youngsters smiled bravely, for they were already engaged in their own battle, fighting to hold back their own tears. It was a time to be off. They kissed their mother one last time and then turning, followed Urien and Myrddin through the gates.

For them the world had suddenly become bigger. No longer were they two boys playing in the clearings of the forest by a limpid stream, but princes marching upon kingdoms, striding between seas. No longer was it sufficient to know which fruits were poisonous, they needed now to watch for men who carried envy and malice in their hearts. The world had become a much more hostile place. So as they rode Urien told them of many things, of their ancestors, of the places they passed and of Prydein itself.

The first to inhabit the land had been the Coraniaid or little people, but from whence they came no one now knew, though their flint arrowheads might yet be found. After them came the first farmers who some said were the first men and they were led by Pwyll. It was they who raised the first shee mounds and made the gates of the Otherworld. Through them Pwyll descended into Annwn, and his son Pryderi was the first swineherd, for pigs are the animals of the Otherworld.

At first the People of Pwyll and the Coraniaid lived peacefully together but a dispute arose and Gwawl, lord of the Coraniaid, was driven onto islands in the western sea where he and his people live still, invisible, and invisible come to work mischief amongst men. It was one of their kings, Llwyd, who tried to avenge Gwawl by hiding the people of Pryderi and Rhiannon, and it was they who were one of the three plagues which Lludd had to master.

After Pwyll came other immigrants, the People of Brigit; the Children of Light. Brigit, whom some call Don and others Dana, was the daughter of Mathonwy the Good. She was the first of the three matriarchs of Prydein for she gave birth to Gwydion, Gilfaethwy, Aranrhod and Gofannon the Smith, for they were the first to work metal though iron was unknown. Aranrhod it was who fathered Dylan of the sea and Leu; and it was Gwydion who killed Pryderi. With Brigit also came Llyr, Nudd, Hefydd, Ulph and Rhiannon, the second of the matriarchs. She it was who married Pwyll and gave birth to Pryderi betraying, some say, her own.

Then came Beli and his sons Ludd, Caswallon, Nyniaw and Llefelys and they ruled in South Prydein.

"What became of the Children of Light?" asked Elphin, "For I have never heard mother speak of them."

"Elven!" spat Myrddin.

Urien looked at Myrddin. "They were driven into the Otherworld too, but some of their women may come forth from the shee mounds to be our brides."

"Your mother is descended from the People of Pwyll," added Myrddin emphatically.

Urien rode on in silence for a while, wondering if such stories really could be true, and why Myrddin hated the Children of Light. It was as if the death of Pryderi was still to be avenged. He turned to Myrddin. "Why if they were elven do you tend the fire of Brigit and pray to the three mothers?"

"Because they were in the land long before the Children of Light came and so they will remain. They are the very elements of our world and cannot be destroyed; disguised but not destroyed. And those who hold to the truth? We have sought sanctaury where we could find it; openly or in secret."

"Why, have sought?" pressed Urien.

Myrddin smiled. "Because the time is coming when the kin of Pwyll will once more rule in Prydein." "And then shall all who have elven blood be driven into the Otherworld," he added to himself.

At Catraeth they turned south, reaching Caer Efrawg on the second day. There Guallauc and Llywarch were already gathered, standing beside Peredur and Gwrgi.

"I had hoped Eleuther would be well enough to welcome my two sons," said Urien as he approached them.

"Have you not heard then that he died five days ago?" asked Guallauc in a hushed voice.

Urien shook his head and sat down. "Eleuther dead!"

After a while he rose. "What news from Deur?"

"None," replied Peredur. "It seems Hussa is unaware of what we plan for him. But there are messengers from the west ... "

From the west? Urien remembered how other messengers had once come to Caer Efrawg from the west and how the Mordei had raided Rheged. Peredur watched Urien's face: so he did suspect them as Guallauc said. From now on they would have to be careful. "Yes, from Kentigern," he continued, signalling to a servant. "Bring in the monks."

The six monks bowed before Urien. "Kentigern, Bishop of Clud and all Cumbroges, sends greetings to his grandfather, High King of the Brython."

"And how is my episcopal governor?"

"He says to tell you he prays for you each day in the quiet of Llanelwy." The monk paused and Urien nodded: Gwynedd was quiet and the Brython would not be stabbed in the back this time. "And our lord abbot has sent gifts in recognition and thanks for the destruction of heresy," continued the monk. "Let them go wherever Arctures goes, let them be carried like Talismans before the Brython that they may triumph over their enemies."

As he spoke four of his colleagues moved forward and spread their gifts upon a table: a silken banner brought from Rome upon which was an image of Mary wrought in gold thread, and a gold brooch in similar likeness. Urien ran his hands over them. What did Kentigern mean, "like the Talismans"? What game did Kentigern play? The monks bowed and, glancing briefly at Guallauc and Peredur, left the hall. Behind them Urien noted the glance: could Kentigern be in league with Guallauc and the others?

"What else was said?" asked Myrddin as Urien told him of what had happened. "Did they speak of the Talismans?"

Urien shook his head. Why he did so he was not sure but something, something told him not to divulge all to the druid. Instead he decided there was no time to lose and the following day they moved eastwards, reaching the first Loegrian settlements in the early afternoon.

As he had anticipated, and Peredur reported, Hussa, King of Deur, had assumed Urien would avenge himself only upon Bryneich. Caught unawares Hussa could mount no serious opposition and had fled northwards.

"Towards Bryneich and Theodoric I bet," argued Gwrgi, like a wolf cheated of a carcass.

"Before long we will see him again, and then you might finish him," countered Urien. "But before then we have other matters to attend to, other booty to find."

Peredur and Guallauc looked at each other. Of what Urien spoke they were not certain but they thought they knew. Let Gwrgi pillage where he would, they and Myrddin would ride with Urien.

After three days they came to that which Urien sought, the Red Stone of which Eleuther had spoken years before: the Spear of Leu. Four, five times the height of mortal men was the monolith; a silent witness to the passing of the Children of Light. In front of them was a broad valley. To the east the ridge of high ground continued for another ten miles before ending in the sea, and from that promonotory the coast swept southwards in a great arc towards the land of Linnuis.

"I thought that was in the north beyond Cathures and Alclud," said Pasgent.

"Aye, there is such a place and a Llwyfein there, too," answered his father. "For like men, many places may carry the same name. So Nudd was one of the companions of Brigit and a Nudd a son of Beli and there might be many Brans, many places where that head lies buried ... " Suddenly he stopped, remembering the words of Modron and Kentigern. What if the Sword of Nudd and the Head of Bran did lie in Caer Lundein? Is that what Kentigern had tried to tell him? "Like" the Talismans?

Urien fingered Kentigern's brooch at his shoulder, wondering, seeking reassurance, and as he did so he recalled again the certainty he had felt in Moel Fre; a certainty that he would not fail, that he was destined to free Prydein. But then the world had been different; Llwyfenydd had been whole and he and Modron happy. Now he had forsaken that valley; Modron was gone and Owen dead. How? Why? He had wished he need not hide Elen away and that wish had come to be: Modron had gone. He had justified the taking of Elen by the need of a king to have more than one heir, and now Owen was dead. It seemed his love for Elen had destroyed his world. Urien shook his head in dismay. He had not meant it to be so: he had not lusted after Elen he had merely ... Urien remembered how Myrddin had come to him in Llwyfenydd, coaxing him, persuading him to meet Elen. The loss of Modron and Owen, they had been Myrddin's doing; but why?

Urien dismissed the others and stood alone with Myrddin by the side of the great stone. He rubbed his hand slowly and thoughtfully across its warm surface, feeling its girth, gazing up at its top silhouetted against the radiant orb of the sun. And in that moment he understood. He was but part of a celestial game of Wooden Wisdom; a High King who needed four guardians to ensure victory and the survival of the land. In that moment he heard again the words of Modron: "The battle of which you have dreamed, seeking out the Talismans, will be of no consequence compared with that which Myrddin plans". Then too, he heard the words of Myrddin, "The time is coming when the kin of Pwyll will once more rule Prydein," and it seemed to Urien the words came from the stone as if an echo, but how could that be when the words had been spoken long ago? Besides, there were other words Urien had not heard before: "Then shall all those who have bred with elven and have elven blood be driven into the Otherworld". Had Myrddin spoken them too?

Suddenly Urien felt angry. "Why have we come here, Myrddin?" he demanded.

"Why have we come here? Surely my lord knows, you brought us here to find the last of the Talismans."

"Aye, but for what purpose? That you might capture them and thus finally destroy the Children of Light?"

Myrddin blinked, momentarily taken aback.

"It is the stone that makes you speak thus, my lord. It is their magic, a trick. Do you not remember how when we first met I told you how they had raised cones of power against my people? Do you not believe that on Samhain they come forth to work mischief amongst men? Why then should they not work mischief here?"

Urien shook his head. "The stone does indeed speak thus, Myrddin, but it is not they who work mischief but you. Was it not you who gave me Elen to drive away Modron? And Owen's death? You needed that so I would bring you here. Is that why Flamdwyn attacked before he was ready, because you tricked him too?"

"And what if I did trick Flamdwyn? Should not a good general entice his enemy to attack before he is ready? But I did not kill Owen. It was his destiny to die when he married Rhiannon. And who was she, but one of them? No, Urien of Llwyfenydd it was not I, nor the Morrigan, that took your son but the Children of Light. Aye, and it was no doubt Rhiannon, too, who stirred up the Picts to raid Llwyfenydd that she and Owen might meet. Did not the Picts come from her land?"

"And it served your purpose too, for by that act you brought me to Elen … "

Urien stopped. Nothing, then, had been chance or an accident. He was but a piece in some great game of Wooden Wisdom where first one side has the advantage and then the other. A game played time out of mind. When Myrddin had given Cynfarch Eurdyl, Avallach had countered by matching Urien with Modron. Morcant's victory over Tudwal had been countered by Kentigern's move against Gwynedd. Eurdyl had driven Owen from Urien but had only succeeded in giving him to Rhiannon … Suddenly Urien began to laugh, a bitter, deriding, triumphant laugh. "Where is the Spear of Leu, Myrddin? I see only a stone? They have indeed tricked you as you say. For only the Children of Light or one who is descended from the People of Brigit can wield the Talismans of Prydein. The Talismans are beyond your reach now. You have driven them from us, like a drowning man whose splashing wafts beyond his reach the plank he seeks to grasp. You have moved me about the board of Prydein that you might corner the Children of Light but in your eagerness you have exposed yourself to counter attack. The next move then is yours."

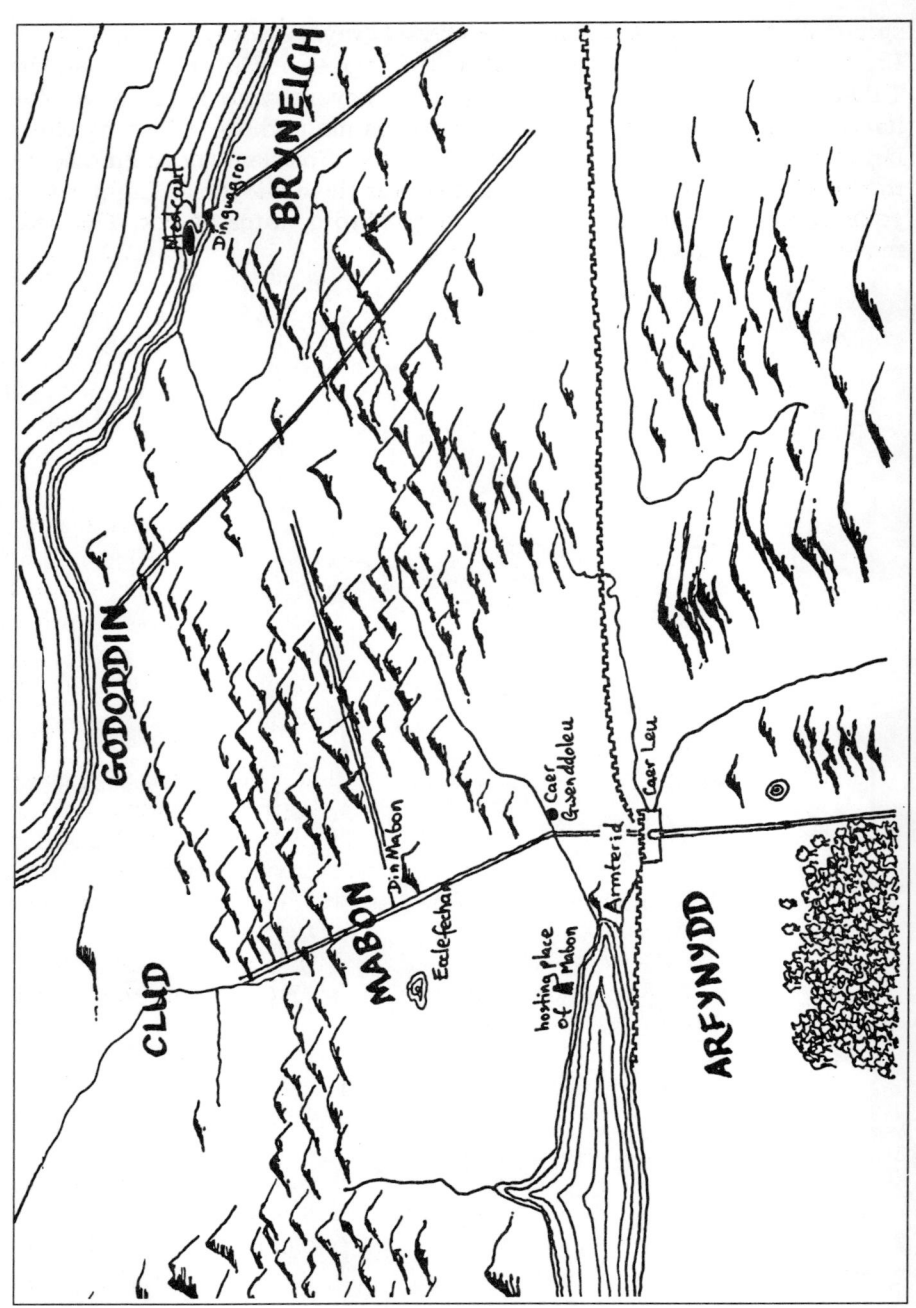

BRYNEICH

GODODDIN

Mencoit
Dinguaroi

CLUD

MABON

Din Mabon

Eidefechan

Caer
Gwendoleu

Arfderid

Caer Leu

hosting place
of Mabon

ARFYNYDD

THE MORRIGAN

Modron, Owen, and now Myrddin had gone and Urien was alone.

"I have failed you, father, and I have failed the Brython ... " He shut his eyes, leaning back against the stone and as he did so he heard his father's voice. "What does it matter? Did you not speak to Myrddin of a great game? What is mortal man's certain destiny, his geis, except that end which the grand players decide for him? Nought he does or says will alter that ... "

"Father?"

Urien looked down at Pasgent and Elphin.

"We saw Myrddin go, so we ran here. You are not angry?"

"We saw him change into a stag and trot off, his head held high," said Pasgent.

"And then he became a merlin flying high," added Elphin in admiration. "Can you do that? Mother said you can do anything"

Urien shook his head. "No, I cannot do those things," he said wistfully. "Not even Owen could do them though men called him a raven. That was because he had no equal upon the field of battle ... "

" ... and his sword brought death to many," added Gwrgi coming up behind the boys.

"Is there anything the matter?" asked Guallauc.

Urien smiled, knowing the concern of the King of Elmet. "No, there is nothing wrong. Myrddin has gone to help prepare our destiny. And so must we. Guallauc, you and your men must stay here whilst I and the others return to Caer Efrawg to await news from Bryneich. When that news comes it will come to you too and you will strike north as we have already discussed."

Guallauc nodded but he did not like it. With him left here, Gwrgi, Peredur or Urien could attack his own lands. "For I trust you as you me," added Urien, reading his thoughts.

"I am going to send the boys home," Urien told Llywarch when they had returned to Caer Efrawg.

"Why cousin? Are you afraid for their safety?"

"Nay, but they are Elen's, Myrddin's".

Llywrach was silent for a moment. When at last he spoke it was with concern. "Must we not make a virtue out of necessity? A king must have sons, nay, be seen to have sons. Who else will come after you but Kentigern, if it be not Elen's?"

Kentigern? Aye, that would suit him, thought Urien. Is that what his game was? His game! Whose game? Whose side would profit from the boys going home? "Aye, you are right. The boys can stay and ride with us." Urien was amused by the idea. Why should he decide? Let the grand players; he would balance Kentigern with the sons of Elen. Then he began to laugh quietly to himself wondering which side had made him choose to let the boys stay.

So they feasted and drank, waiting for news from the north.

"Why wait?" asked Gwrgi impatiently, his thumb feeling the finely honed edge of his sword.

"We wait because I wish the Loegrians to gather their strength into a single place, a place where we might crush them once and for all," replied Urien, the yoke of a broken egg running between the fingers of his fist and down his arm.

Gwrgi continued to thumb his blade. "How will you know when they are gathered?" asked his brother.

"The ravens shall tell me." Urien winked at Pasgent and then, squatting on the floor drew a map. "Hussa has fled to Theodoric; no doubt to ask for help in expelling us from Deur. So what will Theodoric do? He will gather his army and march south towards Caer Efrawg. Should he tempt to stray to the west he will find Gwenddoleu blocking the passes and it is he who will signal by beacon the passing of the host of Bryneich. But they will not be the only ones who come south this summer. Behind them will come Morcant and Ridderch to close the trap."

"And who will guard their lands?"

"Cynfelyn and Dreon, for they lie between Bryneich and Manau, Bryneich and Clud. Besides ... " Urien looked up at Llywarch " ... who would you trust not to burn your lands whilst you were away, Cynfelyn or Morcant? So! We wait."

But they had not long to wait, for the next night messengers were seen in the sky, the fires of men imitating those of the gods. In the morning, at their bidding, the armies of Rheged, Elmet and Caer Efrawg assembled north of the city. Five thousand men were gathered in that place where Constantine had been proclaimed Emperor. Then the world had been made Christian and a new Rome, a new Jerusalem, founded; a bastion against which the barbarian hordes had been broken. Now a new Constantine had arisen and his silken banner fluttered above the gates. To the sound of trumpets Urien and his sons now rode forth, golden helmets upon their heads, scarlet cloaks upon their backs. Through the throng they cantered and the roar was like that of the sea.

174

Urien held up his hand for silence and almost immediately the roar became the murmuring of waves gently lapping a beach. He who had stilled the storm, surveyed those who had come to serve. "Gwyr Y Gogledd, Men of the North, Cumbroges, Fellow Countrymen, ten years ago when my father died I saw a vision of a verdant isle filled with all manner of good things: I saw Prydein free from foreigners. For ten years have I sought that place and now at last it is near. From the sea the Loegrians came, like flotsam upon the beach. Like a stranded carcass rotting in the sun their stench filled the land and the plague laid low our people. For a hundred years the tide has ebbed and flowed; sometimes carrying the flotsam away, now bringing it back; but each time it brought more. How then shall we deal with that which distant lands did not want? Shall we not gather that which came upon the sea and burn it? Cumbroges, this is the moment which will seal the fate of Prydein for generations to come: the moment for which we were born. Who then will ride with me that one day he will be able to say: I was there?"

If Urien had said more it was not heard, his words drowned by the clamour. Five thousand voices, five thousand blades beating rhythmically against shields, ten thousand feet marching northwards. In three columns they marched: two squadrons of cavalry shielding the infantry. To the right were the horsemen of Guallauc and Elmet; to the left Llywarch and the men of Llyfein. Nine abreast marched those on foot, with Urien at their head. On his right was Pasgent, and on his left Elphin and behind was the silken banner of Holy Rome. In front of them rode a vanguard of three great trumpets, their throats coiled like the necks of swans and their mouths fashioned like the heads of boars, and to either side of them were three large drums. And beyond them were three heralds proclaiming the coming of Urien ap Cynfarch, Lord of Rheged and Catraeth, Protector in Aeron, Guledig in Goddeu, Gododdin, Manau and Clud, Llyfein, Elmet and Caer Efrawg, Powys, Glevissig and Gwent, Scourge of Deur and Bryneich. Beneath their feet the ground shook and Annwn knew of their passing: the glory of the Brython.

* * *

Arctures climbed to the top of a low ridge and surveyed the land ahead. He shaded his eyes, searching the ridge which formed the horizon to the north. Between them flowed a wide, lazy river, its sides steep cliffs. In only one place was the slope gentle enough to allow the road to cross and over that bridge the enemy must come.

So they waited until the spears and then the men of Bryneich appeared on the horizon. "Pasgent! Elphin! To the rear and be sharp about it," ordered Urien.

Theodoric and Hussa forded the river, oblivious of the welcome awaiting them. They were pleased with themselves. They had made good time and would soon be able to fall upon the back of the men of Catraeth and link up with those of Deur. Half their men had crossed the bridge when Urien attacked.

"Hold this ground and give the others time to cross!" shouted Theodoric, but his words were lost in the shouts of those swarming towards him. In dismay he watched the countless figures rearing up over the southern horizon and pouring down: it was as if the ridge were covered in ants. With difficulty he cut his way back towards the ford and gained the northern bank. Everywhere the men of Bryneich were falling back, slowly at first but then the trickle became a rush: the retreat, panic.

"Release my Ravens," Urien called and the horsemen leapt forward, their steel talons glinting in the sunlight. Across the fields they sped, towards the running men. Wherever the Loegrians hid the ravens saw them; however fast they ran the ravens caught them. From Catraeth to Dinguagroi the ravens pursued their prey. The Loegrians fell in the fields, they died by the river; they perished in thickets and on the moors, for from the Riders of Rheged there was no escape. Puddles of blood stood in the fields and there was gore in the mud: the hopes of children trampled underfoot.

But it was obvious Morcant and Ridderch had not fallen upon the rear of the Loegrians and that Hussa and Theodoric had escaped. Angrily, Urien followed the trail of corpses northwards. For two days he rode, until at last he came to Dinguagroi; the black rock of Bryneich. There he halted on the crest of a sand dune, the brackish lagoon below reminding him of another, long ago; of memories, of what might have been. His thoughts, however, were interupted by his eldest son pointing excitedly towards the fire which was consuming the palisades of Flamdwyn.

"Flamdwyn! The flamebearer!" mimicked a voice to their left. Urien turned and saw Morcant reining his mount. The lord of Manau looked down at Pasgent and Elphin "So, these are Owen's brothers?"

They bowed, "Did you know him well, were you his friend?"

Morcant laughed, but it was a cruel, mocking laugh and they backed away. "Do you like my fire?" he asked, evading their question, toying with their innocence.

"It is a beacon of our stupidity," retorted Urien. "For easy booty did not Hengist, who was the first of the Loegrians to be settled here, rebel? For easy booty did not the Brython fight amongst themselves, letting the Loegrians grow stronger? And now for easy booty you have let our enemies escape."

Morcant looked Urien in the face, contempt and loathing in his eyes. "Which son will you send to punish me this time, old man? Pasgent? Elphin?" He edged his horse closer to the boys and then spun round laughing. "Such dear ones. Munghu! Will you send Munghu? Nay, even now he pursues Myrddin, disobeying your orders."

"That is enough, Owen should have killed you whilst he had the chance," cried Urien, angrily drawing his sword.

Morcant put up his hand. "Aye, perhaps he should. But he didn't and here I am. Yet do I not wish, like you, to see the Loegrian's driven from our land? Aye, and I have done just that. You castigate me for yonder fire but by it I have driven them into the sea. Come, I will show you the rocks which Hussa and Theodoric now cling to ... "

Climbing onto his horse Morcant led them northwards to the expanse of sands and mudflats which were the ramparts of Medcaut. The sweep of the bay and its sands reminded Morcant of those of Merin Ideo, and the island a coracle bobbing on the waves, but such thoughts were for himself to gnaw upon; reminders of what Urien and his brood had cheated him of. Even so, he knew that for the moment he and Urien needed each other. He pointed to the rocky mass in the centre of the bay. "Yonder lie our prisoners."

If he had hoped for any gratitude, he did not receive it. "And how do you propose we get our prisoners?" Urien asked sarcastically. Beside him Gwrgi drew his sword.

"We just have to wait, like the hound by the fox's earth," snapped Morcant.

"And a long wait, too, that will be," retorted Urien, "For the sea will replenish their larder daily."

The party rode on in silence now, their cloaks wrapped about them by the following wind, and Urien noted with dismay the numerous fires already lit amongst the fringing dunes. Such a large number of men gathered in one place, eager for battle and frustrated, meant danger.

Ridderch came out to greet them and conducted them to a small farm a mile or two from the coast. "It is not ideal for the High King," he told Urien, "But no doubt it will do."

"Even a swineherd's hut would be welcome at this moment," admitted Urien. "I am getting old, Ridderch: getting old."

Urien sank gratefully down by the side of the hearth: he and the boys had hardly slept since they left Catraeth and the soft beds were alluring. Soon they were asleep and it was late the next morning when they finally woke.

In a short time Urien was standing on the beach again, gazing across at the island. In the evening light he had not appreciated how shallow the bay was. Though filled by the tide now, it would be possible to ford the channels at low water, at least for those on horseback. But at what cost? He had planned to crush the Loegrians between himself and Gwenddoleu, but now ... If only they had some ships they could attack from more than one side, aye and ensure no more men reached the island to reinforce it.

The next day Urien outlined his plans to the others and that evening they feasted. Pasgent and Elphin lay curled up at their father's feet, their innocent faces warmed by the glow from the fire. There they dreamed of the small forest kingdom which had once been their whole world and their prison. Urien lay back watching them. "Tomorrow we will finish that task my father laid upon me and fulfill my destiny. Then too shall we show Myrddin was wrong ... "

"And what will you do when it is finished?" asked LLywarch, leaning forward to fill Urien's goblet. Urien was startled: he had not realised he had spoken aloud. He straightened himself and looked about. Here were many of the kings of the Brython. Proud kings, kings not easily commanded; kings who but a few years before were at each others' throats; like Ridderch and Morcant. Urien watched them now, their heads together in quiet conversation, Morcant nodding at some little joke of Ridderch's. Urien chose to ignore Morcant's glance. What would he do when the victory was won? What would he do? Perhaps I shall cross to the continent like Mascen as Theodoric wants, he told himself, dozing. He dreamed then of Llydaw, Gaul and Rome, for all men may dream and in their dreams all is possible.

He awoke just before dawn and leaving the others stood in the entrance to the farmhouse waiting for the sunrise. The pale blue eastern sky was yellow where it met the horizon and the green grass was damp with silver dew. It was cold and he drew his cloak about himself, letting his hand play with the brooch Kentigern had sent him at Caer Efrawg, offering up a prayer to her depicted there. Then turning back into the hut, he woke the boys and with Ridderch and Llywarch behind they rode from the farmhouse towards breakfast and the beach.

Along the banks of the river they rode, the sunlight glistening on their golden, burnished helms; the banner of Rome and Mary ever before them, beckoning. In the morning light Urien and his sons stretched their horses, leaving Ridderch and Llywarch chattering aimlessly.

"My God!" cried Llywarch suddenly, pointing to the thicket ahead and the flailing bodies sihouetted against the eastern sky. Drawing his sword he urged his horse forward. "Morcant's men!" shouted Ridderch, following apace. But it was too late, the bodies of Urien and his sons lay in the mud where they had fallen, their golden helmets and breastplates crushed and torn apart by knives; vanities which had given no protection. Llywarch fell to his knees beside Urien and cupped his cousin's head in his hands, wiping the earth from the brow of Arctures.

He continued to cradle the head for some time. He was alone now, save for Saran, for Ridderch and the others had gone in pursuit of the assassins; evaporating from the Guledig's side like the morning mist from the fields around. Saran bent down and lifted Urien's sword: the sword which Myrddin had fished from the Wailing Tarn and imbued with empty words; promising to keep the Morrigan from Urien's back.

"The sword should be returned whence it came," advised Saran. "And he too should be gone before the others get back." Urien's armour bearer drew the knife from his own belt and offered it to Llywarch.

Llywarch nodded his understanding and turning to his cousin once more began to slice through his throat. In a moment the deed was done and he was standing beside Saran; Urien's head, like that of Bran, held by its silver hair. "He would want to see Modron again and she him," mumbled Llywarch.

Saran managed a wan smile. "Aye, he would have wanted that. You had best be gone. I will see to the rest."

Without looking back, Llywarch gathered his horse and galloped westwards.

For two days he journeyed until at last he reached the bower which Owen had built for himself and Rhiannon. Modron was waiting there now, watching for Urien's return as she used to; before the time of Myrddin, before the time of Elen. Taking the bundle in her arms she folded back the cloth. "Oh Urien, oh my love." Then turning, she walked slowly down the path and into the fields below.

Rhiannon put her hand on Llywarch's elbow. "No, let them go. She takes him to our people, her father, their son ... And you, my lord, have other work to do." Rhiannon pointed to the sword. "You had best return that from whence it came, for it has no place here. It is a false sword given by those who are false. To the water sprite it must be returned."

* * *

179

The coalition of kings had broken up. Ridderch had called for vengeance on Morcant and had marched northwards to seize his lands and thus add to his own. Had Ridderch encouraged Morcant, as Myrddin and others now said? Perhaps, but of those who might have told none now lived, for they had been hunted down and slain by Ridderch's men. Was Guallauc any more innocent? Had he, Peredur and Gwrgi not been anxious to be off? They had claimed they must return to protect their city and lands but was it not to seize Catraeth? Of those who had ridden to Medcaut at the behest of Urien only the men of Rheged had remained to guard the Loegrian scum. But they had been leaderless and those of the Brython who had once been their enemies roamed free. So the army melted away, each man thinking of his own home, leaving the dream of generations to be washed away by the tide of history, like their footprints on the sand.

Elen stood on the rampart, arms folded, her back to Taliesin, watching the swirling waters below. "Urien said man is like a leaf borne upon waters such as these, not knowing where he will be carried, his destiny beyond his control." She turned to look at the young bard. "What will you do now? What will Myrddin do?"

"I will sing to the next king of Rheged if he will have me. As for who that will be and what Myrddin will do I do not know."

"Why not ask him yourself?" said Myrddin, striding towrads Elen. He took her hands in his and looked into her eyes. "I am sorry, my child."

"Did ... could you not warn him?"

Myrddin, still gulping air, shook his head and cast a sideways glance at Taliesin. Clearly she did not know how he and Urien had parted, nor must she. "I was away on other business, I was not there. False business now I know. Nay, do not ask why I could not foretell that, for even I am sometimes tricked by the Children of Light."

"What are you saying?" asked Elen disbelieving. "That Modron had him killed?"

"No, Morcant's men did the deed but I have since learnt that they feasted the night before with Ridderch's, and Ridderch knew whose men wielded the knives before he had reached your husband. And who is behind Ridderch if it is not Kentigern?"

Elen sat down. Could she really trust Myrddin? He had brought her up to tend the Fire of Brigit until she should mate with the new king and she had known no other way; but with the love of Cynfarch's son had grown a feeling of some mistrust. She watched the druid now. What lay behind those hooded eyes she could not tell but it seemed to her he was agitated and more dishevelled than before, as if he had been worsted. No, it was more than that, Myrddin was tired, his face drawn, and there was the hint of fear in his eyes. "Kentigern?" she repeated.

"Did Urien not speak of his distrust for Owen's son?"

"Aye, but ... "

"No buts, there is not time if we are to save you, Morfudd and Rheged. The land needs a new king."

"Of him Taliesin spoke; but why are Morfudd and I threatened? By he who would be King?"

Myrddin nodded and again it seemed to Elen he was agitated if not frightened. "Yes, if we do not act quickly. If I am right, Kentigern will declare himself Urien's heir and who stands in his way but you and Morfudd?" Myrddin paused and gazed down into the waters below as if the future was pictured there. "Besides, there is more to play for than this kingdom. For two thousand years and more we have tended the hearth of Pwyll and kept alive the beliefs of the Old Ones, but now they will try to extinguish those flames. Whilst Urien was alive Modron and Rhiannon could not move against us, but now ... "

"Will they succeed?"

Myrddin smiled grimly. "Not if I can help it. Yet we have grown weak whilst they have maintained their strength. They have sent their women to breed with mortal men and many will be those gathered against us now."

Elen thought of Owen and how happy he had seemed with Rhiannon, of how with her he had found peace of mind and forgiven Urien the wrong done to him. Could Rhiannon really mean her and Morfudd harm?

Perhaps her eyes betrayed her thoughts for Myrddin seemed to know them. "Even if Rhiannon meant you no harm there is Modron and Kentigern. They will not let us live."

Elen turned from the druid and gazed across the meadows to the woods where she had borne Urien's children. She had chided him for not taking them away from there, but now she wished she could go back: she had been happy there. "Why do I and Morfudd, two women, stand between Kentigern and the kingdom? Because we give legitimacy to him you would choose?"

Myrddin smiled reassuringly. "Even as King, Kentigern could not allow Morfudd to live in case she had boys ... "

"Does Kentigern then not want heirs from his grandfather's stock? Or is it that you do not want my children and grandchildren to be brought up by him?"

Myrddin had ceased to smile. Drawing himself up to his full height he began to stare at her. "You will not betray our kind and I will not let you. I will say who shall be King and you will obey."

Elen tried to avoid his eyes but she could not. "Who then will you make King?"

"There is none more fitting than Gwenddoleu."

Elen nodded with relief. If she and Morfudd were to be hostages she would prefer to be Gwenddoleu's rather than anyone else.

"Aye, Urien would like that."

* * *

Gwenddoleu sat silently. He had returned from Medcaut with an empty heart. His friend had perished, his work unfinished, and Gwenddoleu felt he had betrayed him. True he could not have saved Urien from the knives of Morcant's men but he could have taken command and continued the siege, destroying the Loegrians as Urien had planned. But he had not done that; like the other kings he had returned home as soon as he had heard the news. Gwenddoleu shook his head, he would not fail Urien a second time.

"Nor would I," swore Myrddin. "Nor shall we. We must protect Elen and his children from Kentigern as he would have wanted. You must be made King as soon as possible."

"Why did he die?"

"You must be elected King before the remainder of the army disperses, each lord to his own land," persisted Myrddin.

Gwenddoleu brought his fist crashing down on the trestle. "Why did he die?"

"He died because he did not use the Talismans."

The answer seemed to satisfy Gwenddoleu and he sat down again. Then after a moment he looked up. "Why should Kentigern not be King? Was Cadog not a good leader of his people, both prince and bishop?"

"Maelgini too was both bishop and prince, and in Kentigern's heart there burns a passion which consumes him daily; the destruction of our religion and our kind. To him nothing else matters. Was it not he who persuaded Urien he did not need the Talismans, that a Christian brooch and silken banner were Lucks enough? Why, except it was to see Urien dead? No, we cannot entrust the kingdom to Kentigern. You and I must pick up the mantle and rally the Brython, the People of Pwyll. You must be proclaimed King as soon as possible."

Gwenddoleu sighed. "Aye, then perhaps Kentigern and his friends will pull back."

"Did he send Urien to his death to pull back now?" prompted Myrddin. "Has Gwenddoleu grown so old that he does not think to avenge his friend? Shall I bestow upon another the honour of avenging Urien and defending our people?" Myrddin looked at Gwenddoleu, challenging him.

Gwenddoleu shook his head and sighed. "Nay. I will avenge Urien and defend the Brython. I will pick up his mantle and behind my shield and walls I will shelter all those who love that world we have known. At Samhain then, I shall be King."

* * *

That winter was the worst in living memory and the wolves, grown bold by desperation, roamed freely amongst flocks and herds, killing at will. Everywhere men huddled around their hearths and half empty cauldrons to contemplate the future and tell of the past. They had been good days, days of plenty, days of valour: a golden age. Could Urien be really dead? Owen's grave they could point to, but Urien's? True there were those who said Modron had taken him to the land of her father, Avallach; but are those of that Otherworld not able to sally forth at Samhain or bestow gifts and help when needed? With such thoughts men now comforted themselves, secure in the knowledge that in the critical hour which was yet to come Arctures would return to defend them.

But as winter wore on the tales men told began to change: tales told only in whispers, stories of what others had seen. Some, told of a headless horseman leading a phantom army northwards along the slopes of Llwyfenydd. Others, looking anxiously over their shoulders, spoke of a black hag with a single, gleaming eye, whom they had seen stalking the roads and fields, pointing out to her carrion eating familiars this homestead or that. And all who heard tell of that shadow swore it was the Morrigan selecting for her cauldron. In that vessel she, who was both one and three, made the future: when there would be good times she appeared as the voluptuous maiden calling men to her bed, when there would be disaster, war or pestilence, she assumed that form many had now seen. "It was Elen who brought this upon us," was the cry in many a home. The Old Ones were stalking the land and the darkness of fear, dread and uncertainty gripped the hearts of men.

Yet it was not only the Morrigan who journeyed that winter. Kentigern too had travelled northwards, in answer to the call of Modron and Rhiannon. To Mabon, his father's land, he came and with him the men whom Urien had given to guard Gwynedd, for he had returned to claim his inheritance and to fulfil that vow made long ago in Caer Gwenddoleu. To Din Mabon he came, he whose outlawed mother had called "Foremost Prince", and there, within a day's ride of the fort his father had built for Rhiannon, he raised his standard.

There Rhiannon was waiting for him, little Rhun in her arms, and by her side her friend, Cynfelyn. "You look surprised to see me, my lord? But who else was there to guard these two until your coming if it were not I?"

Kentigern returned the greeting. "Aye, it is a job well done but who now guards your lands?"

"Should I need to? Against whom? But since you ask, Cadro guards my lands and hither will he come when Ridderch does, for that is the arrangement; that none might have the advantage."

And so it was. They came from the north, descending through the trees of the valley sides in long columns; mounted men with spears held high. To the small church Kentigern had built they came, calling that place Ecclefechan – Church of the Little Raven. Beyond its encircling bank, built like the sanctuaries of the Children of Light, the men of Clud and Llanelwy assembled; rank upon rank. Then Ridderch, kneeling, swore in the presence of all gathered there that Munghu was the true heir of Coel and Urien and that all should acknowledge, as he himself did, the Bishop of the Cumbroges as Overlord, Foremost Prince.

Munghu, flanked by Cynfelyn, looked down upon his protege and smiled. "Bishop of the Cumbroges and his successors," he corrected, firmly.

The face of Ridderch coloured and he paused before speaking, like a schoolboy deciding whether to obey his teacher. At last he spoke, repeating what he had been told: " ... the Bishop of the Cumbroges and his successors."

"And what of Rhun?" demanded Rhiannon, Cynfelyn still by her side. Kentigern smiled. "Is he not my brother? As a king may appoint a successor in his own lifetime, as Urien did Owen, so I appoint Rhun."

Rhiannon bowed, "Kentigern ap Owen is most generous. In your hands I now leave Rhun, that you shall be his foster father and I might join Modron and my people."

Kentigern looked surprised. "Are you leaving us? I had thought, no, I had hoped, you might join us in the battle, for without your help it will go hard with us."

Rhiannon smiled and shook her head and it seemed to those who watched that droplets of light fell from her tresses. "No, my people will not join you for so they will never be defeated, either by them or you ...

Do not look surprised Kentigern ap Owen; why should I not see your heart when all men are transparent like the Fairie: why should I not read you like the Book you hold-to and which makes you want the Church alone to be victorious? Did you not send Lucks to Urien graven with the image of Mary saying they were like our Talismans? Do you and your kind not follow one you call the Child of Light? Build then your own heaven on this earth, we have our own paradise and there we will live as before, planting our seed in in this world and that. Even so we will be allies like those others who have not yet come ... " Rhiannon laughed " ... no, not quite like them."

What Rhiannon had meant Cynfelyn could only guess until two weeks later Dunawd and Peredur marched into Ecclefechan. Maelgini and Guallauc had, it seemed, come by proxy to add fuel to the fire of civil war and ensure it consumed the house of Rheged for ever. At the sight of them, Cynfelyn wondered if he should not join Gwenddoleu. Certainly Gwenddoleu and Myrddin had not been inactive and they too had summoned allies. To their aid had come Dreon, and from the south Brocmael had sent his son, Dingad. But Dingad's warband was pitifully small, for Powys needed to guard itself against Gwynedd. "Was not that the reason why Kentigern had stripped all six hundred men from Llanelwy, that Gwynedd might be unleashed?" mused Gwenddoleu as he cast a worried eye over those about himself. Myrddin crossed to the rampart and gazed westwards: surely it would not be long before Kentigern would strike?

They had not long to wait. Two days later the sons of Owen and their allies advanced southeastwards, to the crossing of the sands and the hosting place of Mabon where they camped. From there they could either strike directly at Gwenddoleu but ten miles to the east, or march south to Caer Leu, Arfynydd, Llwyfenydd and Catraeth. Which would they do? That night the world waited to know its fate.

* * *

In the morning Kentigern addressed those about him. "Cumbroges, last night I prayed for a sign as to which way we should turn. This morning has that prayer been answered: look behind you and see how the tide blocks our road to the south. Fate then decrees we march eastwards to where Gwenddoleu awaits." Then, digging his heals into the flanks of his horse he drove forward, his sword held high. Behind him rode Cynfelyn, his eyes on Kentigern's sword. "By the sign of the cross shall we conquer," he muttered to himself.

They found Gwenddoleu and his allies gathered about the hill which

185

guards the ford of Armterid at the head of the estuary. There Kentigern rode forward with a herald and Gwenddoleu noticed he spoke with the accent of a man of Clud. "The lord Kentigern ap Owen, Bishop in Cathures and Llanelwy, Vicar in Prydein by authority of Rome, commands all those who envy the salvation of men and oppose the word of God, in the power of the same, to depart instantly from here and to provide no obstacle to those who wish to believe."

But from the cliff top there came no reply save that of prayers offered to those who might hear. Kentigern looked up and saw the figure of Myrddin, naked except for a golden torc about his neck. "It is enough," he said, quietly. "It is enough."

"Is it?" said Peredur easing his horse alongside Kentigern's. "I thought you said Mouric and Gwent had not come to Gwenddoleu's aid." He pointed to the figure of Eurdyl where Myrddin had been standing, a corslet of close fitting chain mail over her slender waist and full breasts so that those who saw her might be overcome by lust. "And if Gwent is here Powys will have no need to guard its southern border, so where she is might we expect Brocmael ... "

Kentigern rounded on Eleuther's son. "Fool. That is not Eurdyl but Myrddin garbed in her likeness: a trick. Often did he tell my grandfather: I am who you want me to be. You wanted to see Mouric and so he obliged. Look!"

Even as Kentigern was speaking the form of Eurdyl was changing. The beautiful apparition which had fired men's loins began to wither, the silvered mail darkened and became a loose black robe, the long slender fingers which might have gently moved over thighs became gnarled talons which could tear flesh apart. Flesh fell from her face until there was nought but a grinning skull. Its jaw dropped and a piercing shriek echoed from the hill, the stench of her breath borne upon the wind. Then with arms outstretched the figure rose into the air, circling over Kentigern.

"It is the Morrigan," cried Peredur, fleeing towards his men who were themselves beginning to fall back. But they found their way blocked by Cynfelyn's men.

"It is a trick," Cynfelyn said calmly, "the art of the Shapechanger. For as Myraddin might inspire confidence by telling some he would keep the Morrigan from their backs so might he imitate her to frighten others. But see, we have tricks of our own ... "

Cynfelyn pointed to the low rise behind them where Clovenhoof stood, and as they watched she shook her mane, letting droplets of light fall to the ground. Then, standing on her hind legs and pawing the air with the others, she began to whinny, and from afar she was answered: Gwenddoleu and his teulu were thrown to the ground as their mounts reared up. Peredur watched in amazement as the enemy were thrown into confusion by the stampeding of their horses.

"Cumbroges," called Kentigern, "since man first came to this island those who would be kings have mated with the speckled race of Mor Greidiawl. See now how those of that race reject Gwenddoleu. The kingship lies not with him, nor shall the victory. Onwards, Cumbroges, onwards ... "

Rhiannon had regained the initiative, fulfilling her promise to Kentigern, and now she left him. Behind her Kentigern's men were streaming across the river and forcing their way onto dry ground, whilst confusion still reigned amongst Gwenddoleu's warband. He had fallen back from the cliff top, rallying his men at a point free of the horses. With Dreon by his side he watched as their former mounts disappeared into the distance and then, blowing on his horn, he counter-attacked, driving Kentigern and his allies back towards the cliff. "Spread out, spread out," shouted Cynfelyn, "so those behind can come to your aid." Kentigern nodded in appreciation, recalling how his grandfather had often told of how he had thrown the Mordei into confusion at the battle of Gwen Ystrad, but then he caught sight of Myrddin amongst a group of naked warriors.

Kentigern's sword flailed right and left, his shield pushed and shoved as, ducking and weaving, he hacked his way towards his enemy. He paused briefly to wipe the sweat from his forehead where it was dripping into his eyes and was surprised to see blood on his forearm. If it was his own he felt no pain, he weighed his sword and advanced again. Suddenly he was lost, Myrddin had gone and he found himself deep amongst the enemy. "Another trick, damn you," he called, but there was no answer save a heavy blow to his shield. "And where the hell is Ridderch, I thought he was supposed to be following," he muttered to himself. Kentigern staggered backwards beneath a hail of blows. Finally the wood of his shield shattered but whilst his assailant was momentarily off balance Kentigern seized his chance; throwing himself to his right he drove his sword deep into the other. But no sooner had he done that than another was upon him. A spear thrust caught the surface of his left arm whilst with his right he parried another. So this was to be his end: betrayed by Ridderch and ensnared by his hatred for Myrddin. Well none could say he had not tried.

Far to his left Gwrgi was enjoying himself as he hacked and hewed. A head, suspended by its hair, dangled from his mouth. He let it fall as he ducked beneath one blow and drove his sword into the bowels of his opponent. "Has anyone else the guts to fight me?" he laughed, nearly tripping over the head at his feet. He pulled a troublesome hair from his mouth and fought on. To his right Peredur was retreating, trying to form his tired men back into shape so that some could get a little rest. He looked over his shoulder expecting to see the ford but found it was far to his left; the seething mass it seemed had turned slowly withershins as Gwenddoleu's men succeeded in driving a wedge towards the river crossing. Now there was no chance of retreat, the men of Caer Efrawg would have to fight on. He wiped the back of his hand across his dried lips; what wouldn't he do now for a cup of water. He shaded his eyes and saw Llywarch a little to his right: Peredur smiled and attacked towards Urien's cousin.

Not far away Gwenddoleu found himself amongst Ridderch's men and, assuming Kentigern was nearby, renewed his attack with increased ferocity, pinning the first men of Clud against their compatriots so that they could not easily move. A swathe of men went down, and then another. Next to him Saran slipped in the gore and Gwenddoleu pulled back, driving to his right where their feet were on firmer ground. Further right still he could see Dreon moving steadily forward in support of Llywarch but of Kentigern there was no sign. And where too was Myrddin?

Cynfelyn paused. They had been fighting for he did not know how long and still neither side had gained the advantage. He watched as two men close by exchanged blows, neither with the strength to finish the other outright, each waiting for the other to fall with fatigue. So would they all soon, aye, and perhaps that would be no bad thing either. He cast his eye over the carnage, the litter of bodies and mangled flesh: each one a Brython. Even so he could not pull back, for if they called a truce now it would only be to fight again. Better to get it finished now than fight again. He pointed to the conical hill not far away. "If we can get to that we might come behind Gwenddoleu," he muttered and waded forward once more, followed by the half of his teulu which remained.

So it was by chance he came across Kentigern just as he was about to fall. Cynfelyn darted forward, throwing his body and shield between Owen's son and his attacker. Gwenddoleu's man momentarily lost his balance, staggered to his feet and collapsed with a sword in his ribs. Cynfelyn picked himself up and stood a little in front of Kentigern. "Get him to the back, someone," he shouted over his shoulder. Once more he pressed forward, his men following in a thin column which threaded its way like a needle through the ranks of the enemy, between groups of exhausted men, around corpses without faces.

Gwenddoleu, sensing the danger, had pulled back, emerging from the melee just as Cynfelyn reached the foot of the hill. Both men halted, their followers behind. "Once we served the same lord," called Cynfelyn.

"Aye and we were pleased to do so," answered Gwenddoleu. "Will you not count me amongst your friends again?"

"Friend yes, but King, no." Cynfelyn advanced slowly, his sword and shield ready, eyes watching Gwenddoleu. Gwenddoleu began to circle, moving in the opposite direction to Cynfelyn before suddenly springing. There was a clang of metal and their blades collided, sending sparks which were but pale imitations of Rhiannon's.

"Surely you do not call Kentigern your king," panted Gwenddoleu. He kicked away a battered helmet lest he should trip over it and stepped over what remained of its owner.

"To his face because it pleases him ... " Cynfelyn swung his sword at Gwenddoleu and shaved a piece of rim from the wooden targe. He swung again, panting heavily " ... .but I fight to protect my Queen." Sweat, dust and blood were caked on his opponents face.

"Rhiannon?"

Cynfelyn lunged and his opponent stepped to one side, countering with a sideways cut which sent a shudder up Cynfelyn's shield arm. "Owen's wife?" repeated Gwenddoleu, standing still for one brief moment. But that moment was enough. Cynfelyn's sword sped downwards, slicing through the shoulder into the torso below. With a roar of surprise Gwenddoleu's left hand moved across as if to feel what was not there: then its owner collapsed into the dust, his lips shaping words which would never be heard. Cynfelyn sank to his knees beside the once proud figure. "It was you or me and should have been neither. What a waste! Foolish was this battle, like boys fighting over a lark's nest were we." He paused and stroked Gwenddoleu's ashen cheek. "Would that I had the Cauldron of Ulph, for then I might put you and all who have fallen here in it that the Brython might be whole again."

* * *

Upon the hill of Armterid was sacrificed the hope of the Brython, the empire of Arctures. When and how Dreon perished none knew, but by evening Cynfelyn, Dunawd and Peredur were able to ride to the top of the hill upon which Myrddin had prayed. From there they could survey their new lands, gazing beyond the dust of whitewashed shields which drifted upwards like incense offered to the gods. Upon that hill were offered many corpses: its green slopes littered with the flower of manhood. The air was filled with the groans of the wounded and dying; prayers of pain offered to deity and spirits, for pain respects neither Christian nor heathen.

But the war was not over and blood did not cease to run upon that single day, for the appetite of the darkness within men and the Morrigan was whetted and demanded to be glutted. Forces of passion had been unleashed which could not be called to heal until all which had survived old Rome and countless centuries had been swept away. Babies were torn from wombs, fathers killed before children, and cows left unmilked before burning homesteads. Everywhere was the smell of putrefaction so that the work of the sword was multiplied by the sickle of pestilence and plague. Everywhere the shrines and groves which Constantine and Pelagius had allowed to remain were destroyed. Springs were defiled and given the names of Christian holymen. Kentigern himself supervised the destruction of the shrine of Cocidius. But of its priest there was no sign.

Kentigern stood amongst the charred timbers. "Where are you Myrddin?" he called. "You cannot escape me."

" ... escape me" echoed his voice from the hills. And from afar, as if borne upon the wind, he thought he heard the voice of Myrddin.

"No I cannot escape you, nor you me. Do you not yet understand? Do you not remember the riddle I set you at Caer Gwenddoleu? As Pwyll could not destroy Hafgan, nor Christ the devil so you cannot destroy me for I am in you and you in me. We are the paradox of creation, the single duality which permeates the universe and which personified is the Morrigan. We are the two aspects of Janus which are in all men, Arawn and Hafgan, good and bad. For there can be no day without night, no healing without disease, no victory without defeat, no salvation without the betrayal of Judas."

GWYR Y GOGLEDD,
THE MEN OF THE NORTH

Llywarch Hen, Llywarch the Old, who had been the shield upon Gwenddoleu's back sat upon the grassy bank of the ford of Forlas looking across the eastern plain. Its woods and fields stretched as far as his dim eyes could see and reminded him, as they had for countless years, of his own land. Now that land was but a distant memory: its stoops of golden corn by the side of bubbling streams, its green pastures and dun moorlands lost in the haze of old age. Llwyfein was no more and its lord was but a shepherd in Powys; an old man guarding the flocks of Cynan. In Powys had gathered the remnants of that once splendid court and The Men of the North. There Llywarch and Taliesin sang in sadness like curlews, but in those mountains the knowledge of Arctures, the Northern Bear, would remain, destined to rise like a phoenix to inspire the Brython and their conquerors. Was not such the destiny of all heroes, that feted in death they should rise again in new guise?

Llywarch turned his face northwards and with tears in his eyes sang gently to himself of glorious battles now past: of Glen, Dubglas, Bonny, Bassas, Celidon, Guinnion, Caer Legion, Tribruit and Breguoin.

"Extol the kings of Rheged, oh my people,
Sing my harp that all the world may heed
How they brandished the spear of battle
That Prydein might be freed."

* * *

Far to the north, in the forest of Celidon, Myrddin wandered as he had since that fateful day … He paused. How many years had it been? Forty or four? Four days or four hours? What did it matter, time was nothing to one condemned to wander without love until the powers that be should grant the reprive of death.

It was autumn again and the dead leaves lay thick upon the ground. The birds had gone and only the sound of water cascading down a small cliff broke the silence of that dying world. It was a damp place and it chilled his bones to the marrow. Not even the thoughts of Beltanes past could bring a flicker of warmth to him now. His feet dragged through the rustling leaves until he found a clearing where the sun had warmed the air and a few green ferns and hardy brambles poked through the gold and red carpet of summer past.

Myrddin slumped against the stump of a once great oak, the rays of the dying sun upon his face. He felt old and frail, his sallow skin dry and wrinkled like the leaves around him: leaves which gathered in the folds of his robe, leaves which would cover him when no man would. A fly tricked by the warmth stirred itself and landed on his torn robe but it did not linger. "Even flies desert me now," he muttered. "Little does Ridderch know tonight in his feast what sleeplessness I suffered last night. Snow up to my hips among the forest wolves, icicles in my hair, spent is my splendour."

The Ravens had perished upon the slopes of Armterid. Rheged had been divided. Ridderch had taken the lands north of the Gweryt, and Cadrod had been given Calchvynyd. Dunawd had regained his father's lands and Rhun, son of Maelgini, had taken all south of the Gweryt. Peredur and Gwrgi had added Catraeth to Caer Efrawg; Theodoric had returned to his land across the seas and the cities of Conmail, Condidon and Farinmail had been taken by the Loegrians. The sacred place of Cocidius had been destroyed and a cross erected there.

The chained birds had been released. The world which Myrddin and his kind had known was gone, gone for ever. He closed his eyes and dreamt. Dreamt of what might be for now he saw the future clearly. Elidyn and Rhun would fight and the armies of Gwynedd would march north to battle on the Gweryt, dissipating still more the strength of the Brython; their blood spilled in worthless sacrifice upon the land they loved. The sons of Eleuther would not hold Catraeth and Caer Efrawg; and Elmet too would be lost. Only those of the Brython who had not fought at Armterid and Gweryt, Powys and the Gododdin, would have the strength to fight off the foreigner but they would not be able to regain Catraeth and the empire of Urien: the Loegrians would be triumphant in Caer Legion. The descendants of Vortigern would triumph over those of Cadell and erect a memorial where Germanus had been victor. Urien's Rhun would write about Germanus and he would succeed Kentigern. He would baptise a king of Bryneich and another would marry Morfudd's daughter. Thus the kings of Bryneich would proclaim themselves Guledig of Prydein, heirs to Coel and Urien. And by the same twist of fate men would remember Myrddin as the wise counsellor of Arctures and, forgetting Eurdyl, say Modron betrayed her husband calling her the Morrigan, Morgan Le Fay.

The Raven Riders had perished and with them the independence of the Brython. Only children would now remember to sing of Coel and learn of the Elven People, of the magic cauldron, of the power of the Morrigan, of Arctures and of Myrddin. Perhaps it had all been but a dream, a figment of the imagination. Even so it was the passing of an age. It was Samhain: the Old World had died, another was just beginning.

SELECT NOTES

p5.   If there were no Roman troops remaining in Britain in AD410 and normal government continued after that date the latter can hardly be said to mark the end of the Romano-British period. A better date for the end of "Roman Britain" might be AD383 (when Magnus Maximus took the bulk of the garrison with him to continental Europe), with the period between that date and the battle of Armterid in AD573 being seen as "subRoman". This subRoman period began with a number of short lived military expeditions and the letter of AD410 should, thus, be seen as simply saying there would be no more.

That the British themselves considered "Roman" Britain to have ended in or before AD383 is suggested by Gildas when he refers to the Romans returning and building walls to protect the independent British; events surely to be equated with the expeditions after that date. If this interpretation is correct then the "expeditions" after AD383 involved restoration of the frontiers and might be the context for the timber repairs and rebuilding of the northern granary at Birdoswald. Equally, the timber buildings which replaced those granaries at Birdoswald should perhaps now be seen as belonging to the period when Gildas says the British themselves continued to man the Wall.

p6.   Gildas (23.1.) seems to say the AngloSaxon *foederati* were deployed against the Picts an arrangement implied by Nennius when he says after "the death of Hengist ... Octha and his son passed from the northern part of Britain" to Kent. If this were so then the "Outigern" referred to by Nennius as having fought against the Angles of Bernicia might be equated with "Vortigern" who, according to Bede, gave the *foederati* lands "in the eastern part of the island". Did the latter mean Bernicia and Deira, lands with which Bede was directly aquainted? Were the *foederati* who eventually formed Bernicia brought in to occupy the area left "empty" by the movement of the British king, Cunedda, to North Wales?

p7.   For discussion of Arctures see Rachel Bromwich 1961, 544.

For a variety of dates for the death of Urien see Jackson 1953,707; Miller 1975,177; Lovecy 1976,31; Shaw 1964,107 and 149. For the probability British material was (wrongly) synchronised with Anglo Saxon dates: see Dumville 1977 and Jackson 1963.

p11.   "The Lake Mountains". This phrase refers to that area we would call the Lake District and I equate with the early Welsh *Yrechwydd*. For the meaning of this word, see Sir Ifor Williams 1968, xli-xliii. He translates it as "fresh water" and suggests it refers to Swaledale; but as an area it might be better seen as refering to a lake or area of lakes, hence I have used it of the Lake District. It is generally accepted the

Llwyfenydd of the early Welsh poems is the modern Lyvenet where a remarkable number of "native farmsteads" survive as earthworks. Is it coincidence?

p12.   I am suggesting the "Round Table" refers to a circular mead-hall.

p15.   For the location of Pabo west of The Lake District see Miller 1975, 107-8.

Urien's wife is not referred to in the poems of Taliesin. This episode is based on Trioedd Ynys Prydein. There, however, the story is identified with the "Ford of Barking" (Rhyd y Gyfarthfa) in Llanferres parish, Clwyd.

p16.   For the location of Modron at Ravenglass see TCWAAS 1924, 256 259.

Tradition says a Swan guards treasure higher up the coast at Moresby.

p17-18. Morris describes the events surrounding Garbaniaum's recovery of his "throne". Because some of his allies, such as Nudd, would also have been natural allies of Rheged, I have suggested the latter lay behind the success of the venture. I have made Morgause Urien's sister. For Urien having a sister Enhinti, who had a son Mouric, we have only Morris. Some Welsh material calls her Eurdyl and because Old Carlisle was known as *Guasmoric* I have, tongue in cheek, located her in that area.

p24.   For Irish links associated with Pabo see Miller 1975,107f.

p25.   A number of writers suggest Brigid was the equivalent of Dana and probably the same as Brigantia. In using the phrase People of Brigit I am suggesting that "the Brigantes" was in reality a grouping of peoples who considered themselves to be "the people of the Goddess".

p36ff. For the ritual(s) associated with kingship, including the use of prehistoric sites, see Byrne. For the idea of inauguration being a symbolic marriage with the Sovereignty of the Land see Dillon and Chadwick.

p39.   The early Welsh form of Carlisle was *Caer Liwelydd*, but I have used "Caer Leu" to show how modern place names do derive from the past. The identification of the city with the Welsh Leu is, however, interesting given that the Roman name was Luguvalium: it confirms Lug and Leu were one and the same.

p42.   "The Lady of the Lake" must be see as a Celtic idea.

There is no evidence for the retreat of Venutius but the marching camps in the Eden valley show one Roman army advanced into the Eden Valley from Scotch Corner. Attention is drawn to the proximity of the latter to the "preRoman" lordship site at Stanwick and the early Welsh lordship site of "Catraeth".

p47.   Gwenddoleu and Brigit – Jocelyn says he worshipped a fire goddess.

p49.   Here "Mabon" is the area north-west of the Esk. This and the forest south of Carlisle I envisage as the land Owen; a kind of "principality" within Rheged. For the idea of "principalities" being alloted to the king's chosen successor see Byrne,36 and TCWAAS 1962,87. Was Edward Ist consciously following a Welsh-British institution when he declared his first born son, "Prince of Wales"?

One Welsh tradition said Gwenddoleu kept chained, supernatural birds. The legend of the Ravens in the Tower of London may have a similar origin. Here I suggest Gwenddoleu's "birds" may be associated with Cocidius. His shrine at Bewcastle must have been in Gwenddoleu's lands and the tiny gold plaques from there can be interpreted as showing a birdman with owl-like face and feathered cloak.

p53-54. There is general agreement *Goddeu* was in the vicinity of Selkirk. As such it would have been a natural ally of Rheged against the English of Bernicia. Local topography would make sub divisions into cantrefs possible and I thus represent it as such, placing Caer Nefenhir in one.

p54. For discussion of when Bamburgh was fortified and the significance of its name see Margaret Faull (51-52). Here I have suggested it was the refortification of the site by Flamebearer – whom I equate with Ida – which broke the "peace" of which Gildas wrote. The date when Ida began his rebellion is usually accepted as AD547 but Kirby (1962,526) argues it was AD558 (adopted here). Urien could be contemporary with either date if Kentigern did die at a ripe old age in AD603 and if Taliesin were a contemporary of Maelgwn.

The *Historia Brittonum* says one Arthurian battle was at "the mouth of the Glen". Here attention is drawn to the Northumberland "Glen" emerging near the Anglian royal site of Yeavering. I have equated the Arthurian battle with Urien's Llwyfein for the latter seems to have been fought with the men of Goddeu against the Anglians. The existence of a number of valleys running towards the Milfeld Basin I equate with Taliesin's reference to Flamdwyn advancing in several columns.

p58. The *Catraeth* of Welsh poems may have been a cantref rather than the old, Roman town. For its continuation as a hosting and lordship centre see Bede (History of the English Church and People) chapter 14.

p77. The story of Owen and Thenew is based on Jocelyn and a, fragmentary, earlier *Life*. The cart into which Thenew was put makes sense as a cult waggon in which a tutelary goddess might ride at certain festivals. The association of Thenew with a spring also suggests a tutelary divinity. The "Lady of the Fountain" tale would seem to be a variant as, indeed, the story of Urien and Modron (chapter 1 here).

p81. There is no evidence the peoples of south western Scotland were called the Mordei – I have simply borrowed the name from the early poems.

p89. Attention is drawn to the strategic position of *Dun Ragit*. That, and the name itself, suggests the fort was built for a military purpose.

p101ff The story of Kentigern's flight is told by Jocelyn, I have merely added he took Ridderch with him; a not unreasonable supposition if the king were restored, as Morris suggests, by Nudd an ally of Rheged.

p106ff Jocelyn's picture of a semi-pagan sixth century Britain rings true, if only because we might expect medieval monks to have believed the land to have been wholly Christian since Roman times.

p113. The *Historia Brittonum* mentions four engagements upon a river called Dubglas. Here attention is drawn to a Douglas being the first river encountered as one descends from Carlisle/Rheged into the Clyde Valley. Taliesin refers to at least one cattle raid by Rheged upon Clud and also implies Urien fought in Manau, where Skene located the Arthurian battle of Tribuit.

p122-3. The strategic importance of Chester is shown by the battle of AD616. Chester is, therefore, a good candidate for the Arthurian Caer Legion. As the AngloSaxons are unlikely to have penetrated that far before AD600 any Arthurian battle must have been between the British. Rheged and Gwynedd would be likely adversaries and later material emmanating from Gwynedd ignores or disparages Rheged whilst it was in Powys, enemy of Gwynedd, that the poems of the *Men of The North* were kept alive.

p123. The idea of a standard surmounted by an animal is derived, by me, from the Roman one found at Vindolanda. There the standard had a horse, here a boar. The idea of animal "badges" should, however, be compared with the epithets applied by Gildas to some British rulers; eg "the Dragon", "the Dog". Compare also the name "Bear", Arctures.

p127. For the possible existence of two contemporary rival dynasties in Powys see Kirby 1976 and Dumville 1977: the latter arguing the line of Cadell was largely invented at a later time.

p128-135 Jocelyn says Kentigern travelled to Wales to hold discourse with Dewi on the Pelagian heresy and established a monastery at *Llanelwy*. A 12th century document of that place (published in Arch. Camb. 1868, 151ff) says, however, Kentigern arrived with three hundred soldiers and clerics. This latter story suggests genuine tradition and the events relating to Kodicum and Maelgwn, also described in that document, I take to be an alternative and elaborated version of events alluded to by Gildas. That it was not unusual for princes and nobles, like Maelgwn, to adopt the monastic life, see Byrne 34. The king might also have been seen as the priest of his people (Byrne 23): a concept which probably explains those prince-bishops like Kentigern and Cadog.

p147. *The Life of St.Cadog* records the Synod of Brefi (held to discuss the Pelagian heresy) occured whilst Cadog was abroad and says this was deliberately timed.

p2149. According to *The Life of St.Cadog* it was after the battle of Caer Tigguid that the Saint invited Mouric to be king. Could this battle be the same as Arthur's Tribruit?

p150-2 Geoffrey of Monmouth has Arthur engaged in a number of campaigns on the continent and the story of Theodoric provides a link between Urien and Brittany. Morris is the source for Mouric of Gwent being related to Urien, but his source is unknown. It was, however, at Caerleon in Gwent that Geoffrey of Monmouth had Arthur set up his court and there that Arthur, "overjoyed by his great success", was crowned by Archbishop Dubricius. Dubricius is also said to have participated in the "Victory Synod" of AD569: the "victory" being the defeat of Pelagianism. It will be recalled: a) Jocelyn said Kentigern journeyed to Wales to counter the heresy; b) Cadog, who gave up his throne to Mouric, was alleged to have been a Pelagian. Finally, the "plenary court" which Geoffrey gives to Arthur at Caerleon, although

198

not without medieval parallels, is surely an oenach.

Geoffrey's Arthur is best interpreted as a High King. Byrne has discussed the hierachy of kingship in Ireland and amongst the "Welsh" material we can glimpse "subkings", like Nudd, and "overkings" or "king of kings", like Ridderch. Urien appears to have belonged to the third and highest grade: "greatest of kings", "king of overkings". These titles can be compared with the names Vortigern and Kentigern meaning, respectively, "high or foremost chief" and "foremost prince".

p166f. Here I have tried to arrange the material of the *Mabinogion* into a form which is the equivalent of the Irish *Book of Invasions*.

p168.   Here I suggest Theodoric and Hussa, for whom we have little evidence, were not successive kings of Bernicia, as is often assumed, but contemporary kings of Bernicia and Deira at a time when those two Anglian states were still separate.

p180.   Welsh tradition, expressed in a poem attributed to Llywarch, speaks of Urien's sons in conflict with Guallauc, Ridderch and others who we might otherwise have considered Urien's allies. That Morcant was involved is accepted by all. Was he Mordred? Geoffrey of Monmouth described Mordred as a prince of Lothian.

p183-4. The return of Kentigern to Hoddam and Mabon, and the acknowledgement of Kentigern's suzerainty by Ridderch, is told by Jocelyn. The events related there only make sense if Kentigern was laying claim to be "Foremostprince" or "king of overkings", and others were backing his claim for their own ends.

p185.   The battle of Arthuret is thus portrayed as a civil war with both sides aided by others. A calling in of neighbours to help in dynastic squabbles does not appear to have been unusual (Byrne, 36). Kentigern's involvement in the battle is suggested by Jocelyn when he reports the speech reproduced here beginning "(I) command that all those who envy the salvation of men ... depart ... oppose no obstacle ... " It is also consistent with later stories that Myrddin was hunted down by Kentigern's men.

p189-90. Kentigern's involvement also explains why the battle of Arthuret is said to have continued for forty days, for Jocelyn records Kentigern showed "that idols were dumb, the vain inventions of men, fitter for fire rather than worship ... " ie the Christian victory was followed by a period in which the pagan shrines were destroyed.

p191.   For the strategic significance of the ford of Forlas see "Rhyn Park Roman Fortress: Excavations 1977", Border Counties Archaeological Group.

A partitioning of Rheged by the victors of Arthuret would seem a reasonable explanation for the late sixth century map of Britain. The northern half was attached to Clud and the diocese of Glasgow, and as such the justification of later Scottish claims to this part of England.

p192-3 It is suggested here that the sudden collapse of the British and the consequent rise of the Arthurian myth, followed the death of Urien. But why did the British collapse when they must have still been numerically superior to the AngloSaxons? One factor may have been that they were depleted by civil war, another that they were unable to unite because of religious divisions. But my story provides another reason: whilst the traditional pattern of Celtic society was one of small kingdoms and local loyalties making conquest difficult (as the English later found in Ireland); Urien created a super-kingdom capable of being annexed or replaced in a single battle.

SELECT BIBLIOGRAPHY

Alcock,L. 1974. Arthur's Britain. London.

Bromwich,R. (ed) 1961. Trioedd Ynys Prydein: The Welsh Triads. Cardiff.

Byrne,F.J. 1973. Irish Kings and High Kings. London.

Dillon,M. & Chadwick,N. 1973. The Celtic Realms. London.

Dornier,A. 1977 Mercian Studies.

Dumville,D.N. 1977. "Sub Roman Britain: History and Legend". History 62.

Faull, M. 1984. "Settlement and Society in north-east England in the fifth century" in Wilson P.R. et al. Settlement and Society in the Roman North. York Arch. Soc.

Jackson,K. 1953. Language and History in Early Britain. Edinburgh.

Jackson,K. 1963. "On the N. British section in Nennius" in Chadwick,N.K. Celt and Saxon. Cambridge.

Kirby, D.P. 1963. "Bede and Northumbrian chronology". English Historical Review.

Kirby,D.P. 1976. "British Dynastic History in the Pre-Viking Period". Bull. Board Celtic Studies.

Lovecy,I. 1976. "The end of Celtic Britain: a sixth century battle near Lindisfarne". Arch.Ael. 31-46.

Miller,M. 1975. "The Commanders at Arthuret". TCWAAS, 96-118.

Morris,J. 1973. The Age of Arthur. London.

Shaw,R.C. Post Roman Carlisle. Preston 1964.

Williams,Sir Ifor. 1968. The poems of Taliesin. Dublin.

SUGGESTED CHRONOLOGY
of Sub-Roman Britain

Conventional dates		Dates used here (where different)
383	Magnus Maximus withdraws the main garrison. Gildas 13-14. "After that Britain was despoiled of her whole army, her governors ... never to return.."	
c396	So, Gildas 15-18. "Britain sent envoys ... to Rome ... requesting a military force to protect them ... vowing whole hearted ... loyalty.."	
c399	Restoration of the frontiers by Stilicho.	
410	Britons ask for another expedition but are told to look after themselves. Gildas 18. Walled frontier maintained.	
440	Continued raids by Scots and Picts. Gildas 19. "Our citizens abandoned the towns and high wall.."	
c443	Britons appeal again to Rome for help. Gildas 20. "But they got no help in return."	
cc445	Famine and invasion from the North. Gildas 20.2.	
c449	Hengist settled by Vortigern against the Picts. Gildas 23. "to beat back the peoples of the North".	
c455	Rebellion. Hengist moves to Kent.	
c490	Saxon advances. Fall of Pevensey.	
518	Battle of Mount Badon.	
549	Ida fortifies Bamburgh. End of Peace in the North.	558.
561	Gildas writes. Peace still in the South. Battle of Caer Legion. Maelgwn returns to throne. Kentigern flees.	
569	Victory Synod. Synod of Brefi.	
573	Death of Ida (who reigned 12 yrs.).	570.
	Death of Owen ap Urien	570.
	Death of Urien.	572.
	Battle of Arthuret. Destruction of Rheged.	
577	Loss of Gloucester area to Saxons.	
c580	Gwrgi dies. Loss of Catraeth to Anglians.	
c590	Attempt to recapture Catraeth. First reference to Arthur.	
595	Dunod dies.	
612	Kentigern dies.	
616	Anglian victory at Chester. Britons finally divided.	

PLACE NAMES

Aeron	The kingdom based on Ayr.
Alauna	Maryport.
Alclud	The Rock of Dumbarton, capital of Clud.
Annwn	The Underworld.
Arfynydd	The Cumberland Plain south west of Carlisle.
Armterid	Arthuret, north of Carlisle.
Bassas	Baschurch.
Brandreth	Tebay.
Brefi	Llandewi Brefi.
Brycheiniog	The kingdom centred on Brecknockshire.
Bryneich	The Anglian kingdom based on the coastal plain of Northumberland.
Caer Beguion	High Rochester.
Caer Daff	Cardiff.
Caer Digoll	Long Mountain in Montgomeryshire.
Caer Efrawg	York.
Caer Gloiu	Gloucester.
Caer Goddeu	Eildon Hill and Melrose.
Caer Guricon	Wroxeter.
Caer Legion	Chester.
Caer Gwent	Caerwent.
Caer Leu	Carlisle.
Caer Lundein	London.
Caer Nefenhir	Rubers Law.
Caer Sergeint	Caernarvon.
Caer Uisc	Caerleon near Newport.
Cathures	Glasgow.
Catraeth	Catterick.
Celidon	The Southern Uplands.
Chalchvynydd	An area near Kelso.
Clud	The Clyde, more properly the kingdom ruled from Alclud.
Coet Celidon	The forest of Celidon.
Dal Riada	The first kingdom of Scots founded by immigrants from Northern Ireland and centred on Argyll.
Deganwy	The capital of Gwynedd, near Llandudno.
Deur	The Anglian kingdom based on East Yorkshire.
Dinas Bran	The hillfort above Llangollen.
Din Eiddyn	Edinburgh.
Dinguagroi	Bamburgh, capital of Bryneich.
Din Mabon	Burnswark.
Din Rheged	Dunragit in Wigtownshire and Rochdale in Lancashire.
Dogfael	The Vale of Clwyd.
Dubglas	Douglas Water, a southern tributary of the River Clyde.
Dumnonia	The kingdom of South West "England".

Dun Pelder	Traprain Law.
Dyfed	The kingdom of South West Wales.
Ecclefechan	Near Locherbie.
Elmet	The kingdom based in the Leeds area.
Ercig	The kingdom in the Upper Wye Valley and north west of Hereford.
Erin	Ireland.
Fort of Cocidius	Bewcastle.
Fort of Frisians	Dumfries.
Glevissig	Glamorgan.
Goddeu	The kingdom based on the Middle Tweed Valley.
Gododdin	The kingdom based on the Lothians.
Guinnion	Kirkby Thore.
Gwen Ystrad	The limestone uplands of the Eden Valley.
Gweryt	The Lune.
Gwy	The Wye.
Gwynedd	The kingdom based in North Wales.
Hafren	The Severn.
Hibernia	Ireland.
Idon	Eden.
Linius	An area between Dal Riada and Clud.
Linnuis	Lincolnshire.
Llan Elwy	St. Asaph.
Lleuddiniawn	Lothian.
Llwyfenydd	The area of the Lyvenet, a tributary of the Eden.
Llwyfein	The lowlands of the Lune Valley and Lancashire.
Llydaw	Brittany.
Luitcoyt	Wall, near Lichfield.
Mabon	The plain east of Dumfries, as in Lochmaben and the Mabenstone.
Maes Cogwy	Oswestry.
Manannan	The Isle of Man.
Manau	Fife, as in Clackmannan.
Medcaut	Lindisfarne.
Meigen	The Vale of Powys.
Merin Iodeo	The Firth of Forth.
Moel Fre	Mallerstang.
Mon	Anglesey.
Morgannwg	The lowland of Glamorgan.
Morvael	Penrith.
Nantcarfen	North West of Barry.
Pengwern	A palace of Powys near the Wrekin.
Penychen	Vale of Glamorgan.
Powys	The kingdom of the Upper Severn Valley, including Shrewsbury.
Powys Fadog	The area north west of Shrewsbury.
Prydein	Britain.

Rheged	Kingdom centred on Cumbria and Carlisle.
Sea of Rheged	Solway Firth.
Tribruit	Sterling.
Tu Hir	The Pennines.
Wailing Tarn	Tarn Wadling near High Hesket, south of Carlisle.
Yrechwydd	The Lake District.

OTHER WORDS

Beltane	May Eve festival.
Brython	British.
Cumbroges	"Fellow countrymen", Cumbrians, Cymri.
Cymri	As in Plaid Cymru; see Cumbroges.
Eoganacht	Irish settlement of Britain during and immediately after Roman rule.
Gael	Irish.
Geiss	Destiny; a person's predestined fate, especially his/her manner of death.
Guledig	High King
Gwyr Y Goggledd	The Men of The North.
Loegrians	"Foreigner" but specifically Anglo-Saxons.
Mordei	Area and people of Dumfries and Galloway.
Oenach	Gathering held every few years. Compare the Olympics.
Prydein	Britain.
Samhain	November Eve festival; New Year.
Shee mound	Ancient burial mound.
Teulu	Personal warhand.

THE GAME OF WOODEN WISDOM

The story The *Dream of Rhonabwy* in The Maginogion includes an episode in which King Arthur and Owen Rheged play a game called "gwyddbwyll" which may be translated as something like "wise wood". Another Welsh story tells of how Gwenddoleu possossed a magic board game.

The details of neither game nor board are known for certain but the story told in The Riders of Rhegged is based on an interpretation/reconstruction. In this interpretation it is assumed the object of the game was to get the High King, symbol of the fertility of the land (eg. pages 38 and 65 here), from the centre of the board to the corner to enable the annual cycle to commence and continue. As such the game begins at Samhain, the pivotal time of the year, with the High King protected by four lesser pieces (eg. p.34-35 here). These four lesser pieces equate with the four Talismans referred to in this book and the High King with a fifth, The Head of Bran (eg. p.42 here).

As indicated above the game is based on the concept of the relationship and importance of the High King to the fertility and survival of the land. On the one hand, therefore, Urien's struggle to defend the Brython assumes the same cosmological significance (eg. p.170 here), and on the other, the board is indeed magical – as players of the game will discover. Called High King or Wooden wisdom and with a board of oak and elm the game is designed to be displayed in home or office. It can be ordered direct from Rheged Books, price £21 including postage and packaging.